Praise for *A Piece of Normal* and *What Comes After Crazy*

"Funny, funny, funny, from page one. You can't help but root for the lovable Maz Lombard, who's surrounded by an eccentric mother, headstrong daughter, deadbeat husband, and way too much whole wheat flour. Sandi Kahn Shelton's writing sparkles with humor and insight."

—Lolly Winston, author of *Good Grief*

"I loved *What Comes After Crazy*. Smart, warm, and hilarious!"

—Jennifer Crusie, author of *Bet Me* and *Faking It*

"A book about slaying dragons (the ultimate toxic mother and lame estranged husband), *What Comes After Crazy* shows that a woman can be the hero of her own life. A comedy with all the avenging and day-saving you can handle, but without any messy bloodshed."

—Valerie Frankel, author of *The Girlfriend Curse* and *The Accidental Virgin*

"A skillfully constructed, economically written novel that is funny, sad, and almost painfully accurate about human failings." —*Boston Globe*

"A zany, affecting first novel. . . . Plenty of laughs here." —*People*

"Shelton delves into family relationships with humor and empathy."

—*Booklist*

"A quirky, funny, graceful story." —*New Haven Register*

"Richly textured, insightful . . . Shelton's humorous, touching story fully engages the reader." —*Library Journal*

"[Shelton] handles her characters and story deftly. . . . A likable heroine and novel." —*Kirkus Reviews*

"[A] fine blend of humor and poignancy." —*Hartford Courant*

"Equal parts energetic comedy and earnest domestic saga. . . . Lovely descriptions often grace the pages, and there are plenty of laughs."

—*Publishers Weekly*

Also by
Sandi Kahn Shelton

FICTION

A Piece of Normal
What Comes After Crazy

NONFICTION

You Might as Well Laugh
Sleeping Through the
Night . . . and Other Lies
Preschool Confidential

Kissing Games of the World

a novel

SANDI
KAHN SHELTON

Three Rivers Press

NEW YORK

Copyright © 2008 by Sandi Kahn Shelton
Reading Group Guide © 2009 by Three Rivers Press, an imprint of the
Crown Publishing Group, a division of Random House, Inc.

Published in the United States by Three Rivers Press, an imprint of the
Crown Publishing Group, a division of Random House, Inc., New York.
www.crownpublishing.com

Three Rivers Press and the Tugboat design are registered trademarks of
Random House, Inc.

Originally published in hardcover in slightly different form in the United States
by Shaye Areheart Books, an imprint of the Crown Publishing Group, a division
of Random House, Inc., New York in 2008.

Library of Congress Cataloging-in-Publication Data

Shelton, Sandi Kahn.
Kissing games of the world: a novel/by Sandi Kahn Shelton. —1st ed.
1. Single mothers—Fiction.   2. Women Artists—Fiction.   3. Widowers—Fiction.
4. Single fathers—Fiction.   I. Title.
PS3619.H4535K57 2008
813'.6—dc22   2008012253

ISBN 978-0-307-39366-1

Printed in the United States of America

Design by Lynne Amft

1 3 5 7 9 10 8 6 4 2

First Paperback Edition

To Helen
This one's for you

Part
One

CHAPTER
I

Harris Goddard's life ran out on an otherwise ordinary afternoon in the middle of May, on the very day it seemed the rest of the planet was pulsating with life. An unexpected warm front had blown toward the coast overnight, pushing out the last remains of the long, wet Connecticut winter and nudging the buds into a frantic, hurried bloom. By 11:00 a.m., the thermometer on the side of the barn read eighty-six damp degrees, and Harris, standing on a ladder and scraping the peeling paint off his house, felt as though he might have missed out on the news flash that the world had slipped into the third circle of hell.

But he was a proud and stubborn old cuss and had never once changed a plan without a fight, so he stayed up there on rung number eight, squinting hard in the sunlight, picking and scratching at the hide of his house, and watching the paint chips drift to the ground like old sunburned skin. By the time he decided to let himself break for lunch, he was cranky and thirsty and his left arm was tingling from holding the scraper.

He still had his winter blood, that was all this was.

"*Hey,* you," said his housemate, Jamie McClintock, when he went inside. Harris let the screen door bang behind him for once and fumbled his way into the sudden dimness, feeling the sweat cooling quickly on his face. Jamie was a blur of pink standing at her easel. Always at her easel in the morning, God bless her.

"Hey, *you,*" he said back. With slight difficulty.

He could feel her looking at him. "Harris, are you all right?"

He nodded and went over to the soapstone sink, where he found he couldn't remember certain things, like exactly how it was you turned on the cold-water faucet. Two bull elephants were standing on his chest, but that was nothing. He'd felt worse. Christ, he'd had *hang-overs* that were worse than this.

"No, really. Are you okay?" she said. He sent over the words *I'm fine,* but they must not have gotten there, because then she said, "I know what. Why don't you sit down a minute? Let me just give Al a call." Al was the doctor. He'd known Harris so long he made house calls for no extra charge, and often stuck around for dinner.

"No. Just *frungy,*" Harris said, and of course Jamie made a big deal out of *that* little slip of the tongue. She came right over, put her hand on his arm, and stared into his eyes like she was looking to see the insides of his brains. He couldn't remember what word he had meant to say. *Fried? Hungry? Grungy?* Actually, nothing made much sense just now.

"Come on, at least let me help you sit," she said. "You don't look right."

"I'm just hot," he said, a little out of breath. "I need a drink."

She turned on the faucet for him, got a glass out of the cabinet, and filled it up. "You want some ice?"

"Nah." As it was, the water she gave him felt like a lump of melted snow going down. Anyway, what he'd meant was that he wanted something with alcohol in it, a gin and tonic, that's what. That and a chance to sit down in the cool, have a little persuasive talk with these damned elephants.

"Whew! So what is it, you think, about a thousand degrees out there?" she said, and even through his haze he could tell she was speaking in that high little voice she used when she was trying to pretend everything was normal. "And wouldn't you know, I sent the boys off to school in corduroy pants and hoodies. Can you imagine? They're going to melt."

"The boys" were Jamie's son, Arley, and Harris's grandson, Christopher. They were five years old, and at the thought of them, Harris's chest tightened even more. If they were here, there'd be none of this sitting around, waiting for the strength to get up and make a gin and tonic. No, he'd be laughing and chasing them around the room, and they'd be giggling and climbing all over him. They saw him as a piece of living, breathing playground equipment, and he didn't try to make them see any different. Every afternoon since they started kindergarten in the fall, he'd met their school bus and spun them around in the driveway, then pretend-raced them to the back door, where Jamie was waiting for them.

It made him tired to think of it.

But he'd be better by 3:15, when the bus came. Of *course* he would. He exhaled, wondered if Jamie would get all crazy-alarmed if he slid down onto the floor, maybe curled up there beside the table until the boys came home. He didn't feel like walking to the couch now, and all he needed was a nap. Jamie was squinting at him, giving him that look that said he was a pathetic old man, which was ridiculous because he was only sixty-eight years old, and he happened to be—he'd actually looked this up—only two days older than Robert Redford. And did he really need to remind her that hardly anybody would dare put Redford in the pathetic category yet? Hell, he still got the girl in most movies.

Harris took another swig of ice-cold water and looked at her, managed one of the sly grins he was sort of famous for. Ever since he'd walked out on his wife and son, back, oh, during the Pleistocene era, and had taken up with the new receptionist at the construction company where he'd worked, he'd somehow had this image to uphold: as somebody who couldn't stay away from women. People in town wouldn't hear of him acting any other way. Even now, tired of it all, he still had to be the town's sexy old rascal, still had to wear his jeans tight and his hair long, and he had to at least leer at younger women, even if he didn't actually *do* anything with them.

But what the hell? As assigned roles went, this one wasn't all that bad. Better than being seen as priggish, like his old business partner, or paranoid, like his friend Frank Cooksey. Besides, Harris still looked damned good, a hell of a lot better than Redford did these days, according to Harris's own private opinion. Redford seemed a little puffy, doughy around the middle, if you looked close. But this rock-hard body Harris had—well, he had a lifetime of doing construction to thank for that, plus the fact that when he got to retirement age, instead of sitting down or going fishing, he had taken on the *real task of life:* raising his grandson.

He'd tell anyone: if you want to stay young, keep up with a toddler when you're in your sixties. That'll either kill you or keep you going. For him, it had been the tonic he needed, saved him from all the guilt that had gnawed away at his insides. Nobody could say that taking on that kid hadn't made up for his litany of crimes against his family. All that—absolved. All those screwed-up days he'd spent around the time he left Maggie, when he just had to leave or else *die* in this house. Die of the boredom, because there was a whole catalog of ways to be bored married to Maggie: sitting in the dining room, listening to the forks clicking on the wedding-present china; listening to the piping voice of little Nate, who always needed *something,* always wanted to play catch outside, always wanted to help Harris bang the hammers on the nails; or listening to Maggie talk on and on, pursing her lips and looking at him across the table, smiling as if she was a member of some smug little Housewives' Club, jabbering on about Olivia's meat loaf recipe, and should we have the Simpsons over; and him thinking, *Yeah, let's do. I slept with June Simpson just last month when I was there redoing her kitchen.* God, it was everything: the heaviness of the light, the future bearing down on him so hard it was like no air was left in the room— but it had been bad to go; they hadn't deserved what he did to them, he knew that now, knew so much more now.

And then, out of the blue, there was the grandbaby coming to save him. It had been horrible, really, the way it happened, this blessing coming in the worst possible way—Nate's wife getting herself smashed up in a car accident when the baby was four days old, and Nate freaking out big time, and Harris, not knowing what to do, aching, panicking, saying to his hollow-eyed son, "Go! Go get yourself together. I'll take the baby for you, and you come back when you're ready." All by himself then, he'd figured out formulas and modern baby bottles and easy-flow nipples and disposable diapers and wipes, not to mention colic and teething—stuff he'd never even had to think about when Nate was born—and then he'd graduated to thinking about baby gates and walkers and tricycles . . . and then preschool, and now the kid was almost through kindergarten, and Harris had grown along with him, now understanding such things as the need for Velcro sneakers that light up and backpacks with monogrammed initials, and DVDs. Yes, DVDs.

People always saying, *Wow, that Harris is something, such a great guy, taking in that baby when his mother died like that and his father ran off.* But he knew it wasn't that simple. The truth was he'd done exactly what he'd wanted to do. He hadn't wanted to give the baby back, simple as that. He'd kept Nate away, slammed the door, and not let him back in.

The elephants kicked him so hard now he nearly buckled, and his eyelids were painted with red and purple flashing stars.

"Maybe you're hungry," Jamie was saying. He brought himself back to the present and saw that she was somehow across the room now, standing by the stove. He was sitting down—when did that happen?—and he was surprised to see that he was still holding his glass of water. "Shall I make you some lunch?" she said.

"Nah." He pointed to his middle, grimaced. "Got some . . . some . . . indigestion."

The light was dappling across the tabletop in a way that made his head hurt.

She was frying up something on the stove, something that smelled evil, like garlic and onions and olive oil, but now she turned off the burner and came over and sat down across from him and studied him. He looked back at her. She had light curly hair that went wild on her—she was always having to whip it into shape with scarves and clips and sometimes even chopsticks—and she had a wide, cream-colored face—the kind of skin his wife would have said was in danger in the sun—and serious gray eyes. Everything about her was serious, was the truth of it. She even *walked* serious. When she'd moved in a year ago, he'd assumed it would be only a matter of time until he slept with her, but he'd been wrong about that. She didn't take nonsense, that was what. Had none of that do-anything-once spirit to her that he found so necessary in the women he slept with. *Lighten up, baby. Smile every once in a while, why don't you?*

"Indigestion, huh?" she said. "Listen, I tell you what. Why don't you go upstairs to my room, the *good* room, and turn on the air conditioner and lie down up there for a while and get cooled off? I'm going to call Al and have him check you out."

"Nah," he said. "Don't."

But she was already heading for the phone, marching over to the counter like somebody who had been prevented long enough from doing what she knew was right.

THEY'D MET LAST year at the Junior Campfire Boys Club for Preschoolers, or whatever the hell it was called. He never could remember the exact name of the thing; it was one of those make-work things people today couldn't get enough of, was his loudly voiced opinion, but apparently you had to join stuff these days if you wanted your kid to make it in the world. Further evidence of the decline of American civilization: you couldn't send kids out to play on their own anymore. You had to *enroll* them in play, arrange all their friendships for them. Playtime had gotten to be like a business meeting.

He and Jamie had been the outsiders right from the beginning.

Everybody knew they were different: they stuck out like the proverbial sore thumb. She was a newcomer to town, a member of the so-called new wave of artists who all the locals said had ruined the downtown, bringing in art galleries and massage therapists and coffeehouses with untenable things like *soy lattes* where there had once been hardware stores and clothing shops. Plus, she dressed as if she'd gone into her closet and started pulling random things out of it and putting them on without looking at them—layers of shirts with lace edges poking out from underneath and wisps of scarves and little crocheted vests, skirts and leggings, or else jeans so old they were torn up and paint-spattered. So naturally nobody knew how to talk to her—all the other women in their khakis and polo shirts, with their folded-down white socks and tennis shoes, turning to look at her as if she had three heads. Even Harris, who was not exactly up on fashion, knew women well enough to know that *nobody* was going to try to befriend her if she insisted on wearing that patchwork skirt.

But what the hell? He didn't fit in himself, being a gray-haired grandfather instead of one of the young dads, so it wasn't as if anybody knew how to act around him either. The whole thing was ridiculous, and he would have left if Christopher hadn't had such a good time there. He dragged himself to the meetings, and stood around feeling out of place, and then one day—might have been at the fourth meeting—he was standing across from her at the back of the room, watching all the ridiculous parents who were trying too hard to make sure their little tykes got to be first and best in everything. He looked over at Jamie, and their eyes met. Her shoulders started shaking with laughter, and she put up her hand to hide her face. He felt himself light up: he was not alone. There was a kindred spirit, even here, in this stupid gymnasium, at this stupid meeting.

It wasn't until after they'd been going to the meetings for a few months and taking the boys out for ice cream afterward that she told him she was looking for a new place to live on account of her sister Lucy had let some guy move into the apartment they shared, and this guy smoked, and Arley had asthma, and oh, it was a big mess over there. She wasn't complaining or anything, just telling him like this was a neutral story about her life. No whining. He liked that. He'd looked down at his hands and cleared his throat a few times and then told her that if she really needed a place . . . well, the fact was he had some room, he and Christopher were pretty much rattling around in that big farmhouse of his. After he said it, he was immediately scared she'd say yes. She didn't. She said she appreciated the offer and she'd like to think about it, was that all right? He'd been both relieved and disappointed, he realized. But then, when she did accept his offer a few days later, he understood it had been a damn good idea, one of his most inspired moments, actually. The boys were already best friends, and even though Harris was doing fine on his own, he was sick of his own cooking and his own company.

A week later, she and Arley had arrived with their stuff, and Harris had even been moved to give her the master bedroom upstairs, the room with the air conditioner; they laughed and called it the "good room." He'd started sleeping on the sunporch, downstairs. He didn't mind. She needed to be near where she could hear her boy breathing in the night.

Harris's friend Cooksey—who also happened to be the police chief, so he had about five times the number of suspicions that other people had—told Harris he'd better be careful, letting some young woman move into his house. "You think it's because you're so irresistible to women, but what if she's one of those New York gold-digger types and is really out to take you for all you've got? Eh? What then?" he'd said. That had cracked Harris up. He'd wiggled his hips suggestively, which made Cooksey madder. Aw, so what? Let Cooksey think that Jamie was hot for him. What the hell did Cooksey and the other old coots know about being friends with a woman anyway? And the part about the gold digging—now, that was a laugh. There wasn't any gold to be dug.

Jamie had had some bad luck with men, but she was down-to-earth and practical, and—how could he ever explain this so Cooksey could understand?—it was great, it was *enough,* to have her standing barefoot in his kitchen at night when the boys were in bed, painting her landscapes from photographs and listening to classical music. Things were calm around her, as if she had her own private force field. Besides that, she cooked wonderful food and she knew how to play with the boys, and she listened, *really* listened to all his stories, and told him stories back, and she laughed at his jokes and poked fun at him. She thought he was wise; so why mess that up by sleeping with her and proving her wrong?

She and the boys—they were his family now, and here was the truth: they'd tamed him. His eyes welled up, thinking about it.

"Harris, go on upstairs," she was saying. "Go on, you crazy old man. Listen. I'll even throw in a back rub."

A back rub. He laughed.

"Yeah. Laugh all you want, you old galoot. I've been trained in them," she said. "Adult-ed course. Nobody better than me at it."

He felt a little flicker of wonder through his haze. Did back rub really mean *back rub* to her, or had she picked this moment, when he was more bent over and washed up than he'd ever been in his whole life, to take things up a notch and . . . well, *do it* with him? That would be some kind of weird but lovely irony, wouldn't it?

He looked over at her, at her wavery gray eyes wide with feeling, saw her brush back her little curlicues of hair and tuck them behind her ears like parentheses. He could barely catch his breath, he felt such a vast expanse of love just then—for her, for everything.

Love, that was all there was. It sounded so ridiculous, but this whole kitchen, this whole *town,* the soy lattes and everything, *every-thing* was made up of it, and he couldn't think why he hadn't seen it before. He saw a flash picture of his wife, Maggie, by the stove, half-laughing at him over something he'd said, the old *wife-o-saurus* he'd called her then; then, *flash,* the picture shifted and he saw Nate standing here cradling the newborn baby and, oh no, Nate is crying, sobbing, wearing an old ratty T-shirt and four days of beard growth; and shift again and it's Harris holding the baby, but the baby isn't poor motherless Christopher, it's *Nate,* who's just been born, and Harris doesn't know how to make him calm, so he's singing his high-school fight song, which doesn't work; *flash,* the red linoleum is all curled up in the corners and he loves it, that and even the worn place where Maggie had stood so many days and nights washing dishes at the sink, and the peeling paint on the walls, the wainscoting coming loose in the corner, all the things he didn't do are still not done, but it doesn't matter. Harris can see all the winters and summers here, all rolled into one big moment: himself walking up the path from the pond the first time he caught a trout, the wood smoke from the stove, the way the buttery sunlight comes slanting in and hits the kitchen cabinets just so on autumn mornings; he feels the snap in the air, and now the heaviness of the wet humidity, so heavy today it slams into you and you can't breathe it in, but it's okay. All of it is good. All so very good. There'd been no need to fix all this; it was right, it was *perfect,* just the way it was. My God, he thought, it was love. Who knew it was love all along?

He leaned forward to touch Jamie, tipping himself into the depths of her slow, patient gray eyes, as wide and deep as ponds, and he said happily—even though his voice felt like it was stuck somewhere in his throat—he said, "One thing to know."

She looked at him. He tried to remember what he had been about to say about all the love.

"I'll help you up the stairs," she said.

"Bring," he said. A moment went by. He started again. "Bring," he said, "a gin and tonic."

"I will," she said.

I will. Like what they say at weddings. He exhaled a long, slow, sacred breath and made his way slowly up the stairs, the beloved, worn wooden stairs.

CHAPTER
2

So he went upstairs and dropped dead.

First, though—and this is the part Jamie thought she would never come to understand or explain to anybody—he took off all his clothes and lay down in the middle of her bed. He sprawled himself out on the Indian-print bedspread and stared up at the ceiling like a man awaiting a visitation from something in the overhead light fixture.

She didn't know this right away. She came into the room—her bedroom, the one he'd given her a year ago—carrying the gin and tonic, with its ice cubes clanking against the side of the glass, her hand shaking a little from the heat, or from nerves. She'd spent the morning thinking about a painting she wanted to do, a new one—she wanted to paint the beat-up old wooden kitchen table, with its scars and cracks, and the daisies sitting in the green glass jelly jar just off-center. She'd been distracted and excited all morning, her mind going over and over the rich catalog of ochres and tans and browns she'd buy at the art-supply store, impatient to begin now that she had the idea— and then Harris had come stumbling inside looking like a bologna sandwich that had been left out in the sun, and she'd once again fallen into the pit of dread. She was the mother of a little boy who got sick suddenly, so she knew this feeling, the fear that everything is going irrevocably wrong and that she's powerless to stop it. It was the familiar territory of her nightmares.

Her room with the shades down was dark and still hot, and the window air conditioner, which Harris must have turned on, was wheezing away as if it was responsible for breathing enough for the two of them and could barely keep up.

"So do you want the back rub first or the drink first?" she was saying as she came in. She'd called Dr. Al's office before she'd come upstairs, but Violet had said the doctor was running far behind today and couldn't come to the phone. Maybe he could come and check Harris out after work. They'd both agreed that would probably be fine, although Jamie had been less sure.

"You feeling any better?" she said, moving toward the bed, but Harris didn't stir. Her eyes slowly adjusted to the darkness, and that's when she realized. She put a hand over her mouth. His eyes were open but unseeing, and he had one arm flung across his chest and the other at a weird angle on the bedspread. Then she saw that he was naked, and she was so startled that for a moment all she could do was stare at him. Naked! What had he been thinking, taking off all his clothes? Could he have imagined that a back rub required nudity? She couldn't help but glance down at his poor old penis, flopped over like a tired featherless bird sitting on its mossy nest. His chest was hairy, with gray brambles rising everywhere, only now it looked caved in, as if somebody had sat on it and dented it. That was it: he looked deflated, like a black-and-white drawing of himself.

She made herself lean down, put her hand on his heart, and feel the silence there. Maybe, she thought, she should try to do CPR, but she couldn't remember what she had learned in that course so long ago, a Girl Scout course back in seventh grade, wasn't it? Why hadn't she ever thought she'd need to know this? And anyway, she knew it wouldn't work. He was already gone. Her blood started whooshing in her ears. She folded her arms close to her body and wished somebody else was there, somebody who could tell her this was going to be okay. And she wished his pants were on. She was shivering, even in the heat, and it was hard to breathe. It was as though the air had grown thorns that caught in her windpipe as it went down.

The phone. She had to call someone. She had to stop standing there being scared and look for the telephone, which had never once been in its stand when she'd needed it. Harris always called the phone charger the mother ship. "Come back, o ye telephone!" he would call out. "Come back to the mother ship!"

The phone turned out to be underneath a pile of her clean laundry on top of her dresser, next to her hairbrush, bottles of moisturizer, tubes of eyeliner, and a bottle of vanilla massage oil. When she could trust herself to speak, she called 911. Her hand was so sweaty and shaky that the phone kept slipping out of her grasp, and finally she had to wrap it up in the hem of her skirt so she could hold on to it. The person who answered already knew her address when she tried to give it. Of course they knew the address. That was what 911 was. She'd called 911 for Arley a couple of times when he'd been having one of his asthma attacks. Once it had been a false alarm—he'd been choking and had gotten panicky, but then he was fine so she had simply hung up the phone without giving an address, but even so, the EMTs showed up, all of them rushing toward her with alertness in their eyes, ready with oxygen and medications, wanting to be of use. She'd wanted to throw her arms around them, serve them tea and cookies, to show how grateful she was for their effort.

When she got off the phone, she stood there and looked at Harris. Then she eased herself down onto the side of the bed, careful not to touch him. The pinkness was leaking out of him now; he was gray and waxy-looking. "Oh my God, I'm so very sorry," she said out loud. "I should have called 911 right when you said you were *frungy*. That is not a real thing people say."

It was hard to look at him, and yet it was also hard to look away.

This was the first time she'd seen a dead person up close this way. *A corpse. The body.* How could he just be . . . gone? Not here anymore, not himself. Just like that! She reached over and touched his arm softly, which already didn't feel like something that was quite alive. She drew her hand away. There were a couple of tiny details she wished they could have discussed. Like, what she should do about Christopher. Why hadn't he turned to her in the kitchen and, instead of talking about a gin and tonic, said something practical to her, like, "Here's what I want you to tell Christopher, and here's what Nate needs to know. And oh, by the way, here's where Nate's phone number is located, and here's where I'm to be buried."

She covered her face with her hands. She had the wild feeling that maybe she could rewind the tape of this day, zoom backward to him and her in the kitchen, do it right this time. She would take him by the hand, she would insist with Violet that Dr. Al come right over, she would find the phone numbers of everyone who needed to know. She was starting to cry now, tears backing up in her throat. Damn. *Where* were Harris's people? How was it that she, a housemate picked because she happened to have a kid the same age as his grandson, had come to be his closest human being?

She could hear the sirens now in the distance. When the ambulance crews came and took over, then she would go and get in her car and drive to the school, and she would tell Christopher as gently as she could that his grandfather had died today. The words would come from somewhere. She wiped at her eyes with the back of her hand. The trouble was not in how to make him understand—he knew plenty about loss—but how to make the world seem like a place where you were safe to love people, when so many had disappeared on him. He was only five, but he'd lost his mom, his dad had run away, and now his grandfather . . . gone. Who could bear to tell a child this?

Harris had told her once that it was only by being with Christopher that he'd learned to forgive himself for all the mistakes he'd made with his wife and his own son. It was only by loving Christopher that he'd learned not go to around having to say, "I'm sorry, I'm sorry," to himself all the time.

"Sometimes you get a second chance," he'd said one night on the porch swing. "And when you get a second chance in life"—she remembered the way he'd stopped and smiled at her—"well, that's just grace, honey, is all that is."

THE SIRENS SCREAMED to a halt outside the house, and she jumped up. What had she been thinking, just sitting there? She should have realized what the rescue people were going to see when they got in here: Harris, nude, stretched out on her bed, and the gin and tonic sitting on the dresser right next to the vanilla massage oil.

Already she could hear the banging on the front door, and then before she could even think to go downstairs and let them in, the ambulance people were coming through the unlocked door, calling, "Hello? Hello?" and pounding the wood floors, as though they were running through the house looking for the trouble they'd come to fix. The house seemed to shake from their footsteps. How many of them had come—the whole town? Everybody who owned a police scanner? She might still be able to put Harris's shorts on him—no, no, she *had* to put his shorts on. All she had to do was flip him up and slide them right up his legs and over the rump, the way you did for little kids. But the voices were getting closer, there was running on the stairs, and then she could hear that the first contingent had arrived upstairs—the first emergency guy was just outside the room, in the hallway. No doubt it wouldn't work to call out, "Just a *min*ute!" in a little singsong voice as if you'd been interrupted in the bathroom.

She grabbed the gin and tonic. At least she could get rid of *this*. She wasn't sure what she was going to do with it—run with it down the stairs, pour it into the trash can, stash it under the bed, *drink it*— she was trying to make up her mind, and then it was too late. The door was flung open, and she was standing over Harris, holding both his pants and the glass in midair, looking toward the doorway with what she knew was a startled, frozen, horrified look stuck there on her face.

The emergency guy looked just as horrified. They stared at each other.

"He's dead," she said. Her voice was so thick she didn't even recognize it. "I think he died."

The room was suddenly full of people, all working on him, talking, hooking him up to things, listening to him, thumping his chest. She was in the way, so she kept moving to the side, fading backward into the woodwork, mashed against the dresser for a while, and then she was in the way there, too. Somewhere she'd let go of his shorts, but she held onto the melty gin and tonic as if for dear life. People were talking, and their walkie-talkies crackled with little bursts of static, perhaps other calls that would probably have to be made at some point when this was over. Occasionally someone would look over at her as though she were a piece of furniture that had acquired the power of movement somehow, and so she kept squeezing herself into smaller and smaller spaces, trying to get herself to the door and out of it. To go down the hall, down the stairs, and out into the sunlight. She absolutely had to go get the boys. That was the main thing now. She couldn't bear the thought of them arriving home on the school bus like on any ordinary day, walking up the driveway with their little lunch boxes swinging, expecting Harris to meet them, and instead finding . . . this.

She finally made it over to the doorway and inched her way out into the hall, where there was air again, and sunlight. She felt so lightheaded she thought she might actually fall down. But then she heard someone mumble from the bedside, perhaps unaware of how voices could carry: "Wow, we know what *this* is, don't we? A clear-cut case of a man being fucked to death."

There was an answering low, dirty laugh. "Yep. Coming and going at the same time."

More laughter, then talk she couldn't hear. She stared into the gin and tonic, wondering if she could stop shaking long enough to go in there and scream, or if it would do any good anyway.

Somebody else said, "So, hey, looks like old Nate the Great is gonna have to come and raise his own kid. Wonder how he's going to take *that*."

"Oh, boohoo," somebody else said.

AND THEN COOKSEY arrived.

Frank Cooksey had been Harris's best friend since the two of them were in second grade, or as Harris had once put it, since God himself was in short pants. They were complete opposites in personality, but after sixty years that probably didn't matter much. By now, they were glued together by history, which was way more important than temperament. Harris was easygoing; he broke things and put them back together all slipshod and never worried about a thing, just drank beer and told long, colorful stories. Cooksey had always specialized in a kind of pessimism, and somehow his ability to worry had driven him straight up through the ranks of the police department, until he'd become chief. At least that's what Harris had told Jamie. Now Cooksey saw himself as the arbiter of the town's deportment, which was a source of constant disappointment to him. All these *artists* moving in and displacing farmers and other decent folks, taxes going up, people drinking lattes instead of regular coffee, and going off getting in car accidents because they didn't have the sense not to talk on their goddamned cell phones while they drove their kids to soccer practice and art lessons. All this change, this *stupidity*—it made him tense, gave him agita.

What was even worse, Harris had told her, what was *really* at the core of Cooksey's personality disorder was that he and his saintly wife, Julia, had raised four daughters, and not one of them had managed to make a go of it out in the world. Go figure. *That* was Cooksey's real grief: the fact that his daughters were constantly coming back home, leaving their husbands and boyfriends or being left by them, weeping and moaning, dragging their children with them, moving back into the spare room so Mama could take care of them. Cooksey never had any peace and quiet. Nobody kept their marriage vows anymore, he liked to say. Half his sentences started with "Kids today . . ." Why, he'd been forced to start organizations like the damned Preschool Campfire Kids just so his grandkids would have some contact with healthy adults. *That* was the trouble. Here all Cooksey wanted was to sit on the porch alone with Julia drinking whiskey sours and raising show dogs, and not have to answer one more emergency phone call. He was sick and tired of saving people from their own stupid mistakes. Why couldn't they act right for a change—suck it up and be adults?

And now this. He came walking in the front door, his uniform all perfectly pressed, as always, his bars and ribbons lined up just right, as always, his bald head gleaming. Jamie had never been so glad to see him.

"Oh, Frank, thank goodness you're here!" she cried out, and then, too late, saw his face, twisted and terrible. His eyes were livid, and as he came up the stairs, she felt the wind go out of her. How could she have forgotten that he didn't like her? He wasn't going to want to join with her in mourning Harris; the truth was he didn't think she had any right to be living there in the first place. *Now* she remembered: Harris had once laughingly told her that Cooksey was sure she was a gold digger and that she and Harris were having wild sex day and night on the kitchen table. They'd had a good laugh over that one.

But the truth was she was so distraught that even though warning bells were going off all over the place, she couldn't stop talking. "It's so terrible! Harris was outside in this heat, working on the house, and I don't know what happened, but he came inside and he could barely talk, and when he did, he said the wrong words—I can't remember what he said, but it was all weird—" She faltered, seeing the way he was glaring at her, and she took a different tack. "He was so *great,* such a wonderful person, but you know how stubborn he was, and he shouldn't have been working outside today on the hottest—"

"*Weird?*" he said, drawing back, as if that had been the only word she'd said, and it was an unbelievable insult. "Harris dies, and that's what you call it? *Weird?* Well, I have a *weird* question for you. Why the hell didn't anybody try to get him out of the hot sun? Huh? Just where were *you* when this was going on?"

"I was—"

He looked down at the drink she was holding, and her eyes followed.

"What's this?" he said. "Enjoying a little toast, were you?" She didn't know what he meant. "Or is this what you killed him with?" He reached over and took it out of her hand, which had begun to shake like crazy. "Matthews, come take this. We'll need to test this in the lab," he said.

What? *What?* He thought she'd killed Harris? She almost started to laugh. She could feel the bubbles of hysterical laughter coming up. "Wait a second," she said. "Now just wait. You—don't thi—"

A cop materialized by her side, and Cooksey handed him the glass. "I want to know what's in this. Run it in for me, will you? And *you* stay right here," he told Jamie. "I don't want you to move a *muscle* until I've checked things out."

He went into the bedroom, which had grown silent. People had all been listening to him talk to her; they had stopped their conversations, and now it seemed they were even falling away from the body, making way for Cooksey to get to the bedside. There was a long, hideously quiet moment, during which Jamie squeezed her eyes shut and leaned against the wall, and then Cooksey said: "*What* the hell is *this?* He was *naked?* What the hell was going on here? Christ in heaven! Scanlon, where are you? Take that woman downstairs and make sure she does not leave the premises. Get her statement, and make it good."

Somebody said something else too low for her to hear, and then Cooksey yelled, "Who the hell knows? Just keep her here for questioning. Find out everything you can. Okay, now get everything wrapped up here. I've gotta go figure out where that son-of-a-bitch son of his got to and notify him. And then I want a squad car to go pick up Christopher Goddard at school and take him to my house. I'll call my wife and tell her to get a bed ready for him." He was silent for a moment, and then he said, "Jesus God in heaven, Harris. What the hell were you thinking, old man?"

People started rushing around. She could see inside the room, where someone had brought the sheet up over Harris and someone else was moving the paramedics' machines to the corner. She wiped her hands on her skirt, smoothed down her hair, and went to the doorway. When she got there, she said, "No." Nobody seemed to hear her so she said it again: "NO."

Two or three of the technicians looked in her direction, little nervous flicks of glances. Cooksey was reading a clipboard, and he ignored her.

Take a deep breath. Don't fall over. "Nobody else needs to pick up Christopher. I'm going to get him," she said in as strong a voice as she could muster. "*I'm* going to get him, and then he's staying with me."

It was unimaginable, being without Christopher tonight. He needed her, and she needed to be with him. Just in the last few months he had started letting her cuddle him at night while she read him and Arley a story. And sometimes lately, every now and then, he'd forget and call her Mom, and then—this broke her heart—he'd dip his head down and lick his lips nervously, as if he was scared of being corrected. He had to be with her! Cooksey could not be allowed to take him away, not on this day of all days. He had to stay here.

Cooksey let out a long sigh. "*No,*" he said. "For once you're going to do what you're told. You don't even know where you're going to be by the end of the day. I might arrest you here and now, you know that?"

"Frank, look at me. You know I didn't do anything to hurt Harris," she said. "He wasn't feeling well, and I offered to give him a back rub, that's what this was—"

"Go on downstairs with Scanlon and fill out your statement. You're not the one calling the shots here. Foster, you go over to the school before it lets out—and, Sullivan, find Nate Goddard, and then call my wife."

"No! *Please*. Listen to me. I'll make out a statement, and I'll tell you exactly what happened," Jamie said, "but then I want to go pick up the boys from school." He had turned away, but she went around him and stood in front of him. "Please! Frank, it's important that Christopher stay with me and with Arley tonight. He's going to be scared enough, and he shouldn't be separated from us."

"Scanlon, take her downstairs."

"We're the people he lives with and knows the best."

"Scanlon!"

"Besides, this is what Harris would have wanted. You know it is, Frank. He'd want Christopher to feel safe and to be at home."

"Harris would have wanted to be alive, too," he said. "But he didn't get that privilege, did he?"

She was quiet for a moment. Then she said, "Why are you doing this? You know I didn't do anything to hurt him. I tried to help him."

"Yeah, I know the kind of *help* you were offering. What the *hell* was Harris doing in your bed with no pants on, Jamie? Try to stand there and tell me I've been wrong about you and Harris all this time."

She looked around, aware that every medical technician and cop in the place had turned to statues. She lowered her voice and stepped closer to Frank, licked her dry lips, tried to summon up moisture in her mouth. "Listen, I know what you're thinking, and it's not true. It wasn't true. We weren't lovers, I promise you that. You know we weren't. I offered him a back rub, and then when I came upstairs—"

"I don't know anything anymore! I know what's in front of my face. What the hell did you want with an old man, anyway?" he said. "Why couldn't you have let him be? You and your sister—what *is* it with the two of you? Why can't you go back to New York, or wherever the hell you came from, and leave this place alone?"

She looked straight into his face, praying that she wasn't going to faint or lose her nerve. He had a little piece of white spittle on his lip, and she stared at that. "Please, Frank. Listen to me. Harris and I were friends, that's all. Good friends. Now let me take Christopher for tonight. He's going to be so scared if he has to go somewhere else. Come on. Please. Just for tonight. Think of what Harris would say— he'd want him to be home with us."

"Oh, you think so? That kid has got a father, you know. Not much good, if you ask me, but he *is* going to be notified, and then he's going to come here and take him, God help us all."

"I know. Just until his father gets here. That's all I ask."

He let out a big sigh, looked skyward, and blinked a few times. Oh, God, he was going to cry. But instead he cleared his throat, turned away, took control of himself. And then, praise the Lord, his cell phone rang, buying her a little more time. He yanked the thing out of his pocket and walked a few steps away so he could talk. She stood there feeling the sweat trickling down the sides of her body, listening to the squawking on the other end of the phone. She didn't have a single intention of losing this battle; she stood there, coolly, staring at him, certain of winning.

By the time he finished the call and snapped the phone shut, she had his number. Here he'd lost his best friend and, instead of letting himself feel bad and join with other people who also felt sad, he needed somebody to blame for it. It was too hard even to *think* that Harris's heart had simply given out. No, it had to be somebody's fault.

He pushed his sunglasses up on top of his bald head and rubbed his eyes. She watched his jaw muscle working back and forth. Then he said heavily, "Goddamn girls. Another one on her way home tonight with three kids." He sighed. "What a day. Of all days." He stared down at the clipboard for a moment and then said in an aggrieved tone, "Okay. You can keep Christopher overnight. But when Harris's son gets here, you're out. You understand that?"

"Sure. Okay."

"Because this is *his* house and *his* boy. I don't know what you were after with this old man, but this isn't yours—none of this is. There's no money for you here, you know that."

"I would never—" she started and then thought better of it. He was an ignorant old man. The world was all black and white to him: everything was either for sex or money. "Yeah. Of course. I never thought . . ."

For a moment he stood looking at her, his eyes sad. "God*damn* it to hell. He just didn't know he was mortal. Thought he could have young chicks all the way into his hundreds." He wiped at his eyes. "Go. Get out of here."

At that moment, Nate Goddard, thirty-six years old and looking like some kind of overgrown schoolboy with his shiny hair, crinkly eyes, and pasted-on Dennis Quaid grin, was sitting in a luxury box at Yankee Stadium, eating shrimp cocktail with a husband-and-wife team of clients, halfway listening to the announcers yammering on in the pregame show, and wearing what his fiancée, Tina, had called his scanning-for-trouble look. He was fifteen minutes away from getting these two to sign a million-dollar contract for a whole nationwide communications system, and he didn't want anything to go wrong. So far everything was picture perfect, tying up with a big red bow four days of almost magical contract-signing luck: today the shrimp was plump and fresh, the champagne came in delicate little flutes that the wife had held up to the light and admired, and there wasn't a cloud in the New York sky. Now, if only the Yankees could work out a win for these folks, he'd be golden. Who did you have to call to fix a game these days? He felt almost powerful enough to make that happen.

He leaned forward, scooped up one of the smaller shrimp, and dipped it lightly into the cocktail sauce. He wasn't hungry, but he'd learned that the clients don't like it if you don't eat the food, too. Makes them feel piggy, and they can't help mentioning it over and over in one way and then another. And these clients—Doug and Denise Morgan, owners of a chain of coffeehouses—were going to sign by the fourth inning, his instinct told him. After five years of doing this work, he knew almost down to the minute how it was all going to go. All he had to do now was keep the smile steady, keep the bright lights on in back of the eyes, and keep the banter so light and fluffy that you'd swear you were in a luxury box full of show poodles—and then there'd be handshakes all around and he'd be out of there, heading to the airport, flying to Chicago for a quick layover with Tina, who was seeing a client there, and then off to San Francisco to see a pharmaceutical CEO about his international network needs. Maybe by the end of the month he'd be able to get to his apartment in L.A., kick back for a couple of days, get his paperwork under control, call on some West Coast customers, say hello to his cactus—the famous cactus, which, he always told people during the required small-talk portion of the sales pitch, was his only dependent.

"You wouldn't want to be there for our reunions," he liked to say. "Man, that bastard likes to hug!" That always got a big laugh. Then, before anybody could muse about why *didn't* he have anyone but a cactus to greet him, he'd carefully steer the conversation back to them, to their wives and children and grandchildren—their second cousins' neighbors, if necessary. People love to talk about themselves, and Nate was one hundred percent up for it. Hell, he'd talk about anyone or anything, and do it in such a way that afterward the people he was talking to thought they and not he were the smartest, cleverest people in the world. Yep, it had taken only one disastrous instance of his mentioning that he was a widower to make him drop that word from his vocabulary forever. For. Ever. That time, he'd spent the rest of the evening being pried open like a clam by the client, a woman who kept urging him to tell her *exactly* how he *felt,* and exactly how the tragedy had happened, and had he gotten some support, and oh, if he was ever in blah blah blah city, he *must* go to this special grief yoga meditation experience class . . . he must, he must.

Never again.

Even when he'd told Tina, he was careful not to use the word *widower,* with its wind-howling-in-the-graveyard sound to it. Nope. He told her very casually, almost offhandedly, in just the right tone. After the third time they'd slept together, he'd watched her get dressed to go catch a plane, and then he'd said, "In the interest of full disclosure and truth in advertising, I suppose if we're going to keep seeing each other, I should tell you that I've been married before."

"Oh," she said, leaning on one arm to wriggle her foot into her shoe. "So you're divorced."

"No. Car accident."

"Oh my God," she said. "You poor man." And then—even though "car accident" should have told her all she needed to know—he'd sketched out the briefest details for her in the time it took her to make two pieces of toast and run out the front door to get a cab. Six months later, right after they'd gotten engaged, he'd added the part about the boy, and how the kid was being raised by his grandfather—happily, *so* happily. An idyllic, perfect little childhood, right there in the house where Nate himself had been raised. It was the first time he'd ever told anybody about Christopher—not even his boss, Howie, who was practically his best friend—and the words were so hard for him that he couldn't look at her while he said them. He'd told her from the hotel bathroom while he pretended he was shaving, calling out the news to her while she got dressed.

There had been a silence, and then she'd come into the bathroom. "That's all very cool, but what's going to happen when he wants to come live with you at some point?"

"Are you kidding me? He doesn't want to have anything to do with me," he said. And then, because he could see she was starting to regard him as someone who went around misplacing loved ones, he added: "Don't worry about him. I send money every month. And my father doesn't want me around. Believe me, this is the happiest boy you'd ever want to hear about. He's got so many people in that hick town I grew up in that the times I've gone to visit him, I could just see that he'd gotten overloaded, just having so many people he had to deal with. His grandfather doesn't even think he should take my phone calls—that's how happy he is without me."

"Hey," she said, "don't tell me this is the way it's going to go with you our whole life, one surprise after another." But she didn't break up with him, although frankly he might have been relieved if she had. He had a piss-poor record, that was for sure. Letting one wife die on his watch, and then losing track of a boy besides. And she didn't even *know* the part about his dad walking away from the family when he was a kid and then his mother dying of cancer while he was downstairs eating a bagel with cream cheese.

That's why the company hadn't hired him for Human Resources, he'd tell her. He *had* no human resources. He was a salesman and problem-solver through and through. A bull's-eye-every-time salesman.

The Yankees led off with a home run, and Denise Morgan said wouldn't it be fun if they emptied their glass every time there was a run. He smiled and poured more champagne into the little flutes.

"And then we'll find out what you're really made of!" she said. "Like, who's the *real* Nate Goddard?"

So he did the cactus bit to fend her off. She laughed. He asked about her kids and grandkids.

"Doug, this guy is a certified workaholic. Are you getting this?" she said. She leaned forward and gave him a sly smile. She was a plump, motherly woman with frosted blond hair that flared out in two little wings and the kind of eyes that looked like they could bore right into you, didn't miss a trick. "Honey, I gotta tell you, no amount of money is going to make up for robbing you of your youth like this."

"What are you talking about, robbing me of my youth?" he said. "What have you heard? My youth is perfectly intact! Hell, I'm having the time of my life! You kidding? I travel all over the country, I meet people like you and Doug and get to hang out with you. Come on, now. You wouldn't let a guy like me spend four days with you if I didn't have something to say about communications, would you? That's just my front, but my main thing is getting to hang out with you."

She wasn't buying it. "You know what you need? You need a wife—a nice, beautiful homebody to get together with at the end of the day," she said and sat back in her chair, looking satisfied at having delivered that pronouncement. Tipsy, not drunk yet, but he'd better start fishing out the pen.

"Well, then you'll be thrilled to know that you're absolutely right and I'm getting married," he said and reached into his briefcase for the contracts. He'd never worked Tina into his routine before; this could be a godsend.

But this didn't shut Denise Morgan up, even though the Yankees just then got a double and the crowd roared to its feet, Doug Morgan along with them.

"Is she beautiful?" Denise needed to know.

"Very." Which she was, if you like a certain type of woman: thin and pointy, all angles. Short black hair all moussed up and sprayed into hard peaks. But even when her hair was just shampooed and not yet lacquered, she was still somebody whose elbows and knees could do real damage if you rolled into them in bed.

"And does she make a nice home?"

He couldn't help laughing at that. He had no idea, hadn't thought to wonder. "Yes, yes, she makes a nice home."

"Where did you meet her?"

He stifled a sigh. "We both work for this company. She travels around, too."

"So you don't see her very much, do you?"

"No."

"Do you *ever* see her?"

"Well," he said, "not so much. Once our planes passed in midair and I waved at her from the window." He laughed. "I held up a sign that said, 'Will you marry me?' And the next week, our planes passed again, and she held up a sign that said, 'Yes.' "

Doug was back in the conversation. "That's a match made in heaven," he said.

Denise threw back her head and laughed so hard Nate was afraid she was going to choke on the shrimp she had put in her mouth.

"Come on, honey," she said to Nate. "Let's get out of this ball game and go somewhere more interesting. I just remembered I hate baseball."

"She does. She hates baseball," Doug said. He shrugged at Nate.

She hates baseball? She begged for these tickets.

"I wanted to come for Doug," she told him, as though his thoughts had been typed out on his forehead. She got to her feet, only slightly unsteadily. "Come on—let's go to the Statue of Liberty. Or a Broadway show! We'll go stand in the TKTS line, and then we'll give Doug a call and tell him what show we're gonna see, and he can join us later for a drink. And then we'll sign the contracts and you can get back on a plane and see if you pass your sweetie in midair."

He looked over at Doug, who gave him another shrug and the thumbs-up sign.

"Okay. Let's sign everything first, and then I can put the briefcase away for good," he said. "Then I can truly have some fun."

Denise paused, as though this was worth considering, but then she shook her head and in a baby voice said, "Nope, nope, nope! You silly man! I know if we do that you won't want to come see a show with us. Ohhh, I *know* your type! Don't think I don't!"

Nate was amazed. He had not seen this coming, not in the least. His scanning for trouble had not even touched upon the idea that Denise Morgan was going to turn out to be a nut job. He laughed. You *had* to laugh. That's what this job was: you had to laugh, switch gears, take charge of the new plan. It was nearly a fucking million dollars hanging in the balance, and he'd worked for four days on this, not to mention all the time he'd spent doing the analysis and drawing up the presentation and figuring out the troubleshooting schedule. The top of his head felt like it maybe had a hinge mechanism to it and was going to flip open and they'd see that his brains were actually smoking.

He made the necessary preparations, made sure Doug was okay with everything, moved the tray of shrimp closer to him, set the champagne bottle just so, and then, with a backward longing look at the game (score: 3–0 Yankees), he and Denise left. She was tottering dangerously on her high heels now, and it was freaking hot out in the stadium. He held her arm, and she babbled on, so pleased with herself for coming up with this new plan.

"I never assert myself," she was saying. "This time I did, but normally I'm just the shy little woman in the background. And then when you told me about your fiancée, I could tell you didn't care one bit about her. You're a big bullshitter, Nate Goddard. You didn't even know if she liked being at home with you. And that's when I decided, This is what women go through. *This* is what being a woman means. And I'm going to get what I want for once."

He gritted his teeth, and when he loosened the lockjaw grip he had on them, he was about to say, "My fiancée gets what she wants all the time. And I still have to find out what being at home even *means*." But then his cell phone rang in his pocket, and instead he said, "Excuse me, Denise."

He leaned against one of the cement portals and flipped open the phone, straining to hear through the static and the cheerful din of conversations around him.

"Is this Nate? Nate Goddard?"

"Yes!" he yelled, put his finger in his other ear, and leaned forward, concentrating. And then there it was, like all the other times: someone was dead and he was being notified. This time he couldn't quite make out who it was because the swarm of bees had already started up in his head, as if they'd been waiting off on the sidelines of his life, biding their time, smoking a few cigarettes, perhaps shooting pool, loitering around waiting until it was time to revisit him. Also there was noise and confusion on the other end: Christopher's name spoken in italics, the hiss of static. He squeezed his eyes shut, waited while his little boy's face swam up again and again—Christopher at two, crying on Harris's shoulder—now silenced, white-faced, drained of life. But no, then it wasn't true. *No.* Not that. Christopher wasn't dead. The scene shifted. It was that Christopher was being *taken care of.* He was going to be taken to someone's house for the night. Chief Cooksey's house. He was fine.

His father. It was his father. Dead. His father was gone.

Air burst back into his lungs. He tried to say something, but a sound resembling a sob was all that came out. Chief Cooksey was talking, saying words that didn't mean anything: *sudden death, collapse, questioning.* Then: *When are you coming?*

He would come. He'd be there. God. The boy is . . . really okay? Oh my God. Yes, I'll come. Later. Tonight. Yes, tonight.

He snapped the phone shut, realized he'd been walking in circles with it, cupping it to his ear.

And then, unable to speak anymore, he calmly walked past Denise Morgan—he saw her open mouth, her wide eyes like black holes sitting there on her face—and he went into the men's room and into a stall, where he very deliberately put down his briefcase on the back of the toilet so it wouldn't get wet on the floor, and then he puked his brains out.

CHAPTER
4

Jamie sat at the picnic table in the backyard, feeling the hot breeze on the nape of her neck, thinking that this is what happens to you when you don't act on your instincts, and wondering if she was going to be able to keep herself from standing up and screaming. Just a little scream, maybe. She settled for digging her fingernails into the palm of her hand as hard as she could, until she could feel them make little half-moon indentations that would last for hours. Damn it, damn it, *damn it,* she'd *known* it was ridiculous for Harris to be outside scraping the house, and she had even told him so when he'd started out. She'd said, "Harris, it is waaay too hot for you to be doing that today! You need to chill out and do something cool today. Scrape the house another day."

Had she really said that? She couldn't remember. But it didn't matter. She'd said *something,* but he was as stubborn as anybody she'd ever met in her life, and if he decided that he was going to scrape and repaint the whole damn house that day, why, then he would, and it didn't matter what arguments she made. In the end, weary of arguing with him, she'd gotten busy doing her own painting: the kind on a canvas.

And now he was dead and the house was full of people—so full that she'd been brought outside for questioning. Which was good, she

supposed. She didn't want everybody overhearing her. It was hard not
to think of this as an interrogation. She sat across from the cop they'd
picked to do this, Scanlon, who was looking at her with that neutral
expression that they must teach them at the police academy—that,
and the way of saying "ma'am" as if he was straight out of an old highway patrol training film. He was two steps away from being Barney
Fife, with that over-earnest way he had of writing down everything
she said on a yellow legal pad, in handwriting that was childish and
big, like a fifth-grader's, with big loops and lots of care taken not to
miss crossing his t's. He bore down so hard that he had to stick part of
his tongue out while he wrote.

Good God.

Several times she had to resist reaching over and grabbing the
legal pad and printing out in huge black letters: THE SUBJECT DID NOT
DO ANYTHING WRONG.

Except—well, she knew that wasn't true. She had done plenty
wrong. She could count it all out on her fingers. She should have called
911 right when Harris came inside. She should not have let him tell her
he was all right. And then she should have insisted to Violet that Al
come right over, not wait until the end of the day. Going even farther
back, she should have hidden Harris's scraper, thrown it into the pond
or something, or tackled him as he was going out the back door. Maybe
she should have pretended that *she* was ill, so he would have had to stay
inside and take care of her. This day needed a big old Rewind button.
One more chance, please, and this time I'll do it all just right.

If she grabbed the legal pad right now, she would write: THE SUB-
JECT ABSOLUTELY DID NOT KILL HARRIS GODDARD. NOT ON PURPOSE, ANYWAY.

Instead, she sat there and, with a mouth so dry that her tongue
kept sticking to her teeth, she answered the questions. She told the cop
exactly what had happened, went through the whole time line in a
polite, restrained voice that did not once scream or sound panicky. It
would not do to break down. Instead, she told about the paint scraping, the coming inside, the phone call she'd made to the doctor, the
glass of water, the trip upstairs. Yes, the unfortunate gin and tonic.

The offer of a back rub. Then she licked her lips, wishing she had a tad more moisture in her body. From out here in the backyard, she could see into the kitchen, see that it was packed with people—all old friends of Harris's, who had flocked there upon hearing the news. For a while, before this baby cop—his name tag said he was Mike Scanlon, not even Michael—had gotten around to interviewing her, she had been the one to answer the door, feeling as though she had somehow become the hostess at a really, really bad party. But all the people streaming through had only briefly registered her presence and had then gone to comfort one another instead. Some of the women hugged her briefly, but it was really each other they were seeking out. Of course. It was almost a forehead-smacking realization: she was a temporary stranger here. A person of not much consequence after all.

"How long did you know Mr. Goddard?" Mike Scanlon said. He had a pleasant, nonauthoritative voice, she thought. It went with his boyish handwriting. He should face the fact now that he could never scare a bad guy. She wondered if he knew this already, and she felt her courage starting to come back.

"One year," she said.

"And what was the nature of your relationship to him?"

"Friend," she said. "Actually, roommate. No, no. *Housemate.* Put down that we were housemates, not roommates."

His pen hovered above the page, waiting.

"See, if you say we were roommates," she said, in her kindest explaining voice, "people who read it are going to think we shared a room—which we didn't. We shared the house. Rather, it's his house, and he let me live here. But we weren't . . . I mean, we didn't sleep in the same room. We both just lived here."

He hesitated a moment, as if this were a distinction he couldn't quite fathom. Then he sighed and said, "Well, *okay,*" as if people were always making wild requests of him. He crossed out the word *roommates* and wrote *housemates* above it, which she thought looked suspicious. He should start over on a new page. But no doubt he wouldn't be talked into *that.* "Now," he said, "how many people live in the house?"

"Four. Harris, me, Christopher, his grandson, and Arley, my son."

"R. Lee?"

"Arley. No, no." She looked at what he was writing. "Not with an *R*. You spell it A-R-L-E-Y. He's named for a village in Great Britain that has wonderful gardens. I did a painting of them while I was pregnant with him, back when I lived in Brooklyn. I didn't really live in Great Britain. I actually painted the gardens from a photograph I saw." *Stop talking. Just please, please stop.*

"Oh!" This fact seemed to make him stop writing. "When did you move here from Brooklyn?"

"When Arley was six weeks old. I came here to live with my sister, Lucy, who teaches yoga here and works as a bartender. *She* would tell you that she rescued me, brought me out of the city and out of a really, really bad relationship. I let her think that. Well, I let her think that because it's really true." She laughed a little and then regretted it. "Don't write that part."

"No," he said. "I won't." He squinted off into the distance, and then looked back at her, his pen poised over the pad. "So what did you do in Brooklyn?"

"What did I *do*?"

"Yeah. Your occupation, I guess."

"Is there really a line for occupation for five years ago? Really?" she asked. Then before he could think she was being difficult, she said, "I'm an artist. I paint pictures, and I teach at the junior college. Just adjunct. And I do some volunteer work, for the Campfire Kids. That's where I met Harris."

She was seized by the idea that she could flood him with facts and then he would know she had nothing to hide, and when he had to present his report, he'd hand it in with the air of someone who is not concerned at all about the person he's interrogated and so he would not set off any unsettling psychological repercussions through the police station's chain of command. So she told him that she'd been born and raised in New Haven, that her mother ran a chain of day-care centers and her father was a history teacher at an inner-city high school—he was maybe a little clinically depressed, as evidenced by the fact that he liked nothing more than making a nest for himself in a sagging armchair and reading history tomes while eating Ritz crackers. Her mother (she didn't tell him this part) used to joke that the warranty on her husband had run out years earlier than she had had any reason to expect it would. Even as a young man, he'd lost his vim and vinegar, she said, and had retired to the corner to read. Maybe, in a way, that's what had happened to Harris, too: he had been in need of repair, and his warranty had simply expired.

The truth was that her mother had lots of wrongheaded opinions about other people's lives. She thought that Jamie should aim to be a business owner, despite the fact that it was clear from an early age that Jamie had no aptitude for organization or keeping track of things. No, she was meant to be an artist—perhaps even a pinecone artist, since when she was a child that had been her favorite medium, gluing little pieces of paper and beads onto the cones she found in her yard. There was the famous family story about the time her mother signed her up for a soccer team, but instead of going to the practices, Jamie sneaked over to the Creative Arts Workshop and started showing up at a beginning painting class, offering to rinse the paintbrushes and hand out the paper towels. They let her stay and do pictures, but the next semester, when they gently told her she had to pay, she handed over the money her mother had given her for the soccer uniform and the team dues.

"Now then. Marital status?" the cop said.

She snapped back to attention. "Oh, single."

"Single never married, or single divorced?"

See? Now here they were, at this part. The truth was not going to sound so good to cops and people who tried to keep society on the right track: she had never gotten married to Trace, Arley's father. He had been her first boyfriend, and they had lived together in Brooklyn for three whole years, but frankly he was not a person anyone would ever have imagined getting married to. He was—or had been, at least, when she last saw him five years ago—a brooding, tortured type, one of those guys to whom art is everything, who simply cannot be led into the family of man. He was a graffiti artist, which he saw as some kind of higher calling. He dressed up in black at night and went out to do what he referred to as "noncommissioned art." She'd had to leave him right after Arley was born, when it was clear that writing the word *eros* in big, shaded, puffy letters on buildings and overpasses was going to be far more important to him than sharing a life with her and the baby. Her friend Shana from college had come and collected her in the middle of the night on the fifth day in a row that Trace had neglected to come home. The heat had been turned off in their tiny, depressing apartment, it was blizzarding outside, the new baby was coughing, and life was about as grim as Jamie thought she could take.

"Single, never married," she said. It was best not to explain about the graffiti and the arguments and the realization that she had to leave. She could go on all day about that stuff.

He must have sensed that she was on the verge of saying more, because he kept looking at her, waiting. And then he cleared his throat and said, "Are you in a relationship with anyone currently?"

It was unbelievable, the questions cops think they have to ask. No. No, she said, she was not.

A moment passed. He looked down at the pad and adjusted his voice. "So you have a sister in the area, you said? What's her name?"

"Lucy McClintock." She looked at his face to see if he'd heard of her, but he stayed blank. *Good.* Sometimes Lucy's name around the police station wasn't so good, especially since—well, especially since she'd started having an affair with Chief Cooksey's son-in-law. It was bad luck is what it was, that Jamie had to be penalized for some stupid guy who never could decide from one day to the next if he was going to stay married to Cooksey's daughter. Handsome Dan perhaps had a little sociopathic decision-making disorder, and Lucy—who could and *did* have any guy she wanted—seemed to be psychiatrically incapable of moving on from this guy.

"What's *her* occupation?"

Jesus. "She's a yoga teacher and a bartender."

"Wow, now that's an interesting combination," he said. "How long has she been here?"

"In Chester? Oh, I don't know. Seven years maybe. She came here with one of her husbands a long time ago."

He blinked. "One of her husbands?"

"Lucy believes in marriage," Jamie said, tugging her skirt down over her knees. She tried out a smile on Officer Scanlon. "That's the way she is. She gets carried away with people, and the next thing you know, she's gone off with some guy, thinking he's going to be the one forever, and they have a ceremony and she settles down. She's very trusting. I'm surprised you haven't met her. Everybody in town knows her."

"I'm actually new in town," he said and smiled. He was shy, she realized. And perhaps flirting with her.

"Oh, well," she said. "Then you'll meet her soon. Everybody in town loves her. They line up to take her yoga classes, and during the shifts she works at the bar, life is one big party over there."

He laughed a little bit and said, "So you and . . . Arley . . . lived with your sister, and then at some point last year you started living with Harris? How did that happen?"

She took a deep breath, as she always did when she talked about Arley's allergies, and told him the story of how Lucy's new boyfriend—whom she did *not* identify as Cooksey's son-in-law—smoked, and how at first Lucy was careful only to meet him elsewhere, but then the relationship got serious and he'd moved in with her. Even though he tried *not* to smoke around Arley, it hadn't really worked out, and so after dealing for a while with the fallout from smoke and being mad about it all the time, Jamie realized it was time for her and Arley to move out. She was teaching by then and selling her paintings at the Momovent Gallery, so she had a little money saved up. Lucy kept saying she should stay at the apartment. Dan could try harder not to smoke there, she really wanted to give Jamie a chance to save her money, blah blah blah, until her art career really kicked in. Please, please stay. But Jamie couldn't take it. All the crowding and the sex going on all the time, the little smirky-smirks at the breakfast table between Dan and Lucy, the smoochings in the hallway, the co-ed showers. *Yuck.* So she'd started looking for an apartment, but all the prices were out of her range, and then one day at a meeting of their little Campfire Kids organization she'd told this older gentleman, Harris, that she was looking for a place to live, and he'd invited her to come live in his farmhouse with him and Christopher, his grandson— and the rest, as they say, was history.

She gave an edited version of this, leaving out the smirks and some of the sex, and Mike nodded and wrote something down on the pad, and then they were quiet. She looked over at the house, and it was as though a sledgehammer had come down on her. *Harris is dead. He's dead!*

She wanted to cry.

"So what will you do now? Go back to your sister?"

She stared off into the distance, trying to think of what to say to this. Who knew what she would do? But he was watching her carefully, so she had to say something. "Oh," she said. "Well, I don't know yet, but I guess I have some options. I have a friend who teaches at a girls' school in Vermont. She's always trying to get me to come up there. The only thing is . . ." She looked down at her hands. "Well, the worst part—by far the worst part is leaving Christopher." Just saying his name made the bottom of her stomach fall out. She didn't want to move to Vermont. She wanted to stay right here. And the other part, which was only now becoming clear in her mind: she wanted to raise Christopher as her own child, even without Harris. Would that be inappropriate to tell the cop? She stood up suddenly, feeling panicky, and licked her dry lips again. It was hot out here, and she'd been talking to him for way too long, and besides that, she had to go. She said, "I really need to go right now and pick up the kids, because the last thing I want is for them to come home and find all these, all these vehicles, all this *emergency* going on. I need to prepare them. I've got to get them *now*."

He looked at his watch. "It's okay. You're good on time. I have a few more of the official questions, and then we'll be done and you can go. Just a few more questions. Was Mr. Goddard on any medications, that you know of?"

She twisted her hands in her lap, trying to think quickly. "No—oh, who knows? I mean, I tried to get him to take vitamins, but he said he'd been living on hot dogs and beer his whole life and he didn't have any trouble, and now that I was making him eat vegetables and stuff, he sure didn't need any more healthy food in him."

He wrote down the word *no*. "Were you aware of any medical conditions he had?"

"No. But believe me, he never would have told me even if he did have any health issues because he was one of those old guys who really, really wanted to be younger than he was. You know? Here he was raising his grandson, which is totally commendable, but, you know, I think he really wanted to be, you know, Christopher's *daddy*. You could see how he hated it when other people would call him Grandpa."

"Oh, really? Did Christopher call him Grandpa?"

"Oh, no. No, he called him Da. And—well, this isn't really funny, it's tragic, but one time I was standing next to the desk and I saw the picture of Harris's son, Christopher's real father, and I asked who it was, and Christopher told me, 'Oh, that's the asshole.' That's what he called his dad. Just very matter of fact, like it wasn't even a bad word. And Harris just laughed."

"Wow," Mike Scanlon said. "If I'd ever said that word when I was five years old, I'd have had my mouth washed out."

"Yeah, well, I think Harris had maybe *taught* him that word. Really. Can I go now?" she said. "It's time. You didn't have any more questions, did you?"

"Just one," he said and looked charmingly flustered. His ears grew red. "Maybe you and I could have dinner sometime? After all this blows over, I mean."

She was a little surprised at this. Who gets asked out by the cop during an interrogation? She was about to go into the spiel she always gave men who asked her out, not that there were all that many, but it did happen on occasion: what it was really like to have a kid who had asthma, and how she didn't really go out with guys because she was nervous the whole time she was gone. It was too nerve-wracking, frankly, being out somewhere and feeling poised to hear the cell phone ringing, alerting her to the next emergency, and knowing that maybe she was too far away or too late to make the mad dash to the hospital emergency room. Most of the time, as she explained to guys, there was nothing standing between her and unmitigated disaster. She'd been on alert for so long she'd forgotten what it meant to be relaxed.

"I wouldn't be any fun," she said. "I'm so flattered that you asked. But I—"

He held up his hand. "No, no. I know it might be a good long time before you're ready to even think about it. But it could be a pla-tonic dinner. We could discuss the good people of Chester and how we newcomers might someday fit in. I mean, if you're going to stay a newcomer. Sounds like you might move, though . . ." He smiled, showing teeth and dimples.

But before she could answer, she was distracted by the sound of yelling. She looked up to see her sister running toward her down the driveway from the street, still dressed in her yoga teacher's clothes—a black leotard, lavender tights, a filmy yellow skirt, and, incongru-ously, high-heeled boots—and she was holding out her arms and cry-ing, "Oh, Jamie! Oh, my God, honey! I just heard!" At which point she stepped in a little pothole, tripped, and sprawled beautifully, in a very yoga-sanctioned way, onto the gravel driveway.

"Ah, my sister," Jamie said, but Mike Scanlon had already gotten to his feet and was rushing to rescue her.

Nate Goddard, post-puke now and sucking on a breath mint, walked out of the men's room to find Denise Morgan standing right where he'd left her, only now she was holding a cup of beer in one hand and leaning against one of the portals, studying the people walking by and working her mouth all around like she was concentrating on them good and hard. He felt the slightest lick of irritation; somehow he'd hoped to return to find her vaporized into thin air or else gone back to her husband so he could figure out what he was going to do. But, no. Here she was still, standing there in her corporate-America standard-issue black pants suit and a pair of black high heels, looking out of place. He wondered again what the hell they were doing there.

But everything looked cockeyed to him now—too hot, too bright, like the day was made up of sharp reflective surfaces and hard edges. He wished he had some shades to put on, something to hide behind. Jesus. He was both motherless *and* fatherless now. An orphan, if middle-aged people could be considered orphans. And when had Denise Morgan started looking like his mother? How come he'd never noticed that before, in all the hours he'd spent with these people? She had the same plump compactness, plus those same bird-like eyes, that looked beady and intense, as if they were internally transcribing and analyzing everything going on. His mom had been dead for more than twenty years now, and suddenly it hit him right in the gut how much he'd missed her tough-talking, take-no-prisoners look, the matter-of-fact way she had of pulling information out of him, making him think thoughts he didn't even know he had.

Goddamn. He was an *orphan*. And that wasn't even the hard, startling part. If he was honest, he knew he'd given up long ago on having anything to do with his father. He'd tried his best to get along with the old man and had failed, and there wasn't anything now that would ever change that. No, the *real* life-changing news—the news that was driving him to his knees, that had had him sprawled out on the floor, clutching the Yankees toilet for dear life—was that Christopher was all his again. Nate Goddard, famous for being the cut-and-run slacker, the guy who was known for his flashes of brilliance and bedazzlement but who couldn't do anything for the long haul, was now going to be an actual father.

This was his shame: he hadn't seen Christopher for three years, since the kid was two years old—and that fifteen-minute visit had gone about as badly as anything could go in the annals of parent-child relations, with the kid screaming at the sight of him, throwing a toy car at his head, kicking him in the kidneys when he'd tried to pick him up, and then refusing even to glance at the bags and bags of sucking-up presents Nate had brought him. He'd bought out the entire Toys R Us, asking advice from the hot moms in there about what a two-year-old might want—and then the kid instantly sizes him up and recognizes him for the opportunistic creep he is, and clings to his grandfather for dear life. And there was Harris, looking so smug, cuddling the hysterical child while saying over his shoulder to Nate, "Well, looks like he sees through *you,* doesn't he? Out of the mouths of babes."

Goddamn if he hadn't spent the entire next year thinking about that horrible visit, as if it had gotten burned into his retinas or some-thing. Could a kid possibly make his hatred clearer? He understood now that he'd waited too long to go see him, that sending money hadn't been enough, that he should have been showing up all along. But he hadn't, okay? He'd fucked up. It happens. And all he had wanted for that one visit was to *see* the kid anyway, to see his own flesh and blood. Was that such an awful thing to do? Granted, he didn't know anything about kids, and he probably shouldn't have shown up with that girlfriend of his—what *was* her name, the one who always kept one hand down the back of his jeans and made kissing noises in public—but didn't it count for anything that he'd *shown up*? Hell, he'd gone there at last with so much goodwill, so much trembling tenderness, wanting to touch his child, to hold him and try to say, "I'm your *father,* and I love you." Shouldn't that have counted for something?

But when he'd tried to gently take him out of Harris's arms, Christopher had shrieked even louder, and the old man had gone downright feral, practically baring his teeth. Afterward, they'd had a terrible fight, with Harris telling him he was a lousy dad, that he'd been a coward from day one—as if his father had never stood in that kitchen and said to him, after the accident, "You need to get out of this town and get yourself a decent job. Leave the kid with me, and go get your head right. We'll be fine here. I'll raise him for you until you can take him." Now it was just: *Get out. Think of the kid and get the fuck out. Look around you and what he has here without you. He's loved. He's having the perfect childhood. Don't fuck it up for him.*

Perfect. Just perfect.

"*OHHH, MY GOODNESS,*" Denise Morgan said in her dry cigarette voice. "What's going *on?* Honey, you look like shit on a stick."

His stomach heaved again and turned over, but he squared his shoulders and headed toward her. He was okay. He was okay. Hell, he was more than okay. One thing he knew for sure: he'd be goddamned if he was going to fall apart. He was not going to sacrifice this sale on the altar of Harris P. Goddard, world-class hate-monger. Just give him this last sale, this last day, and then he'd go figure out what the hell he was supposed to do next. That was the deal he'd made with the toilet.

"Yeah, go ahead," he told her and grinned. "Insult a guy when he's down. I just had a minor disagreement with my breakfast is all."

She held out a plastic cup. "I got you a beer," she said. "From what I hear from my sons who are about your age, beer cures most of what ails a person. Here."

"Really, no. I'm good," he said and patted his stomach.

"A minor disagreement with your breakfast, huh?" she said. "So I take it that was your breakfast that called you on the telephone just then?"

Oh, she was trouble. He threw back his head and laughed that oh-ho-ho laugh he was so good at. "If you must know," he said, "and apparently you *must,* it was my Swiss cheese omelet phoning in, wanting to know if I'd like to revisit those sausages I had. But I'm fine now. *Raring* to go!"

And before she could answer, he reached over and took the beer out of her hand and put away the first sip, in case there was any doubt as to how fine he was. It burned his throat all the way down, but he smiled as he handed it back to her and said, "So, where's *your* beer— or are we sharing this one? Because I've always heard a person should never, ever drink alone." He permitted himself to give her his trademark playfully sexy wink. She'd appreciate that; he hadn't used it on her yet.

Instead she looked at him mildly. "Nate, I'm going to tell you something, and I want you to listen good," she said. "I raised four kids, three of them boys, and so I have a bullshit meter that is nearly one hundred percent on target. And I gotta tell you that it is off the damned charts right now. You are one wreck of a human being, boy. So now, why don't you tell me what happened back there?"

"Absolutely nothing to tell," he said and gave her a smile. He sketched out for her the whole day ahead: they'd drive into Manhattan, go to a museum or shopping on Fifth Avenue, eat a nice lunch at a famous deli in Times Square, get Doug to rejoin them after the game, and then, if they were lucky, he'd get tickets to a show, and when they'd been wined and dined and theatered he'd head out.

He looked at his watch and flashed her a smile. "Shall we?"

She smiled and clapped her hands like a little girl. And then he marched her to the car, talking about the weather and a play he'd seen the last time he was in New York, something he couldn't remember the name of, so he made up something. This is what he was best at.

He opened the car door, and Denise Morgan slid inside, smiling up at him. "You know I'm still going to figure you out, boy," she said. "You know I am."

He laughed and walked around to his side of the car. His cell phone rang again before he got in, and he glanced down at it. Shit. It was Howie, his boss. He thought of not taking the call—but Howie went ballistic on that kind of thing. It was always better to talk to him and fudge things than to try to avoid him.

He punched the button, leaned against the car door. "Hey, boss. Whassup?"

"How's it going, Nate the Man? They sign?"

"It's going great, Howser," he said. He could sense Denise practically leaning out the window so she could hear him. "Just fantastic. But hey, listen . . ." He lowered his voice, turned his body away from the car.

"What?" said Howie. "What else is going on, man?"

"Aw, nothing. It's all right." He remembered in time that he might never have mentioned to Howie that he had a son. Five years ago, when he was hired, that had been a painful subject, and back then he didn't do painful subjects. Hell, he still didn't do painful subjects— and this one was going to take some thinking.

"You sure?"

"Sure."

"Okay," Howie said. "So, listen, buddy, I'll see you on Thursday in L.A. Take a few days to work up the contract for the pharmaceutical guys, and we'll slide 'em a deal end of the week. Like paddling through rocks in a stream, right?"

"Right." Let's see. It was Friday now. Thursday was days and days away. By then, he'd have everything settled. There was the faintest buzzing sound in his head: the residuals from the swarm of bees, the noise of adrenaline kicking in. He propped the cell phone on his shoulder and cracked his knuckles, already working out the peripherals in his head.

"Think Zen," Howie told him.

"Right." He rolled his eyes. Thinking Zen was Howie's solution to everything. It wasn't going to do Nate one tiny piece of good.

The kindergarten room had bright yellow and red construction-paper flowers on the windows and buzzing fluorescent lights, and for a moment, standing in the doorway, Jamie thought life seemed so fragile that she almost couldn't bear it. She looked at the worn red-and-blue hooked rug where the children sat in a circle each morning while they decorated the calendar with smiley-face rain and sunshine stickers. Life is simple, these stickers said. And it wasn't. She blinked, looked around at all the little tables where the children sat, and at the big wooden blocks stacked up on their shelves, and at the housekeeping corner with its little pretend stove and refrigerator. What holds all these things up, she wondered. How is it that the blocks don't cascade down on some kid's head? Why isn't the hook rug labeled a slipping hazard, and the stove and refrigerator removed on grounds that they mislead kids into thinking that life is going to be easy?

She stood there watching while Miss Sullivan, who was fat and bosomy and kind, placidly handed out mimeographed notices to her bouncy Friday-afternoon kindergarteners. If you stood at the door and squinted, they were a blur of color and motion. The air smelled unmistakably of elementary school: kids' sweaty bodies, white paste, floor wax, the whiff of Miss Sullivan's talcum powder, and the leftover smell of overcooked cafeteria vegetable soup.

Arley was the first to turn around and see her there. Immediately his huge blue eyes widened and he jumped up and down on one foot, waggling his head in excitement, and then he balanced himself and leaned over to poke Christopher so he'd look up and see her, too. Christopher, always more reserved, gave her a surreptitious wave and a tiny smile, and then picked up his backpack in a resigned, workmanly sort of way. He was a solemn child. While the rest of the kids banged into one another like puppies, he stood straightening his strap and frowning into the middle distance.

Lucy, who had stopped off to notify the principal—she said the authorities had a right to know there had been a death in the family— came in and stood next to Jamie. "Oh God," she said under her breath.

"I know," Jamie whispered. "It's overwhelming."

"No, I meant what do you have Arley wearing? Is that—is that a *crocheted vest*? And—are those . . . *ladybugs* on it?"

"Don't start on this. He wanted it," she whispered.

"Hey, I know. Why don't you just have him wear a sign that says, 'I'm a hopeless dork. Will you please make fun of me?'" Lucy got a look at Jamie's face and covered her mouth. "I'm sorry, I'm sorry. I know. This is a heart-wrenching occasion. I have to be good. But when this is over, we have to have a talk about the way you dress that child. It's a brand-new century, and no one should have to wear a vest anymore."

"Would you stop it? This is totally inappropriate."

"What's inappropriate is that vest. It's a good thing you're going to move back in with me. This makes it pretty clear you can't be trusted on your own."

"Shhh."

Lucy leaned over and brushed a tendril of Jamie's hair off her forehead. "So, uh, do you know yet what you're going to say to them?"

"Well, I haven't rehearsed a speech, if that's what you mean. I thought I'd just—well, I'd just tell them simply and plainly. What else can I do?"

"What the hell do I know?" Lucy said and sighed. "If it can't be fixed by stretching or drinking alcohol or having sex, I have no idea how to make it better. That's the sad truth of it. You're the artistic, introspective one."

Then the bell rang, and immediately everything erupted into craziness. The children whooped and scrambled for their things, an announcement about buses came on the crackly loudspeaker, and kids spilled out into the hall from everywhere, talking and laughing and shouting to one another.

Christopher and Arley came running over to Jamie, bumping into tables and each other and other children along the way. Christopher got to her first and wrapped her in a hug, standing on her shoes and gazing up into her face the way he did every day, rocking back and forth. And then as usual he sprang away from her as soon as Arley got there, embarrassed, as though Arley might remind him that Jamie was *his* mom. Jamie bent down and gathered both boys to her for as long as they'd let her (three seconds, tops), loving their sweaty little-boy smells, feeling how wiry and strong their bodies were as they wiggled around. Christopher had luscious chubby cheeks and a shock of dark hair to go with his dark eyes, eyes so opaque they looked almost black. Arley—her darling, fragile Arley—was thin and lighter, with wide blue eyes that seemed always to be watering, and a nose red from sniffling. She gave him an extra medicinal hug and listened to his lungs: he was fine. At least now he was fine. Who could guess how this news was going to affect him?

"Why did you come pick us up? Why aren't we going on the bus?" Christopher wanted to know, bouncing up and down on his toes. "Are we getting ice cream?"

Arley poked him. "She came 'cause I need a new inhaler at school."

Damn. That's right—she'd been planning to bring a new one to the school nurse today. Not that the old one was finished, but she didn't like to take any chances. Just let there be a wet, cloudy day, and Arley could run into extra trouble. She'd left it in her car.

"I forgot it, honey. I'll bring it in on Monday," she said—but they were already onto the subject of ice cream. Somehow pickups had turned into trips to get treats. She got busy helping them with their backpacks and notices and jackets, handing Lucy the lizard sculptures they'd made out of papier-mâché, and the lunch boxes. But once all that was done and she'd gotten them outside, the blood started beating hard in her ears. Should she stop on the sidewalk right then and tell them what had happened? Or tell them in the car, once they were belted in?

"Can we go on the swings?" Christopher asked, and Arley said, "Pleasepleasepleaseplease!"

She said yes quickly, even though Lucy frowned at her. She was stalling. But so what if she was? Christopher had the whole rest of his life to know that his grandfather was dead—why not let him swing as high as he could right now?

The boys elephant-walked their way over to the playground behind the school, making trunks out of their arms and shouting and laughing along the way, and Jamie and Lucy followed. The buses left with a roar, and pretty soon the yard was empty of children. The janitor came outside and picked up papers listlessly, glancing over at them, but then after a while he went back inside, too. The boys were on the swings, pumping their little legs as hard as they could and calling out, trying to touch hands as they flew past each other. Jamie kept hugging herself. She was cold, even though there wasn't any breeze and the sun was still hot in the sky.

"You know this is making it *har*-der . . ." said Lucy.

Jamie had been sitting on the ground, but now she stood up. "Okay, time to stop!" she called, and shivered. The children jumped off in the most dramatic, heart-stopping way possible and then rolled out of the way of the crazy-spinning swings, lying there giggling and squirming around in the grass. Lucy took her by the hand and led her over to them. The sun was lower in the sky now but still hot. Jamie sat down, and Lucy gestured with her head, urging her on. After a moment, Jamie bit her lower lip and cleared her throat, and from out of nowhere, she heard herself say, "I'm afraid I have some sad news to tell you."

Her voice sounded shockingly loud to her own ears. Arley's eyes went bright and round, but Christopher was already shrinking down, as if he were trying to make himself so small that the bad news couldn't find him.

She reached her arms toward him and said softly, "Today, Christopher, Da was not feeling very well, and so he needed to go lie down, and then his heart was too tired to keep going, and it stopped beating. And . . . well, I'm afraid he died."

This was all wrong. She should have told him first, shouldn't have let him swing as though the world were still a normal place to be.

In the distance somewhere, a siren screamed. Arley's eyes widened, and he wiped his nose, looking as if he might cry, but to her surprise, Christopher regarded her calmly. "Oh, don't worry. They can make him all right again," he said. "They do that when Arley has to go to the hospital."

"Oh, honey, no. I'm afraid he's not going to be all right," Jamie said and swallowed. "The ambulance came, with the emergency guys and the firemen, and everybody worked to help him for a long time, but they couldn't get his heart to start beating again."

"No," he said with all his little-boy insistence. "It's going to be *okay*. They know how to do that."

"This time they tried, but it didn't work. He had a heart attack."

"No, that's wrong," he said, louder.

"Christopher, honey, she's not wrong," Lucy said. "That's what happened. The workers were very sorry, but it didn't work this time. Sometimes it doesn't."

He got to his feet then, and Jamie saw that his eyes had gone wild, little black dots in a sea of white, like the eyes of an untamed horse she'd seen once. In one springing motion, he took off in the direction of the soccer field in the distance, where he ran in large, looping circles. She could see his red face, his windmilling arms, and she thought she could hear him yelling, and more than anything, she wanted to go and run alongside him, just to be there. But she knew better than to try to force herself on him now. She went closer, as close as she dared go, and watched, and when it was clear he was tiring out, she ran and caught him and held him. He was breathing hard and sobbing, and he fought against her for a bit, until finally he sank against her, breathing hard now, but not crying.

"I—I want my Da to be . . . at home!" he said, gasping.

"I know. It's okay . . . it's okay," she kept saying, and rocking him back and forth, thinking what a stupid thing this was to say, because it was not okay, not okay at all. She could see Lucy and Arley sitting together, talking quietly. Lucy had her arm around him. She wished she'd left the inhaler with Lucy.

"Where is Da now?" Christopher said after a long time.

She didn't know what to say. Did he mean Harris's actual body? Was she supposed to explain funeral homes—or, worse, some sort of afterlife she wasn't sure she believed in? What would Harris have wanted her to say? She couldn't remember if they'd ever talked about that stuff.

"Where is he?" he said.

"He's—they took him away, to the funeral home."

He was silent. She knelt down beside him and stroked his head, patted his brown, chubby little hands. Little-boy hands, with their rim of dirt underneath the fingernails, always there no matter how often she scrubbed them in the bathtub. The hands—the hands melted her.

"Do you want to go back home now?" she said to him at last.

"Okay," he said, and wiped his nose. He pulled away, and she got to her feet and patted the top of his head and smoothed his hair.

He looked down at the ground, poked at something with the toe of his shoe. "Are you going to take care of me now?" he said in a low voice. He wouldn't look at her.

"Well," she said and noticed that a headache was blooming behind her eyes. Here they were, at this moment, so soon. She looked across the soccer field, at the sky so hot it looked white instead of blue. "I am going to take care of you right now. And—guess what! I heard Chief Cooksey say that *your dad* is coming."

His face crumpled. "But I don't want my dad to come! I want you to take care of me!"

She didn't know what to say. "We have to see what happens," she said finally. "Your dad—"

"I'll be good," he said. "I won't do any bad things, and I'll be nice to Arley and let him have the best Lego guy—"

Her heart broke yet again. "No, no, it's not whether you're good or not," she said. "You're always good. It's that your dad is the one who gets to decide. He's your *family*."

He scowled. "My dad is a big asshole."

"Hey," she said, and ruffled his hair again. "Come on, let's give the guy a break. I don't think we should call him that. He's been away for a long time, but I know he's going to want to get to know you, and he's going to love you so much. He wants to come here and be your daddy . . ." She trailed off. The truth was, she had no idea what Nate Goddard might do. What if she got Christopher all excited about his dad, and then the guy came and rejected him and ran off again? What then?

He scowled again and looked away, and she knew she'd failed him, as if she were forcing him to pretend something that he knew simply wasn't true so she'd feel more comfortable. People were always doing that to kids; he already knew that protecting adults from the hard truths was one of the jobs of childhood.

"A bird died today on the window at school," he said. "He crashed into it! *Bam!*" Then, without warning, he dropped down to the ground and rolled around and then started pumping his legs in the air like a bicycle and making engine noises.

"I'm riding a motorcycle!" he said. He screamed out, "Arley! Look at me! I'm riding a motorcycle! ARLEY! Come here, ARLEY!"

Arley, breathing hard, and with his hair flopping in his face, ran across the yard, with Lucy tottering behind him in her high heels, and then, laughing, he lay down in the motorcycle position, too. And then so did Lucy, who could get away with this because, after all, she was wearing a leotard and tights, so it didn't matter.

"Come on," she said to Jamie. "We're all going to ride motorcycles right out of here, right out of Crazytown. Get on your Harley, girl."

Which was nuts. They were out in public, and Jamie had on a long pink skirt, after all. But she did it anyhow: she lay down on the soft soccer-field grass, on all the new light green shoots, and she rode a motorcycle, holding her skirt in place as best she could, while tears trickled steadily into her ears.

At a little after four in the morning, Nate stood on the wooden porch of his childhood home and peered through the gap in the lace curtains and into the front hallway. What had his mother called it? Oh, yeah. The *foyer*. As in: *Don't leave your boots in the foyer, Nate. No playing in the foyer.* Like they were the freaking Rockefellers or something.

She had been funny and furious both, that mother of his. God, she'd been such a fighter. She would have made a great terrorist, actually. His dad had no sooner moved out of the house to move in with that woman he'd met at work, than his mom called in workmen—his dad's competitors, whom Harris had then had to *pay*—and had the whole place redecorated: wallpaper, exterior and interior painting, new light fixtures, everything she'd been nagging his dad to do for years. Ha! It served him right, too—out there in the world, living in the trailer with that new woman with the big boobs and the big hairdo, ignoring his wife and son like they'd never existed. Nate would see him out in town sometimes, gliding by in his fabulous rebuilt Mustang that was his pride and joy, that other woman sitting right up next to him in the front seat, not even riding on the passenger side, scrunched up to him right in the middle—and Harris never even looking in his direction, not even once seeing that his own kid was so close by. How could you *not see* your own kid? Wasn't there supposed to be some kind of electrical impulse, some DNA bond that zapped you when your kid was *right fucking there*?

It still just killed him.

Oh, and then a few years later, when Nate was playing baseball—when everybody thought he was such hot shit, hero of the school's team, putting Chester's sports programs on the fucking map—all he ever wanted was for his dad to come to the games, to come for a little bit, see him play. It was stupid, but he wanted the old man to see how people cheered for him; how, when he rounded the bases, people jumped to their feet and screamed his name. But no, no, he couldn't be bothered. Wouldn't stoop to that kind of thing. It got to where Nate wouldn't even let himself look into the stands, wouldn't search for his dad anymore. But then—how lame was this?—it was as if he couldn't help himself; he'd get so worked up that he'd jump on his bike and ride over to the trailer, all hot and bothered, hoping to see Harris, hoping he could yell at him, throw rocks at the windows or something, *make* him come to the next game or else punish him, get him to feel guilty. But then, like a dork, he'd end up leaving some stupid, whiny note, practically begging him to try to come next time. *Please, please try. Guess what? I hit a triple today, and the coach said* . . .

Pathetic, stupid kid thing to do. Made him want to go out and punch something hard, just remembering.

No wonder his mother was always yelling at him that he had to forget all about his dad, had to get over it, for God's sake. His mother got over it. In fact, she got over the whole man thing altogether. She'd never remarried, never even thought about it. There had been one guy who liked her, Eddy something, who used to take her out to dinner. But then he stopped coming around, and she told Nate she guessed she was all done with that romantic nonsense anyway. She stopped wearing all that fake man-catching stuff like makeup and dresses and high heels. She wore soft, comfy clothes after that, baggy jeans and sweaters, and she even stopped hanging with the boring neighbor PTA moms. She preferred a whole new group of friends—some tough-talking divorced women she'd met in a support group, women who were always dropping by the house, smoking and drinking and telling hilarious stories. Nate secretly called them the Fierce Mad Ladies, and although they halfway terrified him, he adored how cynical and funny they were. They'd sit in the kitchen with their glasses of wine, laughing and talking, cooking up delicious meals and entertaining one another with stories about their lives. They didn't *need* men. He heard one of them say one time, "Just this one *conversation* we're having right this minute—this is waaaay more fun than I ever had with sex!" and they all howled.

Once he was sitting there laughing helplessly along with them when one of them pulled him over onto her lap, giving him noogies and crushing his head against her excitingly ample bosom, saying, "Oh, laugh all you want, but you're going to grow up and be one of them. You're going to go out there and perpetuate the whole system, aren't you, getting some poor girl thinking that love is real, when everybody knows it's all one big lie."

But—well, then his mom got cancer, and it turned out that love wasn't a lie at all. It was that love was really women bringing food and then sitting by his mom's bedside in the dark, driving her to chemo and holding her hair back while she threw up—gifts he didn't know how to give or even how to thank them for.

He sometimes wondered how different his life would have been if his mother hadn't died. How would it be if *right now* she were still here, expecting his return, and then hearing him at the door, she'd come floating down the stairs to let him in? She'd be gray-haired now, probably fatter, but milder, mellower, even smiling—coming to welcome his grown-up self back home. Her life had sucked, and had probably disappointed her in, oh, about two million ways, but you know something? She'd always been ferocious in the way she stayed right in his corner. Never wavering, that one. Protecting him from everything she could think of. Even trying to make him stop loving his dad, so he wouldn't get crushed by the old man the way she had.

If she were here . . .

Yeah, they would say to each other. *Yeah, he died. He was a bad man in his way, but we survived him. You know? We survived. So what did you have for dinner tonight? Are you hungry? You want to go into town and get some eggs at the diner? They're probably just opening up.*

HE TURNED THE doorknob and was surprised that the door was locked. Since when were they locking doors in Chester? No one used to secure anything around here. He couldn't even remember ever having had a key to this place. He cupped his hands around his eyes and peered through the window again, down through the living room, through the little slice of dining room and into the kitchen. There was the soft glow of a light on over the stove. He could see a vase of daisies on the old wooden table and toys scattered on the floor. A robot-looking thingie and some trucks. He swallowed. *Christopher's toys.*

He sat down on the front porch steps and looked around him, trying to think what to do. The wood of the steps was worn down now and splintery. It had once been painted a robin's-egg blue, because that's what his mom had wanted, but now it was chipped, and you couldn't tell it had ever been a color. A drift of melancholy settled over him, much like the mist that seemed to be gathering in the empty field across the road. *Home sweet home.* The place still looked the same, even in the early-morning dimness—still those green-black groves of evergreen trees in the distance, the freshly mown grass in the yard all straggly and growing in clumps, the split-rail fence with rose bushes twining up and around, and of course the same gravel driveway and run-down farmhouse, white with black shutters. Funny how you could leave and then one day come back to the place where every single bad thing had befallen you, and find yourself feeling the same weight on you, as if you'd never gone and had a real life elsewhere.

He shouldn't let himself think. He was too tired for all that ruminating. Automatic pilot, that was the way to go on this one. He was tired, all kinked up, with a crick in his neck from driving so much. He'd walked around the city with Denise Morgan for hours, gone up to the top of the Empire State Building and the Museum of Modern Art, stood in the TKTS line, ridden one of those double-decker buses, taken a hansom cab through Central Park, where Denise had made a little speech about feeling more alive than she'd ever felt in her whole life. He had to hand it to her: for an old lady, the woman was tireless, striding along in her high heels, talking up a blue streak. She was curious about *everything*.

But here was the weird part: he'd actually enjoyed himself. For some reason—he still wasn't sure what had gotten into him—he had ended up telling her about his life. He'd started in jokily enough, saying something lame like, "Well, ha-ha, I just inherited my own son today," and then for once had stood there letting her ask him questions. Normally he loathed any kind of interrogation, hated coming out of character while he was on a sales call. Maybe this was what shock was. That had to be it: he had been reeling from shock, and he'd lost all his protective covering.

Yeah, but so what? So he'd broken his own rule and told her all about his fucked-up life. He would never have to see her again; the contracts were signed and safely tucked away in his briefcase, and other than one single follow-up call he'd make sometime in the next two weeks, they were done with each other.

Damn it to hell, how was he going to get into this stupid house? Was he going to have to sleep the rest of the night in the car? Is that what his life was coming to?

The worst had been telling Denise about Louisa, all the bad stuff he'd done to her. Well, not *truly* bad, evil stuff—not the kind of thing you'd read about in the newspapers. But he knew what he'd done:

he'd been cold and disinterested, and unresponsive to all her hysteria. But she'd *always* been going on about some injustice or some slight that had happened to her. Her sister had been prettier and smarter, and she needed daily reassurance about that. She hated her job, cleaning teeth in a dental office. Who could love *that*? Then she wasn't happy because they didn't own a house. So they'd bought a condo, and that wasn't right either. After that, she wanted to live near her sister, so they sold the condo and moved into a little one-bedroom apartment in Atlanta, and she babysat for her sister's kids while the sister worked. But then there wasn't enough money, and she wanted new living room furniture, and then she wanted her own baby. Then Nate, already half out of his mind with all this incessant *wanting,* had lost his job—a layoff situation—and she got the bright idea that they should leave the sister and move to Connecticut, on some theory that they could help Harris with his construction business, and start a family there. But then the town was too small, the house was too run down, and the pregnancy made her sick, and she didn't have any good friends in the area.

And then—well, they'd had yet another fight four days after Christopher was born. It was routine, wouldn't even have cracked the top ten of their fights if she hadn't stormed out of the house and gotten in her little Triumph convertible and gone tearing down the street and out onto the highway. Only, she went up the exit ramp instead of the entrance ramp, something he knew was on purpose. Nobody makes that kind of mistake. No, no. It was a real *fuck-you* to him and to Harris. And maybe to the baby, as well.

"Jesus," Denise Morgan had said softly when he got to that part, and they'd stood there for a long moment with the crowds of people pressing in around them. Telling her that had been the low point of the day; after that, it had gotten easier. At one point he took the old folded picture of Christopher out of his wallet and showed her: Christopher at about three, eating an ice-cream cone near a pony, looking up at the camera with a goofy, shy smile. She'd pored over the picture for a long time, even got her reading glasses out of her bag and stared at it in the sunlight.

"My, oh my," she said. "He looks just like you. Boy, are you in for it, huh?" Then she looked up at him. "Listen, this is nuts. Let me call my husband on his cell phone and have him come meet me. You need to leave! This boy needs you today."

"No," he said, laughing. "No. No!" He'd reached over and play-fully taken the picture out of her hand, and her purse so she couldn't get out her phone.

She gave him one of her fixed stares and reached over and took her purse back.

"No," he said. He was suddenly panicky. "It's all under control, believe me. The boy's being taken care of by one of my father's dearest friends. The chief of police, as a matter of fact. And my kid doesn't even know me, and he's certainly not missing me. So let's have this day the way it was planned." He couldn't put into words, even to himself, why he didn't want to go there. It seemed that as soon as he left New York City, the life that was waiting for him was going to blow to smithereens all that he now had. Here, the way he was living his life, his *freedom*—there were always so many possibilities. He'd have to work now to protect those possibilities. Didn't she see? He had so many decisions waiting for him. He had to figure out how he could be a father and still be himself. Yes! That was it. How to not be swal-lowed up. Yes.

She nodded and smiled like she understood perfectly. Of course she would. His mother would have known what he meant, too. She insisted on heading to F.A.O. Schwarz, the toy store, and buying Christopher a teddy bear. "You may not know it yet, but you're going to need lots of props," she said.

He hadn't been sure. He still wasn't sure. Boys needed fresh air, bicycles, and adults who loved their work and were passionate about what they did, he told her. He added that what the whole human race needed was *freedom*.

"Let's get a drink," she said. Packages in hand, they went into a bar and slid into a booth in the back. It was an old place, filled with dark wood and wall sconces that offered very little light. She ordered whiskey sours for both of them, and he started telling her his theory about freedom and how work could be something that *fed* that freedom rather than squelched it. He got more and more animated. "This is what my dad never understood. You shouldn't have your work life over here and your real life over here." He moved the salt and pepper shakers far apart, work and life. He was feeling the slightest bit drunk. They'd had beers at lunch. "People in this country—my father, for instance—do work they hate for fifty weeks a year, just so they can stop working and enjoy two weeks a year! How fucked up is that? Me, with my job—well, it's like it's my art or something. It's everything I *am. My life is my job!* And that's what I'll teach my boy— that kind of life is the only life worth living. Where your freedom comes from: your passion and your work."

He leaned back in the booth. God, that insight was so profound he almost wished he could whip out a pen and write it down somewhere. She was smiling at him.

She leaned over and touched his face. Her eyes loomed large in front of him, and he drew back. Was she coming on to him? Older women were always flirting with him, but this seemed truly outlandish. But, no, she was smiling at him, a sad, maternal smile, and he realized she was going to say something motherly and kind.

Instead, she said, "Oh, Nate, that is such bullshit. You know what freedom is? It's something people say they want when they're afraid they can't have what we all really crave: somebody to love. You have no idea what you're in for. To hear you tell it, you had a horrible father and an unhappy mother and then a bad marriage to the wrong woman, and so you ran off and found something you're calling freedom. Right now—no, hear me out—I can see this in your face. You think love is just these little, these little kissing games of the world you play—"

He burst out laughing. "*Kissing games?* May I remind you that I'm engaged to be married? If that isn't giving up freedom, I—"

She dabbed at her eyes with a napkin and laughed. "Oh, don't even start with me about that fiancée of yours. She *is* one of your kissing games, you big lug." She took another big swig of her drink. "If you were really serious about her, don't you think you would have called her by now to tell her about your dad?"

He was stunned. At first he was going to say he had been about to call Tina when things settled down some, when he wasn't on a sales call. But it hit him that, actually, she was right: he'd never even thought about it. Wow. It hadn't even occurred to him that this was something Tina should be told. He looked up and saw Denise was looking right into his eyes and nodding.

"Go home," she told him and gathered up her purse. "I'm calling my husband to meet me. And you—you need to stop playing games with yourself, and go start your real life." She shook her head and crinkled up her eyes at him. "Love is quite the ride. That's what you're going to find out—*if* you don't end up like an asshole and shut it out of your heart."

He didn't know what look must have been on his face, because then she burst out laughing and hit him in the arm. "Oh, you see now? I should *not* be permitted to start drinking champagne in the morning and then continue with booze all day long. It makes me give sermons. Go home! Let's call Doug, and then we'll sign that contract and get the hell out of your way!"

HE'D ARRIVED IN Chester at about two in the morning, driving from New York using the back roads, passing strip malls and barns and old white New England churches, but then once he got to town, for reasons he couldn't imagine, he'd pressed on the accelerator and kept going.

He couldn't breathe the air, that's what it was. All those farms spread out along the road, the trees all bending toward his car as the wind whipped them when he blew past—they were claustrophobic. How did people *live* here? He put the top down, drove through the center of town, opened all the windows, turned on the AC, turned the radio up loud. They were in ruts, that's what. The people here. Stuck.

Way past the town, when he could breathe again, he pulled up to a closed Dairy Queen, reading the signs advertising Blizzards and Dilly Bars and soft-serve cones, and then, to give his adrenaline some productive business to attend to, he got out of the car and picked up pieces of broken asphalt and threw them into the woods, as intent on his task as if he'd been assigned to obliterate all the trees on the planet. When he was exhausted with that, and no trees had fallen down, he shoved aside a bunch of acorns and maple seeds and lay down on top of a picnic table and closed his eyes. His brain felt as if someone had shattered a glass in it, and he had to pick through the shards, being careful not to cut himself.

Deeeep breaths. He needed a plan, that was all. Like anything else. Get a plan together, and then things would go much more smoothly. He'd take Christopher back to L.A. with him—and then see if maybe Tina would want to stop working for a few years and take it easy, live with him in his condo, and be a mom. He could do that. Sure, he could. Hell, they could even have a baby of their own if she thought it was too much to be asked to take care of his. But if she didn't want all that . . . if she didn't . . . well, then he'd take Christopher with him on the road for a while. Why not? Traveling was educational, and they could visit all the historic spots in the towns where Nate had meetings. Kids needed to learn history, didn't they? So instead of hanging out in hotel bars, he'd spend some time in museums. Big deal! Also, it wasn't like he lacked for money. If he had to he could hire a tutor or nanny to meet up with them in hotel rooms, teach Christopher to read and write while Nate was at meetings and on sales calls.

He was a little bit drunk, he realized, but not too drunk to plan this all out. He was the perfect amount of drunk, post-drunk, really, but not yet hungover—just opened up enough to see all the possibilities, to appreciate all the gates swinging open in his brain, leading him to rooms he didn't even know were in there. Hell, he'd find the right people to help him. He'd *delegate*. There were people you could hire who took care of children in hotel rooms while their parents worked. These days you could hire people to do anything for a living. He'd read that you could actually hire people to do your grocery shopping for you, and other people would stand in line for you at the Department of Motor Vehicles, or even put your CDs on your iPod for you. If you could purchase those services, surely you could find some nice lady—an au pair! Wasn't that what they were called?—to teach your kid to read and write while you were on the road.

No question. Harris's death was just the thing he'd needed to get himself moving again. You know, take certain decisions right out of his hands. He could change his life. Of course he could. He would be a father, like the guys you see at millions of Dairy Queens like this one on Saturday afternoons, holding kids on their shoulders and ordering banana splits for the whole baseball team, grinning and laughing like hell while some kid does some cute little impish thing. A *father*.

He'd settled down after that, bunched up his coat in the backseat of the car, and taken a little nap. Just a catnap. Let his body sleep off a little bit of the alcohol, take the edge off this headache that was blooming underneath his eyelids. He'd made his decision, and a kind of peace had settled over him. He'd wake up later, make his way to his father's house, announce his intentions, put on a funeral, and kick things into high gear.

Two hours later, driving down Route 148 with the top down and the freezing cold wind whipping at his face, just to mark the momentousness of the decision, he yelled out the window, *"Yeeeee-hawwwwwwwww!"*

NOW HE WALKED around to the back of the house. The little wet blades of grass stood out as if they'd been rimmed in frosty paint. He stepped in a mud puddle and swore, loudly. The house stood there, a hulking giant in the middle of the field. He looked down where the old orchards had been, now with only a few straggly apple trees left. For a moment he thought of walking down to the pond, his favorite place, with all its reeds and weeds and hiding places—but it was too muddy and still too dark. He'd probably slip and kill himself down there.

Tina. He had to call Tina.

He got his phone out of his pocket and punched in her number. It rang twice, and then there was her voice: "This is Tina Oliver. You know what to do!" He put his mouth close to the phone and said, "*Hellooooooo?*" and waited. Nothing. He said, "God, I wish you'd picked up. Anyway, sorry to call you this late, sweetheart, but some sad news today. Honey, my dad died today . . . and . . . well, my dad had my son, and . . ."

Suddenly he couldn't speak. Something had clotted in his throat, broken glass in there. He snapped the phone shut, furious at himself for a moment, and stood looking at the back of the house—*his* house now—with its peeling paint and dark black windows. All shut up against him. God, he hated this place, the way its memories shoved against you, demanding to be let in. His father walking out of here with his suitcase. His mother dying of cancer and still, even up to the last day, claiming she was getting better. Louisa running out the front door and jumping in the car. All of this contained in this square footage in the middle of Connecticut, this farmland with its squishy backyard. The fence posts. The screened-in back porch with its run-down old glider, and the rickety steps sloping down to the yard. He could smell the loamy odor of the pond. The air was so wet he almost couldn't breathe; it curled up in his lungs, under his fingernails, working its way into his bloodstream.

He stood there, coughing and shivering, miserable. Then he looked up and noticed that one window was actually open a bit, the window to his old bedroom. He wiped his mouth on his sleeve, studied the problem. If he could get up there, he could climb in and get some sleep before he left to find Christopher. Sure as hell better than trying to sleep in the car, or on the glider, which were his two other choices at this hour.

He walked around the side of the house, checking the basement windows to see if perhaps one of them was open, too. And then he stopped walking and stared. A ladder was propped against the side of the house. A ladder! All he had to do was haul it around the back to the open window, and then he could just zip up and in.

He laughed out loud. Was this just like Chester, or what? Lock all the doors but leave a ladder up and a window wide open. He felt almost gleeful. He went over and dragged the thing to his old bedroom window. A couple of times it banged against the house on the way. He *was* awfully tired when you got right down to it. A shower and a nap were going to be just the thing.

Carefully he steadied the ladder against the house, shaking his head at how badly the siding was rotting out—couldn't Harris have taken care of *anything*? And then he started climbing the rungs, one by one, almost dizzy he was so tired.

Now all he had to do was reach in, lift up the screen, and pull himself over the ledge. *Careful . . . don't kick the ladder down . . . ease yourself over, slide through the window like you used to do a million times when you were a teenager coming in late.* As his foot pushed off, the ladder fell to the ground with a loud crash, and his heart started pumping away like a goddamned jackhammer. He had to hang there a minute to catch his breath. Certainly no turning back now. He twisted around to see why it had made so much noise and saw that it had fallen onto a picnic table he'd never even noticed. Christ, he'd lost his touch, that was for sure. Good thing his mother wasn't waiting inside for him this time; she'd have been standing there ready to kill him.

He shimmied himself inside—chuckling now at the thought of being able to do this, pleased to see that he hadn't gotten fat—eased his right leg in and then his left. That's the way . . . eeeeasy does it. He was in!

Then, out of the corner of his eye, he saw something white coming toward him. He instinctively put up his hands to ward it off. A woman was yelling "Oh no, you don't!" He reeled back as something slammed into his jaw, saw a flash of light, and the next thing he knew, he was lying faceup on the floor. His head felt as if it had been splintered into a million pieces, and not only that, but a hundred pound boulder had landed *hard* on his belly.

He wanted to say something, but black squares were starting to organize themselves on the ceiling, blocking out the light, so he lay back and, instead of talking, he swam up to meet the blackness, letting it wash over him like a warm bath.

There were mistakes, and then there were *mistakes*. Jamie, sitting on top of a man she'd never seen before, the one she'd just shattered a lamp on, was beginning to realize that for the second time in less than twenty-four hours, she was in deep trouble.

Shit, shit, shit.

At first, when she'd heard the car pull up on the gravel drive and heard a male voice outside the window, she'd thought perhaps the newspaper delivery boy had brought along company to chat with, but then when she'd felt the cold clunk of the ladder banging against the house outside the window where she was sleeping, a chill had traveled down her spine. Somebody was breaking in.

With the hairs standing up on the back of her neck, she'd gotten out of bed and grabbed the first thing that looked promising as a weapon, a ceramic lamp in the shape of a baseball player. And then she'd waited, hardly breathing, her whole body tensed, for the intruder to make it through the window. He'd come in one leg at a time; then his torso slid inside, bringing with it arms and a head—and she'd run toward him, swinging the lamp through the air, letting it smash into his jaw with a satisfying, bone-crunching sound that had almost made her sick. He'd staggered to the ground, and she threw herself right on top of him.

She felt exhilarated and brave for exactly four seconds. And then she realized what she'd done. *Oh my God.* Even in the dim light from the hallway, anybody could see that this guy was no burglar. He was Harris's son, *Nate.* She'd know that Goddard nose and jaw anywhere. And there he was, passed out, and his jaw was already bleeding and growing a lump the size of a Ping-Pong ball.

Did dead people grow lumps? She should shake him, or call his name. But what if he didn't answer? What if she'd killed him, really *killed* Harris's son? For real. Her teeth started to chatter, and then there were footsteps from far away, and ages passed, and then Lucy appeared at the door, gasping.

"Oh my God!" she said. "What happened? What was that noise?"

Jamie tried to speak, but no sounds came out. Lucy snapped on the overhead light, and for a moment the two of them stared at the man sprawled out on the floor surrounded by the ceramic shards of the baseball lamp. He was dressed in a suit, and his face was so devoid of color that he would have had to darken about six shades even to qualify as pale.

Lucy said, "Oh my God. Am I dreaming this? Did-did this guy climb through the *window?*"

"He did. Yes, that's what he did." Jamie slid off him and sat staring at him.

"But he's dressed up. That's kind of unusual for a burglar, even in Connecticut."

"That's because it's Nate, Harris's son," Jamie said quietly.

"Oh my God. You knocked out Harris's *son?* Why did you do that?"

"Well, what do you think—that I knew it was him? I thought it was a burglar."

"Oh my God. *Jamie.*"

She swallowed. "Well, I heard a car drive up about a half hour ago, and then I heard a man's voice outside, yelling. And then there was a ladder hitting the house, and—and so I got a lamp, and then he just came climbing in the window, so I h-hit him." She leaned closer and stared at his face. Thank God, there was the slightest little movement underneath his eyelids. That was the good news. The bad news was that he was probably going to wake up and kill her with his bare hands. If he wasn't paralyzed, that is.

"Oh my God. Is he breathing?" Lucy said, creeping closer. "You didn't kill him, did you?"

"I think you have to try to stop saying 'oh my God.' "

"Wow. You have, in one day, nearly wiped out the entire Goddard line," Lucy said softly. "I think the authorities are going to insist that Christopher have some real protection from you."

"Well? What was he doing anyway, climbing in the window? Why couldn't he ring the doorbell like other people, if he didn't have a key? And how did he get here so fast, when he lives in California? I thought he wouldn't be here for at least a day or two."

"They have airplanes now, though. Perhaps you forgot that."

"But you have to get reservations. And then it takes hours and hours of flying. You don't get in at three in the morning. Nobody flies in at three in the morning."

"They fly at night now, too. Red-eye flights. Ever hear of 'em?"

"But how is that possible? He would have had to hear the news, rush to the airport, and get right on a plane."

"So? Maybe that's what he did." Lucy leaned over close to him. "Uh-oh. It looks like he's waking up."

There was a crashing sound from the bedroom down the hall. The kids were up. Jamie groaned. "Lucy," she said, "maybe you should shut this door—"

But it was too late. Both Christopher and Arley were standing at the bedroom door, eyes wide.

"Wow!" Arley said. "Is that a bad guy? Did we get a bad guy?"

"Is he dead?" Christopher said.

"No, he's not dead," Jamie said. "He's actually—" *He's actually what? He's actually your father, and he's fine, just taking a little nap here?*

"He *looks* like he's dead."

"Is he a bad guy?" Arley asked again. "Did he come in the window?"

"Why is he here?" Christopher said. He was staring at her. "Hey! Why is the lamp broken? Did the bad guy break the lamp?"

"It's okay," Jamie said. She gave Lucy a pleading look that meant *Take them downstairs. Please.*

"I'm *not* dead, and I'm not a bad guy," the man on the floor said. *Nate.* Jamie had to remember that it was Nate, Christopher's father, not just a man on the floor. They all looked at him. His eyes were open, and although his voice sounded slurred and he was definitely impaired in a lumbering, even Frankenstein's monster kind of way, he seemed determined to get up. Jamie reached over to help him, but he pushed her arm away, then sank back down on the floor, groaning. They watched him in silence. Only Arley was making noise, breathing so loudly through his mouth that the sound filled the room.

"Turn off . . . that light," Nate said.

"Do you need anything? Are you all right?" Jamie asked.

There was a moment's pause, and then he said, "Well, I was a lot better before somebody tried to kill me," he said. "And when that light goes off, I'm going to be fucking splendid." He sounded as if his tongue might be about two sizes too big for his mouth.

Lucy and Jamie glanced at each other, and then Lucy turned off the overhead light, but then it was too dark to see, so Jamie went into her room and got the bedside lamp. She'd been unable to bring herself to sleep in there, where Harris had died; she could imagine the bed still had the indentations from his body. Sleep wasn't really possible anyway; she'd spent most of the night wandering through the house and then had ended up in the room they'd always called the junk room. It wasn't until she'd cleared off the single bed, moving boxes of Christmas decorations, artificial flowers, old baskets, and sewing projects, an ancient sewing machine, and sports equipment, that she'd discovered a little boy's Wild West bedspread, with a real rope stitched on as a lasso in the cowboy's hand. That's when she'd realized this had been Nate's childhood room. She'd finally settled, tossing and turning, into the lumpy bed, and had lain there staring at an old *Barbarella* poster curling up on the walls. The hall light glinted on his baseball trophies on the bookcase. Funny how Harris had never talked about any of this stuff, had never even come into this room.

It made her teary, remembering Harris stretched out in her room, waiting for her to come to him, all that hopefulness and sweetness. Oh God. She'd had way too little sleep for what this day was about to ask of her.

She met Lucy coming out of the bathroom holding a wet washcloth. "His jaw is a little bloody," she said in a low voice. "I think we're going to need to get some ice, maybe a butterfly bandage. I don't think he's going to need stitches, but what do I know? I only see these kinds of things with bar fights, and after the people leave I don't see how the healing goes."

"He's talking, though. I don't think we have to call an ambulance or anything, do you? I really think he's going to be okay, don't you?"

"Well, I'll be happier when he's sitting up."

"*I'll* be happier when he's on the plane, going back to California."

"Yeah, well, good luck with that. In the meantime, I'm going downstairs to get a bag of ice or frozen peas or something."

"Frozen peas?"

"For his eye and jaw. Best thing in the world. They mold to the shape of the face, so they're better than traditional ice packs. Don't you know that?"

"No. You're the one who has all the interesting facts."

"Comes from being a bartender. We keep frozen peas in the freezer in case there's a fistfight."

Jamie had never lived in a world where there were likely to be fistfights—or even people who had to be talked out of fistfights. And yet . . . she had managed somehow to break a lamp on a man's face without even stopping to think. Funny how much could change so quickly. It scared her how satisfying it had been to wield that lamp.

She took the washcloth and the new lamp and went back into the room. She plugged the lamp in the corner socket and put it on the floor, near the bed. It gave off a nice yellowish, homey glow. Things, she decided, seemed less dire in this light. Nate, in fact, *was* sitting up now, leaning against the desk and holding his jaw, which seemed to be expanding, as if he'd swallowed a balloon. A Pinewood Derby car on the desk looked as though it might wobble its way down onto his head, possibly finishing him off, so she went over and moved it farther back and handed him the cloth.

"Am I bleeding?" he said.

"Hardly any," she told him. "I think you're going to be just fine."

He laughed a little at that. A bitter laugh.

The boys were standing together staring at him while he rubbed at his face with the cloth. They jumped when he laughed.

That made him take notice. He leaned over toward Christopher. "Hey, Ace," he said in a thick voice, and tried to pull his son closer. "You know who I am? I'm your dad. Do you remember me? This isn't exactly how I wanted it to be, but here I am. Daddy. Your dad."

Christopher was having none of it. He backed away, scowling.

"Yeah, it's a stunner, I know," Nate said. "But them's the breaks. I'm your dad, like it or not."

"It's okay," Jamie said. "This really is your dad, honey." Then she said to Nate, because she had to say *something,* "I am so, so sorry about this—I woke up hearing a noise . . . and . . . then I . . ."

"Decided to kill me," Nate said. "Sure. Anyone would. It's fine. Fine. I'm just lucky you didn't have an Uzi." He was rubbing his jaw.

"*You* beat him up?" Christopher whispered, looking at Jamie.

"No, no, she did *not* beat me up, Ace," Nate said. "Looks worse than it is. I'm fine, just fine. Not to worry." He touched his jaw tenderly and tried to grin at Christopher, but his face was so lopsided that the grin came off looking like something from a horror movie. Christopher glared at him and said in a low, injured voice, "My name is *Christopher.*"

"I know your name," Nate said, gazing at his son through a Cyclops sort of eye. "And you know why I know it already? Because I *named* you. Yes, sirree. I was there on the ground floor of you. Opening day for Christopher Goddard."

Arley had been smiling the whole time, and now he started jumping up and down on one foot and yelling, "Wow! Wow! This is your *dad*!"

Christopher mumbled something, and Jamie, uncertain if the word *asshole* was about to get tossed about, turned to Nate and said in a loud voice, "Listen, my sister has gone to get you some ice to put on your face. In the meantime, don't you want to lie back down? Get comfortable? Would you like me to get you a pillow?"

He swiveled his head over to her, as if movement had to be a deliberate choice, and gazed at her out of those bloodshot eyes. "Wait. I have a major question. Just who *are* you? And why are you in my old bedroom in the middle of the night, throwing lamps?" He leaned hard on his arms as if he was going to push himself up to a standing position, but then the effort was too much and he grimaced and slumped back down again with his eyes clenched shut like he was in pain.

"Ooh, take it easy!" she said. "Listen, I really think you should rest. Don't try to get up just yet."

He didn't say anything, just stretched his legs farther out into the room. She took the opportunity to study his leather shoes and his dark, thick socks, which were so soft they looked as though they might have come from specially designed sheep. His suit pants still had a sharp crease in them, despite everything they'd been through. Her eyes traveled up to his face, and she was embarrassed to see that his eyes were open again and that he was watching her, amused.

"And *you* are here because . . . ?" he whispered thickly.

She sucked in her breath. "Well, I live here. I'm Jamie McClintock, and my sister is Lucy—she's gone downstairs to get you some ice—and this is my son, Arley. Come over here, Arley, and say hello."

"Hullo," Arley said.

Nate stuck out his hand. "Nice to meet you, Ace."

He laughed. "I'm *Arley*."

"Jeez. Nobody here willing to be called Ace. What a shame," Nate said. He looked back at Jamie through his one non-squinty eye, definitely sizing her up. "So, you *live* here, do you? Since when?"

"Well," she said, and licked her dry lips, "Arley and I have been living here for a year, actually, sharing the house with Harris and Christopher—"

"We're in the Campfire Kids!" Arley said. "And we live at the same house. Me and Christopher!"

"And why might that be?" Nate said. He was smiling.

"Boys," Jamie said. "Could you go and see if Auntie Lucy is getting that bag of peas for Christopher's father's head?"

Once they'd left, she started in with a long explanation about how frozen peas were going to help with the swelling, but he just sat there, unblinking, watching her.

"So you were my father's latest," he said. "Funny thing. Usually they don't have children."

"No," she said, and hated that her face was growing warm. "Not his girlfriend. Not at all. We both just lived here, we shared the house, because the boys were good friends." She started to say something, lost heart, and then started up again. "You see, before that I was living with my sister, whom you met—she's the one getting the bag of peas, you remember. But then, it's a long story, having to do with my sister's boyfriend moving in. Anyway, I needed to move out. And so we were just here, sharing the space. The *house*."

There. That was the truth, painfully told, but still—it was the truth, and there was nothing bad in there. She just wished her voice hadn't sounded so tinny and defensive. It was because of the way he was looking at her, as if he was writing his own version of the story, and that was the one he was always going to believe.

"So," she said. "That's the only reason I'm here."

For a moment he looked as if he was going to argue with her. Then he said slowly, "I . . . I think I need to rest," and closed his eyes.

"No!" she said. "You can't sleep. You might have a concussion."
But he was out cold.

NOW SHE COULDN'T leave him alone. Lucy finally came up with
the frozen peas and said she'd given the boys their Legos to play with,
and she was going back down to make some coffee. Jamie paced back
and forth, stopping every few steps to study his condition as he lay,
faceup, on the floor with his eyes closed. At least now that he had peas
on his face, she didn't have to see him looking at her. But she was
scared. Cooksey was going to have a field day with this. He'd find a
way to charge her with Harris's death and then throw in some assault-
and-battery charges for good measure.

"Look," she said, shaking his arm a little bit. "Are you really hurt
bad? Shall I drive you to the hospital?" *And would you mind if we go to
a hospital way over in another part of the state?*

After a long moment, he said, "Hell, no. No hospital. I'm just
resting my eyes."

"You know," she said, "if you have a concussion, you're really not
supposed to go to sleep. I think you can actually die that way."

"It's not a concussion," he said without opening his eyes. "I'm just
very sleepy."

"Well," she said, "not to argue with you, but you might. You did
pass out, or at least I think you did. And I'm really so sorry, but I did
hit you pretty hard. I didn't know who you were, obviously."

"Bigger women than you have tried to kill me, but I don't die."

"Just for the record, I didn't really try to kill you. I thought you
were a burglar, and I was only trying to stop you from coming in."

He barked out a laugh without opening his eyes. She sat down on
the floor about three feet from him and studied him. He was devastatingly handsome. Just the kind of looks that made her uncomfortable.
Those I-own-the-world looks. Prosperous. Egotistical. She knew the
type. You could tell he'd paid two hundred dollars for that haircut,

which even now lay down perfectly, as if every hair had been nurtured and persuaded to go in the right direction. His hair was straight and brown, a little on the long side, because he was young and hip and no doubt he needed his hair to make that point for him. He had a straight nose, big white teeth that had shown when he'd laughed. Nice bone structure, good jawline, even if part of it had a bag of peas stuck to it at the moment. And the curve of his ear—she had to resist reaching out and touching it, it was so delicate and perfect. Amazing, really.

"So," he said, and she jumped a little because she'd been leaning in toward him, "he was getting 'em young these days. Wasn't he about a hundred and two, a hundred and three by now?"

"I wasn't your father's girlfriend. I told you. I live here because the boys were good friends, and Harris asked me to help him out."

He gave a snort. "Ah! You lived here because the *kids* were good friends. That's a new one. Tell me this. How *was* sex with the old geezer?"

She gathered herself together. "You know, due to the fact that you have a head injury and possible brain damage, I am going to pretend you didn't ask me that."

He laughed. "Ha! So you *did* have sex."

"No. We didn't."

"Not ever? Not even kissing? You had kissing, I'll bet, didn't you?"

"No. What is it with you?"

"I just know my dad, that's all."

"No, actually. You don't."

"Uh, actually. I *do*."

"As a matter of fact, you don't. You haven't been around here for years, and from what Harris told me, you didn't exactly keep in touch—"

"*I* didn't keep in touch? That's what you heard—"

"Well, you haven't kept in touch for the last year! So whatever *opinion* of him you've been harboring since childhood just might not be accurate anymore, did you ever think of that? People do change, you know, and he was a decent, respectful, *wonderful* man who would never have instigated—instigated a sexual thing..." She stopped talking, just ran down because he was laughing so hard.

But then the laughter turned to choking, and she had to go over and help him prop himself up. The package of peas fell on the floor, the cup of water spilled, and she held him up while she pounded him on the back. His breath smelled like booze. Just awful. Maybe, she thought with a little flare of hope, maybe this is more a hangover than a concussion.

He stopped coughing and eased himself down on the floor again, this time with his eyes open. He was watching her, and for a moment she felt like a little mouse in the gaze of some big, playful house cat who could easily reach over and swipe her, leaving bloody claw tracks.

"I'm going downstairs," she said. "You need anything?"

"Okay, listen," he said. "Before you go . . . just tell me. How'd he go, anyway?"

"He had a heart attack," she said.

"Where—was he home when it happened?"

"Yeah," she said. "He was outside working."

"Were *you* with him?"

Well, here we are. "Yes," she said. "Well, I wasn't there at the, you know, *moment* he died. But . . . I was . . . well, I was here. In the house."

He was quiet, thinking that over. "Hmm. So he kicked it right here at home," he said. "Christopher didn't witness it, did he?"

"No. Oh no. The kids were at school." She hesitated and then plunged in. "He was outside scraping the paint off the house, getting ready to paint it. And it was really hot and humid, and so I thought he was just dehydrated when he came inside because he seemed so weak. And so I gave him a drink of water and then sent him to lie down while I called the doctor, and then when I came up to check on him . . ." Her voice faltered for a moment. She wondered if she was going to tell him about the back rub. "Well," she said, and knew she wasn't going to tell, "he wasn't moving. He'd gone."

He exhaled loudly. "Okay, I get it," he said. "Just needed to know the lay of the land. What I'm dealing with here. So it was a heart attack. Anything else I should know?"

She paused. "That's it, I guess. Just a heart attack. Sudden. No pain, they think. I'm going downstairs now. To cook breakfast and stuff. You shouldn't sleep, you know. The concussion thing."

"No, I'm okay. Just tired," he said. "I didn't sleep all night long, except at the Dairy Queen in my car. But then acorns started falling on me, woke me up. Trouble with convertibles."

She cleared her throat. "So you flew in last night from California, after you heard?"

"Fly in? No. Oh. No. I was in New York when I heard. I was at a Yankees game with some clients. In my job, I travel all over. So, it wasn't so far."

She nodded and turned away.

"Wait," he said when she got to the door. "I want to ask you something else as long as you're here."

"What?" *Please not more about the circumstances of Harris's death. Please, not that.*

"So, for real now. You know Christopher pretty well?"

"Yeah."

"What kind of kid is he? What's he like?"

She felt herself softening slightly. "He's great," she started in. "Very creative and funny and—"

He interrupted her. "No, no. Is he easy?"

"Easy?" she said. "You mean, like easygoing?"

"Yeah. Easy to deal with."

"Well, kids are kids, you know. They can't really be put into categor—"

"No, no. Look, I work a lot. I'm trying to figure out how hard this is going to be. I mean, I know I can *do* it. Just look around at all the schmucks that get through it. I just wondered if, you know, he was considered a particularly tough one or not. I can see already that he doesn't have much of a sense of humor . . ."

"Well, he's only five. And he *is* grieving over his grandfather, you know. In fact, I'd say he's been through a lot in his young life."

He didn't seem to take the hint on that one. He said, "Hey, I get it that things haven't been exactly *normal* for him. We all have our problems. But what I'm getting at is—do you think he can adapt to stuff?"

We all have our problems? Had he really just said that? She sighed loudly.

He kept talking. "Because, you know, I travel a lot, and the way I figure it, he and I can pal around together on my business trips, but you gotta be adaptable when you're traveling. I'd guesstimate that at least three, four times a month I spend a whole day at the airport or in the car."

"What? I don't know of any kid who can spend the whole day—"

"Yeah. I know. I hate those days, myself. I figure we can play tic-tac-toe or something. Who knows? Maybe I'll get him a DVD player."

"Excuse me for asking you this, but have you ever even *seen* a five-year-old before now?"

He laughed. "I just want to get a feel for what I'm up against with him."

"Tell me you didn't just say '*up* against.'"

"Scratch that," he said. "Just forget I said 'up against.' I *want* him. I'm really jazzed about getting to know him."

"That's just great," she said slowly.

"Aw, what the hell. I'm getting married soon anyhow, and maybe my new wife will think it's fun to settle down and stay home and raise my kid. You never know."

"No, you never know," she said.

"So." He looked at her. "God, *you* must be bummed. Not only did you lose your boyfriend, but I guess you've gotta make a new living plan kind of quick."

SHE FIXED THE boys pancakes in the shape of sentimental, fat little teddy bears and poured them glasses of chocolate milk, and she didn't even stop them when they poured boysenberry syrup all over the pancakes and squirted their plates with billows of whipped cream. She sat down at the table and curled her hand around her mug of coffee and wondered how she was going to get through the day. It was only six-thirty in the morning, and the weak sunlight was coming in through the kitchen window, falling in a gray-yellow square on the table, shining through the green jelly jar and making wavy patterns. She'd probably never get to paint this now, and the thought of that made her almost as sad as anything else had. Lucy, already dressed and made up, was talking to Arley about Lego dragons or police helicopters or something. Only Jamie and Christopher seemed to know that this morning required gloomy silence.

Finally Christopher looked up at her and said in a low voice, "Is Da still dead?"

"Is he?" Arley said. "Mama, is Harris still dead today?" He was coughing, little dry, barky coughs, but at least he wasn't wheezing.

She smiled at them sadly. "Yes, he's still dead. It's very sad, but he'll always be dead from now on." She thought they'd covered all this last night, when they'd drawn pictures and cried together and done everything they could think of to talk about Harris's death. She'd told them everything: about Harris not feeling well when he came inside, and how he'd gone to lie down and she'd found him there, looking peaceful. She'd told them that she thought Harris's spirit was flying away—and that he looked happy.

Christopher cleared his throat. "Jamie, where is he, really? Tell me where he really is. Where his *self* is."

"Oh, you mean his body," she said. "Well, they took his body to the funeral home. They're getting it ready for the funeral service, which we'll have in a few days, and that's where everybody will get together to say good-bye to him."

Lucy piped up. "They're putting his best suit on him, and some makeup and lipstick so he'll look great when we go see him at the funeral," she said. "Isn't that a funny idea—your grandpa wearing lipstick? I think he's going to look gorgeous. Wonder what color they'll pick for him."

Christopher's face cracked. "I don't think he'd like to have on lipstick."

"You're right," Jamie said. "We'll tell them no lipstick. They wouldn't put lipstick on *Da*!" She looked meaningfully at Lucy, her "maybe you should let me handle this" look. Lucy held up her hands in a "I was just trying to help" response.

"Call them now," he said and started to cry. "Tell them right now that he wouldn't like lipstick." He cut off the teddy bear pancake's head with a sudden violent motion.

"They're not open just yet, sweetheart, but I will. I'll tell them," Jamie said, and she reached over and pulled Christopher onto her lap and murmured little comforting noises into his hair. He tucked himself in, like somebody turning himself into one of those accordion maps folded until it was one-sixteenth its usual size.

"He would *hate* lipstick. He would *hate* it," he said after a moment.

He would hate everything about this, Jamie thought. He'd hate being dead and missing teddy bear pancakes for breakfast. He'd hate it that Nate was milling around upstairs (she could hear his footsteps above them) and hate it that she was scared and that she was going to have to move out and that Christopher was going to have to quit school at age five and learn how to be adaptable in airports. He'd also hate it that he'd missed the best back rub of his life.

Arley put down his fork and looked at Christopher with mild interest. "I know! Why don't you ask your dad to call?" he said. "Your dad could say NO LIPSTICK in a very loud voice."

Christopher buried his head again, and Jamie patted his back and made little soothing noises. "I don't want that bad guy to be my dad," he said, muffled against her.

"Really? You don't want him to be your dad?" Arley asked, surprised.

Christopher burrowed in deeper. "No."

Arley considered this while he wiped his nose on his sleeve.

"Use a tissue, honey," Jamie said. Lucy reached over to give him one.

He ignored both of them. "Why don't you want him to be your dad? He looks like a nice man."

"He *is* a nice man," Lucy said.

"I don't like him."

"Well, *I'd* like a dad," Arley said.

"I don't want one."

Arley ate two more bites of pancake and stared off, out the window, then wiped his nose again on his sleeve. "Wait," he said. "Is it because Mama beat him up? Is that why? You don't want a dad that gets beat up?"

"Now just a minute. I didn't *really* beat him up," Jamie said. "I thought he was somebody breaking into the house—and, Arley, you do have a dad. Everybody has a dad. It's just that he doesn't live with us."

"Where *does* he live?"

"Well, the last time I heard, he was in Brooklyn, in New York," she said.

"I wish my dad would go back to where he lives," Christopher said.

"L.A.," Nate said from the door in a booming voice, and they all jumped, and for a moment Jamie couldn't breathe. He came into the room, still holding the bag of frozen peas to his jaw, and looked around. Standing up and mobile now, he was beyond ominous—your basic entitled, too-handsome-but-beaten-up horror show, tall and smiling and arrogant. Completely out of place and lopsided and yet so full of himself that he seemed to take up the whole room. He reached over and poked Christopher on the elbow.

"Your dad lives in L.A., which is a *very* nice place to live, as you will soon see," he said. "Great place to be. Best place in the world, in fact."

They were all silent at the magnitude of this statement, but then Lucy regained herself, and dimpled at him and said, "So, hi. You're

Nate, right? I didn't get to introduce myself before. I'm Jamie's sister, Lucy, the *nonviolent* one in the family."

"Nice to meet you," Nate said, and Jamie watched his face as he took in the whole Lucy experience: her twinkling little smile and her adorable little leotard and skirt and bright pink lipstick. Christopher snuffled and curled up even tighter against Jamie, squeezing his eyes shut. He was attempting to shrink down to the molecular level, a feat that Jamie could see was not lost on his father, who gave him a puzzled, exasperated look and then went over to Christopher's plate and stared down at the remains of teddy bear pancakes floating in red syrup amid clumps of whipped cream.

"Ewww, what the heck is all this?" he said.

There was silence. Arley said helpfully, "They're teddy bear pancakes."

"Really? It looks like a crime scene," Nate said, and Christopher slid off Jamie's lap and went back to his pancakes, stirring the syrup and whipped cream together. "I am the King Lizard Monster, and I eat the heads of teddy bear pancakes!" he growled.

"The heads are deeeelicious! The best part," Arley said, jumping up and down.

Jamie, now exposed and cold, pulled her blue kimono closed, wishing she'd thought to get dressed before she came downstairs. She felt ragged, too, with her hair tangled and her teeth not brushed.

"Is there any more coffee around here?" Nate said, and she got up to pour him some. There wasn't enough, so she had to start a whole new pot. Out of the corner of her eye, she could see him walking around the kitchen, picking up objects and grimacing, looking as if he'd stumbled into a museum of wreckage and ruin. In a way, she supposed, it *was* like a museum for him, this place of his childhood, old and worn out and, in this morning light, looking somewhat pathetic. She happened to like the look of this place, but now she could see it through his eyes: the peeling paint, the curling linoleum, and worse, the Legos and toys scattered all over the floor. He spent a long moment tugging at a piece of the peeling wallpaper, and then he went over to the old soapstone sink and sighed, mumbling something about how chipped and ratty it looked. "Amazing," he said in disbelief. "This place has gone to hell in a handbasket."

"What is a handbasket?" Arley said.

"Hey, this is just *domesticity,* Nate," Lucy said. "We single people don't know from domesticity, but Jamie's a genius at it. It's called family life." She crossed her legs and beamed at him over the rim of her coffee cup.

"What's a handbasket?" Arley said.

"Nah," Nate growled. "I'm talking about the house. It's like a time machine—The House That Time Forgot. What was my father doing all these years? Couldn't he be bothered to fix anything? I thought he was supposedly in construction."

Jamie managed to keep herself from saying, "What was he *doing* all these years? I believe he was raising *your* kid!" She was in the middle of pouring him a cup of coffee and sloshed it on her thumb. She swore under her breath and set the coffee cup down hard on the table in front of an empty chair. Nate drifted over and sat down, but he still kept looking around in disgust, as though he expected spiders and boa constrictors to be crawling about.

"*What* is a handbasket?" Arley said. "What is a handbasket? What is a hand—?"

"Arley? Honey? It's a basket that you carry in your hand," Jamie said. "Are you done with those pancakes?"

But as often happened with Arley, now that he had one question answered, he was just getting started. "Are you really Christopher's daddy? Did you know that his grandpa died? He was attacked by his heart, and they tried to save him, but this time they couldn't do it." He sidled up next to Nate and proudly showed him the features of the Superman cape he was wearing over his ladybug vest. "Christopher has a Batman suit, but I like to be Superman because he's faster than a train," he said.

"Arley, come over here and sit on my lap," Jamie said quickly. She sat down and motioned him over. "Come on. Now."

He came over and sat on her, but he leaned his elbows on the table, grinning at Nate. "Hey, Christopher's daddy, if you want some pancakes, I have some left. The heads are gone, but the legs taste good."

"Uh, no, thank you," Nate said. "And you don't have to call me Christopher's daddy. You can call me Nate."

"No. You should call him *Mr. Goddard,*" Jamie said.

"How about Natey? Can I call you Natey?" Arley said.

"No," Jamie said. "Mr. Goddard."

"Fine with me," Nate said, and then he looked over at Christopher, ducking his head just slightly. *Why, he's nervous,* Jamie thought. The look on his face was the plain, unvarnished, naked look of a man looking at his own flesh and blood and trying to telegraph to him that they were connected. It made her heart hurt, looking at that.

Nate leaned over and said in a low voice, "Hey. So, Christopher. Earth to Christopher! Look up over here at your old dad. What are *you* going to call me? Dad? Daddy? What's it going to be?"

The silence stretched out. Christopher started making a clicking sound with his tongue, the sound he made when he was determined to tune things out.

Nate picked up his coffee cup and took a sip, never taking his eyes off his son. "Let's see. You can call me Dad, or Daddy, or Pop. How about Pop? I always liked the sound of Pop."

"Me, too!" Lucy said and laughed. "I knew a guy in high school whose dad was Pop to the whole neighborhood. Great name."

Christopher said nothing, but a little stubborn, vacant smile played around his mouth. Jamie knew it was his "you can't make me" smile. She'd seen it once or twice when he was mad. She wished she knew how to help him.

"Okay, well, we'll wait until we know each other better," Nate said at last. "Tell me this. What do you like to do for fun around here? Do you like to play catch?"

Christopher slumped down in his chair.

"What? Will you talk to me, Christopher? I don't hear anything." He looked over at Arley. "What do you say, um . . . Other Child Who Actually Will Talk? What's your name again? Gosh, I used to be able to remember names before I had this serious head wound . . ."

"Arley! I'm Arley."

"So *you* tell me what's fun around here, Arley. Do you . . . um . . . like to race bullfrogs? Do you . . . I don't know . . . pick pockets? Or build rocket ships? Do you like to teach ants to talk? Are you in an indie rock band? What *do* you do?"

Arley's eyes widened and he said, "Well, I *want* to race bullfrogs, but I didn't find any yet. Do you have any bullfrogs I could race?" Dear, sweet Arley. He was jumping up and down and breathing hard, way too excited. "I play Legos and I draw pictures and—yesterday we made lizards at school! I'll go get them!" He tore out of the room, and Nate stirred his coffee and stared surreptitiously at his son. When his cell phone rang out the first notes of Beethoven's Ninth Symphony, he fumbled through his pants pocket and drew it out, glanced at it, then shoved it right back.

Jamie got up and started clearing the table, and when she turned back, Nate was gazing at her. He stood up and reached over to hand her Christopher's plate, but he was off-balance and the plate tipped, wobbling for a second before she managed to catch it on its way down. He laughed, but there wasn't any happiness in it. His eyes looked so filled with fear she had to look away.

That was when she realized she had a slight headache and that she was cold in the kitchen, that she wanted more coffee, and she wished the boys would both come sit in her lap again, and she knew again, in a very real way, that Harris was gone and that this stranger—this guy with the jokes and the arrogance and the wounded tenderness—had been sent to replace him and that he was going to take away everything that mattered to her.

Nate took a nap, although it wasn't much of one, what with kids running back and forth on the hardwood floors, and doors slamming, the doorbell chiming, and the phone ringing incessantly. People kept bringing stuff over the way they always did when somebody died, but he knew perfectly well that what they *really* wanted was to come in and gather more gossip, to speculate about what was going to happen next to the fascinatingly dysfunctional Goddards. He overheard Jamie explain quite a few times that, yes, Nate *was* home, yes, that was his car in the driveway—*no,* he was sleeping now, and no, it wasn't clear yet what was going to happen.

"No one knows," he heard her say to somebody who had asked her if she was staying on in the house.

Really? he wanted to say. *No one knows if you're staying on? It just so happens that I know. You are so out of here, baby.*

He lay in the tangle of sheets in what had been his father's bed— which was surprisingly not in the master bedroom but in the sunporch off the living room, the room that his mother had once decorated with white wicker furniture and seashells on a glass-topped table. The place that had once been kind of an elegant sunlit room filled with houseplants and magazines. Now it was a cluttered mess, with a single bed jammed in alongside a dresser, a desk, and a makeshift rack on which his dad's few clothes hung: flannel shirts, jeans, one pair of decent khakis, his old blue suit he wore on formal occasions. There were piles of T-shirts and sweatshirts folded up on the bookshelf, along with a half-used-up roll of quarters, a bottle of Old Spice after-shave, a copy of the Bible (that was a laugh), a big bowl of popcorn kernels, a calcified apple core.

"What the hell was he doing sleeping *here*?" he'd asked Jamie when she showed him to the room. "What happened to the master bedroom in this place?"

She'd looked embarrassed, and he suspected she had a right to. "Well, actually I sleep up there, because it's next to the boys' room, and I need to hear Arley breathing at night. He has allergies that can lead to asthma, and he often wakes up, and we have to get the inhaler . . ."

"Yep, I have asthma!" Arley said proudly, skating around in his socks on the bare floor once again and looking all too pleased with himself. Nate looked at him. His pale, colorless hair sprouted up in about five cowlicks, his nose was all red and stuffy, and he was wearing some ridiculous get-up: a vest with insects all over it *and* a Superman cape. He was such a bizarre-looking kid that Nate had to laugh. "Christopher doesn't have asthma, but I do, so I have an inhaler that I have to use sometimes. That's why we don't live with Aunt Lucy anymore, because she loves Handsome Dan, and he *smokes,* so we had to move so I could breathe. Ya gotta breathe, ya know."

Nate noticed that Jamie had reached over and put her hand on Arley's shoulder to silence him, but there was no way this kid was going to pipe down. He danced off out of her reach, jumping up and down now, breathing hard but still talking. "I don't have a dad because he's an artist and he doesn't like to be in a family. He didn't see me since I was a baby, and even though he loves me, he can't live with people . . ."

"Arley, Arley," Jamie said. "Really. That's enough. Nate wants to go to sleep now."

"Wait!" the boy said. "Why *can't* he live with people? You're an artist and you live with people."

Gee, this was almost fun. Jamie covered her face with her hands and shook her head, and Nate said, "Yeah, why *can't* he live with people? *You* live with people. And just who is Handsome Dan, anyway? I thought he was the Yale mascot, that bulldog. Don't tell me you had to move out because the Yale bulldog is now a smoker!"

"No, no, no," Jamie said, turning red. "We shouldn't do it, but we call, well, *I* call, Lucy's boyfriend, her former boyfriend, actually—they're always breaking up and getting back together—we call him Handsome Dan because he's just, well, he's a little too full of himself. Please. Don't make me tell you all this stuff. Just go take a nap."

And so he had tried to sleep. Frankly, he'd had better naps while he was driving down the highway. The bed was too squishy and the pillow too flat, and sunlight came in the window and—wait, *here* was the problem, this room was a freaking porch, not a bedroom. But it wasn't only that. The whole damn place was different: little artsy wreaths with dried-up things on them hung on the walls, and there was a cluster of watercolors of flowers painted so close up that a bead of water on a petal took up practically the whole thing. And he'd peeked in the living room, which had once been kind of staid and dignified with leather couches—now there were woven-looking throws on the furniture, big stuffed pillows covered with patches and embroidery sitting on the floor. His father had obviously handed over the whole goddamn place to Jamie and had let her stick up whatever the hell she'd wanted. Meanwhile, who cared that the gutters were coming off the house and the paint was chipped and the floors looked as if they were about to wear through to the basement.

He wondered if Jamie thought she was going to get some money from this little deal here. What had his dad promised her, to get her to come and live out here? It had to be money. A young woman isn't just looking for a guy who'll let her hang wreaths and pinecones on the wall. And she claimed they weren't having sex, although—well, who knew?

He lay there looking at a meandering crack on the ceiling and listening to voices going past the door, no doubt Jamie taking another round of casseroles back to the kitchen with somebody trailing after her, asking how she was doing. Their voices moved away, grew muffled. He closed his eyes, tried to sleep. God*damn* Harris, going off and dying like this. How could he be gone? All those years of trying to fix things with him, all those times he'd thought they'd someday work things out between them—all that was blown away. Over. Done with. Deal with it.

He supposed he should hurt worse than he did. But in the grand scheme of things, in the pantheon of major family deaths he'd been through—well, let's just say this one was by far the easiest. A piece of cake. He was going to be fine. Really.

He turned over, tried to plump up the pillow, which was as lumpy and flat as somebody's purse.

No, he was fine. All he had to do was get through the next few days, get all this furniture out of here, pack up the kid's clothes, and put the house on the market and then get the hell back home. How hard was that? One foot in front of the other, that was all. Completely doable. Jamie and the kid needed to get the message that they had to pack up their stuff, too; he hoped *that* wasn't going to be an ordeal, getting them out of here. He'd manage it if it was. Be firm. *My father is gone, and now you need to move on. Very sad, very sad—but all good things must come to an end. I'm sure he was freaking wonderful to you, but . . . leave your key on the table. Have a nice life. What do you mean, the estate? There* is *no estate, as far as you're concerned.*

He pictured her shocked face, hearing that news. And then, as long as she was right there front and center in his thoughts, he let his mind walk around her a few times, checking her out. He went right up to the thin blue robe thing she'd been wearing this morning when she made the pancakes and gave a good, long look. She had a nice enough body underneath—nothing truly bodacious, but still nice; he'd seen enough of her to know that, with those little boys getting on and off her lap all the time and pulling on her. She wasn't his type, of course. She had kind of that Earth Mother thing going on, all that long, light-colored hair messy and all bunched up with a rubber band on the top. Big eyes, way too serious for his taste, and that pale skin with no makeup on it. True, it had been the middle of the night, and she'd been awakened, and frightened—but even later in the kitchen, he could see that she couldn't care less about how she looked.

He grinned, remembering how she'd looked when she was angry. And oh man, she'd been angry as hell at him for coming in that window and scaring the wits out of her. Even when she was worried that she'd hurt him and was trying to be nice to him, he could still sense daggers right underneath the surface. She was a firecracker, this one—come on now, who hauls off and hits somebody with a *lamp*? Really, now. Who could do that? That takes some brass ones. And it had been cute, the way her weird little kid had embarrassed her just now in the hall, telling secrets. But all in all, she certainly was not the type of woman his father usually went for, all flashing boobs and teased hair. She obviously had adored his dad; maybe that's what had gotten the old man all jazzed up—one more deluded young chick who thought he'd put up the moon.

But what was it *she* liked about the old man? Had to be money. Had to be. Ah, but who cared, really? What did it matter? She was leaving, she and her sniffling little kid with the crazy vest with insects all over it. That kid should sue her for making him wear a getup like that. She was going to pay for that when he grew up and saw old pictures of himself.

He must have slept finally, because he found himself snapping wide awake, swamped with a feeling much like panic. He opened his eyes with a start, not quite sure at first where he was. His cell phone was ringing, Beethoven thundering at him again. He looked at it— Howie, on his third call just this morning. Shit. *Howie, don't you get it? I'm not ready to talk to you. I need some time, man. Back off.* He had to think how to *massage* it just right, line up his explanations for why he'd never managed to quite tell the truth about his previous life. You couldn't dive into that without thinking it through, not with somebody as sharp as Howie.

It was weird that Tina hadn't called him back. He punched in her number and lay back on the pillow while he waited for her sympathy to ooze all over him. *You lost your dad? I'm already on my way!* But no. Voice mail again. He took two deep breaths and said into the phone, "As you probably know by now, if you got my other message, I can't meet you in Cincinnati like we planned. If you could fly into Hartford instead, I could really use you here." He winced—*use* had been an unfortunate choice of words. "Anyway, my dad died, and I'm trying to get things settled. Give me a call. If you don't get me, just leave the flight number. Thanks." After he hung up, it occurred to him that he probably should have told her he loved her. He was always forgetting stuff like that.

God, he had to get up. It was time to pull himself together, get things organized, if he was ever going to get out of this joint. He had to make himself *think,* that was it. Shake off this fuzzy-headedness— didn't matter if it was from a concussion or lack of sleep, it had to be *gone.* Make the most of the time he had, not waste another precious second before he got sucked into the quicksand of this place. Howie, organizational genius that he was, would say he needed to pick three priorities and keep them in the pipeline, stay focused on the main things. That was what he needed to do.

He swung his legs over the side of the bed, sat there blinking and looking at his dad's clothes folded up on the bookshelf. He'd need to take those to the funeral home. This was good. He was starting to think again. He was going to be all right.

Three things, he said to himself. He enumerated them on his fingers.

Funeral home, Realtor, pack up the kid.

Funeral home, Realtor, pack up the kid.

And then . . . well, *then,* the rest of his life—which didn't bear thinking about.

. . .

"MAMA," ARLEY SAID. "Mama, look."

Jamie had her head in the refrigerator, trying to make space for the latest casserole, which had arrived in a deep baking dish, the kind with handles *and* a lid. And taped-on instructions written on an index card that read "Kiss the Cook, Eunice Brantley," with a drawing of a chef with big lips.

"Mama."

"One second, Arley. Here, do you boys want some more chocolate milk? If we finished up this carton, I think I could make this thing fit."

"*Mama.*"

"Just a second, Arley."

The children were sitting at the table, playing with a bowl of blue Play-Doh she'd made for them. For an hour now, they'd been making little beebee-shaped things and putting them in a shallow bowl.

"Look. At the back door. It's Mr. Cooksey."

She spun around, bumping her head on the freezer door. Sure enough, there was Cooksey, standing at the screen, swinging his sunglasses from his index finger and waiting to be noticed. Or perhaps he wasn't waiting to be noticed at all; maybe he was spying on her, hoping to get more evidence against her. Maybe he hoped she'd be explaining to the children exactly how it was they were going to profit from Harris's death. She closed the refrigerator door and went over to him.

"Frank," she said. "For heaven's sake, come on in."

He often came by on Saturday mornings. He and Harris would go outside and smoke cigars together out in the backyard, or sometimes they'd sit in the rocking chairs on the front porch, shooting the breeze, talking about old times. Cooksey always got quiet whenever she came outside to join them, even if it was just to bring them a beer or coffee. He had never wanted her to live there, which Harris had always thought funny. If ever he had to leave her and Cooksey alone together, he'd say, "Okay, you two, sit in chilly silence while I'm gone, you hear? No having any conversation, okay?"

Now Cooksey came inside. "So, where's Nate? That his rental car outside?"

"I believe he's taking a nap," she said.

"A nap? When did he get in?"

"Oh, early this morning. Around four or five, I guess."

"Hmmph," he said. He looked over at the kids and then leaned toward Jamie and said out of the side of his mouth, presumably so they wouldn't hear, "So, he kicked you out of here yet?" Then she saw by the way his teeny little eyes were lit up that he was joking with her—the kind of joking he thought was hilarious. "He must have been surprised to see *you* living here, that's for sure."

"Oh, yeah. He was surprised," she said.

"Harris didn't tell him about you, did he now? I thought not."

A horrible thought occurred to her. *God, if there is a God, could you please, please, please keep Nate Goddard from walking into this kitchen with his huge, puffy, bruised face while Cooksey is here? I'll do anything else you say for the rest of time. Perhaps you could just have the police siren go off about now. Nothing serious; it could even be a false alarm.*

"You got any coffee made?"

"Well," she said. She looked over at the coffee pot. "Actually, I think it's all gone. People have been stopping by all morning with food. And we drank it all up." She could make a new pot. She could feel him thinking that. But then he would stay.

"Just so you know, I read your statement yesterday."

"Yeah."

"Interesting. Very, very interesting. Almost brings up more questions than it answers."

She looked over at the kids, who were starting to toss the Play-Doh balls at the vase of daisies on the table, trying to hit the petals.

"Arley," she said quietly, and when he looked at her, she shook her head.

"It was Christopher's idea," Arley told her. "Why don't you yell at him?"

"I'm not yelling at either of you," she said. "I just don't think that's a good idea."

Really, God . . . just a tiny little inconsequential alarm. A two-alarmer. Even a phone call from Cooksey's wife, calling him home for lunch. Anything. Whatever you've got.

"Your statement, such as it was, brings up the question of why Harris was na— well, I'm not going to talk about it here, with kids," Cooksey said, and then, because God was obviously not taking her calls that morning, that was the moment Nate appeared in the kitchen, materializing out of nowhere, like a ghost in the doorway— the ghost, perhaps, of a prizefighter, with his purple, lumpy eye and jaw. He was holding Harris's suit, folded across his arm. Jamie was sure she saw an alarmed look cross his face at the sight of the police chief. But he covered it up fast, moved the suit to his other arm, and stuck out his hand.

"Chief Cooksey!" he said. "How are you, man? How's the family?"

"Good God!" Cooksey said. "*Nate?* Look at your face. What in the hell happened to you?"

Nate brushed the question off with a ha-ha-ha and mumbled something that had the word *toothache* in it, but then Christopher called out, "Jamie hit him with the lamp! He climbed in the window, and she hit him—*bam! Bam! Pow!*" He jumped around, acting out the whole scenario as though he'd actually seen it. Arley joined in, swinging an imaginary lamp, and then they both fell down on the floor.

"She *hit* you?" Cooksey said and then stared at Jamie. "You hit him?"

"Well, I didn't know it was *him* I was hitting," Jamie said, and Nate interrupted her, saying, "Hey, it's cool. She had to protect the fort. I get it. I thought nobody lived here, and so I climbed in the window—"

Cooksey's eyes had gone all buggy. "This isn't even your place!" he said to Jamie. And then: "Why the hell didn't you call 911 like any *thinking* person would do? What the hell *is* this, some vigilante society? You hear somebody breaking in, missy, you *call the cops*!"

"Hey," Nate said. "Let's all chill. No harm done."

"No harm *done*? Look at yourself." He turned to Jamie, clenching his jaw. She could see a vein pulsing in his forehead. Then in as controlled a voice as he could manage, he said, "I would like you to submit your resignation from the Campfire Kids. Effective immediately."

"All right," she said. He had never wanted her in that organization, and now was his chance. Arley looked up and then came over and stood beside her.

Cooksey turned to Nate. "You see what happens? I start a club for my grandkids to enjoy and then it gets taken over this way. You are *out* of it, young lady. No more of your art projects, and no more bringing that *sister* of yours in to do *yoga* with the kids. Kids don't need yoga! They don't."

"Okay, fine," Jamie said.

"I can't believe this. You hit him with a lamp."

"I thought he was a burglar."

"You and your sister . . ." He shook his head, as if he couldn't even begin on the subject. Then he turned to Nate. "I don't know if you've met the sister yet, but I call them the Dynamic Duo. They're *working* this town." His eyebrows were twitching like they might leap off his face. "Neither one of them has even one scruple about anything."

"Frank—" Jamie said, motioning toward the children. But he was having none of it. He was just getting started. He plopped himself down in one of the chairs at the kitchen table and mopped his forehead, which was glistening with sweat.

"You sure there's not any coffee? If you don't have that, I could take a Diet Coke."

She sighed and went to the refrigerator and got him one. When she turned back, he was saying to Nate, "Now you remember how quiet and shy my daughter Jennifer is, don't you? I think you might have dated her a time or two yourself, heh? Well, after you left, she married a guy, Dan Loomis, nice enough family, from over in Ledyard, father's some kind of research scientist, and—well, I won't go into the whole story now, with all these little whippersnappers around us, but suffice it to say that they have a little rough patch, like a lot of marriages, and then Jamie's *sister* takes it upon herself to get up there in the middle of things, giving quote, unquote *yoga lessons* to Dan—"

"Oh, wait. Is this *Handsome Dan*? The smoker man?" Nate said. He gave a meaningful look to Jamie, obviously enjoying himself. "I think I've heard part of this story."

"Well, I don't know about him being *Handsome* Dan," Cooksey said. "There's been times I'd like to have him professionally punched in the nose, I'll tell you that. But he—"

"Handsome Dan, the smoker man! Handsome Dan, the smoker man!" Arley said.

"Stop," Jamie said to Arley. She clapped her hands. "Come on. Let's see how many of these little round blue Play-Doh balls you can stack in a tower. Who can make the highest tower?"

Cooksey gave her an irritated look. She could tell he wanted her to get those kids upstairs, and to leave the room herself, so he could have a real talk with Nate. But she wasn't going to. She didn't dare let him tell Nate about finding Harris naked in her bed. Let him glower at her all he wanted, she wasn't leaving.

He took a big swig of his Diet Coke and then said, "So, what are your plans, son? Can you see yourself moving back home?"

"Actually," Nate said, "I was thinking that after I take care of business at the funeral home, I'm going to stop by and put up the house for sale. You got any recommendations for a good, quick Realtor around here? Is Todd Haney still the go-to hotshot?"

Jamie felt her hairline freeze.

"You're listing the house. *Now?*" Cooksey said.

"Yeah." Jamie had to hand it to Nate: his crooked, wobbly smile didn't falter, and he gazed at Cooksey with mild eyes. "Then, in a week, when I get all this taken care of, Christopher and I are headed out to Californy. Aren't we, pal?"

"A *week?*" Cooksey said, and it was the only time Jamie had ever felt grateful to him. At least he could point out how ridiculous it was to rip apart everything about a child's life in seven days. "You're not seriously thinking this place will sell in a week, are you?"

Nate smiled. "Oh, I don't know when it will sell," he said. "But I'm emptying it out and putting it on the market. They can drop the check in the mail when it sells."

Cooksey cleared his throat softly and stared up at the ceiling for a moment like he was trying to get control of himself. Then he said, "I would think, out of respect for your dad, not to mention your boy here and your whole *family history* here, son, that you'd want to take some time to think things over . . ."

"Nope, not so much," Nate said. "I guess my contribution to this family history is going to be that I break us out of this town and this rut everybody has been in for generations, and move us westward. Isn't that right, Christopher, my boy? We're going to have us some fun on the road, aren't we?"

"The *road?*" Cooksey said. "What are you talking about?"

"Yeah, Christopher's going to be my new business partner. He's going to come along with me to work, and we're going to visit museums and playgrounds, and we're going to ride in airplanes, and maybe on big boats. Isn't that right, pal?"

Jamie had never seen Cooksey speechless before. He sat there sputtering for a moment, his face turning from red to brown to white while he soaked in this news, and then, as if all he could do was go after a target he knew he could hit, he turned to Jamie and shook his finger at her. "*You,*" he said. "You are out of the Campfire Kids. I mean that, too. And when we have the jamboree this summer, you are not to be there. I know you're already working on it. But you're to do nothing. *Nothing.* You got me? You hear this?"

The jamboree? That was his best shot? Jamie almost had to hide her mouth to keep from laughing out loud. The jamboree was some stupid plan of his, some all-hands-on-deck extravaganza he'd planned for this little organization, nothing more than a hike in the woods with hot dogs cooking on the grill beforehand. He'd been talking it up for weeks now, trying to get the kids excited about it. But the parents were all rolling their eyes. No one wanted a jamboree.

"Believe me, I can stop working on it at any time," she said.

"You better not be doing a *thing.*"

"Not a thing," she agreed.

Arley's face fell. "But I want to go to the jamboree!" he said. "Mama, I *want* to go to the jamboree!"

"Don't worry, sweetie. It's okay. We'll do something more fun than the jamboree," she said.

"I want to go to the jamboree, too!" Christopher said.

"You'll see the consequences, young lady, if you don't do what I say," Cooksey said. He waved his finger in the air.

There was silence. Nate readjusted Harris's clothing in his arms and looked back and forth between them with a happy smile on his lumpy, purple face. "So, on that delightful note, I'm heading to the funeral home. Anybody want anything?"

Once Cooksey and Nate both left, Jamie took the children down to the pond. It was better there, as though the outdoors hadn't yet heard about Harris's death, the way the beds and the furniture and dishes had, absorbing the news with a kind of stony stoicism that didn't allow for argument. Out here, there was a spaciousness that allowed for discussion. She loved this pond—she'd painted several pictures of it that were in the gallery downtown: the pond at sunset, the pond in the heat of the summer, and one, like now, showing it sparkling in the morning sunlight—but nothing quite captured the peace of it, the way the reeds swayed in the breeze, or the wet, slightly sweet feel of the air down here.

She knew she should be upstairs packing their things, getting ready to go back to live at Lucy's house, but instead she sat down on the rusty lawn chair they left out there year-round, holding her cup of coffee and watching as the boys played at the edge of the water. They needed this time, time for things to be a little bit normal before everything got dismantled. They were doing their favorite thing, which was picking up pieces of bark and leaves and floating them like boats. This had a stringent adult attention requirement, because before you quite knew it, both kids could be in the water up to their shoulders, chasing after some errant piece of tree bark with an acorn riding on it as captain.

Her head hurt. She hadn't truly cried yet, that was the trouble. All that grief, all those tears were stuck, backed up behind her eyes. If she'd known that Harris was going to die, even if when she'd made breakfast yesterday morning she'd known that that would be his last meal—well, what then? She didn't know what she would have done differently. But it seemed significant and awful that she had made for him the last bite of eggs he'd ever take, the last swig of coffee, and neither of them had known it. And there had been other lasts that he hadn't seen coming either: the last time he'd sneeze, or laugh out loud, or kiss Christopher good-bye before he caught the bus, the last time he'd see the sun come up. All of it. How do any of us know how much time we have? she wondered. Are we just in some countdown for sunrises, for bites of scrambled egg? Is the total recorded somewhere? You know: *You have 25,478 more bites of egg to take,* and each time you eat an egg, that number gets reduced and you move closer to your end.

Holy shit, it was true: Harris was dead, and she was going to have to move away. Get started on something resembling an adult life, a life with fatter paychecks and rent payments. Car payments. Her mother always had said she'd been foolish to depend on art—she needed something "to fall back on," like teaching. And now it looked as if her mother might have been right. Until she found something else, she and Arley would stay with Lucy, she thought with a sigh. Meanwhile, she'd check around for full-time teaching jobs. Her old college roommate, Shana, the one who had come and rescued her from Brooklyn after Arley was born, was now teaching in a girls' residential school in Vermont, and she was always saying Jamie should come and apply there—it was a great life, providing housing, a social life, and employment all in one simple package. She slumped down, chewed on the string of her hooded sweatshirt. Why resist it? She had to move away, and she might as well go to Vermont and sign up for life at a school where little girls wore uniforms and called her Ms. McClintock and painted inside the lines. She and Arley would live in a small dormitory-type apartment with bookcases and a worn-out Oriental carpet and cups hanging on hooks in the kitchenette, and girls would come by and tell her their problems, and she'd make tea for them and later wake up in the middle of the night to listen to the hiss of the radiators through the freezing Vermont winter and dash through the snow to teach her classes in the building across the quad. She could do that, couldn't she? And she could wait a few years to get back to her art. Lots of people had to do that, and they lived.

She stared up at the sky, at a hawk wheeling around way up high, and blinked back tears.

Christopher was watching her from the edge of the pond. Their eyes met, and he sat back on his haunches and drew something in the mud with a stick. Then he said, "Am I going to move away with my dad?"

"I think so," Arley answered. He was breathing hard, and she automatically felt in her pocket for the inhaler. Just in case. "You have to go to California. That's what he said. Where *is* California, Mama?"

"I'll show you on the map when we go inside," she said.

"But I don't want to go," Christopher said. "I want to stay here."

"I know," she told him.

"You might like it," Arley said. "It might be fun."

"I won't like it. I want to stay here with you. I miss my grandpa, and I don't want to leave here." He kept looking at Jamie, dangerously near tears. She motioned him over, and he came slumping toward her, and then leaned against her when she pulled him onto her lap. He had mud caked on his tennis shoes, and his jeans had the beginning of a hole in the knee. God, she loved this child. Her chest hurt with all that love; it was as painful as pleurisy to love a child who was about to be taken from you.

Arley was standing by the water, looking at them with his owl-like intensity. "But why can't his dad just stay here?" he asked. "Why does he have to live in California?"

"I think that's just where he happens to live," Jamie said. She didn't have the slightest idea why Nate lived where he did. She rubbed her finger along Christopher's elbow and sighed.

"When do I hafta go?" he said after a while.

"Well," she said, kissing the top of his head. She had to try to be more positive, for his sake. She straightened herself up in the chair and made her voice sound more cheerful: "Actually, I heard your daddy say that you and he are going to fly to his house next week, I think. You're going to get to fly on an airplane, Christopher, a big *jet*. With a pilot and flight attendants and *everything*."

There was a long moment while he took this in. She closed her eyes tight and waited. Then he said in a tiny voice, "Will you come, too?"

She squeezed him. "I wish I could, but I'm afraid your daddy wouldn't like that. And anyway, I have to stay here. But, you know something? Did you hear your daddy saying how he's going to get married? You're going to get a new mom. It's going to be great. You'll have your own mom, all to yourself."

"Why can't you come, too?"

"Well . . ." She licked her lips. "Well, because you're going to live with your dad now, and there's no room for a bunch of other people. But I *also* heard him say that the lady he's going to marry is coming here maybe tomorrow. So we'll all get to meet her, and I can tell her all your favorite foods and things, so she'll know just how to take care of you."

He thought about this. "You can't come because you have to stay here in this house," he said. "For when I come back? Is that it?"

She rubbed his head. "Well, no. Not really that, either. Actually, new people are going to come and live in this house, and Arley and I are going to find a new place to live, and you're going to be with your dad and your new stepmom."

"But I have to go to the jamboree!" he said after a moment. Jamie rolled her eyes. Even poor Christopher had been sucked in by Cooksey. "Anyway, I don't want to go to California." He was tracing lines on the palm of her hand.

"I know, sweetie," she said. "But you're going to see that even though it's a big change, it's going to be fine. Your daddy is going to take very good care of you, and he loves you very much."

He slid off her lap, and she could see in his eyes how hard he was working to pull himself together. He knew now that she couldn't save him, that she was useless—even worse than useless, with all that chirpy talk about a new mom and an exciting, adventurous life. He kept hold of her thumb while she walked him down to the water's edge, and then, when she handed him a little piece of bark she'd found, he looked at her and swallowed—that swallow nearly killed her—and said in the bravest voice he had, "Well, will you stay here with me until I have to go on the airplane?"

Like, *Could you at least do* that *before you let my life get totally screwed?*

She stared down at the pond, saw the reeds bowing their willowy heads, heard the sound of a hawk wheeling overhead, squealing with surprise, and then, to her own amazement, she heard herself say, "Yes. Yes, of course I will. We won't leave until you do."

IT HAD BEEN only five and a half years since Nate's wife, Louisa, had died, but there had been big changes at the funeral home since he'd last been there. He remembered fumbling through his wallet to give them a memorial picture, barely holding together as he handed over the pantsuit he'd brought for her to be buried in, being led through the process of picking out caskets and hymns. It was the suit she'd worn on their honeymoon, and he'd brought it even though it had been too tight on her since she gave birth. The funeral director said they could finesse that; it wasn't a problem.

God, the weird little details he remembered—breaking down in tears on her behalf just because her corpse wouldn't fit into the honeymoon suit! Like, who thought of *that*? It was this place that brought it all back, with its blank, benign façade, spotless sidewalk, and neutral dark green shrubbery that looked like it had been formed from giant ice-cream scoops—this place he swore he'd never come to again, after losing both a mother and a wife. But here he was. Hell, he should get special treatment, frequent burial miles, perhaps.

This time, once he got inside and his eyes adjusted to the creepy dimness, he was shocked to see Pamela Nash-Brenner coming out to meet him across the wide expanse of beige carpet, her hand extended toward him in welcome. Her old man, Archie Nash, had retired, she explained, which was too bad because the old guy had a kind of naturalness around grief, as though it weren't any big deal, really. Cry or not cry, it was all the same to him. He was just doing his job, a cog in the wheel of life and death. But Pamela was Nate's age, and in fact, Nate had dated her once or twice in high school—and now she was in *charge*? He and his friends were now running the world, apparently, but didn't the world know they were incompetent, still just playing at life? Once, at a drive-in movie with him, Pamela had started laughing so hard that she'd peed on the front seat of his car, and then had been so embarrassed that he thought she was going to impale herself on the gearshift as a way of distracting him from her mortification. He hadn't minded; he'd actually thought it hilarious that he could make a girl laugh so hard she'd lose muscle control. He had thought it boded well for his future relationships with women.

She probably didn't remember that, in her new incarnation as funeral home director, speaking in that same overprecise way her father used to have, but without the diffidence. She was going to want to dig in to get to his *feelings,* he could see it in the light in her eyes as she came at him and enveloped him in a hug.

"So nice to see—oh my goodness, what happened to you?" she said.

"Bar fight," he said. "Some guy insulted this funeral home, and I leapt to your defense."

She looked at him and blinked a few times, and then laughed

loudly. Oh, he was such a card! Such a cutup! Would he like a little tour of the new renovations, perhaps? No, actually he would prefer not. He laid out the situation for her right away: he had no opinions on any of the questions she was going to ask him—blue satin or green or yellow, hymns or no hymns; whatever she wanted was fine with him. He wanted to get in there, sign the papers, write the check, and get back out, he told her. Smiling.

She smiled back at him. No need for any decisions. Harris had made all his own arrangements. She simply needed the clothes to dress him in—she thanked him for bringing them—and now to arrange the dates for the calling hours and then the service.

"Oh, no. Uh-uh. No calling hours," he said. "Nope. Not even a calling minute."

"Nate," she said. By this time they were sitting down in her office, and now she folded her hands on her desk—white plump hands, no wedding ring—pursed her lips, and frowned in concern. "Nate, it is *customary* to have calling hours. The people of this community would riot if they weren't permitted to come in and visit with each other and with you. It's what we *do*. It's how we as a community process death and get on with the healing."

He didn't need anybody talking to him about processing death or fucking healing. He'd processed enough death to last him. He told her this, and she smiled at him sympathetically, pushed a box of Kleenex across her desk, and said this might be an opportunity for him to really let himself mourn all these losses he'd had. He should take this time that the Nash-Brenner Funeral Home was offering him, and come in for a private viewing—just sit with his father's body and let himself experience *all* his feelings. Because, make no mistake, there *were* going to be calling hours. With him or without him.

Oh, he knew this tack, all right. Just another woman intent on getting him to unburden himself and *talk it all over*. Why in God's name were they all like that? Did this nation have no *end* of women who wanted Nate Goddard to get to the bottom of his feelings?

He stood up and got out his checkbook. She shook her head.

"Your father took care of his own arrangements," she said. "He paid for everything in advance. You just have to show up and mourn him."

"Or not," he said, just to drive her crazy, to see what panic mode would look like on her placid face, worn down by death and arrangements. God, he should just walk around the desk, bend her back over it, and kiss her—that's what he should do. Remind her what *life* is about. Open the blinds of this place, turn up the stereo, *dance. Do something else, get out of this line of work* . . .

But then—oh blessed day!—before he could point out all that was so wrong about a career in death, his cell phone let out its triumphant ring. He took it out of his pocket, saw that it was Tina, gave Pamela Nash-Brenner a wave, and dashed out the front door and into the sunshine. At last! The cavalry was coming to rescue him in his time of need, to save him from having to explain to Pamela that when it came to his father, he *had* no deep feelings he needed to mourn.

"Hey, baby," he said. "Oh my God, I can't wait to get you out here. Tell me you're on a plane right now. No, no. Tell me you just got *off* the plane, and you need me to come pick you up."

She giggled. "Wait, listen to me. I have some amazing news," she said.

His heart sank. As he feared, the amazing news was not that she was arriving soon. It was not even an amazing price on a flight. After a rambling story about a deal she'd been working on in Barcelona and had given up for dead, the amazing news was that it was a go. A *go*!

She wasn't coming. He got to his rental car, unlocked it, sat down, and ran his hands around the leather steering wheel. He had to remember to call the car place and renew the rental deal on this— either that or take this one back and get out his father's Mustang. *Ohhh!* For a moment gold lights flashed in his mind. He could practically hear the Hallelujah Chorus starting up. *The Mustang was his.*

That's *right*. At last he could drive the goddamn Mustang whenever he wanted.

"Ahhh—so you've won a trip to Barcelona instead of to Chester, Connecticut," he said. "Well, well, well."

There was a half-beat of silence, and then she said, "You're angry."

"I'm not angry in the least."

But he *was,* he realized with surprise. Not exactly *angry* angry, but disappointed. She was supposed to come, damn it, and be the fiancée, smiling sadly, keeping her steady hand on his arm. Also, she had to meet Christopher, for God's sake, start trying out that step-mother thing. He swallowed, forced himself to do a one-eighty. It wasn't going to solve things for him to be mad with her. This is who she was: she was about work. That's why she and he were together in the first place. If it had been her father who'd died, and he had a business deal . . . he'd have done the same thing.

"It's great. Great for your career, great for the company . . . it's great. If I had to come up with one word for it . . . *great.* And if I had to put an adjective in front of that word, it'd be *fucking.* It's fucking, fucking great."

"And, you know, it's not like I knew your dad anyway, right? I mean, what would it mean to anyone for me to be there? I never even met the guy."

She paused, but he stayed silent. A little trick he'd learned from being a salesman. Embrace silence, Howie had taught him. It can be your best friend.

"And frankly, I think it might be awkward to have me there, you know? I'm not really good at funerals. I—I don't even know how to do that whole sympathetic schmooze thing that other people know how to do. I didn't get that gene."

He allowed himself to laugh out loud. "Like I did? Sweetheart. *Tina.* Nobody likes to be at funerals, and nobody knows how to do the whole sympathetic schmooze thing, and there is no gene for it."

"See? You are mad. Jesus!"

"No way." He tapped on the steering wheel for a moment before he answered. Stared off at a stand of evergreen trees dark green against the paler greens of the maples and the farmland in the distance. "I'm not mad," he said slowly. "Just busy. I'm running around having to decide about things I don't give a fuck about, like blue satin in the casket or white satin? Church or chapel? Cucumber sandwiches or melon balls?" Here he went, lying again. "*And* now I just came from this funeral home where this chick I used to date is now the *funeral* director . . ."

"Ooh, now *that's* exciting. So maybe you could get a little side action in the old hometown," she said and laughed.

"Yeah, and you'll be in Barcelona making a billion dollars." He looked down at the floor of the car, where he was startled to see the plastic bag from F.A.O. Schwarz with the teddy bear inside, the one he'd picked out yesterday.

Denise Morgan's face swam up in front of him. He wanted to talk to her. Maybe he could call her, say he wanted to make sure she and the mister had gotten back home okay, that they didn't have any questions, act like he was *the* most committed salesguy in the United States. He sighed, ran his hands through his hair, checked his teeth in the rearview mirror. God, he looked awful. Just awful. Like somebody who'd been in a bar fight. Maybe it was a good thing that Tina wasn't coming, to see him like this . . .

"Maybe when I get back from Barcelona," she said, "we can take all my billions and get away somewhere, and maybe I can think of some really fun ways to ease your grief. In case the funeral director hasn't worn you out."

"Right," he said. "Fine. My little son and I will be looking forward to that."

There was a silence. "Oh," she said. "Does he have to come back with you, like, immediately?"

"Oh, well—hey, maybe not. Perhaps I can put him up for adoption just for a couple of days so we can get my grief taken care of. Ya think?"

"Omigod." He heard her sharp intake of breath. "I'm like totally going to be this wicked stepmother, aren't I? AAAAACK! Jesus, Nate, I'm hyperventilating here. I'm way too wacked out to be a step-mom! Holy shit!"

He made his voice light and reassuring. "Oh, you'll be wonderful at it, the way you are at everything," he said. "Watch—you'll have this kid eating out of your hand while I'll have to buy him ponies and trips to Disney World just to get him to take a bath or stop picking his nose."

"But I'm such a workaholic!" she wailed. "And I don't care if people eat their veggies or do their homework or brush their teeth. And yesterday somebody asked me what a Teletubby was, and I had no freaking idea."

"What *is* this Telly Tubba that you speak of?" he said in a foreign accent, and she laughed.

At last he'd made her laugh. Now they could hang up. All he wanted was to get the hell off the phone, get away from this parking lot. Shake loose the fact that his father's body was dead and cold somewhere in this building, and that his old house had been taken over by a woman who looked at him like he was the most clueless guy on earth, and that his own son was not going to give him one frigging inch, not one millimeter of a chance.

The car started up with a satisfying roar of the engine. He pressed so hard on the gas that plumes of smoke came out of the tailpipe and surrounded him in the driver's seat. Fucking rental car. But then he remembered again that he had a 1965 primo Mustang just waiting there for him in the garage. Harris's precious Mustang that he would never, ever let Nate drive—not even when Nate and Louisa had come back to stay at the house before she had the baby. When Nate was a fully grown, responsible adult, about to be a father, Harris was still dangling those keys, withholding the magic, that son of a bitch, with that wicked little smile, telling Louisa *she* could drive the Mustang anytime she wanted, but not Nate. No, no, not the boy who'd wanted that car worse than he'd wanted anything all his life—that little power trip of his, that grin, and Nate feeling himself reduced to being a little kid again, so *mad.* So disappointed. Saying, "I could take that car right now if I wanted, and there wouldn't be a damn thing you could do to stop me." And Louisa, laughing nervously, saying, "Now, now, stop it, you two, or I'm going to go to Las Vegas and have this baby at my sister's house. I can't put up with you two bickering."

When really it was she and Nate who were doing all the serious bickering. The most horrible times of their marriage were in those last few months, everything gone to hell. Maybe that's why he'd been wound so tight all that time, as if a wire were attached to his insides and somebody across the room was yanking it all the time, pulling him taut. God, she'd been so *unhappy.* She'd wanted to come to Connecticut, then she didn't want to come, she'd wanted a baby, but then she didn't want to take care of him. And meanwhile, she would just look at Nate with that stricken expression of hers, that little girl face that said, "You have to take care of me!" And what was *he* supposed to do? What the fuck were you supposed to do when your wife, the one who was pregnant with your child, just . . . loathed you? He'd tried to ask Harris (that was a laugh) and Harris had said—who could forget this, this *sterling* piece of fatherly wisdom—"Son, you'll learn that Goddard men are beloved by women right up until the point when they marry them. Deal with it."

Deal with it. And how were you supposed to do that? Especially when, four days later, she gets up in the morning and drives her car right up onto the highway exit ramp, going up it the wrong way. That was what he was left with: the sick knowledge that it was his own coldness that had killed her was always flickering deep somewhere in him, like a light blinking so dimly he could mostly pretend it wasn't there. But make no mistake: it had been his fault, and Harris had known it.

He sat there for a moment longer, turned off the car engine, and stared out at the trees and the bland, rolling farmland beyond—and then he flipped open his phone and punched in Denise Morgan's cell phone number.

It rang four times and he'd been about to slam the thing shut when she answered with "Why, is this *Nate*? How in the *hell* are things going there?"

So he'd told her how *great* it was all going. But something had gotten lodged in his throat—it was the exhaust from the car, and that smell of the funeral home, both mixing together—and he kept coughing.

"So how's that boy of yours?" she said after a moment. "Did he like the bear we bought him?"

"Oh, the *bear*!" he said and cleared his throat. "Oh, my! Yes, the bear. Yes, he loved it. My God. Just loved it." He looked down at the bag, still sitting on the floor of the car.

"Well . . . good," she said, and behind her he could hear a loud-speaker blaring. "We're at the airport, ready to fly back to Cincinnati. I imagine you're busy with all the arrangements and things. And did you ever call your fiancée?"

They both laughed over that. Then there was unbearable awkwardness during which he wished he hadn't called her. She wasn't his mom, after all. What had he been thinking?

"And did you file the paperwork for the contracts yet?" she said.

"Oh! No. No, I didn't. But it's the weekend, so I have some time. Gotta call Howie and let him know . . . you know . . . what's going on . . ."

"Nate, darlin', you're not all right, are you? What's happening?"

"Me? Oh, sure! *Yeah*. Just great."

"Is Tina coming to help you?"

Wow, she'd even remembered her name. "Oh. Well, yes. I mean, no, she isn't. Not so much."

"What? Why isn't she?"

Oh, they were in a bad area now, he could see that. It had been such a mistake to make this call, to have told Denise Morgan *anything*. She was turning all motherly on him now, telling him something about when you need people they have to be there for you. You have to *tell them* what you need.

He said, "Yeah . . . uh . . . no, you're right . . . thank you. Yeah, well, actually I called to see if *you* were okay, just to see if, you know, you were still feeling fine about the deal we signed . . ."

Oh, God, this was awful. Howie had said you never, ever did this—never expressed doubt, never got the people thinking they might have made a mistake, not in the seventy-two-hour grace period. Jesus, Jesus, what was he thinking?

"I should go," he said. He laughed. "Just wanted to say howdy."

"When's the funeral?"

"Monday. Monday morning."

"Nate," Denise Morgan said. "Listen to me. You are not all right. You need to take a deep, deep breath, darlin', and you need to call your boss and get some time off."

"No," he said. "No, I'm fine. Really."

"Nate," she said. "You need time. I know the signs, honey." Then she was off on another long story, and Nate had to work to get her off the phone after that. He heard her saying, "You call me if you need me," as he clicked the phone shut.

He started up the car with great effort and turned right out of the parking lot, drove a few blocks, and then had to pull over. His heart was thundering so hard in his chest that for a moment all he could think of was that his father had died of a heart attack just the day before. What if it was some kind of congenital thing he'd inherited, and he was dying, too?

He sat there for a while leaning against the steering wheel, watching the downtown going on, people walking past his car. A kid with red hair, wearing those shoes that turn into skates, and the mom with the same red hair, hurrying along beside him. Two old people staring into the window of Simon's coffee shop. Then there was a rapping on the passenger-side window. He looked over to see his old friend, Ron Shiner, grinning in at him, making a face.

"You son of a bitch! I thought that was you! Get out here, you old dog, you!"

He got out, feeling the first instant of gratitude he'd felt in days. Ron said how sorry he was to hear about the old man, but then, that part over, they slapped each other five and then Ron wrapped his big old arms around Nate's shoulder and led him into the bar where they'd hung out as teenagers. It was dark in there and musty, same as it ever was, and there they met Stevo and Johnny Becket, just back from playing baseball over at the high school, an old guys' pickup game, they called it. Beers flowed. Music—the Backstreet Boys and Maroon Five—blared from the crackly old speakers, and Patty, the daytime bartender, gave them a hard time about eating all the peanuts.

Nate had a couple of cold ones, listened to Ron's story about his divorce and then remarriage (happy) to a woman who already had a couple of kids, and then he gave a few details of his own story: the L.A. apartment, the fiancée, the travel all over the world. Everybody listened politely, odd for these guys. Nothing polite about them. Nobody could relate; that was the trouble. What could they say: "How do you think the telecommunications industry is going to fare with the emerging economies of the third world?" Ron was the district manager for a feed company, Stevo worked selling pharmaceuticals to doctors, and Johnny Becket was still farming the land his parents had owned, although he'd had to put in an ice-cream parlor to make the dairy thing worthwhile. No matter. They all knew the same jokes, played pickup basketball every Friday night, barbecued on weekends with one another's families, drank each other's beers.

So they went back to old times: the day Bernie Lumbowski sat on a pencil and had to go to the school nurse to get it removed from his butt; Stokes Jones running the wrong way with the football, *all the way down the fucking field* before he noticed that nobody from the other team was chasing him; the wild rides to New Haven on I-95, the times they'd snuck out with Harris's Mustang in the middle of the night and returned it to his trailer before sunrise and had *never once* gotten caught at it.

"Your dad was a son of a bitch from start to finish, man, from start to finish," Stevo said. "That chick he was living with at the end—you know, she's the sister of one of the bartenders here, Lucy McClintock. You want to tell me he wasn't getting some action from her? Jesus! That old man could get anybody he wanted!"

Nate ordered another beer.

Stevo wasn't finished. "Somebody, *anybody*, tell us—Patty, you knew him: What was his secret? What'd he have that we don't have?"

She appeared to be thinking it over. "You kidding? He had it going on. Everything about him said, 'Let's do it, baby.' You know? And he wasn't eating all the peanuts in here, either. He had class."

"She's *kidding*," Ron Shiner said low in Nate's ear. "He was a washed-up wreck. Trust me."

By the time Nate left the bar and headed back to his car, he was drunk and it was way past dark and Haney's real estate agency was closed down for the day. He'd put the house up for sale tomorrow. But first—he'd made up his mind—he *was* going to go to the calling hours. Yes, he would. He'd sit there and look at the old man's blank, dead face, just so he could finally know for sure he was gone.

THE GROANING WOKE him up at 6:43 the next morning, and after his eyes flew open and he sat up in bed, he was surprised to discover that he was the one making all that noise. He lay back down again, giving way to the throbbing in his head. Calling hours time, and if that wasn't enough to make him want to puke, he just didn't know. It was also the day he needed to move at least fifty tons of crap out of this house. And he needed to freaking bond with his kid. Especially since he'd gotten home so late last night that the kids had already gone to bed, and Jamie had been in her room, with the door closed. Which brought up an interesting question: *When the hell was she moving out?* He had wanted to go ask her that but had talked himself out of it. He'd been too drunk for that kind of discussion.

But now. Now he was going to have to step up to a new level as far as Christopher was concerned, that was for sure. Surely he, with his people skills and the advantage of some shared DNA, could manage to get this shy, scowling little boy to at least look in his direction. Why was it that Arley couldn't get enough of him, and Christopher treated him as if he were Darth Vader?

He sighed, got out of bed, and went upstairs to the bathroom. Then he tiptoed into the boys' room and just stood there, watching them sleep. Christopher was in the bed next to the window, lying on his back, with one arm flung out from underneath the covers, his fingers curled delicately back onto the palm of his hand. His brown hair—the same dark shade as his mother's—flopped down across his eyes, and his mouth was half open, with little wet teeth showing just the slightest bit. Nate leaned down and looked at them closely. Those teeth had grown in while he wasn't here; in fact, all these things had happened: teeth cut through gums, hair grew in and then was cut off; there were trips to the dentist, shots, skinned knees, tears, ice-cream cones falling onto the pavement—all of it taking place while Nate was on airplanes, staying in hotel rooms, meeting clients in darkened bars, standing in front of strange closets deciding which suit to wear. A funny thought, that. When he'd let himself think of Christopher, it had always been an *abstract* boy he'd thought about, not these specific fingernails and baby teeth and brown hair. Not this elbow, surely, or this little thumb. Had Christopher sucked his thumb? Had he cried when he teethed? Had Harris come in at night and rocked him, or had he taught him to be tough? Had Harris even had any clue what a boy needed?

He squatted down next to the bed, reached over gently, and touched his boy's hand. "Christopher," he whispered.

Christopher's eyes fluttered open, at first unseeing, and then he looked right at Nate and started.

Nate smiled at him. "It's okay," he whispered, and put his finger up to his lips. "Come on, let's you and me go on a little adventure. Come on with me." He crooked his finger. "I have an idea."

Christopher closed his eyes again. Nate stood up and waited, but the boy didn't open his eyes back up. He could see the eyeballs moving around underneath the lids. It had to take an incredible amount of determination to keep his eyes closed with somebody standing there staring; he didn't think he could have done it himself. But that was just him. He almost laughed out loud, but then he heard, from the other bed, Arley saying, "Hey, Natey, *I'll* go on a little adventure with you, if you want."

Nate turned and looked at him. Arley was lying on his side grinning at him, his blond hair sticking up all over his head.

Nate swallowed. "No," he said. "No, that's all right."

And he backed out of the room, something in him stinging just as if he'd gone and poured iodine on a cut; he went and took a shower, got dressed, and slipped out of the house, taking the key down from the hook by the back door. He went out to the barn and got Harris's Mustang, which hurt him all over again. It was so clear that it was Jamie's daily car, a thought that had never occurred to him: that *she* would use it. But no, there it was, this off-limits, sacred car, filled now with a stained plastic coffee cup in the cup holder, balled-up Kleenexes on the floor, empty juice box containers, a Thomas the Tank Engine lunch box, and something that looked like a clay lizard.

He hit the steering wheel with both hands. *His car!* The car he'd always wanted so bad, and now, after torturing his own kid about the car for years and years, Harris had obviously turned it over to this, this *idiot* of a woman, who never could have known what she had in her possession.

Damn it, it was his car. He couldn't think about it now, though. It was stupid to care about any of this. He got in it, adjusted the seat, changed the radio to a New York sports station, from the moronic Top Forty station she had it set on, and then started the engine, closing his eyes, feeling the thrumming of the car's pipes running through him.

As if he was a tourist, he drove all through the town, taking in how different everything was from when he used to ride his bike here. Wider sidewalks, nice iron benches and fancy antique streetlights, big planters. The town was becoming self-conscious, trying on a new look to see if it could make everybody forget that it had once been just an old farmers' hangout. He parallel-parked, went into Simon's, and ordered a bold French roast from a red-haired guy who called him sir. A group of scruffy-looking people sat around one table in the back, arguing about Iraq and whether the art gallery should be running an exhibit that had to do with the war, and at first he thought maybe he knew some of them—but no. All of them seemed about his age, but there was no one he knew. After he got his coffee, he walked around the quiet downtown streets peeking into store windows. In the park, the maple trees were all filled in with bright lime-green leaves, still the first fresh leaves of spring. The parking lot at the Congregational Church was full of cars sparkling in the sunshine. He finished his cup of coffee and threw the paper cup in a pretentious-looking little wire litter basket.

Just before eleven, he drove up to the funeral home, sat there in the empty parking lot, turned off his car, and listened to the engine ticking in the sunlight.

When he opened the front door, Pamela Nash-Brenner looked up, unsurprised, and then ushered him to the little side room, where Harris lay. She touched his arm and whispered, "Call me if you need me," and then raised her hand up, before he could answer, and said, "I know, I know! You'll be fine. You won't need anything." She closed the door behind her when she left.

It was a long, wide room, big enough to accommodate the crowd that would no doubt crush in here later, wanting to pay their respects. Nate stood by the door for a long time, and then he took a deep breath and strode over to the casket on the far side of the room.

His dad looked exactly the way Nate knew he would look: like an innocent, seamless mannequin lying in state, the way dead bodies always looked, emptied out of everything you thought you knew about them. Nate was an old pro at this: he felt as if he'd always been standing in this very room, over and over and over again, looking into caskets, gazing at people he was programmed to love, and each time measuring the distance they'd already spiraled off, far away from him.

Todd Haney came by late that afternoon to check out the place. Jamie knew Todd from the Campfire Kids; his boy, Toby, was the same age as Arley and Christopher. She watched Nate and Todd from the second-floor window as they walked around the outside of the house, Todd plodding along in his Realtor suit and tie while Nate walked animatedly ahead, sometimes even walking backward so he could talk, all the while pointing and gesturing, flinging his arms wide to take in the orchard, the pond, the trees, the sky—all that he was so willing to part with.

Harris hadn't liked Todd. He was one of the young rich guys in town, always wearing his hair moussed into little peaks, and—this may have been his worst crime from Harris's point of view—he wore a pinky ring with a diamond. Harris said men should not be putting stuff on their hair that smelled like flowers, and they shouldn't wear rings with stones bigger than their knuckles, rings that looked as though they were just looking for subjects who would come and kiss them.

Jamie was in Nate's old room folding her clothes and putting them on top of the dresser. She'd cleaned all her stuff out of the master bedroom—let Nate and his fiancée move in there, if they wanted.

She'd be glad to take the back room, Nate's old bedroom. In fact, she'd moved out the sewing machine, the exercise bike, stacks of old issues of *Car and Driver* magazine, the ironing board—everything, taken out all the junk and put it in one corner of the basement. Then she'd come back upstairs, rolled up the *Barbarella* poster, swept the floor, and wiped off all the surfaces.

She was *staying*. Let Nate get mad at her. Let Cooksey even come and serve her eviction papers. She was not leaving until Nate and Christopher left, as she'd promised, and that was that.

The boys had been playing in their room, but once she started cleaning, they got restless and whiny, so she put them to work carrying magazines out into the hallway. But then Arley had started wheezing because of all the dust, and she had to sit down with him and do the inhaler even though he protested and kicked. Usually he was so good about this, but she realized there had just been too much going on. She breathed with him while he inhaled, and finally he calmed down. And then she jumped up and started working again, only to have both kids get into a fight over which one of them was Batman and which one had to be Robin.

"Can't you play something else?" she called to them on one of her trips down to the basement. "Play Elmo and Grover or something."

Staying. She was staying.

By the time Nate and Todd came inside, she had gone downstairs and was in the kitchen kneading bread dough, just to give her hands something useful to do. These would be cinnamon rolls for tomorrow's breakfast.

"I gotta be honest, guy," Todd Haney was saying as they walked in. "I think that unless you're willing to put a fortune into fixing all this—and I think you're looking at some fairly serious code work— the only real possibility is to sell it to a developer who'll tear down the house and put up something new. Maybe even condos." He stopped talking and smiled sadly at Jamie. "Hey there, Jamie. How are you? So sad about Harris, isn't it? Lainie and I still can't believe it."

Yes, yes. Very sad.

"It's got a sunporch and three bedrooms," Nate was saying, ignoring them, "and really big closets, which I think is rare for that era . . ."

"Well," Todd said, "it's just that there's no market these days for old farmhouses." He looked at Jamie again. "It's the American tragedy. People want new. They're buying all those crappy McMansions, with their great rooms and their decks and their four bedrooms. Nobody wants a soapstone sink and *linoleum* anymore. They want Italian tile floors, *heated,* and you need at least one more bathroom, and some built-ins. This place is like camping, at least from the point of view of the buyers I'm talking to."

Nate stood there looking around the room, cracking his knuckles, his eyes all blank looking and tired, and then he sighed and said, "Okay. Fine. Great. Get me some developers. Tear the thing down. Put up condos."

"Wait," Todd said. He whistled. "Put the braaaakes on, guy. Baaaack up a second. This isn't something to just rush into right now. You—"

"No. Fuck this. Let's call a meeting," Nate said. "Get me some developers. How soon could we get that together? Tomorrow afternoon? Tuesday at the latest?"

Todd was looking around the room, his pinky ring flashing in the overhead light. Jamie realized with surprise that it had suddenly gotten dark outside, as though night had just pulled the curtain down at last on this long, endless, hellacious day. Nighttime and she was here with a crazy-ass madman who was willing to take this farmland and turn it into condominiums by morning, if there was any possible way. Only Todd Haney and his moussey hair could keep this from happening, and how was that going to work? She looked at Todd, trying to send him a telepathic message to *just say no.* There was no time like the present to start experimenting with ESP.

"Well, Nate, honestly, I don't know," Haney said with an uneasy laugh. "Listen, maybe you need to think about this. Take it easy and not do anything rash right off the bat."

"I think that's a good idea," Jamie said, which of course Nate didn't even bother to respond to. He was acting as though she wasn't there. He said to Todd, "No, really. I'm serious," and he ambled over to the doorway to the dining room and stood up on tiptoe, grabbing onto the metal rod suspended there about five inches from the molding. Jamie had always idly wondered what the thing was, and now she recognized it: a chin bar. Nate stretched his arms up as high as they would go and then hung there by his fingertips. His sweatshirt and T-shirt rose up, showing his flat stomach and hip bones. Jamie wanted to look away but found she couldn't. He'd lost his mind. Next, if you weren't watching carefully enough, he just might swing himself up onto the countertops and then to the wagon-wheel light fixture that hung over the table.

He dropped back down to the floor, breathing hard, and said, "So, how soon can you have somebody over here? I'm here until the end of the week. And my signing fingers are itchy." He held up fingertips still red from supporting all his weight, and laughed out loud.

AFTER TODD HANEY left, the four of them ate dinner together, and that was so awkward that he decided to tackle cleaning out the basement just so he could get away. Going down there was like going back in time, to some damp, mildew-smelling concrete world of childhood, a world ruled over by a heater the size of a T. rex—the kind of oil-burning furnace that thundered on and off all year long, responsible, as it was, for keeping the place furnished with both heat and hot water. No rest for this furnace. As a kid, he'd been afraid of it, the way it roared and sputtered and shook and required his father to come down and beat on it periodically. The basement itself was a well-known home to monsters and zombies. Only one corner of it was even remotely habitable; it had a seedy old black leather armchair and a ragged Oriental carpet and a black-and-white TV set that had probably stopped working years ago.

He made his way down there and, sure enough, it was just as it had always been. He sat in the old chair and ran his hand along its cracks and worn spots. It had been a find when his father dragged it home from a junk shop back when Nate was a little kid, boasting about how it was *real leather,* not something they normally could afford. But Nate's mother had hated it, and insisted it live in the basement, even from the beginning. And there it had gone to stay.

He reached down between the armchair and the wall, and sure enough, there was the box of his father's old *Playboy* magazines, still stuck down there, right where he and Ron had stashed them in seventh grade. They used to sneak down and read them in the afternoons after school. How was it that his mother had never found them? He opened one and idly admired the centerfold, with the staple always in the wrong place.

There was a rustling from the stairs. He didn't look up.

"Hey, Natey, did you know I have a cell phone?" a voice said.

"Excuse me?" He craned his neck around. It was Arley. He was standing there, looking relaxed and companionable, his hair sticking up with its many cowlicks. He looked a lot like his mother—the two of them seemed like slow-moving birds, swooping down to deliver some message and then taking off again.

"I have a cell phone," Arley said. He said it as if he was sure Nate was going to need this intelligence before too much more time had gone by.

"Oh. Well, that's good. Good for you." End of conversation.

"I'm the only one in my kindergarten to have a cell phone."

"Imagine that."

"Do you want to know how I got it?"

"I suppose you're going to tell me anyway, so where did you get it?"

"I found it by the road one day. It doesn't work. I keep waiting for it to ring, but it won't. Mama says somebody prob'ly got mad at it and threw it out of a car."

He didn't say anything. He went back to looking at Miss

November, tried to think of what he and Ron must have thought of her way back when.

Arley studied him. "You know what else I have? I have some other stuff that is just mine, stuff that I found. I know how to find things. I have a rubber band that has *stripes* on it. And I have a tooth that came out of a shark."

"Is that so?"

"My Aunt Lucy is left-handed. Are you left-handed?"

"No."

"I'm not, either. I don't even know what it *means*." He laughed. "Do you know what it means?"

"It means," Nate said, closing the magazine and putting it back, "that you use your left hand for most things, like writing and eating."

"I think I could try that."

"Aren't you supposed to be in bed?"

"No. Not yet." He came down farther, leaned both elbows against the arm of the chair, and smiled at Nate. It was disconcerting, that grin. Relaxed, convivial, and so close up. "So, did you ever invent anything?"

"Invent? Let's see. I don't think so."

"A guy at school says he invented potato chips. But I don't think he did."

Nate couldn't help himself from grinning. "No. I think potato chips have been around for a long time."

"*And* his mom lets him drive the car, but only in their driveway. And he sleeps in his clothes. Every night."

"No! Get out of town! Is that really true?"

Arley's eyes went round. "Yes! He never, *ever* has to put on paja-mas or brush his teeth. He doesn't even own any pajamas, because why would he? That's what he said. His mother told him he could save time in the morning if he didn't have to change his clothes."

Nate laughed.

"And this girl, Angela, in my class—guess what. She has a horse, and sometimes her cat will ride on the horse's back."

"Now *that* I don't know about," Nate said. "Sounds fishy to me."

Arley nodded soberly. "It sounds fishy," he agreed. Then he said, "Did you ever have asthma?"

"No."

"I get asthma sometimes." He said this matter-of-factly. "Then I can't breathe. I'm the only boy I know who can't breathe sometimes."

"Well," Nate said. He ran his hands through his hair. "Well, that's too bad. It must be scary."

"Yeah," Arley said and shrugged. "It's a little bit scary. Well, good-bye. I have to go make something with my Legos now. If you ever want to invent something, let me know because I have some ideas."

CHAPTER
12

"So all this . . . artwork all over the house. I guess that would be
yours?" he said from behind her.

It was unfortunate, that pause before the word *artwork,* as though
he'd had to come up with a polite term to describe it. And she wasn't
in the mood for him right now anyway. She'd put the children to bed,
and now she was washing dishes and weeping. This was the third
night since Harris had died, and each one seemed sadder than the last,
the knowledge really sinking in. Even putting the boys to bed had
been hard; she'd had to answer yet another round of questions about
death and moving—while meanwhile, downstairs, they could hear
Nate throwing things into boxes, dismantling the entire house. No
wonder the tears that had been backed up in her head all day had
started to leak out.

"What artwork?" she managed to say without turning around.

"Oh, you know, all this stuff that's everywhere—on the walls, all
the wreaths and paintings and sewed-up looking things . . ." He was
standing at the top of the stairs that went down to the basement, holding a box.

"Yes," she said. "Yes, it's mine." He started to say something, and she said shortly, "Don't worry. I'll take it all down. You don't have to pack that stuff up."

"And, uh, when do you plan on doing that, do you think?"

"*Tonight.* As soon as I get the kitchen cleaned up. If you can wait that long."

He laughed at her tone of voice and went outside with the box. She heard it landing on the ground with a thud. When he came back, he said, "Also—how should I say this? You *do* plan on moving out, right? I mean, you get it that you can't live here anymore?"

"*Yes.*"

"Great," he said. "I'm only asking because I haven't seen you packing anything yet."

"I'm washing the dishes, in case you didn't notice," she said.

He stood there for a moment longer, perhaps realizing, as she was, that that sentence didn't make any sense. He was looking around the kitchen as if he had never stopped to consider all the dishes and pots and pans and measuring spoons and mixing bowls. He ran his hands through his hair and mumbled something about all this shit that nobody wants, and then he went down to the basement. Out of the corner of her eye, she had noticed that he was wearing a torn, sleeveless Corona T-shirt that she remembered seeing Harris wear sometimes when he was mowing the lawn. The silence while he was gone was breathtaking, but in another moment, he was back with another box. "Hey, so what the hell was the deal with my dad and all these magazines?" he said. "He's like one of those people who dies and you find out he has eight hundred and seventy-six bottles of ketchup and every newspaper since 1934."

She didn't say anything, and he took this box outside too. As soon as he was back, he said, "I now have a new theory. *I* think he used his magazine collection to lure women. Isn't that how it was? Did he say to you, 'Come over to my house, my sweet patootie, and take a look at all my *Popular Science* mags'? And then he imprisoned you here and made you cook meals and take care of his grandson and have sex with him."

God, he made her so tired. It was so much work, just having to be in the same room with him. "Look," she said. "I didn't even know he liked magazines. And, as I told you, we didn't have—"

"I'm *kidding*. Sorry. I was just making a joke about the magazines. That's the best I've got for humor at this time of night." He went over to the refrigerator and looked into it. She let the dishwater drain out of the sink and then stood there staring at the suds that remained. They looked as if they were clinging to the sides of the sink for dear life.

"Actually," he said, "I don't have my A comedy material at all anymore." His head was still in the fridge. "I used to be a fairly amusing guy, but I'm afraid I used it all up on that boy of mine today—to no avail, I might add. He still acts like I'm the biggest loser he's ever seen."

"Here's a thought: maybe you could try being serious."

He resurfaced, and his eyes registered a flicker of interest. "*Be serious?* Wow, that *is* a thought." He made himself look stricken. "Okay. Here. Look at this face, at these lumps. Is this the face of a man who has not known seriousness and suffering?"

She had nothing to say on that topic.

He laughed. "See, what I thought you might tell me, in a comforting sort of way, is,"—he made his voice go into a falsetto here—"'Oh, don't worry about Christopher. He'll come around.' But no. Tough room, I guess," he said. He started taking foil-covered baking dishes out of the refrigerator and putting them on the counter, holding the door open with his hip. "What I'm looking for here is a beer. You wouldn't happen to know if there's likely to be one, would you?"

"I think so. Bottom shelf, behind about fifty casseroles."

"Wow. What is it with all this stuff? They all look like . . . well, like pieces of roadkill or something, floating in who-knows-what kind of sauce." For some reason, the idea of all these sweet old ladies bringing over roadkill casseroles made her laugh, in spite of herself. But then she was sorry, because, encouraged by having an audience, he made a big show of lifting off the foil from a couple of dishes and peering in at them. "Eww. This one is highly suspicious. It has green things floating in some kind of milky stew, *gah*—and *this* one, you don't even want to know. But . . . *aha!* Waaay back here are some beers. You want one?"

"No."

"Why not? Is it breaking some kind of parenting rule I have yet to learn about?" he said. He put on an intoning voice, talking very fast, like an announcer on TV reading the fine print: "When two children are on the premises, at least one adult must be present at all times and be stone-cold sober in case of emergency. If there are *two* adults, and one of them is male and one is female, both must be stone-cold sober, and at least three of their feet must remain on the floor at all times." He grinned at her, obviously pleased with himself. Then he held out a beer to her. "Here, take it. You might as well."

"No. Thank you."

"Why not? You don't drink?"

"I just don't want one."

"Your sister is a bartender, and you don't drink. That's it, isn't it?"

"I drink when I want to."

"Well, then have a beer. Go on, take it."

"Look, I just don't feel like pretending that we're friends here. You've made it clear that you think bad things about me and your dad, and all you want is to see me packing up and getting out of your way, and so I don't think we should sit around drinking beer and acting like we're pals or something."

"I don't think it means we're great pals just because we have a beer together," he said. "I mean, I can have a beer with—" His cell phone rang in his jeans pocket just then. He took it out, looked at it, and then flipped it shut without answering it. This was about the fifth time she'd seen him do that. She felt sorry for all the people who must try to call him. In fact, she felt sorry for anyone who had anything to do with him at all.

She laughed. "My God, do you *ever* bother to answer your cell phone?"

"Oh, this is just my boss. He wants to hear how my sales call went, but I don't want to talk to him until I know what I'm going to say."

"You don't know how your sales call went?" She couldn't believe she was talking to him like this.

"Actually, that's all I *do* know. It went great. But he's going to need to hear a lot more than that from me, and I have to figure out how to tell it just right. So he doesn't, you know, freak out." He started opening drawers, looking in them, and then closing them again. And sighing.

"Freak out? You mean, about your plan to take your five-year-old on all your business trips?"

"Well . . . yes." He opened the drawer with the silverware and stared into it for a minute.

She sighed. "Are you looking for the bottle opener?"

"Yes."

"I think that beer has a twist-off cap. I can't believe you haven't told your boss you have a kid."

"Yeah, well." He tried the beer cap. "So it does. Twist off." He leaned against the counter and took a big swig and then exhaled. "Listen. It's no sweat, believe me, this Christopher thing. I'm fully confident that this is going to work out just great. In fact, if you want to know the truth, I think having a kid there is going to help me burn off some of the stupid, extraneous stuff I'm always having to do with clients. It's going to be good for me." He drank another big sip of beer and said, "So—when *are* you planning to, you know, move out of here?"

"When are *you* moving out?"

"I asked you first."

"Well, I'm moving out when you do. We're going to walk out of here at the same time."

He looked at her and raised his eyebrows. "Why the hell would we want to do that? What are you sticking around for, anyway? I don't know what you've been told, but I don't think there's money for you in the will or anything. And there's some kind of trust that automatically leaves me the house—"

She felt her face flush. "I'm not staying here for money!" she said. She wanted to hit him again. "What is with you? I'm staying here because I promised Christopher that I would. I said I'd stay until he has to get on the airplane. Because—well, I don't know if you've noticed or not, but he doesn't *want* to go off with you. This house is all he's ever known, and he's devastated having to leave. And I'm sick of how you just go along, pretending everything's great, and that it's fine to drag him around to hotel rooms and sales calls and that it'll all be just fine, because . . . because, in your mind, other schmucks have raised kids and so you can, too. It's pathetic, is what it is. It's *horrifying,* in fact. It's like . . . child abuse."

He was silent for a moment, and then he said slowly, "You know, it's interesting because *you're* the one wielding actual weapons and knocking people unconscious. So if we're talking about abuse here, I think *I* would be the one who might actually have a case. Let me assure you, Christopher is going to be just fine with me."

"Well, that's great. But anyway, I'm staying until he goes. You can call the cops on me if you want to. Get Cooksey over here again, if that's what you want to do. Press charges. But I promised Christopher I'd stay, and I'll go to jail before I break that promise to him."

"Whoa. Can we take things down a couple hundred notches?" he said. "Nobody said anything about jail."

"*Fine.*"

"Fine."

They glowered at each other for a moment, and then he took his beer and went back to the basement, where she could hear him crashing around like a wild animal. She went into the living room and started taking down wreaths and paintings and stacking them on the floor. And weeping again. One of these wreaths was one she'd made at Christmas, and then Harris didn't want to take it down when they took down the rest of the decorations, so she took all the little Christmas-y parts off of it and stuck little flowers on it for springtime.

She heard footsteps clumping up the stairs, and then Nate cleared his voice and said, "By the way, I've just now come to an important executive decision. I'm calling the Salvation Army to come and take everything away. I don't want any of it. Nothing. The whole god-damn place. So if there's anything you want from this dump, just take it. They can haul all the rest of this away, and I'll wave good-bye to it from the curb."

She started to say something about how this house held his entire family's past. Harris had told her how it was their homestead. Some of these pieces of furniture had belonged to his grandparents and maybe great-grandparents and should be saved. But then she thought better of it. He cared for nothing. Not a bit of it meant anything to him at all.

"What?" he said.

"Nothing."

"No. You were going to say something."

"No, I wasn't."

"Oh, I think you were. Let me guess." He put his index finger on his chin and did an imitation of someone thinking. "Okay. Got it. You were going to say that I'm no better than the Visigoths, coming in here and trashing the place and putting it up for sale to developers—letting it *go condo*, horror of horrors—and not caring enough to save even one scrap of it. That right? And that, furthermore, you think I'm ruining Christopher's life and deserve to rot in hell for it."

"Actually, I was going to say that you should at least take the photo albums. There are pictures of your mother that Harris showed me. Some are really quite lovely."

"Yeah, well . . ." He looked away. "You're right. I'll mail those to myself. Thank you."

"Good."

A beat of silence. "So, listen," he said and ducked his head kind of endearingly. He was shy, maybe. Or at least aware of the damage he carried around inside. "Even though we're not friends or anything, what the hell? Why can't we just go outside and sit on the porch for a while? It's the night before the funeral and we're never going to have to deal with each other again, so let's call a truce and celebrate the fact that I've decided to donate everything in this house to charity, or that I'm some kind of hopeless idiot who's on the verge of having his head handed to him by a kid. Something like that."

She hesitated. What harm could it do? "Okay," she said.

"And have a beer with me."

"Well . . . okay," she said. "Just one."

"Good," he said. "And I'll have another one."

"So when is your fiancée coming?" she said. He got two more beers out of the refrigerator and she followed him outside. He held the door open with his shoulder so she could pass him.

"Oh. Tina. No, she's not coming after all. Business thing came up." He handed her a beer and rolled his eyes as he said, "Waaaay too important to pass up."

"That's too bad," she said, and meant it. She realized she'd wanted to see the woman whom this guy would be interested in. Outside, the air was cooler and sweeter, and she felt a momentary pang at being there with Nate instead of with Harris; it felt a little like disloyalty, as though she'd somehow chosen the son over the father. A thin sliver of a moon rose up between the trees and she shivered and wrapped her velvet scarf around her throat twice.

"So how long did you say you lived here with the old man, anyway?" Nate said. He settled into the Adirondack chair and left the swing to her. She sat down and tucked her legs up underneath her and sipped her beer.

"A year."

"I probably shouldn't tell you this, but the opinion among my friends is divided about whether or not you and he were . . . you know."

She flushed. "Hey, I am *not* going to talk about this with you."

"Why? Because you think it's none of my business?"

"That, and also that I already told you the truth. I moved in here because I had to move out of my sister's place, and the b—"

"—And the boys were good friends," he finished for her. "I know, I know. But I know my dad. He always had some woman he was buttering up. Even when I moved back here with my *wife*, he hit on her. His own daughter-in-law, and with me right here in the same house. Hitting on her! So you can see why it seems kind of . . ." He trailed off.

"Nope," she said. "He was a complete gentleman at all times." She laughed a little. "Gee, you know, maybe I should be insulted. I wasn't *desirable* enough . . ."

"Maybe he'd lost it. Happens even to old lechers like my dad. I've been packing up all his stuff, and I looked for some Viagra, but—"

"Don't you ever get tired of talking about your dad's sex life? Doesn't that kind of creep you out?"

He laughed and ran his hands through his hair. "I guess it should, huh? But to tell you the truth, my dad was a horndog for as long as I knew him."

"A horndog?" she said.

"Always horny for somebody. Anybody except my mom, that is. He was always making remarks about women's bodies. Had them all rated and ranked and catalogued. Talked about them all the damn time. It was funny, really, but it made my mom *insane*."

She looked down and started peeling off a little section of the label on her beer bottle. It came off easily, in long, wet strips. "You know, I think he might have been really sorry for the things he did to you and your mom."

He stared off into the darkness. "Yeah, well. Good. He should have been. Although it's too late now for any of that to matter, isn't it? He had his chance to make things right."

"He probably didn't know he was running out of time. Maybe he would have."

"Maybe," he said evenly. And then, after a moment, in a completely different voice, he changed the subject. "Okay, I have a question for you. I was having a long talk with your son this evening, and—"

"You were talking with Arley? When did that happen?" She wasn't exactly sure she wanted Nate talking to Arley when she wasn't there.

"*Yes,* with Arley, after dinner, and it kind of got me curious. This isn't going to come out right, but, well, if you don't mind, just who the hell did you mate with to get a kid like that?" He took a drink of his beer, studying her in all seriousness.

"Excuse me?" She laughed. "Who did I *mate* with? Did you really just say that?"

"Yeah. Who *is* this kid's father? You said before that he's some kind of artist who's so special that he can't be expected to live with people, and so what I want to know is if he's some kind of reclusive nut job superstar in the art world that everybody's heard of. Because your kid is certainly an interesting little guy. He told me all about how he knows a girl whose cat rides horses, and oh, yeah, another boy who says he invented potato chips. I never learned so much in a five-minute conversation."

"Oh, really?"

"So what's the deal? Who *is* this dad of his? Is he out somewhere hiding from the paparazzi? Why can't he live with people?"

She laughed again, in spite of herself. "No. He's not really all that special. He's just not domestic, is all. He's a graffiti artist in New York."

"A graffiti artist? Really!" He narrowed his eyes. "Is that a real occupation?"

"Well, he called it 'uncommissioned art.' He saw what he was doing as guerrilla warfare, really—bringing art to the people whether they wanted it or not. It's very political, graffiti art."

"Oh, so I get it—he couldn't be domesticated because all he wanted to do was spray-paint overpasses in his spare time."

"That's right. Hang off overpasses and avoid the cops. But then sometimes it might also seem fun to him to *confront* the cops. You know: have a real showdown."

"Hmm. That doesn't fit in with a good family life, I guess. Even worse than being, ah, a traveling salesman, I would think."

"Well, that remains to be seen," she said. "Neither is great."

"So tell me this. Did you have, you know, a major plan for getting Mr. Graffiti Guy in off the ledges and taming him? A plan that failed?"

She gave him one of her fixed stares. "Why exactly do you care?"

"Oh, I don't know. I just do. As a man about to get married . . . consider it research."

"All right. Although it's not any of your business—no, I didn't plan to tame him. I always knew it was going to be impossible."

"Really? He wasn't tamable?" He leaned forward. "I find that hard to believe, that you were going to give this guy a pass—and after he'd fathered this child. You just let him stay out there with his spray can, never even changing a diaper? Wow, you must have been under quite a spell back then."

She took a sip of her beer and tried not to look at him. "Well, I was," she said quietly. "I was completely crazy about him. He had been my adviser at college, even though he was just a few years older. He was like this boy wonder in the art world, and he kind of *concentrated* on me, even though I was just this nobody. It was very . . . intoxicating. I would say he was the first person who took me seriously as an artist."

"And he was pretty good-looking, I'll bet."

Well. He'd been gorgeous in a careless kind of way. Intense gray eyes, always looking bored and disappointed, but with a smile that spread across his features like the sun coming out. Blindingly white teeth, all straight in a line, *glistening* like they were made of polished marble.

"Oh, yes. All of that. And I was kind of bowled over, because— well, nobody really paid attention to me, not that kind of attention. My sister was the one guys fell all over themselves to get to."

"I find that a little hard to believe," he said.

"Not that I minded," she added quickly. "I was busy doing my art and didn't notice. At prom time I made duct-tape purses for all the girls to take to the prom—I made them all different colors with sequins and everything—and that was *my* prom. I didn't want to go to the actual dance."

"I'll bet if you think back, there were guys who wanted to go out with you."

"I guess so. I don't really remember. My sister was always fixing me up with guys and trying to get me to loosen up, so I could be *popular*. Like that was something good. It just looked like more agony to me, more pressure to be like other people."

"And so then you get to college, and there's this young *adviser* who takes a shine to you? And let me guess, he's broke."

She laughed. "Ohhhh, yes. Very broke."

"Ah. And I'll bet it takes a lot of paint to do an overpass."

She shrugged and looked down. "I quit doing my own art stuff and worked full time to support him. Stupid, but it was kind of our deal. We lived in this dark little horrifying apartment in Brooklyn, with druggies passed out in the halls and cockroaches all over the place, and all our friends were artists. Everybody was sick all the time—it was a very heavy scene. I didn't really fit in, me and my duct-tape creations and my pinecones with glitter. Everybody else was way cooler. They wore all this funky wearable art. All black. You know?"

"Hard to believe anybody dresses any cooler than you. What's that skirt made of? Did you do that?"

"It's batik," she said. "You do it with dyes and wax."

"Nice." He took another sip of his beer and studied her. She could see his eyes shining in the dark, with curiosity. He was such a salesman, so good at talking to anybody, even her. "So, come on, tell me this, and don't take this the wrong way. Are you still crazy about him? Even a little? Like, if you could have him back, would you? Paint bills and all? You would, wouldn't you?"

"No. Oh God, no," she said. "Once I got pregnant, he was just—well, he was a jerk about the whole thing. That's all. Against it from the start. He *reluctantly* came with me to the hospital when it was time for Arley to be born, but then he freaked out at how *medical* the whole place was, and he said they had a mural in there that offended him; paid-for public art always made him nuts. So he walked out when Arley was, like, a half-hour old, and went on some kind of graffiti bender and stayed gone for four nights in a row, and then when Arley was two weeks old, I packed up and left him."

"But you've seen him since, right? Explained his crimes to him. Gotten, as they say, *closure*." He raised his eyebrows to show he was being ironic.

"Well, the great thing was that if you don't marry somebody, then you don't have to divorce him, either. So I just split, didn't leave a forwarding address. That was all the closure I needed. My friend Shana came and picked me up. The electricity had gone out, and I wasn't sure if it was because the bill hadn't been paid or if there was some sort of power outage. Ugh! I just needed to get out of there."

"But do you ever feel bad that your son doesn't know his father?"

She was surprised how angry she felt. "I'm *not* going to run after him, if that's what you mean. He pretty much abandoned us. I'm not going to go looking for him." She pushed off with her bare foot on the porch floor and swung in silence. Then, because he was still looking at her, she said, "So, now *you* tell me your story. What was the deal with you and Christopher's mother?"

He pretended to be shocked, but he was smiling. "Hey, don't you know that you're not supposed to ask questions like that? I'm a *widower,* McClintock. Society doesn't want us widowers to dwell on things like the death itself. You *did* get the memo on the whole death-by-car-smash-up thing, didn't you?"

"Yeah, I heard that she died in a car accident. Which is horrible. But—"

"And I'm sure Harris explained to you how it was all my fault since we were having a fight, and that I somehow provoked her into getting *into* the car when she was mad, and so I am forever and ever to blame and therefore, according to the rules of etiquette for the town of Chester, I should not have to discuss this in casual conversation. No one would ever bring her up to me. Period. I'm pretty sure I have a lifetime pass."

She cleared her throat. "I think that the memo I got didn't mention anything about it being your fault," she said. "And anyway, it's five years later, and what I *meant* was, do you still love her?"

This time he did a spit-take. "*McClintock!* Honestly, where is your *decorum*? First of all, it *was* my fault. Haven't you heard? I'm ghastly when it comes to women, just the way my father was. We Goddard men don't *do* relationships well. And now, watch, your next question will be did I ever love her in the first place? And let me just save you the trouble by telling you that the jury is still out on that. Today's answer is, probably not so much. Certainly not the required amount, or she would be alive right now, wouldn't she?"

Suddenly he jumped up off the Adirondack chair, threw his head back and downed the rest of his beer, sprang off the porch with some kind of rebel yell, and went over and stared intently at the porch steps. Then, to her everlasting shock, he started tearing the boards apart with his bare hands. *Rrippp!* As if they were toothpicks. He'd pull one off and then toss it into the yard over his shoulder.

"What the hell are you doing?"

He straightened up and regarded her. "Look at this wood. All rotted out. These steps are dangerous." He wiped his mouth with his arm. The sweat was already glistening on him. "Have to get them out of here."

"You really are a major lunatic, aren't you?" she said.

"Hey, is there an axe in the barn, do you think?"

"An axe? You shouldn't be trusted with an axe. Would you just stop this? Please. You're making this porch dangerous. We need those steps."

"Hey, I'm fixing this place. Look at it." He yanked off another board with an astonishingly loud crack and stepped back in satisfaction. "You'd never know, to look at this place, that my dad used be a construction guy. Trust me, he didn't allow boards around that even had little splinters showing. He was like a maniac about things being just right—wouldn't even let me do any of it, 'cause I might do it *wrong* or something. No, no. It had to be perfect. Harris Fucking Goddard Standard of Excellence."

"Well, I'm sure you have a lot of father issues you can work out by pulling the house apart with your bare hands, but could I just say that there are two little boys who are most likely going to step on those nails you're throwing around? And besides, we kind of *need* porch steps, when you stop and think about it. Are we supposed to leap off the porch every time we want to leave here?"

"Sure. We can all jump, can't we? Has childhood gotten so pampered that kids can't even take a flying leap anymore?"

She sat there watching him, feeling more and more irritated by the second. "Look, could you at least wait until daylight? You're making way too much noise throwing those boards around."

He stopped and grinned at her. "Hey, why don't you come down here and help me? Huh? Get the old adrenaline pumping?"

Harris had been right about Nate, everything mean he'd said. You couldn't be nice to him; he just was so angry and wounded that he had to trash everything around him in order to make himself feel better. She shouldn't be out here. She knew enough to know that it was her presence that made him think he could dismantle the steps with his bare hands, and if she stayed any longer, he was liable to start smashing windows and pulling apart siding. By morning he'd have kicked the barn down, too, and the whole place would be lying in rubble.

He didn't seem to notice when she went into the house. She rinsed out her beer bottle, and then went upstairs and got into bed. For a long time, she lay there underneath the sheet, staring at the way the back porch light made patterns on the ceiling. She could hear him out back, tearing up boards. *Ccccracccccckkk!* And then finally, after a long time, the light went off, and she heard the sound of the screen door close, and then the big door closed, too. He came up the stairs with plodding footsteps and went into the bathroom and shut the door. The water turned on, the toilet flushed.

She squeezed her eyes shut.

She had never wanted to have sex with somebody so much in her whole life.

The whole town turned out for the funeral. Of course. Jamie had known they would. Among the old-timers here, funerals were social events. Harris, however, had always balked at going to them, and she'd had to remind him of Yogi Berra's famous quote, "Always go to other people's funerals. Otherwise they won't come to yours." That had made him laugh, but he still refused to go. He said he'd rather go down to the pond with a six-pack and think about the times he and the deceased had gone fishing than to go sit in a church.

"The pond," he'd said, "is where I honor *my* dead folks. That's where you can actually get to the memories."

"You mean, that's where you can drink and blot out the memories," she'd said.

But sitting there in the church, shoehorned in among hundreds of people, listening to the young pastor drone on endlessly about life everlasting—the pastor who hadn't ever even met Harris—she knew the old man would say his way had been right after all. He hadn't gone to even one of the five funerals that had been held during the past year, and yet—the place was packed for his. She smiled into her hand, then felt her eyes well up. Arley, wheezing slightly, reached over and tucked his hand in hers, and she had to gaze up at the stained-glass windows to blink away the tears.

Oh, this was one of those roller-coaster days of emotion, all right. Up and down and up and down. Already the morning had been tense at home; the boys hadn't wanted to wear what Christopher called their "scratchy clothes," and instead of getting dressed when she'd told them to, they'd run up and down the hall in their underwear and socks doing heart-stopping dramatic falls at each end until, predictably, Arley had slipped on a little throw rug, almost going sailing over the banister, and had bumped his knee on the newel post. Then, while she was rubbing Arley's knee and discussing whether Band-Aids were of any use when you weren't actually bleeding (she thought no, but he was sure they were), Christopher had come over and gotten on her lap, too, and said he didn't want to go to the place where they put people in the ground.

Nate came upstairs just then to go to the bathroom, and he stopped and shook his head at the three of them, all sitting together on the floor of the hallway. "If I were five years old," he said, "I don't think *I'd* want to be sitting on some *lady's* lap every time something went wrong."

Then later that morning, she'd been ironing her one nice black dress in the kitchen when he came stomping in, holding his suit coat up for her to see a greasy stain on the sleeve. "See this?" he'd said. "This is smashed-up escargot."

"Fascinating," she said.

"Yeah, *you* say fascinating, McClintock. But I'll have you know it was damned delicious. *That* was my life just days ago. I was in New York City, eating escargot with clients."

"And smashing it on your sleeve, apparently," she said. "Luckily, you'll have Christopher to help you with grinding food into your expensive suits from now on."

He acted shocked, and she made a face at him.

"Don't make me start ripping walls out, you," he said after a moment.

"Don't make me come after you with another lamp," she said.

And he'd laughed and gone off, shaking his head. "Makes you wonder why a guy wanted to hang upside down from overpasses instead of coming home," he said. "Can't imagine."

It was overheated and uncomfortable in the church, with people crammed so close into the rows that you could study the hairs that sprouted in their ears and identify the brand of soap they'd washed with that morning. An older woman plopped down in front of Jamie and Arley reeking of perfume. Jamie pulled Arley way back in the pew, giving them both some distance from the scent, put her arm around him, and mouthed, "You okay?" Perfume could be an asthma trigger, and he had already sneezed once or twice when they'd first come in—all those flowers—but he nodded, irritated, and twisted away from her.

"No. Take a deep breath for me, and let me listen," she whispered.

He did; it wasn't great. She glanced at her watch, hoped that the funeral wouldn't take a long time. "Tell me if you have any trouble," she said. The organ was playing, and a soloist was singing "Nearer My God to Thee."

She craned her neck and looked for Nate in the front row. She was about three rows back on the other side, sitting on the aisle on purpose so Christopher could turn and see her if he needed to. He had been miserable that she and Arley weren't allowed to sit with him and his father—that had been another crisis they'd had to get through. "But why *can't* you?" he'd asked at least a hundred times. "Because we're supposed to sit with the friends so we can watch you and wave to you," she'd told him, but she was thinking it wouldn't have killed Nate to include her and Arley in the family pew, especially when Harris was so low on family anyway. Christopher, she could see, was sliding himself around on the slippery wooden pew as though his body were composed of ball bearings. He kept leaning over to wave at Arley, and to grin and make faces, and then his father's hand would land on top of his head and twist him around to face forward again.

. . .

NATE BLINKED AND looked up at the flowers, the endless vases and vases of flowers. He absently turned Christopher to face forward in his seat and forced himself to listen to the sweaty-faced pastor, a lost soul if there ever was one, now flailing about in some kind of pointless homily, trying to come up with something soothing to say to this church full of people, all of whom knew they could do a better job of describing the feel-good, redemptive story they'd manufactured about Harris's life.

Here, *this* is the trouble with small towns, Nate thought. The people here all *knew* the story, and even if it was the wrong one—even if it was patently false, even if it was filled with archetypes instead of human beings, they'd made up the narrative they wanted. Harris Goddard—wild, untamable—got the shy, innocent, boring Maggie Donegan pregnant, and then was forced to marry her. She gave birth to Nate, and although she tried to make the best of things, none of them was ever happy. (Insert tsking sound here.) Harris, bless his heart, couldn't be settled down that easily, and after a few major dalliances, he left Maggie and moved in with some woman who lived in a trailer park across town, when Nate was only nine years old. Oh, and then there was that poor, poor Nate, always trying to get his father's attention but failing at it. Why, he became a baseball star at the high school, just to get his father to be proud of him—but old Harris, may he rest in peace, just couldn't keep his mind off his own pleasure, and he ignored the kid for the most part, which in turn wrecked the child's personality, made him some kind of weak basket case of a human, unable to cope. But *thank God* Harris was able to achieve complete redemption. After Nate's wife died, and Nate flipped out over it like the weak, puny little creature he was raised to be, it was the indefatigable *Harris* who heroically stepped in and took on the raising of his grandchild. At a time in life when most folks want to kick back and drink more, go fishing in their pond and take it easy, there was Harris the Hero learning about disposable diapers and teething rings, then playing Wiffle ball and Frisbee, watching Barney videos, joining Campfire Kids organizations, going to parent-teacher conferences. He wasn't ever seen without that adorable little abandoned boy in tow—even though, oh yes, yes, he still had a (wink, wink) *woman problem*. Always could get the women, that handsome devil, you know how he was, and even at the end, there had been a woman living there with him, a willowy, sexy artist type, another one who just some-how couldn't live without him. Only now—oh, heavy day!—he had died, done in by his own appetites and lusts, that lovable rapscallion, and now they had all gathered in this suffocating church, on a beauti-ful day in May, to say good-bye to the end of an era.

And Nate, sitting there in pew one, wearing his garlic-and-evil-smelling suit, with his little boy sturdily by his side—a little boy who had taken to calling him Natey, when he addressed him at all—knew that he had at best only a supporting role in this little drama. For all the people in this town, the only interesting question about him was whether he would run off again. *Cue the organ.* Or would he do the right thing, in the fashion of his father, become a man, take his place in the routine boringness of life and find Joy and Redemption? And would that adorable little boy sitting so dejectedly beside him have a prayer of growing up sane?

Nate looked down at Christopher's dark little head, which was turned around in the pew, staring, no doubt, at Jamie and Arley. He steered him back to facing forward and whispered, "Please. Pretend you're listening to the minister."

The truth was—he took a deep breath here—he didn't care what these people thought of him or what story they were telling them-selves. Nothing like coming home and being forced to sit alone in church to make a man realize he didn't need his hometown to tell him who he was, or to explain to him his father's behavior. Harris had *not* been a lovable loser who had come to understand the true value of life, damn it. He'd been a prick through and through, and he'd taken way more from his son than he had ever given.

Nate stared straight ahead, squinting, trying to summon his

father's face, to remember what the *real* story was, what it had been like being Harris's son. Could he himself separate the truth from the myths? He tried to recall if he'd ever had the times with his dad that even Christopher had had, the happy Campfire Kids togetherness times. Oh, there had been a couple of Red Sox games when he was seven or eight, and he'd been taken along on a couple of construction jobs when his mother was busy with something else. He could recall a lot of manly strutting around and bluster, and everybody always joking and winking, poking each other in the ribs, looking at Harris admiringly. And damn it, Nate had been so proud of his father—that was what was hitting him now, how proud and how scared of him, too, of that big, booming voice that was full of fun but then could turn on you all of a sudden, the way his laugh could just run dry, like something that had trickled out of a barrel, and then he was mad, standing over you, looking at you as if you were the most pitiful weakling. And those long silences he'd perfected, the way he had of looking bored— bored with you, bored with life. He *used* silence. Oh, that had been painful, those dinnertimes in the house, when he would just withdraw his energy, and Nate's mom would be so blindsided by it, so unequipped to deal with him, trying to pretend it all wasn't happening, being so cheerful and putting a smile on everything—and then he'd hear them later, upstairs in that master bedroom, yelling at each other, and Harris would storm off in the middle of the night, the Mustang door slamming and the gravel being spun out as he flung himself away, and his mom would cry in the bedroom, that sad little sniffling thing she did, until Nate would creep in there to bring her some tea, take her hand, make her laugh.

Nate bowed his head now. He wanted to get up and talk. When they asked who wanted to speak—Pamela had warned him that was coming—he would stand up. He was going to go up there. He didn't know what he would say, but that was okay. He'd look out at the crowd and tell them the truth, even though the truth was complicated. He might have to tell them that . . . that you shouldn't just believe what you think you see in front of you. The truth is always much more mixed up than that.

"Let us now sing 'Amazing Grace,'" the pastor said.

JAMIE REACHED INTO her bag to get the inhaler during the hymn, leaning down so she could listen closely to Arley's wheezing. She wished the woman in front of them could have been prevented from dumping out the *entire* bottle of perfume onto herself. She smelled like a victim of a cosmetics counter explosion.

The organ finished, everybody sat back down, and the pastor said, "Now we'd like to invite anybody who wishes to, to come forward and talk about our friend brother Harris."

In the hushed silence that followed, Arley started wheezing.

"It's okay, baby, you're all right. Let's just breathe in together," Jamie whispered. She was trying to get the inhaler in just the right position, opening and closing her mouth the way she always did automatically, as if she could somehow assist in getting more air for him. Sweat trickled down her back, and she leaned against the pew, trying to get the thing in place.

He obediently held up his head and breathed in while she pushed the button for the puff of air. He took a breath, and she felt relieved. Then she eased him back into the pew so carefully, moving him as far away from the perfumed lady as she could, as if every inch would count, and started fanning herself and him with the program.

From the corner of her eye, she saw Nate stand up and make his way to the front of the church, and she felt a little pulse of alarm.

There was a ripple of surprise through the crowd. Nate walked purposefully with his head down, but once he'd climbed the five steps and was standing at the pulpit, gazing out at the crowd, he bestowed on them what Jamie already thought of as his trademark cynical smile. Her heart was now pounding, and she could not look away. It felt as if everyone in the church had just inhaled and wasn't going to be able to exhale for a long time.

"Wow," Nate said slowly. "Wow." There was a long silence, during which Jamie realized she felt nervous for him. He gripped the sides of the pulpit and his eyes wandered over the room, looked at all of them individually, it seemed. "Wow. Just look at all of you here, coming to say good-bye to my dad. Hey, Mike and Donny. Libby. Wow, so many people from high school. How you guys doin'?" He shook his head, looked around at the church like he'd never seen it before, and once again the silence seemed to stretch out as though time itself had come to a halt. Jamie heard rustling in the back, and someone coughed.

Nate came back to the crowd. "I haven't been in here in so many years," he said slowly. "I guess I don't have to remind all of *you* of that. You all know me. I'm the guy who ran away. I'm the one who couldn't do the *right thing* when tragedy struck." He paused, looked around again. "Oh, now! You don't have to look away. Don't be embarrassed for me, saying up here what all of you are thinking. *I* know my part, believe me. I'm the guy who ran off and left a little newborn baby here for an old man to raise." He grinned at the crowd. "Come on, you know it! You know this."

Jamie put her hand on Arley's arm. The church seemed almost deathly silent.

Nate cleared his throat and said, "Well. I didn't even know until I got here that I wanted to talk, but I guess I just feel the need to set the record straight on a few things. My dad was one of those—I guess you'd call them—*larger-than-life* characters. Isn't that what they say about people like him? I mean, you all knew him as a guy who was funny and fun and a real hell-raiser and a good ol' boy, a real salt-of-the-earth kind of guy, and oh, I know you all have your own stories that you'll stand up here and tell when I get finished. But I'd just like to say that if you were his family, if you were his *son* . . ." He gazed off into space for a moment. "Well, it was a little different, living with that kind of person. He actually"——he stopped and cleared his throat here, looked down for a moment at the pulpit, and then looked back up, blinked his eyes——"well, he actually left my mother and me when I was nine, before I even knew what was going on."

Nate looked out at the faces, which were all staring back at him. "I'm not saying he wasn't right to do what he did. Maybe he was. Maybe he had to do it. Maybe sometimes a marriage just leaches the life out of you, and you've got to save yourself or drown in the pain of it. But from the kid's point of view, if you want to know, it was like he didn't want to have anything to do with me. He was a salt-of-the-earth guy, and I was probably kind of a wuss as a kid, and maybe then I got too tough, just to even things out—heh, Ron? Tough guy, right?—I always wanted him to come to my baseball games, but he said baseball wasn't hard, like construction."

He looked around the room, shook his head, began again. "And then, yeah, my mom died. You all remember my mom. I know you do. She was the one who held things together. I did leave town," he said. "I did. But I came back, and I tried to help my dad out some, because his business was suffering, and I thought we could—well, I thought we could mend things, I guess. That was a kick in the head. And then—well, another big one happened. My wife died right after giving birth to our baby . . . and I couldn't stay." He laughed. "Hey, guys, I know we're in church and all, but do you ever get the idea that there are people that God just might . . . not like? Who he has it in for? Come on, it has to occur to you. You know, that God even maybe holds a grudge toward." He looked heavenward. "God, man, I'm sorry for those lies I told. But let me up off the mat, okay? I said I'm sorry, man!"

Nobody laughed, and Nate started to say something and then faltered and fell silent. There was almost an eerie hush over the congregation. Jamie moved a little bit in the pew, and Nate's eyes swung over to hers and locked there. He reminded her for a moment of someone flailing for a life raft in the middle of a pond, not knowing how he was going to pull through, and she made herself look back at him, steadily. Then she nodded, almost a twitch really, the barest possible movement, but she saw his eyes take that nod as encouragement. He gripped the pulpit then, and looked up at the ceiling fan. When he spoke, his voice was strong again.

"What you might not know," he said, "is that my dad told me he *wanted* to keep the baby, and show him a good life, and that I should just—go off for a while, get my head together. I don't know. Maybe I shouldn't have gone. But I did. And then I tried to come back." He took a deep breath, looked down at the pulpit.

"Yeah," he said at last. "Several times I tried to come back. And maybe I shouldn't have let my dad take over the way he did, maybe I should have fought him . . . but, well, I didn't. I was sending money, and I thought the money was really needed, and so I kept working. And traveling. Which I'm going to *keep* doing because I'm good at it. It's my life now. Only now I'll have my boy with me, and I promise you this: I won't let him out of my sight. I won't give him up again. There. That's it. Now if you want to get up and tell your stories about the good times, you can. I don't mind. I just . . ." Then he cleared his throat again and said, "I just wanted to set the record straight. Oh, and I'm going to be leaving here in a few days. Taking Christopher and putting the old house up for sale—by the way, if any of you want to buy it, come see me after the services, I can get you a good price." There was muffled laughter, and Arley made a sharp, wheezing whistle. Jamie looked down at him in alarm. He was breathing very quickly now, with shallow breaths, so she got out the inhaler again and gave him another puff of air and held onto him tight, locking her eyes with his so he would slow his breathing down to match hers.

He hunched over, as if he was working too hard. In one quick motion, she looped her purse over her shoulder and grabbed Arley by the arm, then she hurried them both down the aisle of the church. Everything was a blur. She could hear Nate still talking, and she heard Christopher screaming, "Arley! Jamie! Wait!" Lucy, who had come late to the funeral, was standing at the back of the church, alongside a man in uniform—and as she went past, she realized that it was that cop, the one who'd interviewed her the other day—but she was running now, holding onto Arley's arm and pulling him out of the hot, oppressive, flowery air of the church and into the safe, breathable, oxygenated sunshine. His breath was roaring in her ears—only, when she got out there, she realized it was her own breath that was making all the noise. He was making shallow little squeaks, and his face had turned white while his eyes were huge, black, frightened holes in his face.

This was the worst, it was the very worst it had ever been.

She had to call 911. She tried to hold onto Arley while she fumbled in her bag for the cell phone, felt it, then lost it in the jumble of her wallet and hairbrush and inhalers and keys—all of which spilled onto the pavement. She got her fingers on it again, pulled it upward, but then Mike Scanlon—there, *that* was his name—Mike Scanlon and Lucy were right beside her, and Mike was taking Arley out of her arms and running with him toward an ambulance that, amazingly, was parked right there, right out in front. She didn't ask why or how it was there, she just made her way to it, running, and then somebody helped them in. Another person came over and put a nebulizer mask onto Arley's face and an oxygen sensor on his finger, there were reassuring beeps, and she leaned down over him, held onto his other hand, and made herself smile at him—the wobbly smile that came up so readily, so automatically when you had a child who was sick.

"You'll be fine, you'll be fine," she started saying, her face right up close to his dear little frightened eyes and nose and mouth, her hand holding onto his. Lucy set her purse down next to her and started doing her own version of it, saying, "It's all right, it's all right," over and over again. They could sing a duet, the two of them—the Asthma Duet, they'd call it. She was suddenly so dumbfoundedly grateful to have her sister there with her. With her free hand, she took hold of Lucy's hand and squeezed.

Lucy said, "Jesus, can you believe . . . ?"

And then, from behind the technician who was monitoring Arley, she heard Christopher say in his tiny, piping little voice, "Is he going to be all right?"

Everybody turned and looked at him. In all the commotion he had managed to get into the ambulance right alongside them.

"Ohhh, Christopher," Jamie said, and her voice was shaking. She sounded hysterical, even to herself. "Oh, honey. I didn't realize you were here, too. Yes, he's going to be all right. He's just going to go to the hospital now."

"I'm going, too," he said.

She glanced down at the oxygen meter and licked her lips nervously. It was ninety-two percent, which was not too bad, but they needed to go.

"No. Honey, this time you need to stay with your daddy . . . Arley's going to be all right." There was something going on out on the sidewalk. The driver, Matt Henson, was leaning out talking to somebody.

"Hey, Jamie. Christopher has to get out," Matt said, turning back to them.

"I know. We know," Jamie said quickly.

Christopher started to cry. "I want to be with Arley," he said. "I don't want to go to the funeral anymore. I don't like it."

"I know, baby," she said, hugging him. The back of the ambulance opened up just then, and Nate was standing there, looking drained and stoic. His eyes met Jamie's, and he gave her a pleading look and held out his arms. "Hey, Christopher," he said. "Come on back inside with me now."

Christopher buried his head in Jamie's shoulder.

She saw Nate's mouth moving. He was saying to her, "Can you help me?" She took a deep breath and tried to sound calm. "Christopher, you should go back and sit with your daddy again. We'll be back soon, and we'll be back to join you at the lunch."

The technician said to Arley, "Okay, take it slow and easy, slow and easy."

Jamie looked back down at Christopher. "Christopher, please. You need to go back and be with your daddy. He needs you."

Christopher whispered, "I can't, Jamie. Tell him I have to go to the hospital."

"Listen," she said to him in a low voice, "Arley's going to be fine. You don't have to worry. You know who really needs you now? Your daddy needs you because he's a little bit sad right now, saying good-bye to Da. He needs to look over at you, and then he'll remember all the good things. Can you go back in there with him and stand next to him? For me?"

"Come on, Christopher," Nate said, smiling tightly. He was leaning into the back of the ambulance with his arms outstretched.

"Daddy, Arley needs me!" Christopher called down. "I *have* to go to the hospital."

"Christopher, come *on,*" Nate said.

"Da would want you there to say good-bye," Jamie whispered to him. "I'd be there to say good-bye if I could. Will you say good-bye to him for me? Would you do that? It's an important job that only you can do. Will you do it?"

He hesitated. He looked over at Arley and then back at Jamie, and then he put his head down. "Okay," he said, almost inaudibly.

"Thank you," she said. On wobbly legs, she walked him to the back of the ambulance, and Nate reached up and took him in his arms and put him down on the pavement. Their eyes met for just an instant and he mouthed, "Thank you." Then he said to her, "Are you—is Arley okay?"

She nodded, fought against buckling under. "Hey, aren't you in the middle of giving a eulogy?" she said.

He laughed a little. "I guess I was, actually. I was talking and then I looked up and saw everybody leaving, and I just walked out of the place myself. There I was, on the verge of taking offers on the house, and then suddenly I was outside."

Christopher was saying, "Could I just run the siren one time like I always do? Can I? Can I run the siren for Arley?"

"Come on up here, you," Matt said. Then he said to Nate, "That was some speech you made, man."

"Thanks. You let Christopher run the siren?" Nate said.

"He sees it as his privilege," Jamie said. "Helps this not be so scary for everybody."

"It's happened before?"

"Well . . . a few times," she said.

Nate went to lift Christopher up, but he refused help. Instead, he turned and walked to the front, where Matt opened the door and helped him inside to activate the siren—two loud whoops. Then he brought him to the back again, and somebody closed the door, the lights flashed on and off, and the ambulance pulled away.

It was all *okay*. It was just that Jamie couldn't get the picture out of her head, the one that came as a blur but then imprinted itself so quickly as the ambulance tore away: Christopher standing there solemnly waving good-bye to them, just before he turned and went back inside the church, a sturdy little boy walking silently beside his father.

Funerals are supposed to make the living feel better, and amazingly, this one seemed to do exactly that. Nate was shocked. In his experience, funerals always made things worse. Maybe it was because he knew he was really and truly leaving town that he felt almost lighthearted once the service was over. Perhaps that was what made the difference this time.

And that might also explain why the townspeople seemed to have suddenly fallen in love with him. Perhaps they, too, couldn't get enough of lavishing him with praise and love now that they saw they were never going to be asked again to contemplate all his deficiencies in person. Not just his old buddies from school, either—although Stevo and Ron had come over and patted him on the back and said they wanted to get another beer with him before he left town. No, it was all the old people, his parents' friends, who crowded around him and Christopher at the reception afterward, touching and pawing them, filling him in on town events that had occurred while he'd been gone, shaking their heads with dismay over the poor way their own Harris had treated him, wishing him well, urging him to stay in touch and to remember where he was from. While the day before, during the calling hours, they had seemed stiff and even judgmental, now it seemed that all they wanted was for Nate to know they understood.

Nate, who fancied himself a private guy, realized at the reception that he'd opened up a door he hadn't meant to, because now people wanted to talk about everything. They were issuing him invitations to dinner and wanting to talk about Harris's perhaps questionable motives for keeping Christopher. The small-town machine was back up and running, already manufacturing new stories to go with the new information. Hey, everybody, Nate Goddard here says he didn't *want* to leave his baby behind. His father *made* him! A new chapter must be written!

People came over and shook his hand, looked into his eyes, told him wonderful things they remembered about his mother. Nobody said they thought he'd been a mama's boy, which he had certainly heard said about him before; no one seemed to recall that Maggie had been "pitifully ordinary" until the day she'd cut all her hair off, and then she became "unhinged," by town standards. All of that was conveniently shelved in the past—at least throughout the luncheon at the Highlander Hotel, which featured stainless-steel trays of roasted herb chicken, sweet potato soufflé, ziti, smashed-up spinach and cream, and plenty of round, hard dinner rolls.

He was heaping his plate high with sweet potatoes when Ron came over and whispered, "So, what happened? Jamie had to go to the hospital, dude?"

"Yeah."

"Tough break for her. Where's she gonna move to, you know?"

He found himself thinking about the way she'd looked at him and nodded when he wasn't able to find the words at the church. Her eyes locked with his, saying, *Go on. You can do it. Tell them what you need to say.* Even though she would have been on the Harris team.

She wasn't ever going to think that Nate could do half as good a job with Christopher, or with anything, for that matter. But still, she could be kind. He appreciated that about her. She was kind, and she was beautiful.

"Um. So do you know where she's gonna move?" Ron was saying.

"Oh! What? No. I have no idea, actually."

"Probably she'll go back with her sister."

"Oh yeah. I mean, probably. Sure."

He looked at his watch. He was done here, but then his dad's lawyer came over to talk about the reading of the will—no surprises, apparently, but something he still had to do. And his old buddies wanted to get together for another beer before he left town again. Todd Haney said he'd already talked with a developer who was interested in coming over to take a look at the property.

"He's just done a massive condo complex in Clinton," he said. "And he told me he'd already done a drive-by of your place and thinks he sees possibilities."

"Great," Nate said.

Haney gave him a long look. "Hey, man, you know you're one crazy son of a bitch to do this now, don't you? I've done some talking around, and these developers are never going to give you what this land is worth, not with the market in the slump it's in now. You should just hold onto that land for a bit. Go condo later on. A year from now you'll see much better money."

"Yeah," Nate said, "but I don't want to be tied to this place a whole year. I want out now. You know that if somebody told me I never had to walk into that house again, I'd be as happy as a pig in shit."

The crowd had thinned out by now, so he said good-bye to the few stragglers and started out to the parking lot, whistling and swinging his keys in his hand.

Then he remembered Christopher. He smacked himself in the forehead, went back inside, sheepish, sure that someone was going to give him a hard time. *You've only had custody of your kid for three days, and already you're walking out without him. What kind of father will you be?* He had his hard, defensive smile all ready—but then it wasn't like that at all. Pamela Nash-Brenner actually was the one who came over and helped him look, and told him her five-year-old daughter was missing, too. "Lord knows they're probably together," she said with one of those exasperated, harried-mom sighs. "She runs off whenever there's the slightest possibility. The only time I know for sure where she is, is in the middle of the night, when she won't sleep in her own bed, so she's in mine."

He laughed his fake social laugh.

"You know," she said. "I really liked what you said back there. In the service. It made a lot of sense to me. I want to wish you the best. I mean, I know you've got lots more to do than think about *this* place, but if for any reason you come back for a visit . . . call me, okay?"

"Okay," he said.

They found the children sitting cross-legged underneath the buffet table, hidden under the white tablecloth, gorging themselves on brownies. Pamela's daughter was wearing a stiff pink organdy dress and little lacy knee socks—her Easter dress, Pamela said, rolling her eyes as if he, a member of the parent club, would get why this was a bad thing—and Nate said something about how Christopher was obviously taking after the family men with his gene for finding pretty girls, ha-ha-ha. The four of them walked out of the hotel together, and Nate felt Pamela's eyes on him the whole way. Sure enough, once they got to her car, she glommed onto him with a big sloppy hug and said it was just too bad, really, that all the single men were always moving out of town. He pretended to be baffled by this, too, and said he just couldn't understand it, and encouraged somehow by this, she suddenly stood up on tiptoes and kissed him on the lips.

It was a quick kiss, a brush-by, really, but suggestive just the same, and he knew it was an invitation. So he smiled at her, and averted his eyes while she figured out that he was saying no, and then said he had to get going, and she said she did, too, and then he walked backward, waving, until it was okay to turn around and head directly for his own car.

It would have been a clean getaway, too, except for the fact that Christopher did not follow him. He stood there as if he was rooted to the spot where they'd been standing.

"Would you *come*?" Nate called to him. He shrugged at Pamela, who was looking concerned. The kid came over, looking as if he was in some kind of a daze, managing somehow to slide his body along the side of three dusty parked cars along the way. Nate let out an exasperated sigh.

"Did you *have* to do that?" he said.

"What?" Christopher looked at him, all liquid brown eyes.

"Nothing. Never mind. Just come on and get in." He waved and smiled to Pamela, who looked as though she wasn't going to permit herself to leave until she made sure that all was well with the Goddard men.

Christopher got into the backseat and sat looking out of the window. From the driver's seat, Nate turned around and said, "Put your seat belt on, big guy."

"Jamie or Da does that for me."

"Well, can't you do it yourself? Oh, never mind." He turned around in the seat, on his knees, leaned way over, and with incredible difficulty, managed to pull the lap belt into place. Of course these would be the old-fashioned kind, before seat belts had gone high tech. Finally he got the thing snapped together, but he was breathing hard when he turned back around to the steering wheel.

"By the way, nice one, Christopher," he said. "This is twice today I've had to go hunt you down someplace."

Christopher stared out of the car window.

"Listen," Nate said, twisting back around. "I would really appreciate it if you could maybe stop trying to disappear on me. I know you don't know me from Adam . . ." His voice trailed off, and he sat there regarding this little boy who looked so much like Louisa that for a moment Nate couldn't breathe. That's what funerals did—they invited all your previously buried people around to remind you that they'd remained dead.

He leaned over and touched Christopher on the knee. This was, he realized, probably the very first time he'd been alone with his boy.

He closed his eyes and willed himself to do a mind shift. "We've got to be partners, you and I," he said. "We can't run away from each other, even if we sometimes want to. I'm your *dad*."

"I just wanted to get Arley some brownies," Christopher said.

"Yeah? You did? Well, that's . . . nice, I guess." He sighed. "So where are they?"

"In my pockets," he said, and pulled out his pockets to show a bunch of smashed-up chocolate. Two little wadded-up balls of chocolate tumbled out onto the once-pristine red leather seats of the Mustang, and Christopher started to cry.

Nate turned around and faced forward, holding onto the steering wheel with both hands. Then he rummaged through the glove compartment and found napkins and a package of wet wipes, got out, went around and opened the car door, helped Christopher out, and wiped off the leather seats.

Christopher was still sniffling.

"What is it now?"

"You're mean."

"I'm not mean. You know what people say about me? Do you think anybody ever thinks I'm mean? They don't. I've never had a mean thought in my whole life. You know what they say? They say I'm *fun*. I'm a fun guy. That's what you're going to find out—that a really great thing happened to you, actually, that you get to come and live with me! You get to live with your father, who is fun and does great stuff and travels all around. I ski—did you even know that? I ski and I know how to scuba dive, and back home I have a sports car, and I go to Hollywood sometimes. And now you get to do that stuff, too. You're actually going to like me."

The kid was silent, stubbornly silent.

"Well?" Nate said after a while. "What do you think? Are you really lucky or are you just plain ordinary lucky?"

Christopher looked down.

"You gotta look on the bright side, dude. You gotta give this a chance. Right? If you say to yourself I can either be *really* lucky or *plain ordinary* lucky, then you don't even have the choice to be *unlucky*. Do you see it?"

Christopher sighed. "I want to go get more brownies for Arley."

Nate sat there for a minute, and then he said, "You're right, dude. This is all just bullshit, isn't it? Come on. Let's go inside and get more brownies."

"You just said a terrible word."

"I know. You might have to get used to that. Let's go back inside. Say, do you know a kid whose cat rides horseback?"

Christopher looked at him warily. "Yeah."

"And the guy who sleeps in his clothes and invented potato chips?"

"Maybe."

"You've got some weird friends, dude."

OTHER THAN MEETING up with illness and fear and mortality, Jamie for the most part liked being in the emergency room. It was a difficult thing to explain, although she had often tried to make Lucy understand it. "When you're here, it's like nothing else bad can touch you," she said. "The worst has already happened, and you're now safe. I actually think I'd like to live here full-time, at least until Arley grows up."

Lucy laughed and wrinkled her nose and took a big bite of her Hershey bar. She was wearing her pink-and-yellow flower-print chemise, the one she called her celebration-of-life dress, which she claimed was way more appropriate for funerals than black because it served to remind people of the great regeneration to come. Or something like that. She had all kinds of theories about death. Jamie blamed yoga.

The two of them were curled up in the visitors' chairs, their legs tucked underneath them, next to Arley's bed in the pediatric ER, waiting for Arley to be declared officially well after his treatment. He was always fidgety and jittery for a little while once he'd had the medication for an asthma attack, but now that had worn off and he was calm, watching a DVD on the overhead television set. Soon the doctor would come in and spring him, and Jamie would have to take him home, back to facing the night once again. That was always the scariest part, leaving the hospital, spending the next few days alert to the sound of his every breath. But for now she was feeling bleary with gratitude. All of it—the funeral; Nate's vulnerability up there in front of the whole silent, stunned church; the asthma attack; and now Lucy sitting here next to her, being sisterly—had reduced her to a fuzzy weepiness. She wanted to go around the ER, dispensing teary hugs and thanking the staff for deciding on careers in medicine.

It would have been perfect, in fact, except that all Lucy wanted to talk about was Nate. "So how's it been, living in the house with him?" she wanted to know. And then, when Jamie didn't answer, "He is devastatingly handsome, isn't he? And you know, I think I felt a little vibe from him about you."

"There's no vibe," Jamie said.

"Uh-*huh*. I know vibes. Trust me on this one, and I've felt it twice with him—the other morning in the kitchen, after you hit him with the lamp, and then most definitely today in the ambulance. He is clearly thinking about you. *I* think that if you wanted to, you could maybe have something with him."

"Do you really think this is the best use of our time here?" Jamie said. "This is a guy who is, first of all, hopelessly arrogant and possibly even clinically deranged in his parenting skills, *and* he's engaged to be married to someone, and besides all that, he's leaving in four days for California, from where he will never return. He hates this town, hates his father, a man I was fond of, and you're sitting here trying to convince me that he has a *vibe* about me and that I should do something about it?"

"I'm not saying you really have to *do* anything about him. I just want some sign of life from you. Some sign that you're not dead."

"I'm *not* dead."

"Yeah, well, you're close."

See, this was the flip side to Lucy. Whenever Jamie was feeling gooey with gratitude over having a sister who had always taken care of her, who had even let her show up with a new baby and live with her for four years, and who had been the best auntie ever—that's when Lucy would do something that reasserted her self-proclaimed right to be the resident expert on Jamie's life. You would think she alone held the owner's manual and was not going to listen to any contradictory information Jamie might have gathered on her own. *No, no, you don't like blueberries—and you never did. Also, you've always been shy around good-looking men, and it's so typical of you, not being able to keep your checkbook balanced.*

Of course, these were minor faults, in the grand scheme of things. Irritations, really. Sure, Lucy laughed at her sister's wardrobe and general funkiness, and it was clear she had never once understood the magnetism of Trace, but nevertheless, she was wholly, fully and one hundred percent in Jamie's corner.

There was a long silence. Then Lucy said, "Here, at least take some of this candy bar before I stuff myself."

"No, thanks."

Lucy sighed, ate the rest of the candy bar, and smoothed down her skirt. "Boy, that eulogy—he did really put his father in his place, didn't he? I mean, did you *know* all that stuff? How he went off and left his wife and son and then wouldn't even *talk* to them? I know you liked Harris a lot, but I think there is just something sick about a man who won't talk to his own kid just because he's getting a divorce from the kid's mother. It's *sick*."

"I don't want to talk about this around . . ." she tilted her head toward Arley.

Lucy leaned over and put headphones on him. He looked up and smiled at her gratefully. He loved nothing better than zoning out in headphones; it was, for him, the best part of the hospital experience. Even better than the nurses bringing him Popsicles.

"Harris wasn't perfect. Nobody ever said he was," Jamie said, a trifle snappishly. "He was good to me, though, and good to Arley, and I liked him for it. And he was funny."

"Well, now I can tell you how worried I always was that you were going to hook up with him. It just gave me the willies to think about it."

"Whew. Glad *that* worry is finally off your plate."

Lucy laughed. "You've got to admit, he was kind of *old*. And not in the good, graceful sense. He was—"

"Could we not have this conversation on the day of his *funeral*?"

"Fine. Whatever. I'm just saying." Lucy was staring at her the way she did when she thought she wasn't getting the full story and was determined to ferret it out. "You ... didn't ever ... though, right?"

Jamie sighed loudly. "*No.*"

"Well, good, because I seriously think that Harris's dying is going to turn out to be the catapult you need to get moving in your life. As long as you had him, for some reason—and I don't even pretend to understand this—you had no incentive to go out and meet guys and get yourself situated."

"Why is it always about guys with you?"

"Because I want you to be happy. And to be happy, you need somebody to love. And to have somebody to love, you need to first start noticing when people feel *that way* about you. Even in theory. Even if they are about to move to California and marry somebody else. You have to *practice*."

This was another thing: Lucy thought the whole world ran on sexual energy alone, and that all people were thinking about was when could they have sex again. Which was so not true. Some people just have no interest in the other fascinating things in life—that's what Jamie had come to feel—and so they turned to sex to fill up the time for them. Pitiful, really. All that intrigue—the whole roller-coaster, the bumpy ride of love and sex, the agony and ecstasy—wasn't it possibly all just a failure of imagination? A regrettable lack of curiosity about the art you could be creating?

On the DVD above the bed, Clifford the Big Red Dog made a silly face, and Arley laughed out loud and then coughed. Lucy watched him for a moment and then leaned closer to Jamie. "So I suppose you've guessed by now . . . about me and Mike Scanlon."

"What?"

"Yes!" Lucy sat back and smiled her wide, red grin, activating dimples. "He's great."

This *was* news. Jamie was accustomed to hearing only about Handsome Dan's latest back-and-forthness. In fact, she had once drawn a cartoon of him as a nomad, head down, dressed in a brown robe, shuffling between the house he had bought with his wife and Lucy's condo, with his toothbrush stuck behind his ear.

"You're kidding me. Mike the cop? The one investigating me for possible murder? And here I thought it was just a coincidence that you two were standing together at the funeral."

Lucy laughed. "Yeah, I'm doing this for you, to keep you out of the hoosegow. It's a personal sacrifice on my part, but I think I can do it." She clapped her hands. "He's . . . well, I won't bore you with that stuff. But you'll see. He's going to come pick us up when we leave here."

"Isn't he about ten years too young for you?"

Lucy laughed. "I'm straying into new territory now that I'm through with Dan. I think both the youth culture *and* the law enforcement field have been tragically overlooked in my experience, and also . . . well, he's cute, don't you think? There's something very sweet and dear about him."

"He looks like he's in fifth grade. I'm surprised his mother signed the permission slip to let him be a cop."

"Oh, stop. He's great," Lucy said. "I really like him."

"Yeah, until you dump him for Dan again."

"No. I'm really done with Dan this time. Really, really done."

"Yeah, so when is Mike moving in?"

Lucy laughed, leaned forward, and touched Jamie on the knee. "I'm hoping that your living with me will keep me from inviting him to live with me, too—before it's time at least. You see, with you there, I won't be lonely." She pulled her skirt down over her knees and smiled. "I've been doing some deep reflection lately, and I think that's my whole problem. I get lonely and then I start going out with the wrong men, or else I go back to Dan. I'm too gregarious."

Jamie laughed, too. "Oh, is that what it is? I knew you were too something."

Nate got home, changed out of his escargot-stained suit, put on khaki shorts and a T-shirt, and then allowed himself a deep breath. Christopher had disappeared somewhere upstairs as soon as they got out of the car, and there was no more denying it: the funeral was over, all the ducks were lining up in a row, and the time had come for Nate to call Howie and let him know the real story.

First, though, he had to get his mind right.

He took his cell phone out to the back porch, flexed his muscles, cracked his knuckles, and did a downward-dog yoga pose that some previous girlfriend had taught him. Then he stood up, almost dizzy, and paced the length of the porch, picked up and put down again a candle that looked like a conch shell. None of this was going to do him a damn bit of good.

Howie Engel was not somebody to take lightly, as Nate, who had been his protégé for the last five years, knew perhaps better than anybody. Howie was a grizzled old former surfer dude from Hawaii—white-haired now and leathery, always grinning, the kind of guy who called waves "pipes" and could explain to you the different personality types of what Nate could only think of as rolling walls of water.

Howie had set up the communications network biz so he could have a rich, comfortable old age for himself and his wife, Leilani. Not for him the typical paycheck-winning grind of employment. Oh, no. He wanted a company that ran on the principles of surfing and New Age karma as well as the Law of Attraction, he said.

Nate had stumbled onto Howie's website one day in a library when he had gone online to look for a job. Louisa had been dead for four months by then, Harris was keeping the baby, and Nate, who had been traveling and doing odd jobs, was just beginning to feel the first sharp, painful sensations of his loss, like when anesthesia starts to wear off. He wanted a job, and a purpose. He called Howie up, and the next thing he knew, he was flown to Oahu, ushered into a bamboo sling chair on the lanai with a good view of the sunset, handed an iced drink, and then, after hours of conversation and philosophy lessons and native Hawaiian food, found himself hired on the ground floor of what sounded like either the biggest bunch of bullshit or the best adventure of his life.

He became a frequent visitor to the house in Hawaii, spent most Thanksgivings and Christmases there, hung out on summer vacations, went there often just to recharge his batteries, get a fix of family and belonging. Along the way, he'd somehow become kind of a surrogate son.

But—well, there was a problem. At the beginning, when he'd first gone there, he'd edited his life story, said he was just starting out in life. Didn't mention the marriage, much less the death or the baby he'd left behind. In fact, it wasn't for eight more months, at the anniversary of Louisa's death, that he'd blurted out that he'd had a wife who'd died. Howie had been shocked that he hadn't known before. Nate could see in his eyes the way Howie was reassessing him, making room for this glaring change in who he was. "You didn't *tell* me this, dude?" he'd said. "I can't believe you carried that all alone, when we were there for you. You just walked around with this huge burden when you didn't need to have it. We're your family, dude!"

They'd had to talk about it for hours and hours, and Howie had actually cried. He was just that crazy.

And then, at the end of the marathon session, he'd said, "Anything else you want to reveal?"

"There is one other thing," Nate said, and he was planning to tell about Christopher. He really was.

"I thought so," Howie said. "I could sense something else brewing in there." But then the phone had rung, and Leilani had called him inside to take an important call, and while he was gone Nate stared over the lanai and watched tiny little surfers way out there, like black insects dotting the waves. He thought of Louisa, how she'd been dead one year, and how weird it was that his life had improved so much since her death—that was the first time he'd admitted this to himself. She'd been unhappy with him, disappointed with him all the time, and this past year would have been a nightmare, with their trying to adjust to parenthood. Already they'd been unable to compromise or get along. And now here he was, in Hawaii, with a great job, making piles of money, sipping rum drinks on a lanai with an old surfer dude who was the wisest, most accepting man he'd ever met and whose esteem he didn't want to lose, no matter what.

When Howie came back on the lanai, he handed Nate another drink and told him about a deal that was going south in Louisiana, and he asked Nate's advice on how to save it. They'd talked about that for a while, and then Howie cleared his throat and said, "So, oh yeah, your further revelation. Let's have it."

"Well," Nate said. He looked out at the surfers again and swallowed hard. "I got a D in high-school physical education, and if I ever got on a surfboard I'd probably kill myself."

"No way!" Howie said, and he'd thrown back his head and roared with laughter. "Get out here, Leilani, and listen to this boy of ours. Turns out he had a wife who died before we got him, *and* he nearly flunked high-school Phys Ed. Let's give him a family hug."

AND SO THE telling did not go well.

Howie already knew. That was the bad part. There was no chance to spin it just right, to massage it so it sounded better. Tina had called him—of course she had, Nate thought with an almost head-smacking realization. She would have had to. She was working on that Barcelona deal instead of meeting him in Cincinnati for their layover, and so she and Howie had been in almost constant communication.

"So you have a son," Howie said in a flat, you-are-now-dead-to-me voice. "Your father is dead, and now it turns out that you have a *son*."

"Well, I—"

"No," Howie said. "There's no qualifying information about it. The fact is, you *have* a son. You came to this job, a widower—a new widower—with a little son. Eh?"

"Well—"

"Yes or no. You came to this job a new widower with a little son."

"Well—"

"FUCKING YES OR NO?"

"If you put it that way, then yes." Nate laughed.

There was a long silence. For a moment it seemed as if maybe the line had gone dead. Then Howie said, "What gets me about this is that you didn't tell me. I'm your *friend*. And now it turns out that amid all the sharing of information and the *trust,* all the trillions of visits and talks and hours spent together, there were some pretty deeply planted seeds of non-trusting going on. It blows my mind, man, that in five years you could not find the trust in me to tell me this very basic piece of information about *who you are*."

"I—"

"You found a way to tell me about your wife dying. *Finally.* It took eight months. But you did finally do it. But the boy—your *baby*—you couldn't tell me that."

"I know," Nate said quietly. "I'm sorry, man. I should have told you."

"Damn *straight* you should have told me. You should have *wanted* to tell me. We were friends."

"Man, I did want to tell you. I just couldn't think of how to . . . after so much time, you know."

There was a long silence. Howie had always said you shouldn't be the first to break a silence. Let it drag on for as long as you can. You learn valuable information from silence. Nate found himself wondering if both of them were acting out of that philosophy, how many minutes would tick away while they stood there on opposite sides of the earth, with their phones held to their ears, waiting for the silence to end.

Howie finally said, "So, let me see if I've got this right. Your wife died and you had this little baby, and so you left him with your father. And now your father has just passed."

"Yes. My father died." Nate realized he hated when people said it that way: *passed.* Like they'd gone around a stalled car on the highway. Also, it sounded vaguely evangelical, hyper-religious. He didn't think Harris had *passed* anything. He had died.

"Well," Howie said. "I have to tell you that this omission of yours, this *non-trust,* kind of changes everything. I don't see how we're going to keep working together, man. I am majorly disappointed."

"Oh, for God's sake," Nate said. It was time for dramatic comeback action. "Don't get all melodramatic on me, Howie, for God's sake. *Okay.* I shoulda told you, but it's not a federal offense. My God! I'm not an axe murderer." He barked out a laugh. "I had a kid, and when he was four days old, his mother goes out and gets herself smashed up on the highway, and I go through a bad time. Okay? And then my dad says he wants to keep the kid, that I should go get my head together, and then he doesn't ever let me come back! I *temporarily* give up seeing my kid, my baby, and then my dad says I'm not ever to come back again, that I'm disruptive, and so I try to put it out of my mind—"

"Nate, let me ask you something. Where's your gratitude, man? I want to hear your gratitude."

Nate stopped. This was definitely a zigzag. One of Howie's

specialties—zig when they think you're going to zag. Christopher came wandering out onto the porch. He was still wearing his grime-covered funeral clothes, with chocolate blobs down the shirt and the dust from the parked cars he'd rubbed against on his pants. "I'm huu-uuungry," he said to Nate.

Nate waved at him. *Wait.*

"I need to eat!" Christopher said.

". . . It's all about the gratitude," Howie was saying. "I want to hear how you accept this gift your father gave you, how it changed you. Talk to me."

Nate swallowed. "My dad was a complex man," he said slowly.

Christopher was picking his nose now. Nate reached over to keep him from putting boogers on the seat cushions of the porch swing. He shook his head at Christopher. God, how he wanted to get off this telephone. Why couldn't he just pay his stupid penalty—whatever Howie was going to require of him—and receive his absolution and get the fuck out of this conversation, which was going nowhere? But now Howie was waxing on about family and gratitude in a sentimental, accusatory way, linking somehow Nate's not telling him and Leilani about the boy to Nate's deep need to be . . . what? He couldn't really follow it. Sometimes he thought Howie had perhaps gotten hit in the head with the surfboard too many times.

"You received this enormous gift from your father, this enormous gift of time and love and energy, and not only do you not acknowledge it in any of your dealings throughout your life—with us, your surrogate family—but even now, now when the gift is over, you're still kicking at it. Still mad at the old guy."

"No, no, I'm just trying to explain—"

"No," Howie said. "That is what a child does. And that is what you've done with me, too. This is a betrayal, Nate. I gave you—my *family* gave you this gift of our friendship, of our confidence, and this is what you did to us, too. Took the gifts you were given and threw them back."

"Wait! Because I didn't tell you? *That's* what you think? That I don't appreciate you? That I don't—no, no, no. That is a serious mis-reading of the situation. God*damn* it, Howie! You know me better than that. I've done everything for this company! Come on, man. Just because I didn't tell you about my—what was going on before I got there. That's *nothing*. You kidding me? Man, I was just fucked up from grief, I couldn't talk about it, and then it felt like it was too late—"

Christopher said, "Those are bad words."

Nate put his hand on top of Christopher's head.

"I seriously wonder if you even have the capacity for grief," Howie said.

"Howie!" He laughed. "Howie, come on. Come back to us, Howie. You're getting maudlin now. Surely you can't be serious about this."

"I wish I weren't serious. I gotta tell you, when your client called and dropped this little bombshell on us, my first instinct was to just fire your ass—"

"What? *What?* My *client?*"

"Yeah. That woman from the coffeehouses, Denise Morgan. She phoned to say that you needed time off, that your life was in turmoil. I have to hear from your client that you have a kid. Can you beat that?"

"Oh, man! Are you *shitting* me?" Nate slammed the palm of his hand against the wall of the porch. A basket of dried flowers fell off a shelf and landed on the wooden floor. Christopher jumped, and then ran into the house and slammed the screen door. Nate paced around the porch. "Denise *Morgan?*" he said. "I can't believe this! This is the most absurd, bizarre thing I've ever heard of! I treated those people like royalty. I did everything they wanted. I spent days and days with them. I talked about their grandchildren. I analyzed their company's needs. I fucking wined them and dined them! Good God in heaven! What is *with* people these days?"

"Are you quite finished?"

"Yeah. No, I'm *not* finished. What was she—you mean, she called *you* up and told you about my *father* and about my little boy? She actually called my *boss?*"

"Yes, my friend, in fact, that's just what she did. And it's a good thing, too."

"Holy fuck." He looked around guiltily for Christopher, and then realized he wasn't there. He craned his neck around to find him.

"Don't blame the messenger, Nate," Howie said. "This was all your doing, and you know it."

"It's *not* my doing! Okay, okay." He tried to modulate his tone. Ah, there was the kid. He could see him through the screen door. Christopher was inside pulling a chair over to the counter and climbing up on it, perching on the edge of the counter and leaning back while he tried to open a cabinet door. "Hold on a minute," he said to Howie, and put his hand over the receiver. "Christopher, *Christopher.* Please get down from there right now. You're going to fall."

The kid just looked at him.

"Get down from there now!" Nate said. "I asked you to wait. Now I'll be off the phone in a—"

"I want crackers. All I want is crackers. Da lets me get *crackers.*" He started to stand up on the counter and then he stepped on his shoelace and very nearly fell backward.

Nate raced into the house and, balancing the phone under his chin, lifted Christopher down and set him on the floor and handed him the box of crackers. He gave him a ferocious look and covered the receiver one more time. "Now, can you try to stay alive for a few minutes while I'm on the phone? Could you *please* just go *sit down somewhere* and keep quiet and out of trouble, for one tiny bit?"

Christopher stared at him, and then he did the thing with poking his lower lip out, which just killed Nate. *Killed* him. Nate stood there a moment more; then he sighed and rubbed his kid's head. "Here, sit down at the table and eat some crackers. But don't eat too many. Five. You can have five."

He walked back out to the porch with the phone. "Okay, Howie. I'm here."

Howie's voice was calm. "This isn't good, Nate. You are out of control. You need to get your life together, buddy. Here's how it's gonna be: I'm giving your L.A. clients to Peter, and I'll have Bob do the training you were going to do with the new hires coming on. The Miami optometrists group can be shuffled off to somebody, and already Tina's on the Barcelona job . . . so you take an unpaid leave of absence and get your life together. We'll talk in the fall about where we are and whether or not you really have a future with this company."

This was worse than Nate had thought. For a moment the top of his head felt as if all the hair follicles had come unglued at one time, but then he settled himself down again, remembered to breathe, willed himself to lose the anger. Play the game, man. Be calm.

"No. Howie, *no*. Those aren't terms I can live with." He slowly walked the length of the porch and back. "I've got too much invested here to just leave all this hanging. Here's what's going to happen, man. I'll meet you in L.A. like we talked about, next week, and then I'm fully capable of doing the new-hires stuff the week after. I *welcome* it, in fact."

"You have a kid, and you are in no position—"

"Listen to me. I know myself. I know my abilities. And I've never let you down before this. Remember the heart of this business, Howie, because I've never forgotten it. *Trust in the universe to bring about the right action*. This is the right action." There was a silence, and then Nate went on. "Okay. I have a son. But I can handle it. Trust me. Nothing is going to change. I can work. I still want to work. Being a father—well, man, it's deepened me, that's for sure. I'm a fuller person now that I know what it is to love and be responsible for somebody." He gestured, one-armed, to the pillars on the porch, his heart hammering in his chest. There should have been a rising crescendo of music as the sound track to this speech. "You know, Howie, I have a reason to work harder and to be the kind of man I want my son to know. You know the kind of man I can be, and I know the kind of man I can be, and now I'm telling you: no matter what you say, *I am coming back to work, and I am going to succeed.*"

He was afraid then that he might have laid it on a little too thick, especially when the silence from the other end went on and on. He heard Howie's breathing, his snuffling. Nate stared up at the eaves and waited. A gnat flew into his ear, and still he waited. He gazed out over the fields, the old orchard that his grandfather had failed at running decades ago, looked at the slope of the land down to the pond. An eon passed, and the earth warmed and cooled a thousand times as the seasons bloomed and died again and again, and then Howie sniffled and buckled under and melted like the polar ice caps, and the continents drifted and crashed into each other. And Nate was forgiven and absolved and brought back into the warm sunshine of Howie's Hawaii surferosity.

Life was good. He made plane reservations for himself and Christopher for the following Saturday and did a couple of handsprings, ripped two more boards from the porch steps, and went into the house and started taking down the wallpaper using an ice scraper he found in a kitchen drawer. He was never going to be so glad to get away from a place in his entire life.

CHAPTER
16

I t was hot in the upstairs bedroom. That's what started it.

It was 2:27 a.m., and there she was, awake and sweaty and thirsty and maddened by life and the night. God, it was stifling in that bed. Even with the window open, the air from outside came and sat on her, like a big waft of dog breath. She probably should have moved to Lucy's air-conditioned condo before the heat wave hit, but she hadn't, and now she was trying to sleep in an upstairs bedroom during a string of nights with temps that never seemed to cool down. Global warming, all taking place right here, right now.

Untenable was what it was.

She took off her nightgown and then sat up in bed, feeling her heart beating so loudly it sounded as if it might leap through her chest. Through the monitor, she heard Arley's breathing—in, out, in, out, gasp. Outside there was such stillness, such intense quiet. How could people sleep through this kind of quiet? Where were the insects, for God's sake? Baked to death, no doubt. The full, round, white moon shone in on a square patch of floor, and she stared at it, mesmerized.

The moon was the other problem. It was too full. Werewolves were baying somewhere in the center of her.

She wasn't sorry she hadn't moved to the condo, not really. She and the kids had been spending most of their time lately down by the pond, she with her sketchbook and they with their Lego men, watching them take boat rides on twigs. Meanwhile, up in the house, Nate, who had most likely lost his mind, was gleefully tearing apart everything that could be torn apart, apparently just for the fun of it. Last she noticed, he had taken to using butter knives and the steam iron on the kitchen wallpaper, unearthing layer after layer of his family's decorative history. As if the wallpaper even mattered anymore. But he had to do it, he said.

In the late afternoon, his need for destruction slaked, he would show up at the pond in a pair of red boxer shorts (he had no bathing trunks, he explained to her), shouting "Woo-*hooo*!" and then he'd jump in and swim around in dizzy-making circles, his brown, strong arms flashing in and out of the water as he swam. She had to stare hard at her drawing pad when he did that.

Then he'd try to get Christopher to play catch with him. "Come on, Ace! You gotta get your practice going if you want to be good enough for the All-states by the time you're in high school!"

"I'm not Ace, and I don't want to go to any states," Christopher would say and then go and sulk on a rock. So then Nate would try to jolly him out of it by letting Arley stand on his shoulders while he spun him around, and then Christopher would finally come over, too, and later, when everybody was tired, Nate would sit down in the muck and dig giant holes with them, the muscles of his arms working hard.

"Tomorrow we're going to play catch until we've caught one hundred balls," he'd say. "*Each.* I've got to turn you into a baseball player because you've already got the genes for it. Who knows? Look at that tiny arm of yours. We've got to toughen you up."

Gah! She had gotten so mad at that remark that she had to pretend to be sleeping in her chair so she could avoid seeing Christopher's disappointed little face.

Now, still naked, she crept out of the bedroom, went into the bathroom, and softly closed the door and turned on the light. For a moment she stood there looking at herself in the mirror. Her face was brown from being outside so much lately—probably she'd get freckled—and her hair, blonder now and strawlike from the sun, was all messed up from sleep. She pinned it up with bobby pins, to get it off her neck, and splashed water on her face and chest, then pressed a wet washcloth on her breasts, letting the cold water trickle down the front of her, pinging all the little nerve endings as it went.

There was a slight noise from the hall, and then the bathroom door opened. She started.

"Oh!" Nate said. "*Oh!* It's you! Sorry."

"You scared me!" she said. Her hand went to her throat, as if she was in a bad horror movie.

That's when everything started going in slow-motion. Instead of backing out of the room and closing the door, Nate—well, just didn't. He stood there, looking at her, his expression changing from shock to something else she couldn't trust herself to name. She pulled the washcloth closer to her breasts, although she wanted to drop it altogether. He mumbled something about the heat. She might have said something cute or funny, to defuse the moment. She might have reached for a towel, laughed, walked past him. But she couldn't breathe, and she was actually thinking, *Why isn't this embarrassing?* and then he crossed the distance between them, and was suddenly right there in front of her. He put his hands on her face where it was still wet from the washcloth, and then he leaned down ever so slowly, his face looming close to hers, and kissed her.

At first she was petrified. And then she wasn't anymore. It was a perfect kiss—perfect, yes. Like, she wanted to tell him, it could go in the museum of kisses. It could give lessons to other kisses. That's how good.

She kissed him back. He smelled like sleep and whiskers and skin and a trace of toothpaste, and it felt so good to sink against him. Body to body, skin to skin. They moved over so he could lean her against the wall, and then they kept kissing. She put her arms around his neck; they pulled close to each other. He reached up and tentatively, questioningly, ran his fingertips in circles around her breasts. She heard herself moaning and tried to stop making that sound but couldn't. He pulled away and smiled at her, and she felt both weak and brave at the same time. When he said, "Oh my God. Jamie? Shall we . . . ? Do you want . . . ?" she wordlessly led him to his old room, where she took off his boxer shorts—or maybe they just fell off—and then lay down with him on the twin bed where she'd been sleeping.

She should have said no. In fact, there were a million reasons to say no, and she couldn't remember even one of them.

"You don't know," he said at one point, laughing a little, "how much I always dreamed about having a girl in this bed with me. Years of that dream—and look, now it's come true."

She laughed and kissed him. This was the best kind of sex— wasn't that what they always said—when you could *laugh* . . . spontaneous passion and laughter together . . . and then . . . well, it hit her: This was *sex*. She was having sex! This was it.

"Nate," she said. "Um. Do you have . . . you know . . . a condom?"

He stopped touching her, raised up his head. "Oh! Of course! Somewhere. I didn't exactly bring one into the can with me."

"I think we need . . ."

"Oh, shit." He sat up, ran his fingers through his hair. "You're right. Jeez, what was I thinking? I *wasn't* thinking."

"Do you have one?"

"Do you?"

"I think so. In my old room. In the bottom drawer. Lucy said I should always have one, in case. She keeps me stocked up."

"Yay for Lucy. I knew I liked her." He ran his fingers delicately across her cheeks. Leaned down and kissed her eyebrows. "Might you, ah, want to go get it?"

"Okay."

She got up off the bed and looked at him lying there. He was so . . . so breathtaking there, on his old cowboy bedspread, that she was clutched with fear that when she returned, he wouldn't be there, and she'd have to spend the whole rest of her life wondering if it had been a dream, or if he'd simply changed his mind about sleeping with her. She bit her lip.

"Go," he said. "Hurry, McClintock. This is spontaneous, throw-down sex. We're not supposed to take breaks."

"Will you come with me?" she whispered.

"Sure."

They got up, and she wrapped herself up in the sheet, but he pulled it off of her and shook his head. "No, no, no. If we have to take a walk, at least I want to look at you. I'll walk behind you."

"No tickling," she said. "And no thinking I have a fat ass." She couldn't believe she'd actually said that out loud.

"You have a perfect ass," he said. "Plump and luscious in all the right places."

"Shhh, we're passing the kids' room."

When they got to the master bedroom, she turned on the lamp and went over to the dresser. Sure enough, in the bottom drawer, there was a condom still in its blue foil wrapper. She handed it to him. He pretended to be astonished by its antiquity, blowing some imaginary dust off of it, then ripped it open with his teeth. She laughed, a shivery laugh.

"I want to take you right here," he whispered. "I have to."

Here? Here, where Harris died?

But then she remembered that Nate didn't actually, in fact, *know* that part, where Harris had died—and besides, stuff was happening to her right then that made her forget everything else, and so she fell down with him on the bed and, well, like the kiss that had already gone to the kiss museum, the lovemaking was mind-boggling. Crazy and perfect and wonderful. Afterward, he brought her close to him and kissed her nose and her forehead and her lips and her cheekbones— hundreds of little kisses. He sighed and said he'd been wanting her so much, he'd thought of nothing but this for *days* now. How could something be so . . . so surprising and yet, and yet . . . so *right,* like it was meant to happen?

So right, she thought, if only you could forget certain facts.

He was leaving in two days, and she would never see him again.

He was going to be doing this with someone else for the rest of his life.

Two things not to think about. That was all. Just two. *Hey, Lucy, you were right about the vibe. And I did it, sweetie. I had a fling.* She'd be so proud. Luckily, though, she wasn't hooked on him; she wasn't signing up for the whole roller-coaster love ride. This was okay, wasn't it? Just to enjoy his body? She closed her eyes, tried not to nestle too closely into his shoulder, to hold herself back just a little, like this was more a case of two friends wandering into each other in the middle of the night. It was all cool.

And then the next thing she knew, she was waking up, and her arm was asleep, and he was breathing into her face while the sun was rising in the window. She lay there, watching him sleep. He was so defenseless, so *unseamed.* It was like watching a child sleep, the fall of the eyelashes against the skin, the soft pouch of the cheeks, the lips gathered so purposefully. His ear, his hair, which was all messed up but glossy just the same. She could forgive him anything, the way he looked so peaceful there, how beautiful he was, the way he had touched her. She smiled at him, and the energy of that smile traveled over to him and woke him up.

He opened his eyes, saw her watching him, and for a moment he smiled, too, and his eyes went soft—and then, as if a switch had been thrown, he looked stunned and upset. He sat up, shook his head, took on the look of a deer in the headlights. "Oh, God," he said. He got up out of the bed and put the sheet around himself. He laughed a little bit, shook his head again. "Good sweet Jesus, Jamie, what the hell were we thinking?"

"I know. Crazy, huh?"

"Oh God." He looked around, his eyes flickering over the scene with a cold, hard gaze. "This is . . ." He stopped. "You know something, I think I hear the kids."

"Oh," she said. She didn't hear anything. And she was a trained mom.

"I'm—I'll go downstairs before they come out of there. I'll make us some coffee," he said. He looked at her for a moment, forced himself to do a gallant smile, and said, "You all right?"

"Sure," she said.

He ran his fingers through his hair and looked around for his boxer shorts and put them on fast. She watched as he transformed himself back into someone she barely knew, and then he shook his head and left the room, mumbling about coffee again. She heard him descending the stairs three at a time, and for a second she rather hoped he would trip and break some very valuable part of his body when he landed.

Then she sank back onto the pillows and stared out the window. For a moment she thought about crying, which she was perfectly within her rights to do. But then she decided she would just hate him instead. It took so much less energy, and besides, she hadn't had all that much sleep.

"LISTEN," HE SAID later, handing her a cup of coffee. "About last night . . ." He laughed a dry little raspy laugh that sounded even to him as if it had gotten stuck somewhere up high in his throat. "Wow, is that a bad cliché, or what? Wasn't there a movie with that name?" He could feel his blood pressure wavering someplace between total annihilation by explosion and mere heart attack. His hand was shaking when he handed her the coffee, and he hoped she wouldn't notice.

She gave him a level look and then a dazzling smile. "Oh *please,*" she said. "Believe me, there's nothing to say. It was ridiculous of us to let that happen." She put two pieces of bread in the toaster and went over to the stairs and called the children. The children! Like the room needed *children* in it just then. He understood then that the discussion was over for her, although he felt that more needed to be said. Just to make everything perfectly clear.

He began again, going back to the talking points he had thought up while he was in the bathroom that morning. "Well, I mean, it wasn't *ridiculous* . . . I'm not prepared to go that far," he said. "It was *great*. I mean, you were great. Really, really great." He growled a little and smiled. "And, hey, under any other circumstances, if I were free . . ." That had been a line he'd been especially proud of; it had *resonated* in the bathroom, with just the right mix of regret and finality.

"No, no. Really. It was just one of those middle-of-the-night things," she said. "Insane. I don't know about you, but I plead insanity." She came back and got the butter out of the refrigerator and, humming now and not looking at him, started buttering the toast. He stared at her ass until Arley and Christopher came thrashing down the stairs, as they always did—as if they'd been shot out of a cannon at the top and had a seventy percent chance of making it to the bottom alive.

Then he sipped his coffee and watched her as she poured cereal into bowls, put toast on plates, listened to the children's chatter, and then agreed that they could watch television while they ate. Just this once. She was wearing that funky long skirt she seemed to like, the one that looked as if it was made out of cobwebs, and she had a lace scarf—a *scarf*! In the morning!—wound around her neck. And a blue tank top. He could see her breasts, which looked as if they'd been formed with an ice cream scoop.

She steered the boys into the living room, balancing their bowls and their toast and shepherding their glasses of orange juice while they attempted to carry them. God, she had been *wild* in bed. Like over-the-top wild. She had had, what? About forty-seven orgasms— well, a few anyway. And she was beautiful. And spontaneous. And adventurous. He felt a tightening even now thinking about it. He adjusted his shorts and his mind flicked briefly over to his father and stuck there for a moment: Had his dad been getting any of this? Of course he was. How could he not have been?

When she came back into the kitchen, he said, "Look, I . . . I really am sorry . . ."

She got a dishrag and went back out to the living room. When she came back, she looked over at him. "It's *fine,* Nate. Leave it alone, why don't you? Why don't you go dismantle the house?"

He barked out a laugh. "Why don't I . . . *what?*"

"Peel wallpaper. Rip the place apart. Isn't that what you want to be doing?" And she took her cup of coffee and went back upstairs. Which was just fine with him.

For the rest of the day she seemed to be avoiding him. If he came into a room where she was, she'd find a reason to leave it. She took the kids down to the pond, and when he stopped picking at the wallpaper and went down there, too, she stood up and declared that it was time for Arley to get inside, out of the sun, before he got sunburned.

"But you put sunscreen on me!" Arley protested.

"Come in anyway. You're getting chilled in the water," she said.

Arley gave Nate a pleading look, as if he wanted him to intervene with this unreasonableness. Nate looked over at her, but there was nothing to indicate that she even saw him. She hauled her son out of the water, and the two of them went up the hill to the house.

That night, after the children were in bed, and after he'd stacked up all the photograph albums, and yes, scraped the wallpaper some more (it was a strangely satisfying thing to do), he found himself alone in the kitchen with her.

"Jamie," he said.

"What?"

"I just want to say again that I'm sor—"

"*Don't,*" she said in a warning voice.

"Don't what? If a man wants to apologize, I think you have to let him."

"Look," she said. "Why don't you stop being sorry about things you can't change? Maybe you could actually spend your time figuring out how to make something work with the one person you actually *need* to get along with for the rest of your life."

Tina? He must have looked blank, because she said tersely, "*Christopher.* Why don't you start getting to know him? Act like you have something of a heart and a conscience."

"I do have a heart and a conscience; that's why I'm taking him and raising him. And he and I are just fine, thank you very much." He got a beer out of the fridge and held one up for her to see, with a questioning look.

She ignored the question, just fixed him with a scary, unblinking stare. "You want to know something? You don't know the first thing about him. Like, you don't have any idea how much he hates it that you call him nicknames all the time, and how uncomfortable it makes him that you're always trying to get him to play catch when he doesn't care anything at all about catch. You don't ever *listen* to him."

"I listen just fine."

"No, now you see, *this* is what frightens me for him. That you *think* you listen when you don't. If you don't even see the stuff that's right in front of you, how are you going to learn the other stuff about him? Like that he doesn't like the peanut butter on his sandwich to be more than one millimeter thick, and that the only jelly he'll eat is grape jelly because it doesn't have any seeds. And that lizards are his favorite animal, and he thinks that Santa Claus takes a magic pill to shrink himself so he can get down chimneys. And his favorite book is *Mike Mulligan and His Steam Shovel,* which he can practically recite by heart, so don't try to skip any of the words when you read it to him— and, oh yeah, if you send him up to brush his teeth, you have to go with him, because he hates doing it and so he'll just wet his toothbrush to make you *think* he did it, and his teeth will rot out. He likes showers instead of baths, and he doesn't like mustard or ketchup on his hamburgers, and he likes half-sour pickles instead of dill. Oh, and don't let him get too hungry because he has complete meltdowns. He can't go to sleep without a night-light. He will wear as many Band-Aids as you can possibly afford, so don't leave a full box of them lying around. And if you ever make spaghetti sauce for him? Don't put any green things in it, like parsley or oregano. He's like a heat-seeking missile, and he can find those in an instant. He hates mushrooms, bran cereal, broccoli, cheddar cheese, and ketchup. Oh, and he eats Oreo cookies by eating the actual cookie part first, in a circle, borders first, which is crazy, but that's the way he does it. And once he fell down and chipped one of his teeth, and his dentist has been watching it to see if it is going to turn black, so you might want to keep an eye on that, too. And oh yeah, he is really scared about shots, so you have to reassure him ahead of time. Maybe offer a reward for after. The reward that really works is M&Ms. He eats them in this order: red, then orange, and then green and yellow, and he leaves all the brown ones because he thinks they're yucky. And when you take him to movies—"

"Okay, okay!" he said. "Would you stop this? I'll get all this. You know I will, so just stop it."

"But I've got it *now,*" she said, and he really did think that she might go off now and get hysterical, maybe start wielding a weapon. "What am I supposed to do with all this knowledge in my head, huh? You think the biggest problem I have is that *you* decided to have sex with me in the middle of the goddamn night and then wished to hell it had never happened when you woke up in the morning? You think I care that you have some . . . some *workaholic* woman somewhere who's supposed to be making you sexually happy, but ohhhh poor you, she couldn't come to relieve your tense little self, couldn't even come to your daddy's funeral, so you slept with me instead?"

"Wait," he said. "That's *not*—"

"Oh, shut up. Believe me, that is *not* the stuff I'm thinking about when I think about you, Nate Goddard. I'm thinking instead that you're an arrogant, clueless, obnoxious, self-loathing guy who never figured out that his biggest problem *isn't* his father—it's the fact that you turned over all your power to a man who was just as flawed and weak as any of the rest of us, and now you can't see that he was a real person who had a *heart* and who was trying his best to make a life for a child. *Your* child. And maybe *that* was so he could make it up to *you*! Did you ever think of that, that maybe he was just trying to get things right with the universe, balance the scales a little bit? Maybe it was out of love and not any sinister plan to rob you of your manhood or your fatherhood?"

"God, would you *stop* this?" he said. "Would you just shut the fuck up?"

"No, I won't shut the fuck up. I'm not going to get another chance to tell you this stuff, because you are going to take this child who means so much to me and fly him way the hell across the country, where you will proceed to wreck what I've been able to give him in about a million different ways—"

He slammed down his bottle of beer, strode over to her, and grabbed her by the shoulders. Once he was there, he couldn't imagine why he had done this, but she looked startled, and then the next thing he knew, they were kissing again. She was flat against the wall and he was pressing against her, grinding into her, shutting her up at last.

At last.

And as soon as he let her go, she bit him on the lip so hard he started to bleed.

Part
Two

CHAPTER
17

Not surprisingly, life became quiet after the airplane took Christopher and Nate away.

The parting from Christopher was heart-wrenching, of course. Devastating.

But then Jamie and Arley moved back to Lucy's condominium, which, as Lucy pointed out cheerfully, did *not* have peeling red linoleum floors and only one room with an air conditioner. Also, you could look out the window through glass that was transparent, not through some thick, wavery substance that stood between you and the world. And the stucco ceilings were high and angled, with beams and skylights. Best of all, Lucy said, instead of a falling-down back porch, there was a balcony—a civilized porch hanging off the side of the building, in line with all the other balconies, one after the other in a row, all containing barbecue grills and window boxes of flowers. There were evenings when you could grill your chicken practically elbow to elbow with a whole population of grillers. Why, you could even get new chicken recipes, maybe even meet a new man—you never know, Lucy said, the love of your life could be out there on one of those balconies, smiling as he turned his chicken thighs with a long fork and described his technique for basting lemon and garlic and butter right over the skin.

Jamie felt as though she'd slipped right back into her old life, as easy as diving into a river and letting the current take her along, as though the farmhouse life had never existed. And there was, she had to admit, much to be grateful for: Lucy was wonderful with Arley, the refrigerator was always stocked with fresh vegetables and Vitamin Water, and she got to attend Lucy's yoga class. Every morning at seven, five women showed up for class, held in the living room. Jamie participated as well. Her abs were tighter. Her mind was clearer. She slept better. She hadn't bitten anyone in a long time.

Kindergarten ended in mid-June with a lovely little graduation ceremony, complete with caps and gowns and rolled-up diplomas. Jamie posted her résumé online and started looking for teaching jobs in earnest. She e-mailed her old friend, Shana, and asked her to look out for a job for her at the girls' school, and Shana e-mailed back: I'M THINKING OF POISONING THE ART TEACHER SO THAT U AND I CAN BE 2GETHER AGAIN LOL. LOOKS LIKE A POSSIBILITY. I'LL LET U NO.

Then she got hired to teach a summer-school painting class each morning at the high school. Although it was temporary and didn't pay much, it was good for her—a foot in the door with the school system, just in case. The kids were lovely and tried hard to paint, and Arley either came with her to the classes or stayed with a woman in the condo who babysat for money. Mike Scanlon, who was now Lucy's official boyfriend, came over nearly every night and hung out with them. He was earnest and sweet, and Jamie could tell by his perpetually frightened expression that he was in way over his head and trying to figure out just what it would take to get Lucy to love him forever. She'd seen that look on the faces of all Lucy's boyfriends, from junior high school onward, as they flailed around during that first flush of love, when they still couldn't believe their good fortune, before Lucy started torturing them with her indifference.

This had always been amusing to watch, and would have been

this time, too, except that Jamie really was fond of Mike and didn't want to see him get smashed up by her sister. There were days when she felt like taking him aside and whispering, "Have you ever even *heard* of the hard-to-get game? You have got to stop giving her flowers and compliments, and for heaven's sake, don't always be so available. Make her work for it."

But he'd have been perfectly within his rights to turn to her and say, "Excuse me? And just what gives you any credentials whatsoever, if you don't mind? You've had, um, *what kind* of relationships with men? And your last one was an abbreviated one-night stand with an engaged-to-be-married lunatic? I see."

"*Fine,*" she said to him in her fantasy conversation. "You'll see what she does with you, how fast you get chewed up and spit out."

Instead, she kept quiet, and it *was* fine. Life was good. She was a tiny bit lonely there on the outskirts of town, but that's where she belonged. She was laying low, staying away from Cooksey and all the memories and the people who thought she was a gold digger, or who *might* have been thinking that, if they believed Cooksey. Which they probably did. The universe, as Lucy kept proclaiming during the morning yoga meditation, quoting "Desiderata," was no doubt unfolding exactly as it should.

Yet . . . and yet . . . every now and then, falling asleep listening to the steady hum of the central air instead of the chaos of a thousand crickets outside, she tried to enumerate all she missed, just so she wouldn't forget anything. It was a little exercise in misery, actually, letting herself strum those memories, plinking each one like a string on a guitar, just to see which one hurt. She missed Harris, of course, and Christopher—she missed him *terribly,* the way his laughter always seemed to catch him by surprise, and the raw tenderness of him, the way he feared she wouldn't love him, and how he was so round-eyed with delight when she let him crawl up on her lap along-side Arley—and yes, she even missed being the only woman in a household full of males, the only one to wear a long dress and to have her hair braided. And how the kitchen had been her domain, how she was queen of the pots and pans, and the way the sun shone in through those yellow curtains, making a buttery circle on the table in the mornings. She missed the back stairs and the coolness of the front parlor, and the way the glider squeaked, and what it was like standing in the kitchen painting, listening to the boys playing with Legos at the table, making up stories; she missed holding her cup of coffee down at the roadside while she and Harris and the boys waited for the school bus to show up; missed the way people stopped over just to talk sometimes; missed taking a blanket down to the pond and watching the boys catching tadpoles.

And then, when her heart was fully and truly sore, she would arrive at thinking about Nate.

And that stupid night.

First of all, it was ridiculous, *beyond* ridiculous, to be a grown woman in the twenty-first century and to be affected so much by a one-night stand, which, let's face it, was nothing more than body parts rubbing together. Penises and vaginas. Big deal. Ho hum. Everybody on the planet was doing it. It was her own policy not to overthink or, worse, *overfeel* anything having to do with men.

One day she was rummaging down at the bottom of her bag for something—down beneath a tube of hand cream, two inhalers, a jar of glitter, a Lego robot, a candy bar, and a couple of fine specimens of pinecones in Baggies—and there was his business card.

NATE GODDARD, it read. And there was his e-mail address and phone number, engraved. She ran her finger over it, then turned the card over. There he'd written in handwriting that was surprisingly open and loopy: "If you ever need me."

If you ever need me.

What the hell did that mean?

"Get over yourself," she said to the mirror. She slipped the card in her pocket, for some reason. What would she need him for?

Lucy had said she should stop obsessing about having slept with Nate, that it just meant that whatever deep-freeze she'd been in for five years was thawing, and she needed to start getting laid again. Blah blah blah . . . the universe is unfolding exactly the way it should . . . he's just a transitional sex object. Get over it.

"I'll look around for somebody eligible that you can date," Lucy said. "Who knows? You could even get married. We could have a wedding in the condo rec room. I know! A *yoga wedding*. We'll figure out what that could be like. Cheer up! Smile. Men are going to adore you."

ONE NIGHT WHEN she was putting Arley to bed, he said to her, "Mama, do you like living here in the condo?"

He was propped up on his Spider-Man pillow, all scrubbed and in his cowboy pajamas, and she had just read him two stories and sung him a song, and was stretched out next to him in the darkness, having their togetherness time before sleep. Occasionally headlights swept across the white walls of his room as a car turned into the condo complex. There was the sound of a television muffled through the wall, and somewhere water rushed through the pipes of the building and a door slammed. Down in the living room, two rooms away, Mike and Lucy were laughing about something. Mike had a nervous, high-pitched laugh. Even from here, Jamie could tell he was trying too hard. She sighed on his behalf.

"Yeah," she said. "Do you?"

"I like it," Arley said, after a while of thinking, "but I want to go back to the other house." He turned over on his side, and she could see his face, which suddenly looked older than five. "This place doesn't have any rabbits hopping around outside. And there's just a pool instead of a pond, and yesterday I saw a ladybug on the window, and Lucy said I shouldn't put it in my bug jar because it's just a boring bug, she said. Not an interesting bug. And there's nobody to talk to in my room if I wake up in the night."

"Aw, I'm sorry. You must miss Christopher so much," she said.

He sniffled, which broke her heart. "I don't see why he had to go and stay in Ellay. Can't he come back here?"

"Well, he has to live where his dad lives now. That's the way it goes."

He thought about this. "I like his dad."

"Yeah. I know you do."

"He was funny."

"Yeah, he was a laugh riot."

"What's a laugh riot?"

"Never mind."

He sat up in bed and picked at the threads on the bedspread. "I want him to come back here, and I want him to live in the old house again, and I want to go down by the pond and catch tadpoles. One time we saw a dead raccoon down there, and his eyeballs were all gross, with that white stuff . . ."

"I know. I remember."

"Could I call up Christopher on the phone?"

"Well . . . I guess we could do that sometime."

"Could we do it right now?"

She actually thought about it for a moment, wondered what it would be like, calling Nate on the phone. She'd have to have something to say to him. Something official, not just, *How's it going?* And maybe his fiancée was with him. That would be awkward.

"No," she said. "It's bedtime."

"Come on! Let's call!"

"Not now. What do you want to tell him?"

"I want to tell him that we should live in the old house again, and that the day the raccoon died, I went over and poked his fur with a big stick, and he didn't move."

"I think Christopher was there and that he remembers that."

He gave her a withering look. "I want to *remind* him."

"Oh," she said.

"Maybe we could go swim in the pond, and I could find a lizard for him. You know, I want to send him my vest. Could we send him my vest sometime?"

"Which vest?"

"The ladybug one. I want Christopher to have it."

"Well, maybe."

From the living room, Lucy suddenly laughed out loud and said, "Oh, Mikey, honey! Come on—hasn't *any* woman ever shown you the one-handed bra-removal technique?"

Mike said something she couldn't hear, and then there was more laughter.

"What are they doing?" Arley said.

"I don't know," Jamie said. "But it's time for you to go to sleep."

"Is Mike going to sleep over again?"

"Maybe." *Certainly sounds like it.*

"How come you never have any sleepovers like Aunt Lucy does?"

"Shhh. Go to sleep now."

"Tomorrow, can we call Christopher?"

"Maybe."

Maybe, maybe, maybe. The whole world was made up of one big maybe, and it made her sick.

She went into her bedroom, flipped on the computer, and wrote a note to Shana: USE THE POISON, BUT DON'T GET URSELF CAUGHT. I MUST GET A REAL LIFE, HOPEFULLY INVOLVING A PAYCHECK! YOU THOUGHT TRACE WAS BAD, BUT NOW I'VE SLEPT W/ THE VERY WRONGEST MAN POSSIBLE AGAIN. MISERABLE, JUST MISERABLE. XOXO, JAMIE.

Shana was the one who had been there when Jamie, a freshman in college—no, scratch that—a *completely inexperienced and idiotic freshman in college,* had come back to the dorm filled up with the moon after having slept with Trace for the very first time. He was her TA. He hadn't wooed her with food or wine, or even, heaven forbid, the promise of a good grade in the course. He'd simply told her that she, like him, was a misunderstood, underappreciated artistic genius . . . and that so far she was the only person he'd ever met who really *got* him.

Shana had rolled her eyes at the time. "Ha!" she said. "Just wait.

He'll have you supporting him and putting your own art aside in no time. That so-called *genius* of yours isn't going to mean a thing to him when he wants you to go off to work at Wal-Mart so he'll have enough money to pay for paint."

Sure enough, by the end of junior year, that was exactly what happened. And then, five years later—well, that's when little Arley came thundering into the world. When Trace kept forgetting to come home, Shana was the one who came for Jamie and Arley in a pickup truck and drove them to her sister's. And now she was going to have to come again.

MIKE SCANLON WAS still there when the yoga class started the next morning. Which was ha-ha funny. The yoga ladies were always amused when he came creeping out of Lucy's room and into the living room, wearing his uniform and a shit-eating grin. He usually did a mock salute as he made his way through the crowd to the front door, stopping to kiss Lucy on whatever appendage of hers might be most available. One morning she'd been in the downward dog position, with her butt up in the air, and the yoga ladies *loved* it that he pretended to stop, perplexed, while he contemplated kissing it.

But this morning, Jamie noticed that instead of leaving, he looked right at *her,* lifted his eyebrows, and then headed instead for the kitchen. She waited a few moments, and then she got up and slipped away from the meditation exercise and went to the kitchen. He had the coffeepot on and was searching in the cabinet for mugs.

"Hi," she said, and he jumped. "Sorry. I didn't mean to scare you."

He smiled. "Actually," he said, "I wasn't sure you got my signal. But I wanted to ask you something."

"Sure. Fire away."

"It's about Lucy . . ."

"Uh-oh."

"What's wrong?"

"You just gotta keep in mind that there's a sister code I'm forced to operate under, and that she will cheerfully break both my legs if I say anything to embarrass her." She was smiling at him.

"No, no, it's nothing like that. I just wondered . . . ah . . . well . . . I might as well just say it. I mean, okay, you know how I feel about her, right? I think she's just incredible, and I know I'm kind of out of my league here with her, but she seems—well, she seems to feel something for me, too, so I have a lot of hope, but . . . well . . . would you just, you know, give me a heads-up if you see the end coming? Like, if she starts calling Dan again, would you just give me some kind of sign?"

She blinked. "Dan? Oh seriously, I think she's really through with Dan." Poor sucker—he didn't realize that his competition, when it came, would be from some direction he had never even contemplated worrying about. A guy who wandered into the bar who looked interesting. Some purple-haired yoga master on retreat, perhaps driving a Harley and wearing cowboy boots.

"Okay," he said, and nodded like somebody in a trance. He'd probably been marinating in love and gloom all morning. She reached over and touched his arm, and said, "Hey, you'll be okay."

"I'm already in this so deep that no advance warning is going to give me time to protect myself."

Well, *duh*. She almost told him she thought the hard-to-get game might be a good possibility for him; he should look up the rules. But the class was breaking up, and Lucy would come breezing in here in a moment, sweaty and glowing and peaceful.

"Do you think she likes me? I mean, really likes me?" he said, and then he smacked himself on the forehead and said, "God, this sounds like junior high all over again, doesn't it?"

"Don't worry about it," Jamie said. "Love does that to people. Reduces everybody to seventh grade again. It's just awful."

They both laughed. And then, inexplicably, he said, "So, have you heard from Nate?" as if the two things were in the same category.

"No," she said.

"I'd just be curious, if I were you, how he's getting along. That's a wild plan he had."

"True."

"He's bound to be missing this place by now."

Getting out of Chester was more of a relief than Nate could have ever predicted. A person could actually *be a father* once he got his kid away from all those people who expected him to do it wrong. In fact, Nate had never found a job he was more enthusiastic about than fatherhood—not right from the start, at least. All that uncertainty and doubt he'd felt about it while he was back in Chester? That sick feeling he'd gotten when Jamie was trying to bludgeon him with all the stuff he didn't know? Ha! That's what he said to that: Ha! Now that he actually had the kid to himself, everything was different. Clean slate. And with just himself and Christopher to worry about— well, they were natural allies, that's what.

Natural allies in *fun.* That was the most important skill he had going for him: he was going to be a fun dad.

Even on the plane. There was Christopher riffling through the seat pocket in front of him and getting sort of restless, and Nate knew what to do.

"You know," he said to his son, "we're on an adventure, you and I." He squeezed the kid's arm. "You see this airplane? We're going to be on *lots* of them, just like this. Did you like the takeoff? Because a lot of people are scared of taking off, they're wusses like that. But you and I—we like it, don't we? That whoosh as you go up. I love it." He pantomimed an airplane going up into the sky. "Did you like it?"

Nate was talking too much. He'd had two cups of coffee. Christopher silently nodded and kicked at the seat in front of him. Then he said, "I have to go to the bathroom."

"Ah," Nate said. "Wow. Airline bathrooms are *great.* I just want to tell you in advance—you're going to have an interesting time in there. Now, you have to latch the door. That's important. One time I went into the airline bathroom and there was already somebody in there, and when I opened the door—well, you don't want to know, but it was hilarious."

"No, Natey! I have to go *now.*"

"Okay, okay, pal. Just go to the back of the plane, and you'll see the doors. They have signs on them. If it says 'Vacant,' then you can push the door to the side . . ." He stopped talking, seeing Christopher's face. "Wait. I should come with you, huh?"

The kid shrugged, so Nate unbuckled their seat belts and clambered out over the legs of the woman sitting on the other side of him, in the aisle seat, a nice-enough-looking woman who had been giving him encouraging little smiles since they sat down. She had nodded when Nate said he should go with Christopher to the bathroom. The world was full of women who knew just what Nate Goddard should be doing with his kid moments before he himself got it. But hey, at least he got it.

By the time they got back to their seats, Christopher was hungry, so Nate got out the little thermal pack Jamie had fixed for him, with a peanut butter sandwich, crackers, and cheese inside. "Kids get hungry at unscheduled times," she'd said as she handed it to him.

The woman in the aisle seat now leaned over and held out her hand to be shaken and said her name was Emily. She praised Nate for his astonishing foresight in bringing food, and he was in such a good mood that he took complete credit for thinking of this, even though when Jamie handed him the thermal pack, all he could think of was that it was such a pain having to bring one more thing along. He said, "Well, Emily, you just have to think ahead with kids," and she smiled back at him. She was kind of cute, in that mom kind of way, with short, pixie-cut hair. She said her husband would never have thought to do something like that. Their kids could starve, and their father wouldn't even *think* of how he might prevent that. Then she laughed, and Nate shook his head. *Men.*

Christopher was sliding the tray table back and forth, back and forth, in a way that was clearly annoying the person in front of him, so Nate leaned over and quietly intervened. He pointed to some lovely scenery out the window, the way the clouds were piled up in interesting mashed-potato formations. When he turned back, Emily was looking at him with her high beams on. She said, "So what do you think that I, as a mom, can do to get my husband to be more involved like you are? Or is this some instinct you have that most guys don't get? I'll bet you were wonderful from day one!"

So! There was going to be parental flirting. This was a category he was just learning about. He leaned back, wondering for a tiny moment what it would be like to tell the absolute truth on this one, if it might be fun to watch her recoil in horror instead of drool all over him. He was juggling the bunch of different responses that all came up in his mind unbidden, when little Christopher suddenly broke out of his spaced-out stupor. He'd been tapping on the window of the plane and muttering little nonsense rhymes to himself, but now he turned and gave Emily a big, shy smile.

"You're sooo cute!" she said, and leaned across Nate to touch Christopher's arm. The slightest little tip of her breast grazed Nate's arm. "So tell me. Is your daddy just the best daddy in the whole wide world?"

Nate found himself holding his breath.

Christopher looked as if he might vanish back into his five-year-old world without comment, but Emily clearly wasn't going to let that happen. "Are you just the luckiest boy, having such a good dad?"

Christopher said, with a coy smile, "Well, Da is *really* the best. But he . . ."

"Christopher . . ." Nate said. He gave the merest shake of his head.

And Emily-on-the-aisle sighed happily and said, "See? That's what I'm talking about. A kid knows. He really knows. His Da is the best."

"Natey, can I have some more peanuts?"

"Ooh," Emily said and wrinkled up her nose as if she was preparing to be charmed. "What is that other name he calls you?"

"Oh, he just heard someone call me that nickname . . ." Nate said, and decided that he would instantly need to cut off all conversation with this woman for the remainder of the flight. He showed Christopher the headphones and the cool children's music to be listened to, and then he put a pair on himself, closed his eyes, and plugged himself into jazz.

THE APARTMENT LOOKED just the way he'd left it. Which was unfortunate. He'd never paid that much attention to this place before, but walking in there that first night with Christopher and about a thousand pounds of luggage, it was suddenly clear to him that he had been living all this time in a small white box: white carpeting, white tile floor, white walls, white horizontal blinds on the windows. Not even any pictures on the walls, just a calendar stuck up on the fridge. The whole place consisted of one bedroom with a double bed and a dresser, a tiny kitchenette, and a living room that contained an old leather couch and a scarred-up table he'd bought from a second-hand furniture store. There was the requisite sliding door out to a balcony overlooking the parking lot, furnished with an aluminum lawn chair.

"Ta-*da!* So here's our new home!" he said to Christopher, who stood there blinking in the fluorescent light and looking as though he might cry. Nate stooped down and started picking up the pile of take-out menus and junk mail that covered the floor of the "entryway," a one-yard-by-one-yard square tiled area before the carpeting officially started. "Now listen. Don't freak out on me. I know it doesn't look like much. It's just a *guy's* bachelor pad, so don't think our whole life is going to be a certain way just because of what you see here, okay? This is just the *before,* not the after."

Christopher looked at him as if he didn't know what he was talking about, with those round saucer eyes. "Where's your TV set?"

"Well, it's broken right now, actually, so I put it in the closet. You see, I don't spend a lot of time here." He put the menus in the trash can under the kitchen sink. "I mean, all that might change somewhat—you know, with the marriage thing coming up with Tina, I've sort of been waiting to see what things we'd have together. Not much point in fixing an old TV if we're going to get an HD one. You know?"

"You don't have a TV set?"

"I have one, but it's broken." He stood up and ran his fingers through his hair and looked at the kid.

"So what are we going to do here?"

"What are we going to *do*?" Nate laughed. "Well, we're going to live here, presumably. This is our house. Our *home.* You should come farther into the room, not just stand there in the entryway. Come on. It's okay. It's a friendly little place, despite how it looks." He went over and turned on a pole lamp next to the couch, picked up a *Car and Driver* magazine off the table. "Wow. It's been a while since anybody was in here, that's for sure. This is the March issue of this thing."

"Who lives here with you?"

"Nobody. It's just me and you. And oh yeah, my cactus, Joe. Let me introduce you to my cactus. He used to be the only dependent I had, but now I have you. Big improvement right there. He's in the bedroom. Come on, I'll show you."

Christopher did manage then to actually enter the apartment, although he still looked waiflike, as though he expected something to jump out at him and scare him to death. Nate went over and put his arm around him and gently led him down the two-foot hallway into the bedroom, and flicked on the light. His cactus was sitting on the bedside table.

"This is Joe Cactus," Nate said. "Joe Cactus, this is Christopher. You are now no longer going to have to pretend to be my only companion here, Mr. Joe Cactus. I have a real boy to talk to now." He laughed.

Christopher stared glumly.

"Come on now, dude. That's funny stuff, don't you think? I used to have only this cactus to talk to, and now I have you. So, okay. You tired? Hungry? Anything? You got questions for me? What's going on in that little head of yours?"

"I have to go to the bathroom."

"Okay, one bathroom coming up! Here it is. Here, conveniently located, may I point out, directly across the hall from the bedroom. Two steps, and you're there! Go right ahead in."

Christopher was gone for a long time with the door closed, and when he came out, he announced that the tub had brown stuff in it.

"That's okay. That's just—well, it's probably dirty. We can clean that up. Don't worry."

Christopher stared off into space, hugged himself as if he wished he could disappear himself. "Why were there so many papers on your floor when we came in?"

"Papers on the floor? Oh, the menus. People just shove those under the door. It's one of the things about living in an apartment. People come by sometimes, and they want you to have their menus so you'll order food from them. And then they bring it to you."

"They bring you food? How?"

"In their cars, I guess. You call their number, and then you say what you want, and then a little while passes, and then they knock on the door, and they have your food for you. Here. You want something? A pizza? Some chicken tenders or something? We could order something. That could be fun."

Christopher shrugged.

"Let's get a pizza. I'll call Pizza Man. What do you like? Pepperoni? Sausage? I like meat on a pizza. How about you?"

"I like cheese."

"No meat at all? Really? You don't like *any* meat?"

"Cheese."

"Wow. Just cheese. What kind of stuff did my dad teach you? Huh? Or—oh, maybe this was Jamie's influence."

"What?"

"Nothing, dude. We'll do cheese for now. I can show you the finer things of life later." He went and rifled through the menus, looking for the one from Pizza Man. His hand was shaking a little. It was only eight-thirty, and the sky was still light outside, but he felt as if he could slip happily into a coma. Oh, but that's right. They were operating on Eastern time, so it was really eleven-thirty. No wonder Christopher looked as if he was ready to fall down, or worse, burst into tears. It was way past his bedtime.

"You know, we probably shouldn't get a pizza at this time of night," Nate said. "It's crazy. You need to get some sleep."

"I don't want to go to sleep!"

"I know. But you're tired, dude."

"Don't call me dude. And I'm *not tired.*"

"Let's see, where are we going to put you to sleep? And I've got to clean up that tub, I guess . . . you don't actually want a bath, do you?"

"You don't have a *bed* for me?"

"No, no, I do. Obviously you have a *bed* here."

"But I don't have a bedroom, do I? There's no bedroom for me! And I am never, *ever* going to get in that tub with the brown stuff. I can't take a bath *ever!*"

"Okay, okay. Just settle down. You don't have to take a bath. Things are going to be all right."

"They're *not* all right! I want a pizza!"

"Fine," Nate said. "A pizza you shall have. Let's not freak out, go all medieval here, okay, dude? Cool heads, cool heads." He called and ordered the pizza, but by the time it arrived, Christopher was asleep at the foot of the bed, looking like a soldier felled in battle. Nate had wondered what the sleeping arrangements were going to be, and here was his answer. Slowly, carefully, he lifted Christopher up and placed him on the right side of the bed, where the kid promptly flung out both his arms and legs as though they'd been spring-loaded.

Nate sat there for a long time watching his son sleeping. He was tired. And then at last, when he was bored and tired beyond belief and had nothing else to do that wouldn't make noise, he slipped into bed himself, into the four square inches that were unoccupied on the mattress, and tried hard to go to sleep.

"I THINK WE have to have a talk about the rules," he said to Christopher the next day. "The rules are . . ." he spread his hands wide and grinned, ". . . there *are* no rules! We're just two guys together in life. Two men! How's that?"

They were having breakfast in a diner, which seemed preferable to any kind of cooking he might do. Eating out, after all, was a treat. He had let Christopher order strawberry waffles with piles of whipped cream, and then, when Christopher had been confused about just what a delicacy this was, he had allowed him to eat all the strawberries separately and then put butter and syrup on the waffles, blending it just so with the whipped cream. The plate was an utter disaster, which made Nate so happy he couldn't think straight. You see? This was fatherhood. And these were the stories he'd tell somebody, anybody who might listen.

"Slap me five," he said, and Christopher held up a sticky, strawberry juice–stained hand.

"Naw, that's okay. No, wait. Yes. Let's high-five anyway. I'll use the water in my glass here to unstick myself from you, if necessary."

They high-fived, and Christopher went back to tearing apart the waffles as though they were wild animals he had to vanquish. Nate sipped his coffee and averted his eyes. It was both horrifying and fascinating what a little kid could do to a plate of food.

"So. Now, let's talk about what's going to happen," he said. "Today we're going to go out and buy us a TV set, so we have something to watch to help us fall asleep easier at night. And *then* we might get ourselves a little blowup bed for one of us to sleep on so we don't get backaches sharing our bed . . ."

"What's a blowup bed?"

"Oh, it's cool. It's like one of those floats you can use in a pool. It'll make a nice bed for you in the living room."

"The living room!"

"Yeah. That way you'll have your own room. And your own bed."

"I have to *sleep* in the living room?"

"Yeah."

"I don't want to. I want to sleep in your room. In the big bed."

"See, little man, I think we need to look at this another way. Maybe take a moment for an attitude adjustment, okay? Now, close your eyes, and let's think this through. What if sleeping in the living room were the biggest treat you could have? What if it were like a special, special thing that you only got to do sometimes? Then you would *want* that, right?"

The waitress came by with a pot of coffee. "More?"

"Sure," Nate said. He grinned at her and winked. "Tell me something," he said to her. "Did you ever get to sleep in the *living room* when you were a kid? Wouldn't that have been the most special thing?"

She looked quizzical at first, but then he winked at her again, and she laughed and said, "Oh, we never could do that! It would be waaay too special to do."

"Exactly," Nate said. "But this is my boy here, and he's just come to live with me, and we are out celebrating the fact that we are going to have a house of just us, and we are not going to have any rules at all. None! And this guy will even get to sleep in the living room!"

"I don't want to," Christopher said.

"Well," the waitress said. "Good luck." And she moved off with her coffeepot, no help at all.

"What do you want to do today?" Nate asked after a while.

"I . . . I know! I want to go to the pond with Arley."

"No-oooo, you don't! Get out of town!" Nate said in his most fun, you're-being-silly voice. "What do you really want to do?"

"I want to go play with Arley."

"But, dude, we're in California now. Arley's not here. You know that."

"My name is not dude. And you asked me what I want."

"I tell you what. Let's go buy a television set, and then maybe we'll go to the park, and then we'll get a blowup bed, and then we'll . . . I don't know . . . get prepared for our meeting with Howie tomorrow. I've got to tell you about Howie. He's kind of a trippy guy, but he doesn't seem to think that you and I are going to be able to go to meetings together, so we've got to prove him wrong. We've got to show him we're a team. Right?"

Christopher was just sitting there. He poked out his lower lip. "I just want to go back home, and see Jamie and Arley and . . . and . . . Da. When is Da coming back? Will he come here and see me?"

"No. Remember? We had the funeral and all that? He died. He passed away, I mean, and when people pass away, that's it."

"But I want him to come back."

"I know. But I'm afraid he can't."

Christopher started to cry in earnest then, and people in the other booths turned around to look. Nate took his napkin and leaned over and wiped some of the top layer of syrup and snot off Christopher's face before it all combined and dried there. He didn't know what to say. "I know, I know," was all he could think of. "Come on. Let's get out of here before everybody in here thinks this strawberry stuff is blood and that I'm some kind of monster and we've been in a huge fight or something."

To his surprise, this idea made Christopher laugh. He started laughing and crying and hiccupping, and then he took a drink of milk, but he was laughing so hard that milk came out of his nose. Nate took the last swig from his coffee cup and hurried the kid out of there and into the car, hugging him and kissing him all over his damp, sticky little face. He could make this kid laugh so hard that he'd spew milk! At that moment this seemed to be a golden milestone. They were going to make it. Once he got him belted into the car, he knelt down on the floor of the backseat and looked at Christopher. Basked in him.

"Okay, guy, here's the deal," he said. "Today we're having fun, because tomorrow, *tomorrow* we have an important day ahead of us. Do you remember that we're going to a meeting together, and you're going to be a big boy and show my boss and everybody at the meeting just how grown-up you can be? Right? And we'll get some toys and books for you to take, so you can play while Daddy's at the meeting. Right?"

Christopher turned his head and looked out the window.

"Because we're in this together, right? And so we get the TV set for you, and then for *me,* well, I get your promise to cooperate. Right? Do you see how this works? We both help each other. That's the rule."

"You said there are no rules."

Nate blinked. "Smart boy. Okay, I was wrong. Turns out there is just the one rule. The rule of helping. The rule of we're-in-this-together. Okay?"

No answer.

"Okay?"

"I want Jamie and Arley to come to the meeting, too."

Nate rolled his eyes and looked up at the sky. At what age did kids finally understand that some things are absolutely impossible?

"Well, they can't," he said when he could trust himself to speak without sounding mean. "It's up to you and me. It can be hard, or it can be easy. Whichever you pick. Hard or easy. Lucky or unlucky. It's up to you, dude."

No answer.

"Do you want to pick?"

"I don't want to pick."

"Well, then I'll pick for you. I pick easy, and I pick lucky. We're going to have a good attitude, man. Because that's eighty percent of the battle. Maybe ninety percent. You'll meet Howie, and you'll see where I get all this stuff from. He's a great guy. Pick easy and lucky, and you'll always be on the right side of trouble." He straightened up and patted Christopher on the knee. Then he closed the car door and walked around to the driver's side. He was sweating when he got into his seat.

"What if I pick hard?" Christopher said.

"Well, then, it'll be hard, I guess," Nate answered. And he started up the car and drove silently to the first traffic light. There, in the next car, was a woman who reminded him of Tina. That's what he needed: a partner. An audience. Someone to remind him that life wasn't just going to be grueling conversations with an inscrutable five-year-old from now on. That was it: he needed a woman and a pep talk and, yes, some sex. Definitely some sex.

At the next traffic light, he called Tina, and to his amazement, she picked up.

"Hellooooo, baby," he said, mimicking a TV show they'd once seen and thought was funny, some dorky guy trying to pick up a cool girl.

"I'm kind of in a meeting," she said in a low voice. "What's going on?"

"Nothing much. Me and my main man are settling in, in L.A. And we're ready for some action. *You* know." He grinned at Christopher in the rearview mirror. Christopher was looking out the window scowling, probably because there were a million ways that L.A. wasn't Chester, Connecticut.

"Let me call you back later," she whispered.

"Just say you're coming to rescue me," he said. "That's all you have to say."

"I don't know."

"Pretend, then."

"Okay. I'll pretend I'm coming. Now I've gotta run. Seriously."

From the backseat: "Let's go to the pond," Christopher said. "Isn't there a pond here?"

Nate wanted to crash his head against the steering wheel of the car. But he didn't do it. Instead, he took deep breaths. This was just one of the trials of being a single parent. He could overcome this. Why, he'd take the kid to the beach! To Santa Monica. Show him how great California could be. Smoothly, he pushed a button and let the top down on the convertible, turned the car around, and headed for the freeway.

They had a wonderful day. Sand and waves and cold water could improve anything. Iced Cokes. They had to stop off first, of course, and get themselves some brand-new bathing suits and beach towels, and a couple of floaty things that he then had to blow up. But it was good. Christopher asked a million questions, everything from why there were so many cars on the freeway to why people needed to eat food, to where Da was really. Nate called him Christopher the Inquisitor.

On the way home, late that afternoon, practically delirious with happiness, he stopped off at Target and bought a blowup bed, a TV set, a home Sno-Kone machine, a drum of kettle corn, four frozen pizzas, a boom box, nineteen DVDs, Batman and Robin sheets, four board games, a baseball, a football, and a basketball, lawn darts (you never know when you might find a lawn), and about five hundred dollars' worth of toys and books.

"Tomorrow morning, before the meeting," he said as they were driving back to the condo, "we'll get you some spiffy, conference-worthy clothes and a California haircut, and we'll practice saying,

'Howie, I'm so pleased to meet you.' Can you say that now? Do it convincingly, will you? Howie has a bullshit detector—oops, I mean, Howie can tell insincerity a mile away. Say it after me. ALOHA, HOWIE. I AM SO PLEASED TO MEET YOU. And oh, one more thing: Could you please, you know, just call me Daddy?"

But Christopher was sound asleep.

CHAPTER
19

Teaching high-school kids was mostly okay, Jamie thought, except when it wasn't. And usually when it wasn't it was because Arley had come with her instead of staying with the babysitter, and often he grew tired and crabby in the classroom. It didn't matter what she did or how many toys she brought along. Sometimes she could buy him off by allowing him to take off his shoes and do sock-skating in the gleaming, newly waxed hallway, or by letting him eat packages and packages of peanut butter crackers and drink juice boxes or do his little air-guitar, rock 'n' roll act for the high-schoolers to laugh at.

But one Friday afternoon, none of that was enough. It was hot and humid, even in the classroom, and Arley was whiny and clingy. It was after he was elephant-walking and knocked into one of the students and spilled her paint box all over the floor that he fell apart. And then when Jamie asked him to help her wipe up the paint, he burst into loud, spurting tears and screamed that he hated everybody in the whole world. So she took him out into the hallway and sat down next to him on the floor.

"What gives here, bunny? Why is everything so hard today?"

He picked at a scab on his knee and wouldn't answer. When she leaned over and touched his arm, he said, "Because I'm sad and I hate everybody."

"Wow. That sounds pretty awful."

He glared at her.

"Is there anything that would help you feel better?"

He stared at the floor for a long time. And then he said, in a voice she could barely hear, "I want to go back to the old house."

She sighed. She'd been thinking about this for a few days herself. "Would a visit there help? Would you like to go, say, swim in the pond this afternoon?"

He wiped his tears with the back of his hand. "Yes," he said, barely audibly.

"Okay, then," she said. After the class was over, they went to the condo and got their bathing suits and towels. For a moment, she contemplated talking him out of it, letting him watch television for the rest of the day instead. She felt a little strange just showing up at the farmhouse again. But then she squared her shoulders. Come on, she said to herself, it's not like I'm doing anything *wrong*. The place was just sitting there waiting to be sold. She might as well use the pond.

But as soon as she swung the car into the driveway, bouncing over the old familiar ruts, her heart started pounding. There was the Realtor Todd Haney's car, parked right by the barn. And oh, God—not Todd's wife, Lainie, too! Lainie Haney, the woman with the most ridiculous name in town, sitting up there in the passenger seat all by herself, fingering her poofy hair while she looked at herself in the rearview mirror. Jamie wanted to slam the car in reverse and take off down the street, but of course she'd been spotted. Then she remembered: Lainie was now the head of the Campfire Kids organization this year—and oh, Cooksey must have told her such awful, awful things!

Sure enough, Lainie was now getting out of the car and coming over to Jamie, but she had a big—and probably fake—smile on her face. Jamie felt herself shrinking. *Shit, shit, shit.*

"Hiiiiii!" Lainie said. "It is so good to see you! What in the world are you doing back here?"

"Oh," Jamie said, wishing she could have avoided this whole problem. It was all she could do to meet Lainie's eyes. "Arley just wanted to see the place again. You know how it is with kids. They don't really *get* when things change."

"We're going for a swim in the pond!" Arley said. "We got our bathing suits!"

Lainie's eyes grew wider, and she smiled at him and ruffled his hair. "What a good idea!" she said. "We're just here because Todd is inside showing the place to a *rather big-deal developer,* who is *very interested* in the *property.*" She'd always had a habit of twisting her mouth and dropping her voice into italicized whispers whenever possible, as if her whole life with her husband revolved around keeping real-estate transactions secret. "I'm just waiting outside in case they need any of the *stats* on the place, you know. He'll be out in a minute, I'm sure."

Arley was pulling on Jamie's arm. "Come on, Mo-ommmm. Let's go swimming."

"Just a minute, honey," Jamie said. She looked at Lainie and tried to think of something wonderfully small-talky to say. Her brain cells seemed to have deserted her.

"Here, I'll walk down to the pond with you," Lainie said. "The truth is, I've been about to call you for days now, so it's good I ran into you."

They made their way through the unmowed grass and down the little hill and over to the pond, which was shining in the sunlight. For a moment, it was so beautiful there that Jamie thought she might not be able to breathe, but Lainie was chirping on and on about kids and summer and the Campfire Kids and how Cooksey was ruining everything.

"When the group heard that he'd—well, what he *said* to you, we were just outraged," she said. "And even his daughter Sue, the one whose kid he started the organization for—well, she was just horrified. She called me the other day and said you should be invited back, and that the kids all loved doing art projects with you, and so it would be really great if you felt like coming back. Would you?"

"Welllll . . ." Jamie said. "I don't know how Cooksey would take that. He made me promise . . ."

"We're standing up to Cooksey," said Lainie. "It's ridiculous how we've let him dictate all the rules. Even his own kids think it's time he let the whole thing go."

"Also, I might be moving away . . ."

"Oh," Lainie said. This seemed to set her back for a moment. But then she said, "Well, what about until you do move? You shouldn't have to lose everything, all your friends, just because Harris died." She reached over and touched Jamie on the arm. "We're your friends, Jamie! Here, you've already lost so much—your *house* and your good *friend* Harris, and I hear Christopher has been taken away . . . here, darling, take a tissue from my purse. Oh, see, I've made you cry, haven't I? I'm sorry. Look, we just want you to come back and be with us. And Arley shouldn't miss out on the good stuff we have planned. Why, we've got the jamboree in another month! As a matter of fact, we're really being selfish here, because we *need* you! Please say you'll come back. For whatever time until you move. The summer, at least. Give us the summer."

"Well," Jamie said. "I don't know. I'm still dealing with so much, and Cooksey really will go ballistic . . ."

"Don't let Cooksey stop you. His daughter is going to handle him. There's a bunch of us who want him out of the whole organization in the first place. We find him really . . . redundant."

Redundant. Jamie laughed.

Lainie's mouth twisted around again. "And anyway, God forgive me, but now that your *sister* isn't seeing Cooksey's *son-in-law,* we have a lot of hope that he'll let up on things. I think that was all it was, really. How could he not like *you?*"

At that moment, Todd Haney came walking down the slope wearing his Realtor suit and expensive-looking shoes and seeming pleased with himself. "Here you are!" he said to his wife. "I leave you in the car, and the next thing I know, you've disappeared on me. Hi, Jamie."

"Hi," she said shyly.

"I was doing good works," Lainie said to her husband. "I think I've just convinced Jamie to come back to the Campfire Kids. And did you finalize with this guy? You're smiling. You did, didn't you?"

"Well, this guy has big plans, so we'll see," Todd said. "He's done some oceanfront properties in Milford and other towns, so he's excited about all this. He's got the capital; he just has to see about some of the permissions. Usual stuff." He stopped and smiled at Jamie and shook her hand. "Good to see you. You doing all right?"

She probably looked like hell, after all that blubbering over being wanted again. She shook his hand and nodded, but tears were so dangerously near the surface that she didn't trust herself to speak.

"Arley and Jamie came to swim in the pond," Lainie said. "I walked them down while you were wrapping up."

"We were actually just going to walk down and *look* at the pond," Jamie said. "Maybe dip a toe in and then head back. Otherwise I would have called you . . . to make sure it was okay for us to be here."

"No, no. Do what you like," he said. "Come swim whenever you feel like it. That's a great idea. Keeps the weeds trampled down so the place looks lived-in."

"What I want is to *sleep* here by the pond!" said Mr. Always Upping the Ante Arley. He was spinning around in circles and jumping up and down, chasing little flashes of minnows in the shallow water and leaping about like a demented elf. His ladybug vest was flapping wildly around his waist. Jamie reached out to pull him over to her, but he skittered, crablike, away from her.

Todd leaned over to her and lowered his voice. "If you *want to* . . . ," he said. "You're welcome to pitch a tent and sleep out here by

the pond. Why not? Hey, you're one of the Campfire Kid families.
That's what that's all about, isn't it? Forget the yoga and the art
projects we put these kids through. Let's see you pitch a tent and do
the summer up right, is what I say. Make a little fire, cook you some
hot dogs and marshmallows. Yum!"

"Well," she said. "Maybe . . ."

"I've got my kids' tent in the car," he said. "Take it. Use it." He
laughed and cupped one hand around his mouth and stage-
whispered, "Keep me from having to take my guys out camping. Better you than me. I need a good bed."

AND SO SHE borrowed the tent and went back to Lucy's and got
sleeping bags and a flashlight. Lucy still wasn't home, so she packed
hot dogs and marshmallows and matches, brought along some blan-
kets and a cooler—and left a note: WE'RE HAVING A CAMPING ADVEN-
TURE. WHO KNEW WE HAD IT IN US? I'LL TALK TO YOU TOMORROW.
SMOOCHES, JAMIE AND ARLEY.

It was lovely, being out there. They put up the tent together, amid
a flurry of disasters involving zippers and tent stakes not working,
which required cussing. But then they triumphed, which included
running in circles around the tent shouting, "Whoo-hooo!" They
swam a little bit in the pond at dusk, and then later they lay on their
backs on the beach and looked up at the constellations. She found at
least four clusters of stars that could possibly be the Big Dipper. The
day's heat seemed to be absorbed back into the earth, and a breeze
came up and tickled their faces. There was the music of crickets and
frogs, and they built a little fire in the sand, using the old wood from
the porch steps.

By the time it had been dark for an hour, the two of them were
ready for bed. They snuggled up in their sleeping bags, and she read
him stories until she was so tired she could barely see the page or hear
her voice over the sound of the peepers and crickets.

"I want to do this every night," Arley said as he drifted off to sleep, and she lay there watching his sweet little face and measuring his breaths until she couldn't stay awake.

They didn't go back home for three days.

"ARE YOU IN danger of becoming peculiar?" Lucy demanded on the fourth day, when Jamie and Arley returned. "Good God. Look at you. You are, aren't you? You're going totally weird on me."

Jamie was in the condo kitchen unpacking the cooler, which was filled with melty ice and some cheese slices, a couple of hot dogs, and some red grapes floating around in it. She looked up and laughed, thinking her sister was teasing her. "Peculiar?"

But she wasn't. "Yeah. I mean, I can see you leading up to some— I don't know—serious psychological *break* with reality, where you don't live with civilization anymore, and you eat nothing but nuts and berries that you've trained your child to forage for you. Because I can't take that. I'm giving you fair warning."

Jamie put the hot dogs in the refrigerator. "Hey, it's called *camping*. And it's fun. If there had been more room in the tent, and if I thought you'd behave yourself, I'd say you should come and join us."

"But you don't even *like* camping." There: another example of being told what she liked and didn't like. "You're just there because of that man. And look at your legs. Ugh. You have a ton of bug bites."

Jamie looked down. "I forgot the mosquito repellent the first night, that's all. I'm fine, believe me."

"And you can't tell me this is good for Arley's asthma. Out in that night air. Sleeping in a tent." Lucy grabbed at a waterlogged grape and munched it down.

"I'm watching him, don't worry," Jamie said. "I'm very attuned to his breathing, you know, and I sleep with the inhaler right beside me. He's doing fine."

"Do you even bother to go to your teaching job anymore?"

"Wait," she said. "Are we having a jokey conversation about my camping out, or is this really something more? Because, of course I go to my teaching job. What's the matter with you?"

"What do *you* think?" Lucy started down the hall to her bedroom, calling back over her shoulder, "Come with me. I have to get ready. I've got actual civilized human beings to deal with. People who wear suits and sleep in real beds."

"Are you going to work?"

"Welllll . . . no." She was rummaging through a drawer, with her back to Jamie. Jamie sat down on the bed, which was still rumpled and unmade. She had to admit that after a few nights of sleeping on the hard ground, the idea of a mattress seemed pretty good. And— she smiled—it was interesting that there was a pair of jockey shorts right in the middle of all this unmade chaos. Bright red ones, too. Not the kind of thing you'd imagine a police officer wearing. But, she mused, that was just the kind of transforming effect her sister had on men: she souped 'em up.

"So . . . really, it's been fun out there sleeping by the pond," she said, stretching out on the bed. "I never knew that camping could be so great, you know? All the stars and the pond noises . . . Oh, and did I tell you? I've been invited back into the Campfire Kids. Lainie Haney told me that she and the group are sort of *phasing* out Cooksey. She said—well, actually, you'll find this amusing—she said that since *you* aren't having your little thing with Handsome Dan anymore, they think Cooksey is more likely not to be such an asshole about my being in the group again. Which is probably wishful thinking, of course, but still . . ."

She stopped talking because Lucy slammed her drawer shut. For a moment, it seemed as if she might be mad, and so Jamie automatically stopped talking and waited. Her sister pulled on a black knit T-shirt that said BEBE on it in rhinestones, and started combing her hair in the mirror.

Jamie got up and started making up the bed, just to give herself something to do. She held up the jockey shorts by her thumb and forefinger and laughed. "Whoo-hoo, look at these babies! Do you suppose that Mike Scanlon is out somewhere patrolling our town without any underwear on? Is he *going commando* while on command?"

"You know, if you'd made just a little more effort, those red undies could be in *your* bed, you know," Lucy said. She saw Jamie's blank face and said, "Mike told me that he'd asked you out first, and you turned him down flat."

Jamie laughed. "Yeah, but he was the cop investigating me for possible homicide. It didn't seem appropriate at the time. Besides—"

"Oh, come on, let's face it. You were never a suspect, and anyway, that's not why you turned him down."

"Okay." Jamie sighed. "Tell me. Why did I turn him down?"

"Because you turn *everybody* down. You're the queen of Just Say No."

"And *why* am I the Queen of Just Say No?"

"Oh, stop being impossible. Who cares about why? You know, I think you need to think about settling down. These are your good years—and look at you. You're spending them dressing like a hobo, hanging out with old guys who drop dead, and now it looks like you've taken up living in the woods in a tent."

"I—"

"No, now hear me out. Just listen to this. I haven't wanted to say anything, but Arley needs a man in his life. Can't you do that for Arley, if not for yourself? I mean, it was bad enough when you were a kid and all you wanted to do was go off by yourself and glue feathers onto pinecones and make purses out of duct tape so other girls could take them to the prom. But, my God, you're grown up now. Don't you want more for yourself than *this*? I mean this in the kindest possible way, Jamie. Is this all you're going to ask of life—for you and your boy?"

Jamie looked down at her hands. Her head felt light, as if maybe there was a hole in it somewhere and all the life force was being whisked away from her. She opened her mouth.

"I mean, here you went and slept with Nate, and I really thought that could have been a *good, healing thing* for you, sort of a launching back into the adult world—but apparently, it's plunged you back into something even more unhealthy. There you are, back at the scene of the crime, as it were . . . and *mooning* over him, mooning over his *father*—I won't even let myself *think* about which one of those men got to you the most. I think you're just stuck, sweetie, and if you're not careful, you're going to turn into one of those peculiar old women who keeps five cats and plays the didgeridoo and . . . and only wants to talk about whether the pinecones are more plentiful this year than last—"

"Stop, please just stop," Jamie said.

"Arley deserves more than that."

Jamie could feel herself getting more mentally ill by the moment. Lucy was right. Arley had been pathetic around Nate. Needy and show-offy and trying too hard—how often had she had to call him off Nate, remind him to use his inside voice or let Christopher answer some of Nate's questions? Hell, he'd even been weird with Todd Haney at the pond. Oh my God. She'd failed him. He was only five years old, and already she'd made his life a catastrophe. She should have stayed with Trace. Or maybe she should have taken off her clothes for the veterinarian she had half a date with three years ago. But he was covered in dog hair! And she hadn't liked him that much! She said in a small voice, "I don't know how."

"You've got to get out there and—did you just say you didn't know how?"

"Yes."

"You don't know *how*? You're kidding, right? Everybody knows how. You smile and flirt and dress cute. You listen to guys when they talk. You act *interested*. And you don't keep looking for reasons to reject them right off the bat. How is it that you don't know this?"

"I just don't. I'm an introvert. I like peace and quiet and not having to do much in a social situation. I'm not like you."

Lucy drew herself up and combed out her hair again. "Okay. Listen. I shouldn't yell at you. I'm sorry. The main thing—the main thing, if you want to meet a guy, is that you just don't say *no* all the time. You know, like with Mike. You didn't even give him a chance . . ."

"Ha-ha! Well, you should be glad I didn't. Maybe I knew he'd be better for you."

"I'm sure that's not what you were thinking. And who knows who he'd be better for? You know?"

"What are you saying? You're crazy about him."

"Yeah. Yeah, I am. He's great. But now we're talking about you."

"Wait. You're *not* crazy about him?"

"Jamie, we are talking about you."

Jamie shut up.

"Now. Here's what I think you should do. Sit down and figure out first what you want in a man—which is a father for Arley, I would think, as well as somebody who's going to be madly in love with *you*—and then go where those guys are. Guys who like kids." She smiled. "You gotta work it a little, honey. That's all. And forgive me, but I don't think you're going to meet a guy out there sleeping next to Nate's pond. Not anybody who's not a psychopathic maniac, at least."

"You're probably right," Jamie said.

"You'd have better luck putting on your bikini top and going out and grilling some chicken on the balcony here," Lucy said, and she wasn't even half-kidding. "Comb out your hair, put on some lipstick, and go outside and say, 'Does anybody know how to get my grill started?' and you'll have somebody in five seconds."

"Ha. I am so not going to ask a man to get my grill started. I'd rather throw myself off the balcony first."

Lucy was studying her as if she was a science project gone seriously awry. "Just take off those ratty clothes, will you, and put on something cute. And some lipstick. Would that *kill* you?"

THE FOLLOWING WEDNESDAY night, Jamie went to a meeting of the Campfire Kids at Lainie Haney's request, and was welcomed back by the group. Todd Haney even stood up and said, with a wink, that he had it on good intelligence that she'd been camping out in a tent at the old Goddard place (how had it already become the *old* Goddard place, she wondered), and that tonight, on that basis *alone,* he'd like to welcome her back by insisting she become the coordinator for the jamboree.

"Already she's braver and knows more about campfires and camping than the rest of us!" he said. "In fact, in what has got to be the best coup I ever pulled, I even gave her *my* tent to use out there, so when my kids whine about wanting to camp in the backyard, I can say in good conscience that our tent is not around!"

Ha-ha-ha. Everybody thought this was hilarious. And what a good idea, to plan the jamboree with a camping component to it. There could be a hike *and* a campout, *and* cooking over the campfire, of course. They got busy, passing around sign-up sheets. They promised to help. They patted her on the back. They praised her for being so brave, sleeping outside. Wow! If only *they* had that kind of time . . . and patience . . . hoo, boy!

And then, when the meeting was over and she was heading out to the parking lot with Arley, who was doing his Hopalong Cassidy walk beside her, one of the fathers sprinted over and caught up with her. He was Brian Spangler, a dermatologist in New Haven whom she'd never talked to before. He always looked at people as if he was studying the lines in their skin and would recommend some wrinkle cream just as soon as they indicated even the slightest interest. His daughter, Gabriella, was fantastic in art, and Jamie had often helped her with her crafts projects.

"Hey, nice job on taking on the jamboree," he said. He had a voice like a morning disk jockey's, smooth and—well, almost oily. But you see, this was exactly the kind of thing Lucy had been talking about. She had to not rule people out right at the beginning by finding fault.

She smiled at him.

"Soooo . . . do you do a lot of camping?"

She said she didn't, but she enjoyed it. And him? Well, he'd done a bit. Hard work, really, camping. And he didn't have much time for it, especially now that he was a *single parent*. There was a beat of silence. And then—hey, would she maybe like to grab a bite sometime?

Now? She couldn't hide her dismay.

No, not now. Goodness. They had the *kids*. He meant the kind of grabbing a bite that included . . . well, a nice restaurant maybe. Perhaps alcohol would be involved. He smiled at her, lifting his eyebrows in a suggestive sort of way.

How bad could this be? Maybe Lucy had been right. Maybe there *were* actually guys out there who had been waiting for her—besides this one, even, who really did sound as though he was playing the part of the phony, debonair, smooth-voiced seducer in some film from the 1950s. Harris would have doubled over laughing to think she was even contemplating going out with Brian Spangler.

But she had to stop thinking of how Harris would react to everything she did. Now that she'd slept with his son, which would have been waaay high on his list of appalling things, she really had to let his opinion waft away. That was it—like the house and the peace and quiet and the laughter . . . just waft away. She was in a new phase of life now. The phase of life in which she was going to run the jamboree and date guys who talked smoothly.

"Okay," she said, and took a deep breath. "Sure. I'll go out with you."

CHAPTER
20

Christopher was charming and adorable at the meeting with Howie. Bright and curious, talkative—and bouncy. Opinionated.

And living up to his reputation as Christopher the Inquisitor, he even asked a million questions.

Okay. So it didn't go all that well, Nate had to admit. True, the kid *had* actually charmed Howie with his little pressed khaki pants and white shirt, and the way he held out his hand and said, "Aloha, Howie. Pleased to meet you." It had been a tad robot-like, but at least he had said it. Nate held his breath as Howie's glance flickered over the kid for a longish moment. Then Howie had ruffled Christopher's hair a bit and said, "Looks like you, Nate. Nice work. So, who's minding him while we get down to brass tacks? We've got a lot of work to do here."

And then, of course, there *wasn't* anybody, so Nate had to proclaim that there wasn't any need, that Christopher was actually a consultant in training—ha-ha-ha—picking up some valuable tips from meeting Howie like this. His ace in the hole—which he was very proud of, as he whispered to Howie—was the portable DVD player he'd brought along, just in case Christopher really wasn't going to be able to sit quietly.

It had been genius to buy that. Nate figured that Christopher could do at least an hour of drawing pictures and wandering around the perimeter of the room before he got bored—and then for the second and third hours (Howie tended to be long-winded), the kid could watch a movie. Nate had bought some cartoon about a character who was a giant sponge or something, and he planned to stick Christopher off in a corner, plug in the player, and . . . voilà! Nate could resume his career as a contributing adult member of a sales team.

And it might have worked, except that Howie had invited along four other sales associates, all of whom needed to discuss their schedules and protocols, and who didn't find it fascinating that Christopher wanted to tell them that his birthday was next month and that he didn't like to take showers, because the water banged on his head too hard.

And then, when Nate had redirected this line of talk, Christopher needed to sit in a swivel chair right next to Nate and spin in circles until he screamed with joy. And then he needed to go to the bathroom five separate times, during which he sang loud songs to himself in the stall and would not be rushed. And then the DVD player, once it was actually going, had a mysterious tendency to suddenly be turned up to full volume, requiring Nate to go over and turn it down and plead with it not to mysteriously do that again.

None of this was *horrible,* exactly. It wasn't as if Christopher had let loose a full-throated temper tantrum, or had thrown up on Howie's natty Hawaiian shirt. It was just that Nate had been a wreck before, during, and after the meeting, and, although he thought that Christopher had been splendid, he found himself uncomfortably enduring the disbelieving stares of his colleagues as the meeting kept getting interrupted.

Yeah. That's the way he himself would have felt before, too, if somebody had brought a kid to a sales meeting. He knew.

But there was even worse to come. He was handed a list of five new clients, all of whom needed immediate attention, of the in-person variety.

He and Christopher—and five hundred dollars' worth of toys—were going on the road. Starting next Tuesday, four days away.

The meeting had broken up, and Nate had stood there sweating and watching as Christopher carefully walked across the seats of each swivel chair, from one to the next, holding his arms aloft and emitting little screechy noises as he made his way along.

"You want my advice? You've got to get yourself a nanny, boy," Howie said. His eyes were cold now, as if he'd completely forgotten that Nate was his protégé, practically his son.

"TINA," HE SAID into her voice mail at three in the morning, from the blowup bed in the living room. "Tina, I know you're in Barcelona, where it is a decent time of day. I know you're probably awake. I have to insist that you come to California immediately and marry me this afternoon and be a mother to my child. Correction: a *stay-at-home mother to my child.* It will be the most rewarding thing you will ever do in your whole life." He waited. "Good-bye now. I am going to go beat my head against the wall."

He flipped the phone shut, smacked himself on the forehead, then called her back.

"I think I might have forgotten to say that I love you."

His hand hovered over the phone after he'd hung up. He almost called Jamie. She would love the story about Christopher saying that showers hurt his head too much. He pictured how she'd look when she laughed.

He punched in the area code and then clicked off.

It wasn't right to call a woman ten seconds after you'd told another woman you loved her. The woman you'd cheated on with her. That, as the dreaded Denise Morgan would no doubt have pointed out to him, was just further evidence that he was still playing kissing games.

· . . .

SO HE WAS going to have to hire a nanny. Howie had told him a long time ago that when you are looking to employ somebody, you had to hire from the gut. "I look 'em in the eyes, and if I feel the gut say yes, then I sign 'em," he'd said.

Nate wasn't positive he had a gut for nannies—and to read Internet sites about the subject, it seemed the general consensus was that hiring a nanny was akin to getting married. You had to find the perfect fit. Not just anybody who could prove she wasn't an axe murderer would do. There had to be *chemistry.*

Lorelei Swinson was perfect. He had found her card on the bulletin board at the grocery store, and she'd come right over when he called. He was a little unnerved by how nicely displayed her boobs were, and the fact that she was wearing boots (white ones) in the summertime—but what the hell? What was he, a style cop? She had red hair all in ringlets and bright blue, blue eyes, and she said she had lots of experience taking care of her little nephews every summer. When she gushed over Christopher, he hired her on the spot.

But then it turned out she didn't have a car and had lost her license anyway—and as much as Nate hated to think of Christopher being ferried about on the freeways of L.A. by a stranger, he could *not* picture his son trapped in this hellhole of an apartment for days at a time. So, after an evening of thinking about it, he had to call Lorelei back and rescind the offer.

After that, he entered a stretch of bad-hiring karma. The hire-from-the-gut gods were apparently not easy to appease.

There was Pauline, who believed in spanking. "Why else is your hand the same size as a kid's bottom, eh?"

And Edna, who was so old her knees cracked whenever she walked. She spent an hour explaining that the avian flu was going to kill off a third of the population in another five years, and that after that there would be widespread rioting as people fought for food and killed off another third of the population. Also, she said, she would need a better mattress. She had arthur-itis, she said.

Linda said she'd gotten fired from her last job because they had a nanny cam, which was so totally unfair. The camera *distorts* things so much, you know. Nate didn't want to know.

He settled into a low-grade panic. He was starting to wake up in the middle of the night noticing that the heft of the air was keeping him awake. And Christopher had all but taken over the double bed in the bedroom—but so what? At least with the kid in the bedroom, Nate could close the door and turn on the television without waking him up. And he could heat himself up some frozen French fries in the kitchen, guzzle milk straight from the carton, walk around in his underwear, drink beer, read his notes for his upcoming consults, scratch his privates—do *whatever.* Watch the news, even, without having to explain why people killed each other all the time, or why banks got robbed, and why that man said that bad word.

They had accomplished a lot together in their first week of living on their own. They'd done their laundry at the Laundromat, they'd cooked hot dogs and hamburgers in the apartment kitchen, and they'd gotten haircuts together. Nate had learned that kids don't shampoo their hair without being threatened. He'd discussed poops that were too stubborn to come out, and prescribed patience and a book to read. Three times he'd been tempted to call Jamie when things got a little squirrelly—like when he couldn't remember the rule about peanut butter sandwiches, or which rewards worked to get Christopher to do things, or what you were supposed to say about the problem of nightmares.

But he had managed not to call her. If there was any hardship to this life, it was this: that he was tired, so very achingly tired of having to do it all himself. Of even answering the questions. Christopher must have asked him at least five thousand a day, many of them along the lines of "Can a ferret tell when he has run a whole mile, or does he think he just went an inch?" and "Why don't animals have last names?" and "Why do they have ponies when they already have horses?" Really. He should categorize this stuff, get a tape-recording of himself saying, "I DO NOT KNOW."

THEN, ON THE national news, a story broke about a nanny and her boyfriend strangling a kid. And although he would have been the first to point out that in 99.9 percent of the cases, nannies were fine—still, he quit looking.

And so Tuesday morning came, and finding themselves nanny-less, the two Goddard men packed up their suitcases and drove to the airport for their flight to San Francisco. It was five o'clock in the morning, and for a guy who'd stayed up all night tossing and turning on the blowup bed, Nate was irrationally happy. The plan, carefully worked out, was this: they would stay three days in San Francisco while Nate did his thing for a small pharmaceutical company, then head to San Antonio for a couple of days with a guy who owned a baseball team, and then off to Cleveland, where a chain of vegan health-food stores awaited him—and then there'd be a few days off and they would meet up with Tina in Boston.

That was why he was cheerful. There would be a hotel room, there would be someone to eat meals with in the restaurant, and as a bonus, there would be someone to answer even a third of the five thousand questions Christopher posed. Even if she just fielded the occasional inquiry, it would be heaven.

He looked over at Christopher, sitting quietly on the seat next to him, playing with Nate's BlackBerry. Punching buttons and frowning at the thing. God, he thought, this whole arrangement was *so* going to work. So what that he didn't have a nanny? He had a great kid and a good attitude, and he was smart, and more and more, it was looking like he *could* do this job and raise the kid at the same time. For one thing, he'd been working for Howie's company so long it was second nature to him; hell, he didn't *have* to spend all his time studying up the stats like the young guys did. He was *ready,* baby. Ready for anything.

And wasn't it fucking wonderful to have his kid along with him, rather than having left him behind in that apartment, worrying that he was with somebody like Lorelei Swinson, who surely would not strangle anybody but who was quite likely to pick up a man at the corner and let him have wild sex with her.

Sex. Wow. This may have been the *real* reason he was so cheerful at this hour of the morning: once Tina got there, they could have *sex*. Real, two-people kind of sex.

He looked down at his laptop, where he was taking a few minutes to brush up on sales stats for the pharmaceutical company while he waited for the plane to board. The BlackBerry chimed the way it did when there was a new e-mail.

"Hey, pal, you gotta hand it over when it makes that noise, remember," he said.

"But give it back to me," Christopher said. He had become obsessed with the thing.

Nate scrolled down absently, and then there it was: an e-mail from Jamie. He stared at her name lit up on the small screen: Jamie McClintock. *Speaking of sex,* he thought. He thought of her in that bed, and his groin tightened. He shifted in his seat, gave his laptop a new strategic placement. He knew he should feel guilty for having cheated on Tina that way, but he didn't. Not one bit.

DEAR NATE, she'd written. HOPE ALL IS GOOD WITH FATHERHOOD AND THE DREAM OF THE SALESMAN/VAGABOND LIFE. ARLEY WANTED ME TO LET HIM WRITE A MESSAGE TO CHRISTOPHER. HERE'S WHAT HE'S DICTATING TO ME: CHRISTOPHER, YOU MUST WRITE BACK AND TELL ME IF YOU WANT MY LADYBUG VEST BECAUSE I AM NOW GOING TO BE A LIZARD BOY. I HOPE YOU LIKE L.A. DID YOU GET A NEW MOM YET? ARE YOU GOING TO COME BACK WHEN IT'S YOUR BIRTHDAY? WE COULD GO RIDE THE PONIES AGAIN LIKE LAST TIME. LAST NIGHT I ATE PIZZA AND THE CHEESE FELL ON MY SHOE.

He read it aloud to Christopher, who then insisted on taking the BlackBerry back and studying it, as if for clues. "Why does he want to know if I have a new mom yet?"

"Don't know, pal."

"Am I still getting a new mom?"

"Well . . . sure. If she ever gets here. Someday." He looked up to see a woman overhearing him. She smiled shyly and turned away.

"*Am* I going to ride ponies on my birthday?"

"Could be. We don't know. Your birthday isn't for another month."

"You have to reserve the ponies, you know. You can't just show up and ask for a pony just because it's your birthday."

Nate looked at him. "We don't know where we'll be. That's the part about our travel life that makes it so *interesting,* remember? Maybe we'll be riding the ponies in San Francisco or San Antonio. That's why our lives are more exciting and fun than other people's. Remember?"

"*No.*" Christopher stubbed his toe into the floor and then slumped down in his seat. "I think I want a BlackBerry of my very own. And I want to go see Arley."

"Yeah, well, we'll just have to see about *that,*" Nate said. The woman turned back and smiled at him again. She had the same kind of hair Jamie did.

God, he needed Tina to come so much. He took back the Black-Berry, over Christopher's howls, and e-mailed her: TWO MORE WEEKS. HOPE YOU'RE READY FOR ME.

"Now write to Arley," Christopher commanded. "Tell him this: I don't have a new mom. I ride on airplanes all the time. I want the lady-bug vest. And I want to come home for a pony ride. I want to see Jamie. Bye." He stopped and looked at Nate. "*Write it,*" he commanded.

He wrote it and then he added, DEAR JAMIE, SITTING IN AIRPORT, WRITING TO U ON MY B-BERRY. ON THE WAY TO SAN FRAN, THEN SAN ANTONE, THEN CLEVELAND. BOY IN TOW. HE'S GREAT. WHO KNEW THIS COULD WORK? OH, YEAH. ME. ☺ He thought a minute, then typed: WORK'G ON GETT'G HIM TO EAT OREOS LIKE NORMAL BOY. HIGH HOPES. ALSO — DO NOT SEND LADYBUG VEST. NO NO NO. LOL. After a moment of deep thought, he typed, xoxo, n.

And then wished he had taken at least one of the xo's back before pressing the Send button.

CHAPTER
21

Jamie had to dress up to go out with Brian Spangler. Every single time. Lucy insisted. In fact, the way Lucy carried on, you would have thought that any evening now, Brian was going to suggest they swing by the justice of the peace and have a quickie wedding right after dinner, and Jamie should look presentable for it. She did a parody of an ethnic mom: "Dahlink, he's a *doctor*. Be noice to him!"

Lucy, who had taken on Jamie's love life as her personal project, even insisted on drawing up a list of topics Jamie and Brian could discuss—and even though it was embarrassing, really it helped out a lot. Here were the categories Lucy said would be acceptable: the beauty of nature, possible future art projects, the surprising resilience of children, funny things kids say, puppies and kittens. The latter she'd added just to be amusing. Ha-ha-ha.

"And don't forget skin diseases," Jamie said. "I'm sure that's what a dermatologist would rather talk about. I could brush up on my rashes, if I really cared."

"You know, you really do have a bad attitude," Lucy said. "If in doubt, you can always fall back on the weather. People love to discuss weather. But, really, stay away from current events, politics, religion, money, and your past bad relationships with men. And if he wants to talk about his ex-wife, let him. But do not judge her. This is very important."

Nothing that happened between her and Brian ever felt as if it was going to lead to a visit to the justice of the peace, however. He was a nice enough man, Jamie thought, but he did tend to drone on about his ex-wife and her new boyfriend and how that made him feel. (It made him feel bad.) All he cared about were people's outside surfaces. He told her nearly everyone would benefit by having cosmetic work done.

When she asked him why, he said, "Why not? It's easy, it's inexpensive these days, and it can make a huge difference in how a person feels about aging. The human race doesn't have to look so *tired,* you know."

She sat across from him in restaurants or next to him at the movies and felt like an imposter. She was tired, and she was sure she must look it—even though she was wearing makeup, and clothes she would never normally wear: dresses and silk things that belonged to Lucy. One night she realized she had forgotten to do her nails, and so she spent the entire evening with her fingers curled under so he wouldn't notice.

After the third date she decided this was a ridiculous way to feel and that she shouldn't be dating him anymore. Besides, she didn't like the way he kissed, and she suspected she wouldn't like anything else he did to her body, either. So after they finished dinner, when he suggested they go over to his place, she said quietly, "I think, Brian, that I just want to go home, if you don't mind."

"Go home? But the night is still young," he said. A grim line settled across his features as if a shadow had fallen. If he had seen himself in the mirror just then, he would have probably suggested he have a little facial work done himself.

Possibly, she thought, this grimness had to do with the money he'd spent on her. Here he'd bought her dinner three times, and now, as horrible as it sounded, it was time for the payoff. He always mentioned money whenever he talked about his ex-wife. It was one of his issues. No doubt he'd tallied up the cost of the meals and now he expected her to sleep with him.

Only she couldn't. Not only because she didn't want to, but also because she was wearing a stupid padded bra that belonged to Lucy. It had occurred to her that he was just the type to be disappointed when *that* came off and she proved to be so . . . inadequate. And besides that, her hair was sprayed nearly to rigor mortis, and even her eyelashes felt as if they had been coated with tar. She wanted to go home and take all of this off and stand underneath a hot, steamy shower until she forgot what his face looked like.

"I'm sorry," she said. "I'm just a mess. I shouldn't be inflicting myself on nice people anymore."

"No, it's okay," he said tightly. "I completely understand the grief response."

"The . . . grief response?"

"Yeah. Your boyfriend *died*. That's gotta hurt a lot."

"My boyfriend?" she said blankly. For a moment she couldn't imagine what he meant.

"Harris Goddard?" he said. "Your boyfriend."

"Oh, no, he wasn't my boyfriend," she said. "We were just friends."

"Yeah," he said. "Okay."

"No, really."

"Oh, so you just don't like me then, huh?" he said with a bitter little laugh.

"No, no! Oh, God no. It's not you at all. Really. It's me."

"Forget it."

"No. You know what it is? I feel like a fake here. Look at me. See my hair? It's all sprayed up into these stupid curls. And these eyelashes—you think these are the way my eyelashes really are? These are about ten times heavier than mine. And my face is coated with all this goopy makeup my sister made me wear because you're a dermatologist and she said I had to look good. Isn't that laughable? Like you can't see through makeup! And—also, well, I hate to tell you, but this bra is like ninety percent foam rubber." She laughed and could hear the hysteria in her voice. "I'm ridiculous here! I don't even own this dress! I don't own *any* of the dresses I've gone out with you in. I wear stupid-looking long skirts and T-shirts all the time, and I spend my days covered in paint and glue."

In the movies, the man would have turned and said, "But I don't care about any of that. Oh, you poor thing! Didn't you know that it was *you* I wanted all along, not these stupid clothes and eyelashes of yours?"

Instead, Brian Spangler let out a high-pitched, half-hysterical laugh as he pulled over to the curb in front of Lucy's condo. She hadn't even realized he'd changed course and was driving her home. But there they were. He sat in the car staring at his hands. He looked as if he was mortified for her. Then he said, "You want me to walk you to the door? I will."

"No!" she said. "No, I'm fine. I'll walk myself."

"Okay," he said.

She got out of the car. She started to say she was sorry, but in fact, she wasn't all that sorry. If she'd had money, she would have written him a check right there for the dinners he'd paid for. But, you know, them's the breaks. Besides, she'd listened to a whole bunch of stories about his wife. She'd even given him advice.

Maybe they were even.

"Well . . . good-bye," she said. She got out of the car . . . and he was off.

She felt better with each step she took toward Lucy's apartment. By the time she reached the door and was putting her key in the lock, she was quite giddy over the idea of bursting out of her dress, flinging her padded bra skyward, ripping off the black lace undies (the "just-in-case, third-date undies," Lucy had called them) and sticking her head in the sink to rinse out the hairspray.

"Lucy!" she called when she walked into the air-conditioned coolness of the apartment. "Lucy, you're going to be so ashamed of me, but I'm free! Lord almighty, I'm free at last!"

She bounded up the stairs to the second floor of the condo, and then came to a dead halt.

Handsome Dan, dressed in a red wife-beater T-shirt and jockey shorts and holding an unlit cigarette, was standing before her, a tight smile on his glazed-over, robot-like features.

"I'm baaaack," he said, and laughed. "Wow, you look different! You actually look good."

"Bite me," she said.

That night, she sat down and e-mailed Shana: PLEASE, PLEASE SAY THERE IS GOING TO BE AN OPENING FOR AN ART TEACHER AT PENDLETON. I HAVE APPARENTLY USED UP BOTH NEW YORK AND CONNECTICUT, AND NOW MUST START ON VERMONT. PLEAD MY CASE! ARLEY AND I NEED A NICE RESIDENTIAL SCHOOL TO ESCAPE TO.

The next morning Shana e-mailed her back: GR8 NEWS. ART TEACHER IS PREGO AND NOW LOOKS LIKE SHE'S TAKG A YR OFF INSTEAD OF 6 WKS. UR NAME GOES IN HOPPER TOMORROW.☺

Tina, thank God, was still exactly his type. He had been traveling with Christopher for nearly three weeks, and now he and
Tina had three days together in a hotel in Boston, before he had to be
in Miami, and all he wanted was to fall down on the marble floor of
the hotel lobby and weep from gratitude at the sight of her. Gratitude
and exhaustion. Because you never know about that kind of thing, if
people will stay the way you left them.

But here she was, still the same perky made-to-order woman
she'd been when he'd last seen her. Her skinny, taut body was
poured into a black sundress, and her long, tanned legs were
carrying her quickly toward him, across the lobby. She was clean and
put-together and unencumbered, and her black hair was sticking up
in little points, all moussed together like hair from the future. Someday everybody would have such cute, sticking-up hair; they just
hadn't figured out yet how to get it like Tina had. She looked, in
fact, like a character from a very edgy, fun cartoon, peeking
out through almost impossibly wide eyes beneath strands of spiky
bangs.

"Here she is," he said to Christopher, as Tina threaded her way through the potted plants and the ambling tourists. "God, just look at her. Isn't she beautiful?"

"Why does her hair stick up like that?" Christopher said before she got close to them. Nate couldn't answer; he was busy falling on Tina as if she was a piece of bologna and he was a junkyard dog. After he forced himself to stop hugging and kissing her, he thrust Christopher forward, as if he was offering a momentous present at a time of great portent.

"*This,*" he said, hating himself for the way his voice trembled, "is my son. Christopher Harris Goddard, say hello to Tina."

There was a long silence. Tina held out her hand and then put it down again.

"Ummmmm . . . I don't really want to," the kid said.

"Come on! Come *on*. You've been waiting to meet her. Of *course* you want to say hello."

"I haven't been waiting to meet her! And I *don't* want to say hello." Christopher started play-marching around Nate, smiling to himself as if he was imitating some crazy person hearing voices.

Nate could feel himself starting to lose it. "Well, do it anyway. Do it because I say so."

"No! No! No!" Christopher was grinning, holding onto Nate's hand and standing on his feet, twisting himself around in a circle that almost pulled the two of them to the floor. That's when Nate spotted his BlackBerry in Christopher's pocket. He snatched it back. The kid howled, as if he'd been struck.

"I'm not giving it back to you until you say hello to Tina! I'm not!" He held it up over his head.

"GIVE IT BACK TO ME! GIVE IT BACK!"

People in the lobby were starting to step around them, looking alarmed.

"No, no, no," Tina said. "Hold on. This isn't the right way for things to go."

Nate looked at her, mute with thankfulness. She was going to be the grown-up they needed here. She would know just how to take over and fix things. He and Christopher had been traveling for too long and they needed civilizing. Last night they'd had a burping contest in bed. If they were left alone for even one more day, who knew what would become of them?

Tina linked her arm into Nate's and said in a little singsong, "If he doesn't want to say hello to me, then fine. I won't say hello to him, either! Let's all of us just go into the hotel bar and I'll tell you all about Barcelona, and we'll ignore Christopher until he wants to be a good boy and join us. Maybe he should even sit at another table and we won't talk to him or look at him."

Nate had a moment of shock, but Christopher said, "Good. And give me back the BlackBerry."

THE HOTEL RESERVATION was for a suite—so Christopher could sleep in a separate room and Nate and Tina could have some privacy, but there was a convention going on, and—well, the reservation had gone missing.

"Mistakes were made," the desk manager said in the bored tone of somebody who did not have the slightest intention of solving anything. "We're very sorry, sir. All we can offer you is a regular room, and we'll bring in a cot."

Nate could feel the muscle in his jaw pulsing and his Adam's apple going in and out like it might explode. He wanted to take the clerk, with his knowing little pig-faced expression, and push his nose in. He wanted to take off his shoe and start banging it on the marble counter. After twelve days of taking Christopher to every sales meeting, after trying to talk to clients about their telecommunications needs while his child danced about the room or darted out in the hallways, or else breathed on the clients, he wanted to take the guy by the collar and say, "Find me a suite so I can be alone with this woman, and I will pay you a million dollars!"

"Couldn't we just put him out in the hallway?" Tina joked. At least, Nate *assumed* she was joking.

When they got up to the room, Christopher performed the newly discovered ritual he had come to reserve for hotel rooms: he opened and closed all the closet doors and dresser drawers, ran and turned on the water in the sink and the shower, hid in the closet while Nate pretended to look for him, turned on the TV set and the radio, punched the buttons on the telephone until Nate told him to stop, then lay on the floor and looked underneath the beds in case anybody had left anything there. In San Antonio he had found a quarter, two torn-up credit card receipts, and a picture of a baby. These were now his treasures, which he carried every day in his pockets. *Had* to have them. He and Nate couldn't leave a hotel room until these items were secured.

Once all this had been accomplished, Nate found some children's cartoon show on the television and insisted that Christopher watch it. Tina announced that the very worst part of having a boy in the same room was that she would now have to dress and undress in the dinky little bathroom, and it was such a drag to have to carry all her clothing in there each and every time.

"That's not the worst part," Nate whispered, and snaked his arm around her waist and kissed her on the nose. "That is by far not the worst part. Remember back to naked couplings on the hotel floor while we drank room-service daiquiris, and then you'll have some idea of the worst part."

She kissed him back on his nose, and then moved away from him and brushed her bangs out of her eyes. "What *are* we going to do having him with us every second?"

"I've been asking myself that now for three whole weeks," he said and flopped down on the bed. "We've done museums, we've visited malls and toy stores. I think I've eaten in half the Chuck E. Cheese restaurants in America . . ."

"Chuckie what?" she said, and then held her hand up. "Wait. Don't tell me. I don't even *want* to know."

"You know, baby, he *does* go to sleep eventually . . . and he'll have a cot. We can, you know, when that finally happens . . ." He pulled her over to him on the bed. Christopher was sitting on the floor, staring at the TV, which was blaring ridiculous flute music while a big blue dog romped around on the screen.

Tina was distracted and irritated. "You don't think I'm going to be able to relax enough for *that* with a kid in the same room, do you?"

"Under the circumstances—that it's been *weeks* since we've had at each other—I'd say *maybe* you could manage," he said in a low voice, playing with the strap of her sundress. "You know . . . in the dark, deep of night, when we know he's safely off to dreamland. Couldn't you? Hmmm?" He kissed her shoulder.

"I don't know. It seems a little pervy to me."

"Pervy? Are you insane, woman? We're not inviting him to join us. *That* would be pervy. We're being . . . cleverly opportunistic. That's the way it is in the parent game. You take what you can get. Believe me, he sleeps like a log. Besides, it'll be exciting."

To his delight, she suddenly stretched out beside him on the bed. "Speaking of exciting, I have two verrry major exciting things to tell you," she said. "One, I really *nailed* it in Barcelona. I had those guys eating out of my hand, and I want to tell you all about it because you'll be so proud of me! And *two*—this you're *really* going to find exciting—"

"I find *you* exciting," he said. "And I may just need to hunt down those Barcelona guys and tell them no more eating out of your hand, or anything else."

"Oh, stop. The *second* thing is—"

"Oh, baby, I can't wait."

"I bought a BMW convertible!"

He settled himself back on the pillows and looked at her, trying not to let the disappointment play on his features.

"*Did* you now?" he said, and she smiled, held his hand, and proceeded to tell him about the sales meetings at which she'd triumphed, culminating in the unexpected flourish with the signing of the contracts, which segued nicely into the recounting of all the *Consumer Reports* reading she'd done before she'd bought the BMW, *then* shopping for it in her very limited spare time, and what her father thought of the car, and her brother, and her uncle Fred, and how she'd picked the color, and the fact that she'd gotten the five-year warranty instead of the three . . .

Just when he thought his head was going to explode into a million pieces from hearing about all this and pretending he gave a fuck, the TV show ended and Christopher climbed up on the bed and said he was hungry. If Nate had learned anything in the last three weeks, it was that Jamie had been right: don't let the kid get overhungry. Total meltdown. Nate leapt off the bed, and with Tina blinking and saying she had never eaten dinner this early in her life, he guided the two of them out of the hotel, onto the street and into the first place he saw that had a kids' meal special.

THERE WAS YET another thing looming on his personal learning curve: a single guy with a kid can talk his squeamish girlfriend into having sex with him when they share a room with the kid. It's just that the sex has to take place in a hotel bathroom. And it requires a whole carload of candles and some rose-scented bubble bath, and a locked door.

He leaned her up against the wall of the bathroom while candles flickered on every possible surface. Twenty-six votive candles. She was fretting over every aspect, including that the tile was cold against her back, that Christopher might hear them and wake up, that the candles might set off the smoke alarms in the hotel, and that the bubble bath she'd just taken was going to dry out her skin.

He finally started laughing and placed his index finger over her lips. "Shhh, you," he said. "I know what you're really anxious about. That I'm going to turn into a different person now that I have a kid. But I'm the same guy. I tell you, I swear to you, everything is just the same."

"How can you say that?" she whispered. "Nothing is the same."

He took off his clothes and turned around, flexed his muscles, did a little butt-waggling. "Look at me. Same."

"Well, *that's* the same. But nothing else is. Besides that, your kid hates me."

"He hates me, too, and it's still going to be okay," he said. He placed both his hands against the wall near her head and leaned down and kissed her nose. "Believe me, if I can do it, you can, too. Anyway, you're *great* with him. Tonight, when he wanted cheese pizza, and I wanted mushroom and onion, and you offered to share the cheese one with him, that was so nice of you."

"I can't believe you have to reach that far down to find something I did right," she said. "I couldn't even get him to say hello to me."

"Aw, it was just that he was tired from being on the plane, and he was trying to assert himself," Nate said. He ran his finger along her jawline and brushed back her bangs, which were so stiff they bounced right back into place. He laughed. "What—do you spring-load these things or something? Are they made of human materials?"

"Stop it," she said. "What if I never become friends with him? What then?"

"Well . . . ," he said slowly. He traced her nipple with his index finger. "Well, if you never become friends with him, then we'll be like nine tenths of other American families, I guess, where people have problems and they have to try harder. Like the family I grew up in. But it's not going to come to that. He's *great.* And you're great. And it'll all work out. You'll be the only mom he knows."

"You really think we should still get married?" she said.

"Let's not try to figure everything out tonight. This is just day one, you silly little woman, you. How many people hit it out of the park at their first at-bat? Now could we . . . you know . . . like *do it*?"

"Okay, but we can't make any noise," she said.

He smiled at her. "Okay, so we'll pantomime. Now, would you like me to make a bed for us on the floor with the towels?"

"I don't know. I'm nervous. I guess so."

He made them a bed with all the fluffy white towels and lowered her down onto it. He was nearly out of his mind with desire by the time he positioned himself above her, his head practically knocking into the sink and his feet in the shower.

Just as he leaned down to kiss her, there were footsteps running across the floor, and then the door opened. *The locked door just opened.* Tina squealed and grabbed a towel and put it over herself.

"I hafta go to the bathroom," Christopher said. "And why does it smell like matches in here?"

OVER THE NEXT few days, they did everything tourists with kids do while in Boston: they visited the children's museum, Faneuil Hall, Paul Revere's house. They went to the Boston Tea Party site. They ate hot dogs and peanut butter sandwiches for lunch.

The only trouble was, it was Nate and Christopher doing these things alone most of the time. Tina claimed she was not all that enthusiastic about history, and she hated standing in line and dealing with crowds. She wanted to sleep late, she said. Besides, she had work calls to make. Her hair needed cutting. She wanted a manicure and a pedicure, and needed to go to the tanning salon.

"Besides, you guys need some male bonding time," she said. Late at night, when they were back in the hotel room and Christopher was asleep, she said that while she *loved* kids in the abstract, she could see that Christopher didn't really like her. He *glared* at her when Nate wasn't looking. The only question he'd ever directly asked her was why her hair had to stick up like that.

"What did you tell him?" Nate asked her, grinning. "Come on. Lots of people want to know how you get your hair to do *that.* It's the talk of the streets."

She didn't smile. "This is a big problem, Nate," she said. "He doesn't like me, and he doesn't want me around. Believe me, I'm doing you a favor when I don't come along."

Nate was so tired that he didn't know what was a problem and what wasn't anymore. He would have liked to suggest that she not speak to Christopher in baby talk. And that she might think of fun things they could do once in a while, and maybe not look so tragic when she didn't get her way. Instead, as they were sitting one night on the tile floor of the candlelit bathroom, he said to her that he knew Christopher was a hard kid. He said again that these things took time, that she shouldn't feel bad about herself.

"Listen," she said. "I'm going to fly out tomorrow. I know it's a day earlier than we agreed, but I want to get to Portland early for my meeting, maybe meet with some of the company people ahead of time. And I just think it's best for the time being, you and me being . . . you know . . ."

"Okay," he said.

She suddenly laughed and poked him with her big toe. "Hey, look at you! Look at that long face. You know, I just can't get over what father material you turned out to be. You're, like, amazing with him. You never lose your patience."

He knew what that meant. It meant you never lost your patience when anybody could see that you should have.

AND THEN, THE next morning, something happened that changed everything. Nate just wished to hell he knew what it was.

He'd left the two of them alone in the morning while he ran out for breakfast, and when he came back to the hotel room a half hour later, anxious and sweaty but bearing coffees and juices and plenty of warm, chewy bagels, the air had changed somehow. He knew how to suss out a mood change. In fact, if he'd been on a sales call and these were clients, on the basis of this mood alone, he would have gotten the signing pen ready and started pulling the contracts out of his briefcase.

Tina was sitting on the floor next to Christopher looking at his treasures as if they were remnants of the Holy Grail. The torn receipts, the quarter, and the picture of a baby were being held on display for her approval and—get this!—she was *giving it,* and not in a condescending way, either. She was leaning over them and studying them very seriously. And Christopher, although still hanging back just a little bit, was at least *talking*.

Nate looked from one of them to the other, and then he spread out the feast on the floor on a blanket. Tina actually ate half a bagel with cream cheese and didn't once complain about how it was going to make her fat. And—surprise of surprises—when Nate went in a bit later to get in the shower, she showed up in the stall next to him. Naked and ready to soap him up.

"Where's Christopher?" he said to her, blinking in surprise.

"Watching cartoons. I didn't think you'd mind." She handed him the bar of Ivory so he could soap her breasts, which he very willingly did.

They had sex in the shower while the water ran down on top of them and between them. He wouldn't characterize this as "making love," no matter how you looked at it. It took all his concentration to keep from sliding down and dying by banging his head against the tile, but if this was the sex being offered—hell, he could adjust.

When it was over, she nibbled on his ear and whispered, "So tell me. Have you been getting any action since I saw you last? Did you end up taking that funeral director up on her offer?"

"Funeral director?"

"The one you dated in high school, silly."

"Oh! Pamela Nash-Brenner. Oh, ha-ha-ha. That's right. I told you about her. No. No, nothing. Good God, no."

She stroked him and smiled up into his eyes. "And how about *Jamie*?"

"Jamie?"

"Yeah. You kinda failed to mention *her* to me. I had to hear from Christopher that there was a woman you were staying with . . ."

"Oh, did I forget to tell you about Jamie? Oh, yeah. She was just my father's friend. Turned out she was living in the house with him." Her face swam up in front of him; her *whole body* swam up in front of him. *Go away.*

Tina was looking at him closely and smiling in a weird way. God only knew what she thought she was seeing on his face. He consciously relaxed his features, made his breathing regular.

She leaned over and kissed him and started walking her fingers along his chest hair. "And I hear she's a young mom. Christopher told me that she's beee-yooo-tiful, and that his Da loved her, and that she is the mom of somebody named Arley, and that he misses her, and that she paints pictures and—ooh, what else did I learn? Oh, that she knows how to make pancakes that look like bears, and that she likes *you*."

"He told you all that? My, he's gotten quite talkative."

"Yeah, and that you sign your e-mails to her 'xoxo.' Not even just *one x* and one *o*. Two!"

"Wha—? *What?* Now, I *know* he didn't tell you that."

"Christopher was showing off your BlackBerry," she said. "He's quite obsessed with it, you know."

"I know that, but—"

"And I read what you wrote to her," she said. "I know that was naughty of me. But then even naughtier, I read what she wrote back to you."

"What she wrote back to me?" he said. Jamie hadn't written back to him. Too late, he realized Tina was staring at him, measuring something in his expression.

"She wrote a whole long letter back to you," she said in baby talk. Her eyes were dancing. "How much she *wuvs* you and how she wants to marry you and have babies with you and fly with you all over the world."

"Ha-ha," he said.

"Oh, and there's something about a ladybug vest. But I want to make love again," she said.

"I—can't. We just did it. What's gotten into you anyway? You wouldn't even touch me for the last three days—"

"I've gotten used to the situation. And maybe I decided I *can* be a stepmother. You know?"

He felt overwhelmed for a moment. He wanted to put her in suspended animation for a moment, to step out of the picture, shake the water from his ears, maybe knock himself in the head a few times, figure out what fucked-up impulse all this was coming from. This couldn't be real. Worse, he wanted to go and find his BlackBerry and find out what the hell Jamie *had* said to him.

But there was no time. She needed kissing *bad,* and he took care of that. Later that afternoon, when her plane took off, he was still shaking a little from the throw-down hug and kiss she'd given him at the airport and the way she'd grabbed little Christopher and spun him around in near delirium before she left for the security line.

"I'll see *you . . . soon!*" she'd said to him. And then she was off, calling them "my men," and then merrily waving to them until the last possible second. As soon as she was out of sight, Nate thought that perhaps most of the oxygen had gone along with her. He opened the BlackBerry. Sure enough, there was a note from Jamie. It said: N: SO GLAD CHRISTOPHER IS BECOMING AN EXECUTIVE. I THINK HE NEEDS THE LADYBUG VEST. REMIND HIM OF HIS ROOTS. DON'T SWEAT THE OREO THING. ECCENTRICITY IS GOOD. J.

No *xoxo.*

"Whew," he said to Christopher and jammed his hands down in his pockets. Tomorrow they were headed to Miami, and then back to L.A. for a few days, and then he was due next week in Philly, then New Jersey and New York. He was worn out, but he'd figured out something he hadn't really taken in before: Tina was the most competitive person he'd ever met in his life. His head was still spinning from her turnaround.

He stood there, letting the knowledge of that settle over him like a net. "Well," he said and ruffled Christopher's hair. "We shouldn't overthink things, I guess. Right, pal?"

"I don't like her. I want to go home and see Jamie and Arley," Christopher said.

The day after discovering Handsome Dan preening on the second floor in his underwear, Jamie had a huge fight with Lucy. It started in the morning before she left to teach, and then kept erupting and re-erupting after she came home, like an underground fire that was still smoldering even when the main blaze had been vanquished. Arley was off on a playdate, thank goodness, because this fight moved with them from room to room, and from decade to decade, taking on age-old layers of anger.

Lucy was maddeningly opaque, the way she always got when she was cornered. *Yes,* she'd been seeing Dan again, but it was nobody's damn business. She thrust out her chin and put her hand on her hip. Nobody was going to tell her how to live, especially not some younger sister who was too chicken to even *have* a life, who ran from men and romance and complications. Who was supposedly an *artist,* a creative person, but who kept herself practically virginal.

"I do have a child," Jamie said acidly. "So it's a well-known fact that I am not a virgin. Just because I don't sleep around doesn't mean I haven't had relationships, and you know it."

"Oho! Don't get me *started* on your nonexistent relationships with men! If it weren't for me, you'd still be living in New York, being a slave to that idiot graffiti guy of yours," Lucy said, and apparently she really wanted to do a major review, because she then went galloping down the whole tiresome list of all Jamie's failed and unfortunate romances. She started with the son of one of their parents' friends, who in third grade had hit Jamie with a baseball and then asked her to a square dance, and whom Jamie had then hit; then careened through the unfortunate story of Trace, the brief thing with the veterinarian who was covered in dog hair, then *Nate,* and finished up with the rich doctor Jamie had escaped from the night before. There were a few more that Lucy didn't even know about, but they were nothing to be proud of, either.

So then Jamie pointed out that the fight wasn't about *her* relationships. It was about Handsome Dan being the most odious, robotic, empty, soulless creature that had ever crawled out from under a rock.

And furthermore, she said, it was about the flabbergasting thought that he got to call all the shots in so many people's lives— his wife's, Lucy's, and now even Jamie's and Arley's. That he could just snap his stupid, nicotine-stained fingers and Lucy would go back to him.

"Why does he get to say how all the rest of us have to live?" Jamie said, building up steam now. "Just because of his casual decision to come over here and stir things up again with his terrible cigarette smoke, *I* have to find someplace else to live! I just want to know one thing: Why did you even beg me to come back here?"

"Because I love you, and obviously I forgot what a pain in the ass you are, and the way you try to run my life!"

"I am not trying to run your life," she said quietly. "All I'm trying to do is to protect my son from cigarette smoke."

Then Lucy, in her best full-throated, apoplectic channeling of Linda Blair, screamed, *"He only smokes on the balcony! You can't keep people from smoking all over the earth, you know! You don't have control of the fucking air!"*

"Well, I did have control over my living space until *now*."

"Why don't you grow up and realize that you have to coexist with people?" Lucy wanted to know. Then she said that Dan had been over lots of times lately—he'd even slept over while Jamie was camping out—and Jamie hadn't even known about it, and had Arley had any bad reaction? Well, *had he*?

"Wait a minute," Jamie said. "Those were Handsome Dan's red bikini briefs in the bed, weren't they? They weren't Mike Scanlon's at all!"

Lucy looked a little rattled.

"Wait. Exactly how long *have* you been seeing him again?" Jamie demanded.

Lucy looked away.

"Oh my God," Jamie said. "You never really stopped seeing him, did you?" She started laughing, feeling the hysteria rising in her chest. "You didn't ever stop. Oh my God. And here I told Mike Scanlon that I was sure that this time you had."

"Oh, Mike Scanlon is just a kid. And he had a good time with me. Don't worry about him."

"No, no. He's in love with you. In fact, poor guy, he begged me to let him know if I ever suspected that you were going to leave him, so he could protect himself. And I said, 'Oh, no, she's over that—'"

"God*damn*, what is it with you people? You can't protect yourself from feeling things! What kind of stupid life is that, where you don't let yourself take any chances and have any feelings? That's you all over. Take out an insurance policy against getting hurt. You know what? Why don't you call him up and go on and marry him? Go ahead. You guys would make a perfect little couple, just sliding through life, trying to figure out how you can feel as little pain as possible."

"You can't just roll over people and then blame them for getting hurt by you," Jamie said.

"You know what? I can do whatever I want. This is *my* condo, this is *my* life, and Dan is *my* lover—and you can go take a flying leap somewhere, if you can't deal with that. And take Mike Scanlon with you, why don't you?"

"I can't stay here any longer," Jamie said. She hated the way her voice was shaking. "Arley and I have to leave. I don't care if Dan's not going to smoke here or not, I can't live here under these conditions."

"Fine. Do whatever you want. I don't care anymore."

Jamie went into the bedroom and got down a suitcase and started putting her stuff into it. She could hear Lucy banging things around in the kitchen. In a moment, surely Lucy was going to come in and say, "What could I have been thinking? Listen, you're right. I just remembered Dan's a big fat jerk anyway, and also I really, really love Mike Scanlon, like I've been claiming for the past three weeks!"

But she didn't.

Jamie closed the door to the bedroom and leaned against it, thinking so hard it made her head hurt. She had two weeks of summer school still to go, and then another week until the jamboree. After that, maybe she should get in the car with Arley and drive up to Vermont and see for herself about that possible teaching job. And if that job at Pendleton didn't come through, maybe she could find something else up there. At least she could live near Shana; she'd have a friend. But until then . . . well, the only thing to do was to camp. That was it: she and Arley were going to camp out.

It might even be fun. *Lots* of people camp all summer long. They love it! She squared her shoulders. What was a few more weeks? They'd loved their three days there. They could *totally* do it for twenty-one more days. They could shower at the neighbors' houses. She'd make arrangements.

She looked at herself in the mirror. God, this was getting to be a bizarre life. Very, very soon she was going to have to sit down and take stock and figure out how to get things normal again. She'd have plenty of time to do this at the pond. Her hands were shaking a little as she opened up her top drawer and emptied all her underwear out onto the bed.

It was when she went into Arley's room to get his things together that Lucy came to make amends. For a moment she stood in the bedroom doorway with her arms folded. *Now* it was going to happen. *Now* she would say she'd come to her senses, and she couldn't bear to lose them.

"Please stay," she'd say, and try as she might to hold back, Jamie knew she would readily agree to stay. They'd hug and kiss, and Jamie would make a wonderful dinner for them, and Handsome Dan would be consigned to life's dustbin once again.

But Lucy leaned against the doorjamb, cleared her throat, and said in a raspy voice, "Okay, I've got to tell you the truth. Dan both breaks my heart and makes me happy. I don't know why I feel this way about him, but I don't think I can leave him just now." She'd been crying.

"Why?" Jamie said. "Does he have terminal cancer or something from all those cigarettes?"

"Stop it. You're just being mean. If you want to know the truth, I went to a psychic, and she said I'm addicted to him and there's nothing I can do."

Jamie stopped emptying a drawerful of Arley's shorts into a bag and laughed. "You're *addicted* to him."

"Yes. I'd had one of my major realizations, and the psychic helped me see that he and I are meant to be together, and she said it was going to be hard—maybe the hardest thing I ever did, she said— but she said I need to hold on right now. For him and for me."

"I cannot believe this."

"I know what you're thinking, that it's crazy. I know you hate him." She laughed suddenly, and Jamie saw that she was starting to cry again. "But you know, when there's true love, you have to go with it. I think we're bound together, like from different lifetimes or something."

"Oh, *please*," Jamie said. "Spare me this previous-lifetimes shit. Just take responsibility, will you, for the fact that you're letting this guy use you to cheat on his wife! Will you at least do that?"

"This is bigger than that. It's beyond that."

"Beyond him cheating on his wife? I don't think so. Just tell me this. How did you, a feminist and a strong woman, let a guy do this to you? That's what I don't understand. Isn't there anything else in life that you want? Just for *you*?"

"Sure there is, lots of things, but I can't have any of it."

"Why not? What is it you want?"

The vein in Lucy's temple was throbbing. "All right, you want to know what I want? I want to have my own theater production company, and I want to run a whole yoga institute, and I always wanted to be a ballerina. Did you really think all I wanted out of life was to grow up and be a bartender? Is that what you thought? Did you ever even care what I wanted? You're the one who does what she wants. You have your *art*. And you don't do anything you don't want to. Anything that's just for money. It's *me* who has to worry about the mortgage and the bills. I've always had to take care of you, even from the time we were little and you were too shy to get to know anybody. It's always been me, me, me!"

Jamie felt as if the top of her head had been lifted off and her brains were now exposed to the elements. She didn't know whether to hug Lucy or shake her.

"Let me get this straight," she said finally. "You are addicted to a married guy, and it's *my* fault because you never got to do what you wanted with your life while I do my art and make almost no money."

Lucy started hiccupping then. "I've been supporting you, subsidizing your art. Don't you realize that? By letting you live here and taking care of you, I've been the one who's made it all possible. And now *you* stand here judging the man I'm in love with, the one guy who actually makes me happy."

"He has never made you happy. He makes you crazy."

"You see? That's how little you know about me."

Jamie stared at her. "Well, let me just correct this deplorable situation right now," she said. "I'll get completely out of your way. I certainly don't want to be a burden to you any longer."

She gathered up Arley's trucks and cars and flung them into a cardboard box. Then she carried the cardboard box and suitcases out to the car and slammed the door.

"It's so easy for you!" Lucy yelled at her from the balcony as she left. "When you block out love, all of life is just a string of tolerable Tuesday afternoons, isn't it? Who the hell wants a life like that?"

"I do!" Jamie shouted over the noise of the engine.

IF CAMPING OUT had been fun before, now that it was a necessity, it was horrible. She was still angry with Lucy when she and Arley put up the tent, and then she cooked hamburgers on the hibachi with Lucy's voice hammering inside her head. She and Arley ate quietly, sitting on folding chairs down by the pond. The sky turned from a dull gray to a dull black, with little holes for stars. The crickets were deafening, and a swarm of mosquitoes soon chased them into the tent for the rest of the evening.

In the tiny three-foot-square space, she read her son stories by the light of the lantern, and then sat up awake, staring at the branches of the tree overhead through the screened-in window of the tent after he fell asleep. When the first rumbles of thunder started up in the middle of the night, she was surprised to find that she'd actually fallen asleep and that the lantern was dim, the batteries slowly giving out. There was going to be so much to keep track of, living this way. Batteries, daily bags of ice for the cooler, trips to town to use the bathroom, matches, thermoses of water, bug repellent.

And now there was a thunderstorm.

As the heat lightning came nearer and then started being followed by increasingly loud claps of thunder, she knew they had to get out of the tent and go to the car. She woke up Arley and wrapped him in a blanket and ran up the hill with him as the first raindrops spattered on them. By the time she got them in the car and settled, the rain was a steady drumming on the roof, and they sat huddled in the backseat, among the suitcases and garbage bags filled with their clothes, listening for it to stop. The car smelled like fermented apple juice, and she remembered that a juice box had spilled on the seat over a week ago, on their way to class. The windows fogged up from their breathing.

"Isn't this fun?" she said and cuddled him to her. "We are having a genuine adventure, aren't we?"

"I can't sleep in the car," he said. "It's hot in here."

Lightning flashed, lighting up the farmhouse just like in a horror movie, and thunder rocked the whole car.

"Can you open the window?" he said.

"No, we'll get wet," she said. "We just have to sit here. We can sing some songs. What do you want to sing? 'Moon River'? 'You Are My Sunshine'?"

He snuggled closer to her. "I know what," he said. "Let's go back to Aunt Lucy's house to sleep."

She couldn't tell him why they weren't going to do that. But then, after a moment, an incredible thought occurred to her, and it was as if the sun had come out and harps started playing: there was a key to the farmhouse in the glove compartment of the car, a key Harris had put there, underneath the maps and the service receipts.

"Wait," she said, and scrambled into the front seat. Sure enough, there it was.

"We have a key," she told him. "We can go inside."

He clapped his hands.

Was this wrong to do? She couldn't think. As soon as the lightning and thunder let up a bit, she opened the car door, and she and Arley ran to the back porch and she hoisted him up and then jumped up after him. (Damn that Nate, ripping out the stairs with no plan of putting more in.) The windows rattled with a loud clap of thunder and she hurriedly turned the key in the lock and stepped inside.

The light switch worked! The house had that shut-up feel to it, but it was welcoming just the same. Most of the furniture was still there—Nate never had gotten around to calling the Salvation Army to come get it—so they could actually stay there. They would be comfortable. All the dishes and pots and pans—those he'd thrown out, but for some reason, he'd left everything else just the way it was. They could sleep in their old beds, cook on the stove, put food in the refrigerator, use the toilet upstairs instead of having to travel to the one at the gas station.

They explored the house, shivering at how empty and lonely it looked, and then she tucked him back into his old bed and went down the hall to her old room and lay down. Lightning flashed at the windows until nearly three o'clock, when she finally fell asleep.

T hree days later, Nate realized he was a beaten man.

Maybe, he thought, he was a moron or something, but he had not seen this coming. He knew he was frazzled, sure. Tired, even. *Toast* was a word that came to mind when he considered his mental state. But he had no idea that he was so completely drained until he lost the sale in Miami because he simply could not concentrate.

This had never happened to him before. He was dealing with a family business, importers, and twice he had called the patriarch/CEO Mario when his name was Luís. *Very bad.* A mistake that made him seem not only clueless but ethnically insensitive as well. He'd also lost a folder with all the important research papers in it, and when he'd tried to gain the CEO's sympathies by telling amusing stories about his past few crazy weeks, he was met with stony silence. Worse, Christopher had stuck to him throughout the meeting, singing tuneless songs under his breath and tapping on the conference table, spilling a box of apple-cranberry juice all over the table and onto an upholstered chair. And *then*—when Nate had managed to remove him to a corner of the room and handed over his BlackBerry to appease the kid— Christopher had managed to dial, hang up, and then redial Howie's number twenty-three times, until Howie himself called and suggested that Nate put his kid in some kind of straitjacket until he was forty-seven years old.

Then, on the plane going back, there was what he liked to think of as the "international terrorism incident," when, unbeknownst to Nate, Christopher smuggled the BlackBerry into the airplane lavatory with him and dropped it into the toilet without telling anyone, thus causing the flight crew, when they discovered a clog, to enact all the alarms worthy of a terrorist attack, including landing the plane at the nearest airport, interrogating the passengers, having the bomb squad take apart the toilet system, and then, in a moment of supreme humiliation, disposing of Nate's drenched and smelly BlackBerry while Christopher had a public meltdown.

All of his contact information—gone. Business records. Upcoming sales call schedule. E-mails.

Luckily, he still had his cell phone with him. That was how, when walking from the terminal gate to the parking lot at LAX, he was able to get the news from Todd Haney that Smith & Golden Development Corporation had failed to get the necessary permissions to go forward with building condos on his dad's property, and were withdrawing their applications. The place was not going condo.

And that was it. He had to stop walking for a minute and lean against somebody's minivan while Todd kept talking to him. Everything he said was a blur of words, all adding up to *No can do.*

The smog in L.A. was so thick that he could hardly catch his breath.

"So what do you suggest now, O Great Haneymeister? Do we blow up the place?" he said. He looked up to make sure a piece of the parking garage wasn't going to come crashing down on their heads. It was that kind of day.

"I don't know, man," Todd said. "I think just fix it up and sell it as a single-family."

"Are there other companies we can go to?"

There was a long silence, and then Todd Haney cleared his throat. "I don't think you're getting the big picture here, man. The *Planning and Zoning Commission* is not going to give the permissions, no matter who the developer is."

The old Nate—the one who was not beaten and bloodied and who had not very nearly been charged with trying to blow up an airliner with a BlackBerry—would have said that there was always a way.

The new Nate said, "Okay. List it."

"As is?"

"As is, a fixer-upper. Who cares? I don't give a damn. Do whatever."

"We'll talk another time," Todd said, using the kid gloves tone of voice that Nate recognized from his career as a salesman. *Former* career.

After he hung up, he looked down at Christopher as though he were seeing him for the first time. The kid looked like a poster child for parental neglect. His face was still tear-streaked from today's loss of the BlackBerry, his shirt was stained with apple juice and chocolate, one of his shoes was untied, and he was shuffling along like an old, tired man, worried and bereft. For the last few days he had been asking so many questions about his grandfather and his mother; he wanted to know if they were together. Nate had said he didn't know, he had no idea, and now he tried to remember the last time he and Christopher had sat down and had a real meal, a meal that wasn't just a bag of something handed to them by an airline employee.

He put down his briefcase, the one that hours ago had been emptied in front of him while every piece of paper was studied by the airport authorities. He felt lousier than he could remember feeling in years, and his boy must feel even worse. The kid was *grieving*. This was what grief looked like.

People pushed past them in the parking lot, trundling suitcases behind them, not even stopping to notice that the two unhappiest people in the world had come to a dead halt in the middle of long-term parking at LAX. There was a little curb surrounding a beat-up old palm tree. Nate sat down on the curb, in his suit, and pulled Christopher over to him. A woman in a suit looked at them in dismay. They must look like homeless people. Nate realized he didn't care.

"Do you want to go home?" he said.

Christopher wiped his nose. "Isn't this L.A.?"

"No, dude. *Home* home. To Connecticut."

"To see Jamie and Arley?"

"Hell, I don't know. Maybe. We need to shake things up. Rethink things. You know what I think we should do? Fix up the house. Save some money. Hell, I don't know. Work on getting Tina to come and live with us. Grow tomatoes in the garden and eat them standing over the sink. Practice our burps. You need some serious work on your belches. We are just not able to get that belch work done while we're on the road."

"Are we going to stay there?"

"Now why do you want to ask such hard questions right off the bat? Who knows? What does *stay* even mean?" Nate sighed and stood up. He picked up the suitcase. "Come on, keep walking. I guess you wouldn't be Christopher the Inquisitor if you didn't ask things like that, would you? You'd be Christopher the Boring. Or Christopher the Monkey. Come on, let's go find the car."

AND SO IT was that he called Howie and announced that he needed time off, only to be told by his boss that he had already been placed on an involuntary, don't-call-us-we'll-call-you leave of absence. He closed up his L.A. apartment, gave away the cactus, swept up the menus and the dust, threw away the moldy hot dogs in the fridge, threw out the frozen pizzas, boxed up his and Christopher's clothes and the toys and the TV set, and shipped them to Connecticut. He wasn't terribly sure he could face another trip on a plane just yet, and for a day he toyed with the idea of driving his car across the country. But the thought of three thousand miles in the company of Christopher the Inquisitor defeated him in the end. He pictured a gruesome scene between the two of them somewhere in the desert along Route 70, when Nate's last nerve was sure to snap. So he sold his car to a neighbor in the condo, wrote a check for the rest of his lease, and on Friday morning, their plane left LAX for the last time.

Whatever life was going to ask of him next, it surely wouldn't ask him to be in L.A. Frankly, he never wanted to see another six-lane-freeway snarl-up in his life.

Christopher was restless on the plane, twisting around in his seat and trashing the magazine in the seat pocket. He had to be stopped from kicking the seat in front of his, and then from bringing the tray table up and down again and again. Then as soon as the seat belt light went off, he said, "I'm going to go to the bathroom by myself, okay, Natey?"

Nate felt the top of his head contract and expand. "No, you're going to stay right here," he said. "And you're going to stop annoying everybody around you."

"But I hafta go to *the bathroom*!"

"No, you don't. You went in the terminal. Now sit there quietly. If you want to do something, you can put your headphones on. But you have to be quiet."

Christopher stared at him and then launched one more kick at the seat in front of his. Nate gave him his dangerous look.

"I wish you still had your BlackBerry," the kid said and folded his arms and stuck out his lower lip.

"Yeah, well, you and me both."

"Da would let me kick if I wanted to."

"No, he wouldn't."

"I bet my mommy would. Wouldn't she?"

Nate looked over his son's head and out the window into the clouds.

"Wouldn't she let me kick if I wanted to?"

"I—I don't know," he said. "We just don't know."

"She would. I know."

Nate laughed and shook his head, then sat back and stroked his chin and looked down. That's when he realized that he had forgotten to shave, his shirt was buttoned all wrong, his jeans had a hole in the knee, and his socks didn't match. When he turned and smiled at the woman next to him, she turned away and closed her eyes tight.

Go ahead and think I'm a lousy father. You don't know the half of it. He didn't care. He stared out again at the piles of clouds. Piles and piles of clouds. He was going home, or to the last place that had ever felt like home to him, and he would throw himself into fixing up the house and selling it. After some time had gone by, he'd talk Howie into letting him work from the East Coast for a change, and eventually he'd find a nanny for Christopher.

But now—right now—he was going to concentrate on being grateful that he was being allowed back on an American airliner and that he didn't have a BlackBerry that could be tossed into the toilet. It wasn't a lot to be grateful for, but it was a start.

CHAPTER
25

At first it was creepy being back in the house, and Jamie was sure she and Arley would return to camping by the pond any minute. It seemed wrong to be there, somehow, possibly even illegal— like trespassing. Well, it *was,* in fact, trespassing. But then the next night it started to rain again, just after midnight, and Arley was wheezing a little bit, so they trudged back up the hill to the house and settled back into their old beds, which were so comfortable, just the way they used to be. And it was so familiar, the way the sun came in the windows and made patches of warm light on the hardwood floors, now cleaned of all extraneous stuff.

And so the next day—well, she went out and bought plastic plates and cups, and a cheap set of flatware, some pots and pans. On the fourth day she stocked the refrigerator with eggs and butter and cheese and milk. In the basement she found an old mayonnaise jar that had had nails in it, and filled it with water and daisies from the garden and set it on the kitchen table. She guessed she'd moved back in.

It had been ridiculous, she now saw, to assume that they could actually live in a tent until after the jamboree, when she could leave for Vermont. A person, at minimum, needed a shower, a toilet, and a stove. A hibachi wasn't going to cut it. She should probably ask permission to be there, but whose? She certainly didn't want Nate to know she'd had to come crawling back. Plus, he hadn't answered her last e-mail. She meant to call Todd Haney, just to make sure it would be okay. But then she just didn't. It was temporary anyway, her being there. He wouldn't mind. She put it out of her head.

And then, wouldn't you know, three days later she was standing in the kitchen, painting at last the scene she'd always wanted to do—the table with the daisies in the mayonnaise jar—when she heard the unmistakable sound of a key turning in the lock and the front door opening. She heard a man's low, muffled voice.

"Todd?" she called. She held her paintbrush between her teeth and tried to wind up her hair into her scrunchy. "Todd? Is that you?"

"It looks different," a child's voice said.

"*Christopher?*" she said. Her heart started beating so hard she thought it was likely to be heard all the way in the living room. She put down the paintbrush and brushed out her hair and tried to straighten her clothes, and hurried to the front of the house. Sure enough, there they were in the hall: Nate and Christopher.

At first Nate didn't see her—he was facing the front door, putting two huge suitcases down in the corner—and she had a frantic moment of wanting to dart, unseen, right back to the kitchen, slip out the back door, and run like hell to nowhere. But she was frozen. She knew for a fact that she had turned purple and that in a nanosecond he was going to look up and she would be like a moth that had just smashed itself against the smooth hotness of a lightbulb.

And then Christopher made a squeaking noise, and Nate turned. He went ashen. "*Wha—?*" he said, and then, "What the hell are *you* doing here?" And—this was the worst part—there wasn't any pleasure in his voice. He appeared shocked through and through.

"Hi," she said. She looked like hell; her hair was half up and half down, the tank top she was wearing had holes and paint splatters on it, and her denim shorts were too tight. "I'm not—"

"*JAAAAAA-meeee!*" Christopher let out a shout and then attacked her, spinning her around and around, and then Arley came thundering down the stairs, yelling, too—and for a moment, everything was simple pandemonium. The boys were jumping up and down and running around like maniacs, and then Arley grabbed Nate about the thighs and squealed, "My Natey is back! Natey Man! Natey Man!" Nate, who kept staring at Jamie, seemed as if he was going to peel him off, but then he just kind of patted him on the head and said hello. Arley launched into one of his long explanations about how they'd been in a tent, but then a big storm came so they came inside, and he finished with, "So we live here now! Do you still live in Ellay?"

"No! I moved back!" Christopher said at a decibel level associated with airplanes taking off. "I'm going to live here now, too!"

Then they fell over each other like puppies, all arms and legs tumbling and scuffling, and then grabbed their parents by the legs, pulling and shoving, pushing them together.

Jamie swallowed and looked at Nate. He seemed so different, so *rumpled,* and maybe lost. He stood there trying not to be toppled over by children and running his fingers through his hair and looking disgruntled and confused, and then he nodded, motioning her out of the chaos and toward the kitchen. They managed to disentangle themselves from the children, who went instead to jump up and down on the couch, and she followed him. Already her mind was racing, trying to formulate an explanation that could make some sense. She knew, though, what it was going to come to: she had to get out of here. Maybe she could make up with Lucy, or perhaps it would make more sense to find a substitute for her teaching job and then to go to Vermont early. But she didn't have the job in Vermont yet. God, how was it that she'd come to living this irresponsible, derelict life? Why hadn't she grown up and become the kind of person who didn't depend on others all the time? Lucy may have had a point.

When they got to the kitchen, she said the only thing she'd been able to work out so far, which was, "Just so you know, this isn't what it looks like."

He looked weary and amused. "Oh, really? It's not that you and Arley are here in my house? What is it, then?"

"No. We're here. I mean, obviously . . . we're here. It's just . . . well, we haven't been here the whole time. I did move out."

"You did? Well, isn't that nice. And just what factors prevented you from continuing on that course? Just the fact that you're a rascal of the highest order?" he said.

This was a good sign: a joke. There were worse things than being called a rascal. And anyway, he was grinning at her now, so she smiled back at him.

"It's kind of a long story," she said, "having to do with a bunch of boring things you probably wouldn't care about. Things with my sister and her love life and all that." She leaned against the counter for strength. "Hey, and how about *you*? What are you doing back here? With big suitcases, too, I see."

"Well, I do sort of happen to *belong* here," he said. "I have the deed to the place and all that."

"Funny, that never carried much weight with you before."

"Yeah, well . . . ," he said. "Everything's different now. You're looking at a humbled man."

She burst out laughing. "You do look like shit."

"I know. What can I say? I've given up." He looked around, taking in the painting she was doing, and the breakfast dishes on the counter, along with a carton of milk. "Are you sure you really moved out, or did you just walk out the door with us, and then move right back in once we were around the corner? That's what you did, isn't it?"

"Listen, you have every right to be mad at me, but I want you to know that I was here only temporarily. Lucy started up with Handsome Dan again, and so then Arley and I borrowed a tent from Todd Haney and we were sleeping out there by the pond—but then it started to storm, and so I happened to remember that I had a key in the glove compartment of the car. Harris had—" She stopped, seeing his expression, which was glazing over. "Sorry. I'm not making sense. I need to get out of here now. Arley and I can go back to Lucy's— wait, you don't care about where we go, but that's what we'll do. There's a tent down by the pond, and I'll come back for that. And listen, if you want Arley and Christopher to play together sometime, just call, and I'm sorry about all this. It's terrible. I'm really sorry."

"Wait, wait," he said. "Stop a minute. Just stop talking, okay?" He looked out the window, then sighed. "Actually, the truth is—well, I'm glad to see you. Sit down. Let's talk for a minute."

"No, really. I just want to go."

"No, no. Please. I've been sarcastic again, and I'm sorry. I didn't mean to act like that. I was just surprised, that's all, but I'm working on not being so tight-assed all the time." He smiled at her and pointed to a chair. "Will you . . . please?"

She hesitated a moment, and then sat down.

He took a deep breath, started drawing little circles on the table with his fingertip. "I've left the company and moved out of L.A.," he said. "Taken a leave of absence. This place didn't sell to developers after all, and so it's going to have to be a single-family house. Say, you didn't have anything to do with *that,* did you?"

"No."

"Sorry. There I go again. I'm *kidding,* McClintock. Anyway, Todd just told me the developer didn't get the permissions he needed to go condo, and since most people are not going to like all this funky red linoleum and broken-down windowsills, while I'm waiting for Christopher to grow up into a sane person, I figured I might as well come home and live here and kind of fix it up. Regroup."

"Wait. Christopher's not a sane person?"

He laughed and leaned across the table toward her. His eyes fastened on her, and she couldn't look away. She was a goner, such a goner. "Ahhh, *no,*" he said, and just the way his laugh was dry and raspy, just the way his fingers were drumming on the table, the way he was leaning toward her, including her in the joke. "Not so much. Not even close. But it's my fault, thinking a kid—a grieving kid, yet—could go to meetings and fly on airplanes without dropping electronics down the toilet and nearly getting us arrested." He dropped his voice. "You know, McClintock, it's waaaay worse than just that he eats Oreos weird. You didn't tell me half of it."

"You wouldn't listen," she said, barely able to breathe.

"Well, now I'm a beaten man, McClintock. Beaten and bloodied and bowed."

"So . . . you really quit your job? You're here to stay?"

He leaned back. "Well, I took a leave. Was *given* a leave. So . . . well, actually, I'm going to be working a lot on the house. That's my plan, anyway." He looked around, squinted at the moldings and the paint chips and the peeling wallpaper. "Not that I know what I'm doing. But as you've noticed, I have a lot of confidence in my ability to do things that I know nothing whatsoever about."

"You'll do it," she said.

He got up and went over to the refrigerator suddenly and opened it. "Wow. You've got it pretty well stocked for somebody who's not really living here."

"Please—" she said, and he held up his hand.

"No, no, I'm saying that as a good thing," he said. "I know I'm a little dazed still, but let me just throw something out here." He rubbed his head. "I actually have to do a lot of work here on the house, so I don't know how you feel about this, but maybe we could share this house, like you and my dad did." He cleared his throat. "Same deal, kind of. I could work on the house, and you could help me with Christopher, and we could, you know, eat dinner and stuff. You being the cook."

"Well, I'm moving to Vermont in September," she said, just so he would know she wasn't a pushover. "Teaching job."

He kept looking at her too long and too steadily. "Okay," he said finally. "September works for me. Are you in?" Then, as she nodded, he looked concerned and said, "Hey, how's Arley doing? I've been thinking of that little guy. How's the asthma? Has he been okay?"

"He's okay," she said, barely audibly. *He was thinking of* Arley? *Really?*

"Good," he said. He stood there rubbing his head and looking at her with a little half-smile. Then he shook his head. "You're something, you know that? I can't believe you, moving back in here like this. No, no. I mean, it's great. It's going to work out perfect. It was such a bold move, that's all. But I'm *glad,* believe me. It's . . . good to see you again."

She couldn't breathe. Oh, she was going to be in such trouble. She wanted to put her head down on the table. The real truth settled on her like a blanket: she wanted nothing more than for Nate to come over and kiss her the way he had before.

"All right," she said in a low voice, when she could trust herself to speak.

"SO WHEN IS Howie taking you back? Has he said?" Tina wanted to know. Her voice had to fight its way through international static, since she was calling from somewhere in Mexico, but even through the fuzziness, Nate could tell she was irritated.

Irritated, shmirritated. What the hell? The truth was he was lying alone in the grass—in the weeds, really—and it was nine o'clock at night, and ticks were probably about to bite him, taking up where the mosquitoes had left off, and he didn't care about any of it. He had knocked off work after trying, in vain, to rebuild the porch steps, and since then he'd been on his back looking at shooting stars with the kids and, oh yes, Jamie. They'd been outside eating melting Popsicles, racing to get them devoured while purple syrup ran down their arms. "This is what comes of eating grape Popsicles while lying down," he'd said grimly, and Jamie had laughed out loud, which had startled him in its spontaneity. And musicality. And oh God—whatever. *Stop analyzing stuff.* Anyway, they'd all been out there, craning their necks to see the meteor shower, but then the combination of sticky hands and faces, as well as a sudden swarm of mosquitoes, had caused Jamie to jump up and declare that the limit of fun had been reached and that the kids had to go inside.

And then Tina called.

"I mean, what is Howie *thinking?* It's so unfair, punishing you because you're a parent now. He's got to *understand.* I think you should fly to Hawaii and sit down with him and Leilani and just *explain* what's going on."

"Nah," he said. "Forget it."

"But what *are* you going to do?"

"Well, I'm planning to fix up this house and raise my kid for a while, and then . . . well, we'll see what comes next. What are *you* going to do?"

Somebody else was talking to her. There was music in the distance, the clinking of glasses. "Yeah, another mojito," she said. *"Un otro."* She came back to him. "I just wish you were here with me. We could be having so much fun."

He closed his eyes.

Her voice changed. "So, I almost hate to ask this, but have you heard from Jamie?"

"Yeah. She's around." He looked up at the back of the house, half-expecting to see her at the window looking out at him.

"She's around, huh?" Tina said. "I'll bet she is. I think she's got it going on for you, you know what I'm saying?"

"She's watching Christopher," he said. "So I can do the house."

"What? Wait. Is she staying there?"

"She is. She's staying here, she and her son."

"Oh my God. Am I going to have to catch a plane and get over there and rescue you? For God's sake, Nate, go to Hawaii and talk to Howie! You want me to talk to him for you? This is crazy."

"Look, I'm working on the house," he said. "Jamie's here helping. It makes it all go faster. She's good with kids. What can I say?"

"Aha! So this is just outsourcing," Tina said. She laughed her tinkly little laugh. "You're outsourcing Christopher. That's brilliant!"

For a long time after he closed his phone, he lay there in the dark like the idiot he was. He was so tired he could have fallen asleep.

IT TOOK ABOUT a week before it hit him: he was living in very interesting times indeed.

Here he was, sharing a house with a woman he'd once slept with during a moment of huge mistakenness, if that was a word. *And* now they were together every day, doing the most intimate of things— everything but having sex, that is. Bathing children, sharing a bathroom, eating every meal, heading off to separate bedrooms. It got to him.

Life had settled into something that bordered on chaos—and yet, nothing seemed to rattle Jamie; she moved through the catastrophe of everyday life as though she were enjoying a constant Valium drip. Nate would wake up in the morning to find that she'd made chocolate chip muffins for breakfast, and sometimes, when he was working, she'd show up with smoothies or glasses of lemonade. And she looked, unbelievably, as if she was having fun—as if taking the kids to the pond, teaching them to swim, then cuddling with them on the glider, telling them stories in the late afternoon while she shucked corn or peeled potatoes, were just the greatest things anybody could do. He felt like some kind of inept whiner around her—everything was always too hard. These freaking steps, for instance. What had he been thinking, ripping them apart without measuring the boards and knowing how he was going to build new ones?

At night, after the kids were in bed, sometimes she'd help him with inside projects—peeling back layers of flowered wallpaper dating back to the time when apes roamed the earth—and they'd talk. She told him about some hilariously doomed dates with one of the Campfire dads, a loser dermatologist, and also how she'd gotten snookered into running the jamboree thing; and he told her stories about Christopher in L.A. and Christopher on the road. There were times they were laughing so hard they could barely operate their scrapers. One time she got so hysterical that she had to lean against the wall for support, and then she slid all the way down to the floor. It was all he could do not to slide down next to her and hold onto her.

But no. They weren't doing that anymore. He kept busy, tackling the house as if the siding and the floorboards and the linoleum were all his sworn personal enemies, long-term enemies that he alone could vanquish. During the days, he stayed outside, scraping and painting, and in the evenings, he swam in the cold pond before he fell asleep in his old bed. He was exhausted, but in a good way. For once, he didn't have to plan how he was going to win over the next client, and the one after that. His mind felt blank; all it needed to do was concentrate on one brushstroke after another.

One day he was up on a ladder painting the side of the house when he happened to look in and see Jamie in her room. It wasn't that she was undressed. It was *worse* than that. She was twirling around in a circle, *dancing*—and it took his breath away. She looked so damned unprotected, so innocent, so free with her body and so *artless*. It was almost as if he was seeing her real essence, even more than if she'd been stark naked. She was dancing, in front of the mirror! He couldn't get over it.

Another time she was sitting cross-legged on the kitchen floor, sticking a hook into a string of yarn and wrapping it around and around, her fingers moving like lightning. He stood there with a cup of coffee, watching her, and then said, "What in the world are you doing?"

"Crocheting a vest for your son," she said, without looking up.

"No, no, no!" he said. "The boys are *not* going to wear crocheted vests anymore, woman! Are you trying to turn them into objects of ridicule and scorn? Do you want them beaten up by fourth-graders on the school bus *every* day?"

She looked up at him mildly. "I'm *kidding,* Nate."

And it was the weirdest thing, but for a long moment he stood there wondering if he'd ever heard her say his name before.

THEN ONE DAY he walked into the barn, which had been Harris's sanctuary, the place where he kept all his sacred tools. The sun was streaming through a dusty window, shining on the rows and rows of wrenches and screwdrivers and awls and saws, everything in its place. Outside the barn, he could hear the kids shouting as they ran around chasing little brown frogs. How many times as a boy had he come in here and been told by his father to get the hell out, that he would break things? This was where Harris escaped to, it was the impenetrable fortress he locked himself in when he didn't want to deal with his family. *Women and stupid kids,* was the way he put it. *Goddamn kids—they just break everything, and what they don't manage to break, they lose.* Nate remembered his mom saying, "Harris, why don't you *teach* him how to use the tools, and then he won't break them?" and his dad saying, "Let him go hit baseballs. He's not coming in here!"

Nate walked around inside the barn watching the dust motes drift down through a beam of sunshine. He ran his hand across an old calendar tacked up on the board over the workbench, moved a sack of empty beer bottles, and then picked up one of his dad's old T-shirts, which looked as if it had been used as a rag.

And for some reason, that's what did it. It hit him, like a blow to the gut, that his dad was gone. It wasn't the funeral, the house, even the rows of tools that brought him to this—who would have thought it would end up being simply the sight and the feel of this old soft shirt balled up in the corner of the workbench, with its holes and oil stains? The fact of it stunned him: he wasn't ever going to talk to his father again.

For a moment he just stood there, then he kicked the workbench as hard as he could and went back outside to face the fact that he had ripped off the porch steps and now had to build new ones, and that he didn't know what the hell he was doing, that he'd *never* known what the hell he was doing, and probably Harris hadn't either. Just generations of men bumbling along in their stupid, prideful little lives, getting it wrong over and over again.

And then they died, maybe never getting much of it right. *Fuck.* How were you supposed to live with *that*?

LUCKILY FOR HIM, his buddy Ron got some time off from work, so he came over and helped Nate build the porch steps. It was clear that

the job required two people, at least one of whom knew how to measure boards. For a while Arley pestered them by trying to help, but
finally Jamie called him inside. After she left, Ron stood for a moment
in silence, and then he said, "So how's this arrangement of yours
working out?"

"Arrangement?"

"Yeah. Arrangement with Jamie."

Nate was careful not to look at him. He pretended to be measuring the step for the fourth time. "With Jamie? I guess it's fine. So far, at
least."

"Her kid certainly seems to have taken to you."

"Yeah. Tell me about it. My own kid won't give me the time of
day, but Arley is like my personal shadow. He gives me news bulletins
all the time—like if you pet a raccoon, you immediately have to go get
twenty-three shots in the stomach."

Ron laughed. Nate pounded his thumb with a hammer, but
not hard enough to make him stop working. Ron didn't seem to notice.

After a while, Ron said, "So how does your fiancée feel about this?"

"I don't think she pets raccoons much."

Ron said, "Don't make me throw something at you. How does
she feel about your living situation?"

"What about it?" Nate said.

"You dog, you." Ron was married for the second time, this time
to a woman who had an eight-year-old boy, and for him, life was black
and white. He'd explained his theories while they built the steps: You
loved someone; you married her. If it didn't work out, you got
divorced as amicably as possible, and then you moved on, and tried
again. It was like finding the right lock for your particular key. The
locksmith theory of marriage, he called it.

They worked in silence for a while, and then Ron said, "Your
fiancée must really be something if she's better than what you've got
going on right here."

Nate stayed silent.

"Are we ever going to get to meet her?"

"I dunno. I guess she'll come here eventually."

"Has she met Christopher yet?"

"What's with all these questions? *Yes,* she's met Christopher. We spent three days together in Boston, okay? In one hotel room with a faulty lock on the bathroom door. She's a busy woman. She has a *career.* Now is there anything else about my life that you need to know before we can put this last step on?"

Ron was grinning at him. "Yeah. There is, actually. When did you get to be such an A-one dickhead?" He went over and picked up the hose, turned it on, and started spraying Nate with it. Nate lunged at him and chased him around the yard, getting sprayed in the face the whole time. He finally got the hose away from Ron and soaked him with it, and the two of them yelled and laughed and carried on like they had when they were ten.

"I'm gonna kill you, you son of a bitch!" Nate was hollering, and Ron screamed, "Yeah, and die trying!"

When they were both soaking wet and breathing hard, they flopped down on the grass, gasping.

"That's more like it," Ron said. "Christ, I was afraid you didn't have any stuffing left in you anymore, man. You've turned into some kind of corporate tight-ass wuss, you know that?"

Nate was lying on his back looking up at the sky, at the clouds passing. "Yeah, that's me. Out trying to make money when I could be getting chased with the hose in my old hometown. What was I thinking?"

"Like that was any kind of life. You wanna know the truth, man, I think you got saved, comin' back here when you did."

"Yeah, always a pleasure to remember how fucked-up the past was."

"Oh, boo hoo."

Nate picked up an old stick and hurled it in Ron's direction. "Just tell me this. My old man: Was he or was he not the biggest jerk in the world to me?"

"He was."

"He didn't come to my games, and he didn't do stuff with me, and after he moved out, he avoided me. Right?"

"Right."

"But then everybody says he was so great with Christopher. Now is that not fucked-up or what?"

Ron seemed to be thinking for a while. "Who knows what went on in his head, man? He was great with Christopher. I kinda wish you coulda seen it. It was like he got to be his better self at last. I think at some point you and he could have come to the same place, you know?"

Nate watched a cloud sail across the sky. When he spoke again he had to take a deep breath to get this question out. "So was that—that *change*—was that, you think, because he was screwing Jamie?"

Ron rolled over on his stomach and stared at Nate and laughed. "Are you out of your friggin' mind, man? You're serious, aren't you?"

"Come on. You know how my dad was."

"Yeah, but this is *Jamie* we're talking about."

"So? She had kind of a thing for him, it sounds like to me."

"But not that kind of thing. Your dad was an old guy, Nate. Jamie's young and good-looking, and she's got some intelligence to her."

"So? I've seen some pretty young and intelligent women go for that guy."

"Yeah, according to *him*. I don't think he really had all that much luck with women in his, uh, later years, if you want to know the truth. I think he was all talk. Like a lot of guys of his generation."

"So . . . not Jamie. You're sure."

"Jesus, you are something. No. No, no, no. Yuuuck! I can't even think about that for too long or it makes my brain freeze up. No, he was not making it with Jamie. God! Bite your tongue, man."

NATE WOKE UP in the middle of the night needing a drink of water. He'd spent the evening with Mike and Ron and Stevo, drinking beers and shooting hoops in Ron's driveway, just like when they were in high school, only now Ron owned the house and it was his wife and kids inside sleeping that required they be quiet. After a while his wife had come and sat on the steps with them, drinking a beer and talking and laughing. She was a good sport, funny and self-deprecating, sitting there in her sweatpants and a T-shirt, and it was clear that Ron loved having her out there with them.

Happy marriages. Who knew there could be such a thing?

It was 2:32. He lay there staring at those red numerals in the darkness. When the clock clicked over to 2:33, it made a little groaning sound, like it might be actually physically painful for it to mark the time. 2:33. So that meant it was 11:33 in L.A. Tina was probably just settling into bed, putting on her teddy, getting ready to watch Letterman. He closed his eyes, tried to picture her slipping underneath the sheets, flicking on the remote, her face expectant, waiting to be entertained. She always slept with a glass of Pepsi next to her on the bedside table. What kind of person did that? Only crazy people, that's who. Caffeine addicts.

He punched in her number.

"Hiiiii," he said when she answered.

"Is anything wrong?" she wanted to know. He could hear Letterman in the background. Opening monologue, the audience laughing.

"No," he whispered. "I just wanted to hear your voice. To say goodnight."

"Oh." He thought he heard her brighten somewhat.

"I miss you," he said. "I just woke up from a dream, and you were here." This was a lie, but it was a good one. "And we were having the most amazing sex . . ."

She laughed. "Uh-huh. What did you eat before you went to sleep?"

"I miss you."

"You do? Really?"

"Yes," he said. "God, *yes*. What do you think?"

"I don't know. I just don't understand you lately. You've been so distant, and it just feels like you won't do anything about getting your job back. Won't even *talk* to Howie."

"I'm doing the house," he said. "You should come here." A cloudy picture arose in his mind then, of Tina standing in this horrible, rundown house looking around disapprovingly at the chipped paint on the exterior, and the damned half-up, half-down linoleum floor, and then he got a picture of Christopher being rude to her again, and Jamie breezing through the room. His mind halted dead at the thought of Jamie in the same room with Tina.

"Do you really, really want me to?"

"Of course I do," he said, but it was already a lie.

"I'll look at my schedule and see when I can come," she said. "If you really think I should."

"You kidding? It'll be great."

"Okay, I'll look at flights tomorrow," she said, and her voice took on a tinge of excitement that scared him. Then she told him fourteen things about work that he had to struggle to make himself listen to, and then he yawned and said he was awfully tired, and she was still chirping away when he insisted they hang up.

Afterward he lay there looking up at the ceiling, hyperventilating and kicking himself. But then he ticked off on his fingers all the reasons it was a good thing for Tina to visit: (a) they *were* going to get married, (b) if she was going to be his wife, then she had to see his full self, his real life, and (c) having her here would be just the thing he needed to propel himself out of this dump. Remind him of who he really was: a guy who wore suits and showed up at meetings sure that people would sign contracts at his command. If nothing else, it would get him going on the house and get him out of there.

And, well, there was (d): maybe she'd keep him from wanting to sleep with Jamie.

CHAPTER
26

"Okay, don't hang up on me." It was Lucy calling on Jamie's cell phone. Her voice was shaking as she said in a big rush, "And don't tell me that you knew this was going to happen. But I can't stand the idea of you and Arley camping out for weeks on end, so... well, you can move back. I mean, I want you to move back."

"Actually—" Jamie said. She was holding the cell phone propped under her chin, washing dishes.

"And Dan is gone. *Really* gone. I want you to know that, too."

"Oh, my—"

"And *do not* say that I always say he's *really* gone, because this time it's different. He really is."

"Okay. I won't." Jamie waited, running her hands through the dishwater. Out the kitchen window she could see Nate and the children in the doorway of the barn. It was late in the afternoon, and he'd stopped painting the side of the house and was now running what he called a Learning to Build school, which was when he let the kids hit nails into boards. This was theoretically great, although she was sure that any minute now Arley was going to either have an asthma attack from being in the barn or break his thumb with a hammer. She couldn't decide which emergency would befall him first.

"Well," Lucy said—and then burst into tears. "I've missed you so much, and I just can't make it work out with this, this *creep*. It's just not going to work, no matter what I do. You know? He keeps saying how confused he is, and how he knows he's ruining my life, and he can't take it. And now—you're not going to believe this—but now Jennifer is *pregnant,* and . . . well, how did *that* happen, is what I want to know? *When* exactly were they so lovey-dovey that she could get pregnant? He's been lying to me."

"Ohhhh no. Oh my poor Lucy."

There was a lot of sniffling. "And I just don't know what else I can do. I hate him so much! And the worst part is that I know that I made such a mistake letting a *man* come between you and me yet *again,* and I'm so, so sorry, and I can't sleep for thinking about you and Arley camping and living outside all this time. It's horrible, what I've done. And I want you to come back."

"Well, as a matter of fact, we're not camping, so don't even worry about us," Jamie said. Then she told her how she'd remembered there was a key in the glove compartment and had gotten into the house, and then how Nate and Christopher had come home, and what a shock that had been, and how they'd come up with a new deal of sharing the house and the child care.

Lucy was silent. Then she said, in her regular non-crying voice: "So you're all just living there happily-ever-after style? Back in the house, all together?"

Out the window, Jamie saw Nate lean over and look at something on Arley's finger, and just the sight of him bending down to her son, and then ruffling his hair—well, it jolted through her like electricity. This morning, when she'd gone into the bathroom to brush her teeth, she'd stood there looking at the little whiskers of his that had collected in the sink, glossy short brown hairs, which she picked up and studied. Then she'd slowly run her finger along the handle of his razor, and his toothbrush, and the towel he'd used, before she realized what she was doing and made herself stop. It was ridiculous.

"Back in the house, all together," she said to Lucy. "Maybe not happily ever after, but temporarily happy, I guess."

There was a silence, and then Lucy said, "So, oh God, you're sleeping with him, aren't you?"

"No," Jamie said quietly. And then, because she was met with what she recognized as a disbelieving silence, she said it more emphatically, "*No.*"

Lucy said, "But you want to be. And you will, at the first opportunity." Then she laughed. "Oh my, oh my. Love makes idiots of us all, doesn't it? Well, hey, if you agree not to say, 'I told you so,' I'll save *you* the embarrassment of having to recant your little speech about women needing to do their own thing and not letting men define them."

"Hey, I'm totally not letting Nate define me. And we're *not* sleeping together, and he still is engaged, *and* I'm still planning to move to Vermont when that job comes through. He's on the premises, but we're not together."

"Yeah, right. Don't get all huffy. I'm still your big sister, and I still get to be the expert on men. And besides that, I actually called for two reasons—one was to tell you that you can move back in, which I now see you *obviously* don't want to do, and the other was to tell you that a guy came into the bar the other night who looked exactly like Trace. Dead ringer for him, in fact."

"My Trace?"

"How many Traces do you think I know? *Yes,* your Trace."

"How would you know what Trace looked like? You only saw him two times, I think. Also, what in the world would he be doing in Connecticut? He doesn't know there's a world outside New York."

"Yeah, well, it was him. I've seen *pictures* of him. And this guy had the same nose, the same chin, the same way of walking. He was with a whole group of guys, and they were on motorcycles, and they all ordered beers and sat in the back for hours."

"Well, then, that settles it. It wasn't him. For one thing, Trace wouldn't get on a motorcycle. And Connecticut doesn't have enough overpasses for him. And for another thing, he would never hang around with a group of *people*. He wasn't a group kind of a guy."

"Okay, suit yourself," Lucy said and yawned. "But I say it was him."

"It was not him," Jamie said.

"Suit yourself," Lucy said again, but just then there was a yell from the barn, and Jamie had to hurry outside, possibly to save Arley's life.

EXCEPT THAT ARLEY was really fine. He was just running around the barn, flapping his arms and screeching like the maniac he really was—like all children were. Nate stood in the middle, smiling grimly through a headache as he watched the two boys wreak havoc on Harris's sanctuary. Then Jamie was at the door, with a funny look on her face, as if she was expecting trouble. That was what was wrong with her, basically: she was always expecting trouble. Every time she came upon him with the kids, she looked as though she was stunned to find them all still alive.

"He's fine," he called to her. "They're yelling because they've thought of new and louder ways to torture me. See? They hammered a bunch of nails, and now they're running around the barn like the crazy hyena-monkeys they are."

"I'll get Arley out of your hair." She called over the din, "Arley, I have to go to the grocery store. You need to come with me."

"No, no, no! I want to stay here with my Natey." He ran over and grabbed Nate around the middle and tried to stand on the tops of his sneakers.

"No. You have to come with me."

And then it went that way, predictably, for a while—*Yes, you have to come . . . No, please could I stay*—until Nate had to step in and practically beg to keep the kid. And even then Jamie looked uncertain. Finally she put her hand on her hip and said, "Will you really watch him? I'm just worried about an asthma attack in the barn. It's awfully dusty in here."

"Actually, I was planning on going outside and giving him some dynamite in a minute," Nate said. "You don't mind if he lights the fuse, do you, ma'am?" She grimaced at him, and he said tiredly, "Of *course* I'll watch him," when, really, he was so sick of kids, so tired of their yelling and their inability to hammer nails. His head was throbbing.

"Wow! *Dyn-o-mite?*" Arley said. "I get *dyn-o-mite?*"

"Ha-ha-ha," she said and walked away. When she reappeared a few minutes later, she had changed into a pair of jeans without rips and a blue blouse with little beads stuck all over it, including some intriguing ones right around her boob area. Her hair was pinned up with little shiny things, and she was holding her purse. "All right," she said. "If you're sure you don't mind, Nate, I'll just go alone to the store. Arley, if your chest starts to feel tight, I want you to promise me you'll tell Nate."

"Aw shucks, ma'am, you're trusting me with your *boy?*" Nate said. "What did I ever do to earn so much trust?"

She gave him a look and walked over and handed him an inhaler and briefly showed him how to use it. He was busy smirking at her and trying to figure out how the beads on her blouse had gotten attached there. "Keep this with you. At all times. Please," she said. When she got to the car door, she called back to him, "Wait. Do you know my cell phone number?"

"For criminy sakes, it's in the kitchen by the phone, isn't it?"

"I know the number," Arley said.

"Will you just go?" Nate said. "I may not be much in the way of competence, but I do think I can keep two children alive for an hour."

"Oh, I won't be gone that long."

"All the better then. My odds are increasing."

Once she'd gone, and his blood pressure had returned to something approaching normal, he said they could knock off work and go down to the pond so the Lego men could go for a swim. He was sick of watching them dismantle Harris's workspace. He was sick of *everything*.

It was a hot, overcast day, and for a while the two boys stood, dazed, in the water, letting the little Lego men drift around in the weeds. Nate plopped down in a chair with an ancient copy of *Time* magazine he'd found in the barn. The sun beat down on his arms, and the air was filled with the slow buzzing of insects. The kids seemed squabbly and overheated. Arley was making annoying zooming noises, pushing his Lego man around on a piece of bark, arguing with Christopher about which Lego man was the one he had made. And Christopher was scratching mosquito bites and griping because his Lego man wouldn't bend at the waist to ride on the bark boat. Nate watched them for a while, and then the sunlight started making green and yellow patterns on his eyelids, and he drifted off. Somewhere far away there was the sound of coughing.

He brought himself back to awakeness. "Are you okay, Arley?" he asked.

There was another cough, and Christopher said, "Da liked pancakes." Which was just the kind of thing Nate would never get about kids—that whole non sequitur thing. You never knew which direction their brains were going, or why.

He closed his eyes again. Christopher was saying something about a kid at school who ate too many orange peanut candies. "Remember when he barfed all over the desk? Wasn't that funny, Arley?"

The sun was so hot, and he could feel sweat trickling down his back. A bug landed on the hairs on his arms. He swatted at it, and there was now more coughing. Against Nate's eyelids was a big vomiting bear, with orange peanuts. He slid away somewhere.

To the land of coughing.

Christopher said, "Natey! Look at Arley!"

His eyes flew open. He didn't know how much time had passed, but Arley was wading farther out in the water, and he was coughing so hard he was doubled over.

"Arley, come back over here. I think you should sit down," Nate said, but then Christopher said, "Arley needs his inhaler," and Nate realized he'd thought that right at the same time. He sprang up and felt for it in his jeans pocket, but it wasn't there. Shit—had he left it in the barn?

"Are you having an asthma attack?" he asked, but that was ridiculous. Of course the kid was having an attack. He ran into the water and picked him up, and led him up to the chair. The kid was wheezing bad now, and his eyes were panicking.

"Christopher!" Nate said. "I need you to run to the barn and get the inhaler." But no, that was wrong. A five-year-old wasn't going to run fast enough, and then what if he couldn't find the thing? "No, never mind. Come on with me. We're going to go back to the barn. I think I left the inhaler."

"No!" Christopher said.

"Yes. You have to come with me. I'm going to carry Arley, and you have to run fast with me."

"No, no, the inhaler is here!" Christopher said. "It fell out on the sand. By your chair." He was jumping up and down.

"Okay, okay." Nate set Arley down on his lap in the chair and reached for the inhaler, knocked the sand off it. It must have fallen out of his pocket when he sat down. Christ, he hadn't been paying much attention when Jamie had shown him this thing. He had never in a million years expected this would happen, that was the truth of it. He stuck the thing in Arley's mouth and pressed the button, but the stuff seemed to come right back out. These things had to be operated *correctly*. Whatever correctly meant. Why, why, why hadn't he paid attention for the two seconds it would have taken him?

"Come on!" he said loudly. He didn't know if he was saying this to the inhaler or to Arley, who was looking worse by the second.

"You put it in his mouth," Christopher said, "and then you press the button."

Arley was taking short, shallow, openmouthed breaths. Nate, feeling an ice-cold squeeze around his heart, tried once again to put the inhaler in the right place. "Okay, breeeeeeathe," he said. "Take it slow. Breeeathe."

Arley, wide-eyed, shook his head and kept making a noise as if he couldn't get breath.

Nate stared at him. This could not be happening. His heart was pounding, and for a flash, all the deaths rose up in his head: Harris having a heart attack, here alone; his mother dying of cancer in the upstairs bedroom; Louisa ramming her car into some concrete barrier at a hundred miles an hour. He didn't think he could breathe, himself. He tried one last time.

He put his face up close to Arley's, staring right into his eyes. "Breeeeeeathe, slowly and evenly," he said, and waited. "In and out . . . eeeeeasy does it . . . in, out. In, out."

And this time it worked. Arley took in the medicine from the inhaler—Nate could almost feel the flow of oxygen entering him. He smiled at Arley, who smiled back at him. The child's eyes were watering. Nate pulled him over next to him, wrapped his arms around him.

He'd done it. Mr. Flashes of Brilliance comes through once again.

Still, he was shaking, and he didn't think he wanted to let go of Arley for a while. In fact, his arms and legs felt so heavy and shaky that he didn't think he'd be able to move from this spot for about two hundred years. That's how Jamie found them when she came back from the store. Nate had no idea how much time had passed. The bangles on her blouse twinkled in the sunlight when he tried to look up at her. He had to shade his eyes.

She was smiling, but she looked quizzical. "I brought us some fried chicken for din—hey, what's going on here?" she said.

"Oh, nothing much," Nate said. "We're enjoying the summer afternoon."

"Arley had an asthma attack!" Christopher yelled. He was squatting down, pushing his Lego man around in the weeds. "He was in the water and he couldn't breathe, and he needed the inhaler!"

Jamie's eyes clouded up. She leaned down and looked closely at Arley, diagnosing him. "Oh, my goodness, what happened? You're fine now?" She turned to Nate. "You had to do the inhaler?"

"Yeah," he said and shrugged, as if it had been nothing.

"Wow. And you did it? It worked and everything?"

"Worked fine," he said. "After a few tries. We were just sitting here . . . recovering." He laughed and held out one hand, which was still shaking a little bit. She laughed, too.

"Yeah, it's a heart-stopper, isn't it?" she said. She hugged Arley and Christopher, and then after a little while she went and got the fried chicken out of the car, and Nate managed to go get some drinks and dishes and a picnic blanket, and they all came back to the pond and sat there on the blanket eating for a long time afterward.

Nate was surprised to see that he wasn't restless, that it was okay just sitting here with the three of them, not taking down wallpaper or figuring out how to build things or painting the house. He just sat there smiling idiotically. The children clambered over the laps of the adults and asked them a million questions about the sky, and wouldn't it be something if a spaceship came down and landed right now, and what if everyone had superpowers and could fly, and Jamie and Nate nodded and smiled above the kids' heads. And at last the sun went down and the stars came out, looking like little hard, bright things that might hurt you but weren't going to—at least not for a while.

LATER THAT NIGHT, after they put the kids to bed together, they went downstairs to the kitchen. The dishes from the picnic were still on the table, and Jamie started to clear them off, but her head was still filled up with the moon. She could see it rising, fat and orange, through the kitchen window. Nate went into the living room and turned on the stereo. She smiled when she heard "I Heard It Through the Grapevine" playing—that was his song, the one he had listened to over and over while he was packing up the house.

After a moment, he came into the kitchen and, out of the corner of her eye, she could see him getting a beer out of the refrigerator. She was standing at the sink, filling it with warm, sudsy water and watching the bubbles, as if she was in some kind of trance. He came over close to her and then reached around her and turned off the water, and she did not move. Then he gently took her hands out of the dishwater and dried them off with a towel and turned her around to face him.

"Here's a beer for you," he whispered. "Take a sip."

She took it out of his hands and drank some, and then he took the bottle and put it on the counter. He was staring at her, so close to her she could hear his heart beating, but she couldn't bring herself to look up at him. He put his arms around her tentatively and started dancing with her. She moved against him in time to the music. She had always loved this song. Her breath was high in her chest.

"Jamie," he said and buried his head in her neck. "I am so sorry about everything."

"What are you sorry about?"

"What? Now you want a list?" he said, teasing. Then he said, "Well, for starters, today. The whole asthma thing. I didn't really get how awful it is," he said. Another song had come on now, a slower one she couldn't quite make out, and he pulled her closer and danced her into the middle of the kitchen. He kissed her neck.

"But you handled it," she said.

"I know," he said. "But I wasn't smooth at it. It took me a long time to realize he was having an attack, and then I couldn't find the inhaler, and then I realized I didn't really know how to work it."

She didn't say anything. He swallowed and looked at her with his huge brown eyes, as if he was waiting to be screamed at. She didn't scream.

"I just never realized how quickly things can go wrong," he said. "I should have been paying more attention when you told me how to work the thing. I never in a million years thought that was going to happen."

"It's okay," she whispered. "That's how it is for me, too, sometimes."

"And, okay, while we're on the subject of things going wrong, I'm sorry about . . . my dad . . . and the things I thought about . . . you know, about you and him. And I'm sorry about before . . . when we made love . . . and then I . . ."

She laughed and shook her head. "Oh, don't give me that. Now you're going too far."

He laughed, too. "And, well, *now* I'm sorry about how right now I'm killing off a perfectly good seduction scene with all this guilt. Jeez! Somebody send in the hook and stop me from this."

"Wait. This is a seduction scene?" she said, looking right into his eyes.

"Yes," he said, smiling. "Is there something wrong with me, that you don't know that?" They started dancing again, which helped because she could put her head against his chest and not have to look at him. It was almost too much, looking at him, like looking into the sun or something. She wanted a moment to think.

"What do you say?" he said into her ear. "The real truth is that I know I've been rotten to you, and I'm all out of clever things to say to make you want me, and so I'm running on here like an idiot." He traced her cheekbone with his index finger. "The other truth is that I've never wanted anybody so much in my whole life as I want you right now."

"You do?" she said.

"Yes," he said. "Yes, yes, yes. What do you think this is? This is me, falling at your feet."

THEY MADE LOVE, and then it was too hot to sleep.

He told her about being a suspected terrorist, during the Black-Berry incident, and she told him about living in Brooklyn and always being afraid the cops were going to come and take Trace away—and how, months later, it occurred to her that maybe they actually had. Maybe that's why he hadn't returned. She stroked his arm and smiled at him. He was propped on the pillows with his hand resting on her hip, lazily making circles on her hipbone and then her stomach.

"Do you know what porn movies get wrong?" he said suddenly.

She laughed. "What?"

"This. They never show this part, where two people are just touching each other and looking. They don't care about the looking."

"Oh really? I was under the impression they were all about looking."

"No, see? Obviously you've been watching the wrong kind of movies. The ones I've seen are more about spurting. I saw one once where they just showed a guy coming again and again, in slow motion."

She laughed.

"But the way people really touch . . . the lazy, erotic way of just stroking each other's parts while they're talking—not so much of that." He reached over and held her breasts and kissed each of them. "Like these. They're so delicious they each deserve their own name."

"Lefty and Righty?"

"Are you kidding me? More like Lulu and Gigi. They're show-girls, these breasts." He stopped kissing them and looked up at her. "Wait. You gotta tell me. Did they already have names? Some other guy has probably already christened them, huh? What did that guy—what's his name, Chase?—what did he call them?" He kissed them both again.

"Trace. I don't think he called them anything."

"He was too busy painting them on overpasses, huh?"

She laughed again. "And what did you call your wife's? Or do I want to know? She didn't have Lulu and Gigi, did she?"

"My wife," he said, and settled back onto the pillows. He got a faraway look for a moment, and she was sorry she'd brought her up, half-expecting he'd go crazy on her again, like before. But she was curious, and besides that, you couldn't just not mention someone for the rest of your life.

"Wow," he said. "How scary is it that I don't think that much about her? What do you think that means, that I almost never talk about her? Even to Christopher. It occurred to me the other day, when I was painting the front door of the house, that that was the last place I ever saw her alive, and yet I've walked in there ten thousand times since then and . . . nothing. I'm a fucked-up guy, you know that? I know I should tell Christopher more about his mom. Every day I should tell him one more thing, and yet I can't think of a thing to say."

"I don't think that means you're fucked up," she said. "Maybe you've just worked it all through in your head." She knew as she said it that it wasn't true.

"No, no, you have to look at the whole picture to know how fucked up I am. Like my dad. They say you miss your parents when they're gone, no matter how bad they were. And I look around here and think, he's *here*, and he's *here*, and he's over there, too, and how can I get him out of here even faster?" He sat up and ran his fingers through his hair and looked at her with his eyes wide and intense. "I gotta say, it's so much better here without the *dishes* and glassware, isn't it? Life here is so much better on paper plates. It's fine that the furniture is here because that's all new stuff that my mom bought when my dad left, but somehow those dishes reminded me of him and me staying here after Louisa died. He was *in those dishes,* I tell you, and now that they're gone, I'm better here."

"Ah, he was haunting the dishes. I didn't know that." She'd been about to say that she thought of Harris as haunting this bedroom, this bed, where he died, but she stopped herself in time, changed gears.

He laughed. "But they're gone now. He'll be haunting some

other poor soul who won't know what hit her. But at least he's outta here."

"Also," she said, and ran her fingers around his cheekbones, "there's the fact that you're single-handedly dismantling the place. That's got to be getting rid of him here."

She should just come clean, say it. Tell him about the circumstances of Harris's death. After all, he'd apologized for everything bad, so she should, too. She could take a deep breath and say, "There's something you should know," and then she could explain about how the whole incident was innocent but that it had looked bad, at least to the paramedics who'd shown up that day. Maybe he'd even laugh. It might be a story he'd find amusing.

"I always forget that you really had a whole relationship with him, that you knew him when he had turned into Harris, Patron Saint of Children and Community Life, not when he was Harris, Patron Saint of Assholes," he said.

She started to say something then, but he turned to her and she was taken aback by how intense he looked. "I hafta tell you, McClintock, it makes me unendingly happy that you and my dad weren't lovers. You know? I couldn't do this if I ever thought . . ." He rolled over on top of her and started passionately kissing her face all over, hundreds of little kisses along her hairline and then down by her jaw, and then ending with her mouth, which he kissed over and over again. Then he looked at her and smiled so happily it was like a child's amazed smile.

"Come on. We've used up all our bodily fluids. Come downstairs naked with me. We need drink and sustenance if we're to go on."

"Okay," she said, "but shouldn't we sleep a little? The morning is going to come and we're going to be dragged by children into the day."

He was already standing up and pulling her off the bed. He held her close and said softly in her ear, "I think I'm too happy to sleep."

"I know," she said. "I'm that way, too."

"Are you?" he said. "Really?" He searched her face.

"Yes."

"Then come on. Let's go downstairs."

It was startling, being naked in the kitchen in the middle of the night, as if the night had somehow shifted into an alternate universe. The clock on the stove read 3:45. When she was a child, she believed that when the numbers were consecutive that way, you could make the same number of wishes as the lowest number. She got plastic cups out of the cabinet while he cut up lemons and strawberries and got ice out of the freezer. He said they were going to drink fortified water, fortified with colors and vitamins.

"I don't want any alcohol, do you?" he said. "I want to have all this without that buzzy feeling."

"Yeah."

"I mean, this is buzzy enough."

"We have to make three wishes quickly," she said and looked at the clock.

"I don't need any wishes," he said. "I have everything good—oh, except for one thing. I wish Christopher would call me Dad."

"Aw," she said. "Then maybe you should wish that three times. Makes it more powerful that way."

"We have to do an Arley wish. Let's wish that Arley's asthma gets cured, and the third wish will be that he decides never again to wear his ladybug vest." He ducked out of her way, laughing, as she reached out to clobber him.

"What about we wish that you get over yourself?" she said.

"No, no!" He grabbed her butt and enveloped her in another hug. "How about we wish that *you* don't take some stupid job in Vermont and that life goes on like this for a while?"

She started to say something, but he covered her mouth with his to shut her up. When he'd stopped kissing her, she tried again, but he laughed and kissed her again and again, each time pushing back every single fear she had.

Finally, laughing, she started beating on his chest so that he'd let up.

"I have to say something!" she said.

"Nothing about your new job in Vermont, okay?"

"No. I just want to ask you something. Are you going to help me with the jamboree?"

He was cradling her as though they were waltzing and he was just about to dip her. He stared at her, looking like he was going to burst out laughing. "Yes, of course I'm going to help with the jamboree," he said. "But just tell me one thing. Is this how you plan to get all your helpers?"

"No," she said, "but I figure this gets you to be at least a hike leader and maybe to arrange for the hamburger concession."

"Oh, Jamie, Jamie," he said, leaning her over backward and pretending he really might drop her on the floor. And then, just at the last second, as her hair was brushing against the linoleum, he swooped her up and kissed her again. The sky was just getting light when they went back upstairs and got in her bed.

She realized when he got in and pulled the covers up over the two of them that this whole time she had been expecting he'd go back to his own room, and had steeled herself for it, and now that he hadn't—well, all that holding herself together just seemed to dissolve. She curled herself up into him, and he brought his body around hers and they slept.

Nate's cell phone was ringing when he woke up the second time. The first time was when both boys came plundering into the bedroom at 7:38, cannonballing themselves right into his kidneys and then bouncing around on his sheet-covered private parts, claiming they wanted teddy bear pancakes, Sponge Bob Squarepants videos, and later, to swim the length of the pond with their floaties on.

He had expected to be asked to explain his presence there in Jamie's bed—he'd even readied a small speech on the topic—but apparently this rated low on the scale of interesting things of the morning. Jamie was laughing and already pulling on her T-shirt, which was somehow right on hand, and she smiled at him when he opened one eye.

"I'll get this one," she said, and he mumbled, "God bless you, woman."

She leaned over and said into his ear, "But it'll cost you. You are now officially leading a hike at the jamboree, running the hamburger concession, *and* if I say it's necessary, you have to protect me from Chief Cooksey. You may have to kill him for me."

"I'm on it," he said, and she laughed and herded the boys down-stairs. They chattered as they went. Christopher was asking her if she could make the pancakes this time with *no heads* at all so he wouldn't have to eat them off.

"I think the heads taste funny," he was saying, and Jamie was good-naturedly explaining that the heads are made of the same batter the bodies were made from. Christopher wasn't buying it. "They taste yuck," he said. "I don't eat those."

Nate smiled and fell back to sleep. When he woke up again, his cell phone was ringing, and Christopher was standing over him, hold-ing it in midair.

"Here. Jamie said I should bring this to you. You got a call."

"Look at the little screen and tell me who it is."

Christopher said, "It starts with a *T* and then there's an *I* and . . ."

The phone had stopped ringing. "Oh Jesus. Here, hand it to me." He flipped the thing open and checked. *Tina.* Jesus, did that woman have an instinct for the wrong time to call or what? He sank back against the pillows, feeling the slightest twinge of guilt, and looked at Christopher, who was rearranging things on Jamie's dresser and hum-ming a maddening little song.

"So, how you doing, pal?" Nate said.

"Good."

"Are you having fun, now that we're back here?"

"Yeah."

"You know something? I was just thinking how much you look like your mom." He wanted to tell him about his mother, how sorry he was that he'd made her so mad at him the day she died. He'd add that she'd been so happy about having a baby. It was just that she had this temper—but could you tell a kid that? It was crazy to say that stuff. That she was a lovely woman with some anger management issues and that she was massively, cosmically, hysterically disap-pointed by ninety percent of the things her husband did and said. And while he was at it, he'd tell him that Tina was perhaps a mistake, maybe she wasn't going to be his stepmother after all, and now he'd done this thing with Jamie and he felt happy this morning, but who knew what it was going to lead to? He was the king of the dazzling start-up, he'd tell him, not known for his effective long-term staying power. But maybe he could change. Maybe.

I might change.

Christopher was stacking hair clips on the dresser. He turned and looked at his father. "Oh, yeah," he said. "I'm s'posed to tell you that Jamie is taking me and Arley to a place you go to rent tents. For the jamboree. We'll be back soon, and she wants to know do you want anything for the burger stand. Or something."

Nate laughed. Then he cleared his throat. "Hey, kiddo, by the way, were you wondering why I slept in here last night?"

"Nope," Christopher said, and scampered out the door and down the hall.

LATER, HE WAS working outside, standing on the ladder and painting the last of the trim on the front of the house, when he heard a car door slam in the driveway, and there was Frank Cooksey striding across the lawn, dressed in his cop uniform with his aviator sunglasses flashing in the sunshine. Jamie and the kids were still gone, and Nate had figured if he worked steadily, he could finish up this last part today.

"Hey, chief," he said.

"How's it going, Nate?" Cooksey called as he came up the walk and then climbed the three front steps with some difficulty.

"Good, good," Nate said. He did one last swipe of paint and then put down the brush on top of the can of paint. "How are you?"

"Don't stop. Far be it from me to stop a man who's being productive," Cooksey said. "I just came by to say hello, welcome you back to town. Things didn't work out so hot in L.A., I gather."

"Wellll, I guess you could say that," Nate said. He didn't want to say it. Not wanting to stay up there with his butt to Cooksey, he came down from the ladder and wiped his hands on a rag. "Mostly I came back because I wanted to take some time off to get the house in order." He squinted up at it, feeling a little proud of all he'd accomplished. "Looks pretty good, all things considered."

"So you selling it?"

"Well, now, I don't know what I'm doing. Everything's kind of up in the air."

"Uh-huh." Cooksey looked at him as if he knew the inside of Nate's head better than even Nate did. "Say, you got any coffee? Jamie make any before she left?"

Their eyes met. This was, Nate knew, a direct shot, to make it clear that he knew Jamie was living there, too.

"Yeah," Cooksey said, since Nate must have looked blank. "I ran into her downtown, at the rental place. She was getting a tent for the jamboree. I guess she's running that thing now. My daughter Sue told me it's time for me to retire and let the young people take over."

"I haven't heard much about that," Nate said. "I'm just fixing up the house best I can. She watches the kids. And does that stuff. Clubs and all. And the cooking."

"Is that so? You got any coffee?"

"I don't know. We can go see." Nate opened the front door reluctantly, and Cooksey went in, looking around as if he was taking notes. They made their way back to the kitchen, where, sure enough, the coffeepot was still on. Nate got out a Styrofoam cup and poured coffee in it and handed it to the chief.

Cooksey looked at it quizzically.

"Oh! Sorry. You want cream and sugar?"

"Nah. Where are your cups? Your real cups?"

"We got rid of all the dishes," said Nate. "Gave 'em away. We didn't know we'd be back."

"Oh, *we* didn't, did we?"

"Christopher and I. We."

Cooksey took a sip of his coffee, regarding Nate the whole time. When he'd swallowed, he said, "You know, don't you, her sister Lucy is back living with my son-in-law. That's been pretty rough on my family, I'll tell you that. Jennifer is trying to keep up the apartment, but she's lonely and miserable and pregnant, so my wife is trying to get her to move back home." He shook his head and rubbed at his eyes. "I don't think I understand people as well as I used to. Why would a woman even want a guy who's married to someone else who's having his child? What's the point there? Is it just the thrill of the chase? Of winning? What? Where's the morality? The sanctity of the family!"

"I don't know," Nate said and sighed. His paintbrush was drying out on the porch. "Want to bring your coffee back out to the front? I'm afraid I'm a man on a mission. Gotta finish up the porch."

"Yeah, finish it up so you can sell the place and get busy moving out and taking your kid to God knows where. You're just like all the rest of the young people: heading into trouble, never staying put." Cooksey looked around and shook his head. "And just look at *this* place. Toys everywhere. Now with the Styrofoam cups. Pure chaos all the time. This is the way it was when your father was alive, like the children owned the place. Just tell me this. Do you ever ask yourself: *What does she want? Why is this woman sticking around?*"

Nate laughed. "Let's go back outside, shall we?" He ushered Cooksey back through the house and out the front door.

The whole time, the old guy was saying, "I know, I'm just a crazy old man. But I think things. I'm a police chief, so I'm trained in thinking things. My wife says if I weren't a cop I'd just be an ordinary paranoid guy that nobody would want to have anything to do with, but I believe in asking questions. I look around and say this: Why, why, why would an attractive young woman want to come live with an old man? A man who was doing perfectly well until she started feeding him all these rich, unhealthy foods and desserts, and then she started acting all sexy with him, wearing these torn little tank tops or whatever they are, and then pretty soon she got him hot for her, and after leading him on, she screwed him and gave him a heart attack. And then when she got around to calling 911 and we come—well, never mind." He spat on the ground, over the side of the porch.

"Frank, I can't let you—"

"Oh, so now it's *Frank,* is it? Is that how it is? You realize that's the first time you've ever done that, called me by my given name? You've lost all respect for me, haven't you?" He stared at Nate, and for a moment it looked as if his rheumy old eyes were going to start tearing up. He looked away and then he said, "Bah. Don't mind me. It's just life, that's all, and I've got to get over it. Just like I've got to get over my little girl getting married in some big-deal, twenty-five-thousand-dollar ceremony to a guy who can't seem to live at home for longer than three months before he runs off to be with another woman."

"Well, that one really is too bad. For everybody." Nate went over to the paint can and got his brush out and examined it.

"Yeah, it really is too bad," Cooksey said and he spat again. "Your father would be alive today, you know. Not that that means anything to you. You didn't talk to him anyway. But still. He got done in by that woman."

"No, he didn't." Nate sighed.

"He did. I know it for a fact. He was sleeping with her."

"In his dreams he was! Listen, my dad may have wanted to have a romance with Jamie, but he absolutely did not have that kind of relationship with her. Believe me. I've talked to Jamie about this, and I've talked to Ron Shiner, who used to come and visit all the time, and they both have made it very clear: my dad and Jamie were good friends. And anyway, this is just ridiculous. He's dead. What does it matter anyway?"

"Oh. I see. It doesn't matter a bit. The fact that your father was naked in her bed when he died—I suppose that was just some kind of friendly visit he was making. Maybe trying out the sheets in her room, that's all. I'm glad you could explain that for me. Because I'd been wondering how to think about it."

Nate felt his insides do a slow turnover.

"And let me tell you something else, too—that I'm sure doesn't prove a thing to you, since you know everything for yourself. She calls 911 when he's already dead, and we get there, go running upstairs, and she's standing there over the dead body looking like a deer in the headlights and holding a glass of gin, like she's looking for someplace to pour it out, and she's got his *shorts* in her other hand, and she's looking guilty as hell. And there's a bottle of *massage oil* on the bed, vanilla massage oil. And all she can say to us is, 'Oh, I think he died.'"

"That does not mean—"

"No. You're right. It doesn't mean a damn thing. Spare me your legal analysis." Cooksey tossed his empty cup into an empty paint can. It made a satisfying crunch. "But you're not going to stand here and tell me that you already knew about your dad being found naked in her bed. She didn't bother to tell you that part, did she? Eh? I can tell by the look on your face. But just ask her. She'll tell you. It ought to make for an interesting conversation. Wish I could be around when you have it." And he reached in his pocket and put his sunglasses back on and strode across the lawn and got into his squad car.

SHE KNEW RIGHT away that something was wrong. One doesn't live with parents who have spent thirty years in a seething, nonverbal war zone without learning every subtle symptom of unrest. For starters, his face looked terrible. And she knew something was horribly wrong when he didn't greet her or the boys when they got home; he just kept working away, up and down, up and down with the brush strokes, facing the porch wall as if he were a robot programmed for one thing only. She said, "Wow, this looks great." He didn't answer.

Well, fine then. He obviously was a guy who had some severe intimacy issues. Couldn't make love and then stay nice. What *was* that all about?

Arley was jumping up and down, telling Nate about the tent they were going to rent and about the big coffee machine for the grown-ups and the "bijantic" fold-up metal tables—so big that people could put all their stuff on them *and* still eat their hot dogs and hamburgers.

"That's great," Nate said, in as controlled a voice as Jamie had ever heard. She shooed the boys away by promising them a trip to the pond, and then she went upstairs and changed into her bathing suit and got towels for the three of them and went down with her lawn chair to sit on the beach. But she was restless there; she kept listening for Nate to come down and join them, kept going back to the hill to see what was happening at the house. The house was just sitting there, silent and sullen. There was no movement. But what did she expect? He was painting the front porch. She wasn't going to see anything from the back of the house.

And then, as she was helping the boys build a sand castle, it suddenly came to her what had happened. She'd seen Cooksey today at the rental place, and he'd looked shocked to see her with Christopher. Had he come over after that and told Nate about Harris's being in her bed when he died? Such a stupid, inconsequential thing—but oh, he would just love to be the bearer of that news, wouldn't he? He'd been waiting for his chance to tell this.

Shit. She felt this horrible, guilty emptiness in the pit of her stomach, exactly as if a swarm of bugs had taken up residence there. She should have told Nate herself before now, back when it didn't matter so much, even last night. But he'd always been so weird about her and his dad, always so prickly. But surely she could have found the right way to explain it at some point. It had only been a proposed back rub. Surely she could have explained that so Nate could understand. But now Cooksey had taken it upon himself, no doubt, to fill Nate in on the details—and oh, this was ridiculous. Just ridiculous! They were *adults.* Why did everything have to get so complicated?

The children looked at her, worried, when she pounded one of the towers of the sand castle too hard in frustration and cried out. Arley came over and gave her a hug, and Christopher said it was the best castle they'd ever made, and it didn't matter about the tower.

She stayed down at the pond until it was quite late, and then she took the children up to the house, promising them hot dogs and potato chips for supper. The house was dark, and for a moment she felt dread so strong it was like a palpable thing that had moved into her body. She went inside and looked through the house for him, but he wasn't anywhere. Then she checked outside. Sure enough, his car was gone.

He had left. Somehow that made it easier.

She fixed dinner, feeling cold and hot all over. She couldn't eat, so she watched the children finish their supper, and then she took them upstairs and allowed herself to be talked out of making them take baths. The house seemed vast and cold, even though it was a warm evening. She noticed that she walked with her arms crossed over her chest, and that her stomach hurt. Every time there was a little sound, she jumped. After the children were in bed, it was hard to be in the kitchen, where last night they had danced naked.

Imagine! Dancing naked and laughing, eating strawberries and drinking water so they wouldn't dull the memory of the whole thing by using alcohol. She could barely imagine that mood now. She sat down on the floor, leaning against the cabinets and holding her head, but then scrambled to her feet when she heard his car door slam outside.

He came in through the back door and turned on the overhead light.

"Hi," she said. She wiped her hands on her skirt.

He looked at her.

She said, "You talked to Cooksey today, I guess."

"Yeah."

"I hate it that I didn't tell you the whole thing first."

"Yeah, I hate that, too," he said. "It was kind of rough, standing there defending you when I'd been told by you just this morning that I might have to be ready to kill him for you—and then it turned out, hey! He was right, and you were wrong."

"But it's still not what he thinks. Your father and I weren't lovers."

"Spare me, okay?" he said. "It was bad enough that I had to find out that the old guy was naked in your bed."

"I know he told you that, but—"

"Oh, yeah. All about it. And the massage oil and the gin. And the fact that when the rescue people came, there you were, holding his shorts." She started to say something, but he held up his hand. "Don't. Don't. I'm sure there are fourteen thousand reasonable explanations for all this that Cooksey never considered, and I'm sure that we could sit here and you could convince me that nothing whatsoever was going on. But you know something? I don't want to hear it."

"You don't even want to know what I have to say about this?"

"Nope. That's a kick in the head, isn't it? I don't want to hear it. It's not worth it to me, because what I figured out today, after I heard about this, is that this is just one more time my old man inserted himself into *my* life, and took away some good thing that I thought I had going for myself. And if he can still do that to me after he's dead, then I am far too fucked up for a relationship. You know what I'm saying? So it doesn't *matter* to me whether or not you were fucking him, or whether you used the vanilla massage oil or Crisco, or whether there is some perfectly innocent explanation for everything, because *I don't care*. I don't care anymore. I'm out. Over. That's it. We've saved ourselves a lot of time and aggravation and heartbreak, because, number one, I'm no damn good, and number two, I'm not a stick-to-it kind of guy anyway, and number three, I'm *no damn good*. Are you getting that? Because if I can't handle *this* now, then what's the hope that I can handle any other thing that comes along?"

"Would you get a grip?" she said. "What is the matter with you?"

"Who knows?" he said. "But something is. Maybe I have a big sign on me that says, 'Nate Goddard wishes you would just kick the shit out of him now.' Do I? Because I don't remember putting it on, but it can't be a coincidence that every single person figures out that they can get away with this. Anyway, I said I'm done, and I am done. Good night, good-bye, whatever."

"No," she said, and laughed. "No. You're being insane. This is crazy!"

"No doubt it is."

"You would really just stop . . . with me . . . because . . . ?"

"Stop what?" he said. His eyes had gone reptilian. "Exactly what did we have going, in your mind? We've had sex exactly two times and major fights after both of them. I think that's a track record that speaks for itself, don't you?"

"I don't think it speaks for itself," she said softly. She went over to him, as if maybe she could touch him and things would be okay again. "I just want you to know that your father *was* naked in my bed when he died, and I didn't tell you before because it meant nothing, he was just waiting for me to give him a back rub because he didn't feel well—and then when I came upstairs, he was already dead."

He smiled at her, showing teeth. "Feel better? Got that off your chest? *Fine.* Now let me tell you: It doesn't matter. I do not care. Get it? It changes exactly nothing."

"Why won't you listen?" she said, and started to cry. "Why can't you see that this is not something you need to worry about?"

"What makes you think I'm worried about this? I'm disgusted by it, if you want to know the truth. I'm repulsed."

"Oh, come off it. There's nothing to be disgusted by! It was going to be a *back rub*. Nothing more. You've got to stop this. You're going to hurt Christopher if you go around your whole life with this chip on your shoulder."

"Excuse me, but aren't you going to get a job in Vermont?" he said. "Aren't you leaving anyway? What right have you to start talking to me about what's right for Christopher? You're leaving. I'm leaving. And by the way, I put the house on the market today—*not* with Todd Haney, since he's completely ineffective. I'm just going to sell it as is. And I'm getting out of here."

She was leaning against the cabinets. For a moment she felt him looking at her and had a wild thought that he might come over and reach for her. She could explain again about Harris. She could make him see. He would tell her he understood and that he didn't need any more explanations. He would say, "Let's put all this behind us." And she would try, she really would try.

But then she heard his footsteps on the stairs. He had gone to bed.

CHAPTER
28

I f there was anything Jamie knew how to do, it was keep up appear-
ances. She became relentlessly cheerful around the kids, to show
them that nothing was wrong, although the effort of it exhausted her.
Nate, true to his word, finished painting the house but spent most of
his time on the computer or the telephone, off in his room with the
door closed. She supposed he had business deals he was working on.
One day she overheard him in the kitchen, apparently talking to an
agency about getting a nanny. Another time, from the hallway, she
could hear him on the phone with a headhunter. He was looking for a
new job.

"Yes, I've had lots of experience in the telecommunications field,"
he was saying. There was a silence. "Well, travel is a little bit problem-
atic . . . I prefer to work locally from a home base, but that base can be
anywhere. I don't care where I go."

And then his floor had creaked, and she was afraid he would
throw open the bedroom door and find her there, eavesdropping like
a child.

As for her, she'd stepped up her efforts for the Vermont job. As
soon as the teaching gig was over, she was planning a trip there. Shana

said the school was still trying to hire from within for the art teacher's job, but there wasn't anybody truly qualified who wanted the job, was the truth of it.

"I think if you came here and they saw that you're a real person who knows something about art and is nice to children, I think you could get it," she said with a sigh. "I keep trying to impress upon them that time is running out, but it's just that the headmaster is a little gun-shy because he's made some personnel mistakes in the past."

So she was depressed thinking about this, and also about keeping life normal for Arley and Christopher, and meanwhile she was getting bags under her eyes and her stomach was in knots most of the time. Nate was distant but polite to her, but what made her most crazy—and most angry—was that it was so unnecessary, this male pride, this wounded tenderness. Why couldn't he see through to the things that were really important? Why did he let his feelings about his father dictate his whole life? Then she'd think maybe he wasn't really doing that at all: maybe it had to do with her. She was intrinsically unlovable, that's what she said to Lucy. She was the kind of woman that men got excited about, and then abandoned. She was too opinionated, too caught up with her child, too overprotective, too *needy*. No one was going to ever really love her, and she might as well accept that and get back to what was important in her life: doing her art and taking care of Arley. And now, making money.

And Lucy said all the right, sisterly things: "No, no, no, sweetie. This is just the way men are sometimes. They fight their feelings. It's a doomed system, I've decided, this man-woman thing." Handsome Dan had gone back to Jennifer; they were picking out nursery furniture.

Then one day Jamie was in a rush getting to the high school to teach her class, and as she got to the building, nudging Arley along with all his papers and books and crayons, she saw out of the corner of her eye a figure rise up from the shaded edge of the steps where he'd been sitting.

"Jamie," he said, and she jumped. The guy had on a black leather motorcycle jacket. He strode over to her, holding out his hand. At first, as he came out of the shadows, she thought he was just the parent of a student, but then her body recognized him before her mind caught up, and she instinctively reached down and grabbed Arley's hand.

"Trace," she said in barely a whisper. Her fingertips lost all feeling.

"Hey," he said and smiled his beaming good-looks smile, exhibiting those Chiclet-perfect teeth and some rather attractive mellowing laugh lines around his eyes. "So, you look great. Things are good for you." It was a statement, not a question.

"Thank you," she managed. She took Arley's hand in hers. Arley was looking at her face and then at Trace, back and forth, back and forth. She would have to tell him something in a moment, turn to him and say, "Arley, you wanted to know your father? Here he is." Why did that feel so unthinkable? But she was going to have to; in fact, that moment she'd never even imagined before was speeding fast at her. She heard herself say, "So how are you?" and Trace laughed a little bit, a lazy kind of laugh she remembered. His eyes were still that ice-blue color, so pale they looked barely tinted.

"Wow," he said. He was grinning in kind of a dazed, surprised way, shaking his head in amazement. "I'm good, I'm good. Real good." He looked much older now—maybe because he wasn't wearing his hair long anymore; it was clipped close to his head in that style she always considered kind of ominous-looking in a POW-camp sort of way, and she saw little flecks of gray interspersed with the blond now, and in his whiskers, too. He was dressed just the same as always, black leather jacket and boots and dark jeans. His cheekbones were like Arley's—high and sticking out—and she watched a little muscle in his jaw flex back and forth as he looked back and forth from her to Arley. She waited to feel something for him—she had loved him for so long, or thought she had, anyway—and yet it all felt too difficult to sort out now. Her arms felt so heavy she was sure she was going to drop all the art supplies she was carrying.

"What are you doing here?" she said, and didn't like it that there was a little high note of something almost slightly hysterical in her voice.

"So this is him, isn't it?" he said, tilting his head toward Arley. "The bay-bay." That had been a joke between them when she was pregnant, the way he said it. "Hi," he said to Arley.

"Listen," she said, "I have to go inside and teach a class."

Trace laughed. "Yeah, I know," he said. "I've been coming through town a lot lately, and I figured this was the place where you taught." He smiled, including her in the joke: "I *Googled* you. Found out you're teaching. And selling some of your paintings in galleries. Good for you!"

"How did you get here?" she asked him, which was ridiculous, because what she wanted to say was "Why the hell were you looking for me?" Arley was looking at Trace curiously, yet shrinking back behind her. He'd missed the reference to himself as the "bay-bay."

"Oh, I have a bike now." Trace pointed his thumb at the parking lot she'd come from, rocked up and down on his heels. "Yeah, I've kinda had to give up the art thing for a while, due to some . . . disagreements with the law, you know." He barked out a hard chunk of laughter. "So I've been traveling around for a while now. Passing through, looking at places, thinking about us. After I saw your name on the school's website, I called and told them I was a parent who was interested in having my kid take an art class, and they told me when you were teaching. So I knew you were here, and I figured one of these days I'd just run into you. I mean, I know where you live and all, but I didn't want to scare you by showing up at your house, just like that."

At the mention of his knowing where she lived, she went a little numb.

"Mom," Arley said, pulling on her hand, trying to get free.

"Heard in town that you were living with a rich old man who died," Trace said. Now he looked down at Arley. "Hi," he said, extending his hand. He squatted down. "And what's your name? Let me guess. Does it happen to be . . . let's see . . . *Arley*?"

"Yes." Arley's eyes widened.

"Do you know how I knew that?"

She shifted her weight. This was not happening. This could not be happening. "I said I have to go in and teach now," she said.

Trace knelt down on the sidewalk and took Arley's hand in his. He said very softly, "I'm your father, Arley. I'm Dad."

Arley looked up at her with his wide, questioning eyes, and she nodded at him and swallowed. There was a lump in her throat.

"Oh," he said quietly. "You're my dad? You *are*? Really? Really?" He looked up at Jamie, one of those *You've been holding out on me* looks. She could tell he was reacting, as everyone did, to Trace's hand-someness and, yes, to the charm he had when he felt like bestowing it.

"Yeah, and you look like me, you know that?" He reached out his hand and touched the boy's cheekbones and eyebrows, and Jamie felt herself draw back. "I haven't seen you since you were a newborn baby. Wow. This is heavy." He looked back up at Jamie, rubbed his eye with the edge of his thumb, took a deep breath. "Hey, what if I take him for you while you teach your class? He and I could walk around or go get some ice cream."

"No," she said. "No, that would not be possible."

"People can't keep me because I have asthma," Arley explained, as if he didn't want his father to think Jamie was simply being rude. "And they have to know how to work the inhaler, and sometimes I have to go to the hospital. So nobody keeps me but Lucy and Nate sometimes, but he just started and he didn't know how to work the inhaler and I almost died. Harris could keep me, but he died."

"Arley," Jamie said.

"It's okay," Trace said. He stood up, smiling with his eyes through a nest of wrinkles. He looked as if he might cry. "I just wanted to see him and hear him talk. I'm a nice guy. Maybe you remember that. You *liked* me."

She nodded. She had a chalky taste in her mouth. He smiled at her again, as if he knew he'd blown his whole life and was just getting around to realizing it, but he knew all that was hopeless. His arms hung at his sides, in their long black sleeves. She saw his fingers curling and uncurling, black underneath the fingernails. She remembered that: the paint under the fingernails, and deep in the lines of his hands. But there was something else about him now: an unpleasant edge, a soullessness in the eyes.

"Well, maybe when you're done with your class, we could talk," he said. "We could all get ice cream."

"I don't know," she said. "I have to be someplace."

"Jamie, Jamie," he said, and smiled at her with his pale blue eyes. "I'm not going to do anything bad. I just want to talk to you, baby. I know you think I was bad to you, but it was just that I got picked up by the cops, and when I got back to the house, you were gone . . ."

"No, no, no. That's not how it was!" she said. He stared at her. "Listen, I—I have to think about it," she said. Arley was looking back and forth between them, starting to breathe harder. She clutched his hand more tightly.

"It's sudden," Trace said. "I didn't mean to startle you. I just want to talk. Don't worry."

He stepped then to the side and let them walk by him, and when she passed him, he reached over and touched her arm with his rough fingertips, and she jumped back.

"Easy," he said, and laughed. "Jesus, you're wound tight."

Fortunately, he had gone by the time the class was over. She had half expected to find him still on the steps, or waiting beside the car. She felt a quick relief, but then realized the larger picture: Trace was around. He had found her. On the way home, Arley said, "I like him. I really like him. He's my dad. Is he really my dad? Like Natey is Christopher's dad?"

"Yes," she said. "He is your dad."

He leaned across the front seat, breathing onto her neck. "Really,

really? Is he going to come and live with us? Like Natey did with Christopher? Let's see. We could have a house with two kids, two dads, and one mom. That would be fun, wouldn't it? Wait until Christopher sees that I have a dad, too. I have a dad! I have a dad!"

"Really, really. *Please* sit back in your seat. I'm going to get a ticket if you don't have your seat belt on."

"But wait. You said I wouldn't ever see him. Why did I see him when you said I wouldn't ever see him?"

"I don't know. It was a surprise to me. Sit back."

"Where does he live now? Call him on the cell phone and tell him I would like him to come to our house and see Christopher and Natey. Okay?"

She pulled the car over to the side of the road and turned it off. "Okay, I'm going to tell you about him."

She told him how he had been her teacher in college, and how they'd fallen in love, but that he had a very strange job: he painted things on buildings. Words. Words that people don't want to see on buildings sometimes. His eyes had widened at that. It's not a very smart thing to do, she said. People get mad about it. She told him about how Trace always said it was art that people would look at and it would make them think about things in new ways. Sometimes, she said, that's what art does. Makes you think. And so that's why he did it. But then he was staying out longer and longer hours, and he didn't really have the money to help them pay the bills, and so when Arley was born, the apartment was very cold and dark, and she needed somebody to come and take care of her, so a friend came and took her to Aunt Lucy, and they decided it would be the best thing if she and Arley lived in Connecticut, where Arley could have an aunt nearby and a whole group of people who would love him.

He thought about this. Then he leaned over, and patted her cheek. "But *now* I need a dad," he said. "Christopher has a dad, and now I have one, too."

She didn't know what to say. She twisted her hands on the steering

wheel. "Well, I would love it if you could have ... some kind of relationship with him, maybe," she said finally. "But even though he's your
father, I think he appreciates ... a different kind of life, that doesn't
include other people. That's just the way it is. He likes the city, and he
likes painting on the sides of buildings. There aren't really enough
buildings here for him to paint on." This was all idiotic; she didn't even
know what she was saying.

He looked out the window. A fly buzzed inside and then regretted it, buzzing and throwing itself at the car window.

"We have buildings if he really wants to paint them," he said at
last.

"Well," she said. "I don't think it's that easy, kiddo."

"Could we go through the car wash and scream while the water
hits the car, and then go home and tell Christopher I have a dad?"

"Okay, sure," she said. Screaming in the car wash might actually
be of use.

CHAPTER
29

Fifty times a day now Nate wished he wasn't such an idiot. Hell, he might even be depressed. Was that what this crushing, go-nowhere feeling was? The urge to do nothing? He'd finished painting the outside of the house, the steps had been built, the wallpaper removed, and whenever he had the energy, he was going to sand down the walls and paint the kitchen. But for now, he seemed to be in some kind of weird suspended animation. He was waiting to hear from two separate headhunters about jobs; also, he sometimes had to talk on the phone with Tina, who had finished up her docket of work and was now intent on coming, even though during every phone conversation she made it clear how she was mad at him for not groveling to Howie to get his job back. *And* the house was on the market, but no one was coming by to look at it. The new Realtor had come over to visit and surveyed all the work Nate had done, and said the house really needed a second bathroom. He'd given her his heavy-lidded stare and said, "So sell it to people who'll put one in." She'd tightened her lips at that and said that in this kind of market, people didn't want to put in their own second bathrooms.

He said, "You know, that's *exactly* the position in which I find myself, too. I don't *want* to put in a second bathroom, especially for somebody else." And then he'd performed a chin-up on the bar in the kitchen, just to indicate that this was the end of the conversation. And sure enough, she'd packed up her big Lady Realtor purse and marched herself out of there.

He stayed home every day with Christopher, poor kid. Arley went with Jamie to school, but Nate wasn't having any of that for *his* kid. They had to learn again to be together, just the two of them, father and son, damn it. One day he'd gone into the kitchen to make the kid a simple peanut butter sandwich, and he'd apparently done the crusts all wrong, or the cutting—it hadn't been in triangles, the way Jamie did it. And Christopher had turned all dark and puffy, like a storm was brewing in the middle of his head. Wouldn't take the sandwich, wouldn't say what was wrong. *Gah!* It had been months already. When was this so-called *bonding* going to happen, if not now?

At first he'd tried again to get the kid to throw balls in the yard, but Christopher would just stand there listlessly and then start picking dandelions and blowing the fluff all around the yard. So finally they'd settled on something that worked for both of them: eating Cheez Doodles in their underwear on the living room couch while they watched cartoons.

One day Nate had looked over at his son and said, "You got a good burp yet?"

The kid looked startled.

"No. I mean it. We've got to work on your belching skills now. Lemme hear what you got."

Christopher had tried his hardest, but only a squeak came out. They both laughed.

"No, like this." Nate swallowed a big boatload of air and then opened his mouth and let out one of his finest. It was the belch that had won contests back in junior high. Ron still deferred to him on all matters having to do with processing air.

Christopher practiced, but finally Nate remembered that drinking soda helped, so he went to the kitchen and poured them both big paper cups filled with Coke. "Now, swallow it and hold it in, and then let 'er rip!" When Christopher had finally gotten the hang of that, Nate had showed him some of his other major tricks: how to make a farting sound using the palm of your hand in your armpit, stuff like that.

This was progress.

So that's what they would do in the mornings from now on. Sit on the couch and burp. And as soon as they heard Jamie and Arley pulling up in the driveway, they leapt up and put their clothes on, threw the empty Cheez Doodle bag in the trash, and pretended they had plenty of good stuff to do. Not that they were fooling anybody. But it was a start, Nate thought.

This was male bonding at its finest.

ONE DAY HE and Christopher were sitting on the couch scratching themselves and eating orange cheese snacks, when they heard the car door slam too many times. Three times, to be exact. They leapt up and did their little Keystone Kops throw-away-the-evidence routine (which was strictly for fun, not because Nate had anything to feel bad about, as he'd explained to himself). Through the kitchen door, they could hear Jamie saying, "Well, yes, you're right, we are doing quite a bit of work to the house . . . yes . . . and this is the kitchen . . ."

Arley said, "I want to show you my room! Come upstairs! And these are my Lego men! Come on, come upstairs!"

There was a man's low voice, saying something that Nate couldn't quite hear, and he and Christopher looked at each other. Nate shrugged and crumpled up the bag.

"Christopher! Natey!" Arley yelled. "Guess who's here! My *dad* is here!"

Nate snapped his jeans shorts and quickly pulled a respectable, only minimally stained T-shirt over his head, brushed his hair with his hands very fast, and then sauntered into the kitchen to get a look at this guy. Arley's dad, huh? This didn't sit right with him.

And sure enough, there was a guy dressed all in black, an older-looking dude, smiling, with big white teeth, and looking around the room with hesitation in his eyes. Nate almost laughed. *This guy?* he wanted to say. He pictured a comedy routine where he'd say, *Well, here's your problem, ma'am. This is who you decided to have a kid with?* Although, who was *he* to talk, sitting here in his ragged jeans shorts with his hair not combed and orange cheese powder on his hands? He didn't know what he'd expected this supposed great love of Jamie's life to look like, but definitely like somebody a little more alpha, with less of the starving artist look. A guy with some meat on him, whom you could picture swinging from billboards and subway trestles.

Nate stuck out his hand. "Hi. I'm Nate Goddard," he said.

"Trace Forrester." The guy shook his hand but didn't meet his eyes.

"Natey, this is my dad. This is my dad," Arley said, jumping up and down, and looking back and forth between Nate and the other guy, who wasn't looking at him at all, but instead was looking like he'd made a wrong turn somewhere and wished he could remember the instructions for how to operate his invisibility cloak.

Jamie looked terrible, just terrible. She was bustling around, not meeting his eye, acting as if she'd been taken over by a tornado of emotions, opening up cabinets, getting out cups, then going to the freezer and rattling ice cubes, asking people what they would *like,* and not getting any answers because nobody was going to get what he would *like.* That was obvious. She meant drinks, of course—what would they like to *drink,* and finally Nate had to come to her rescue to get it all sorted out. Lemonade for the two boys, plain tap water for this guy Trace (although he did ask about beer, but that request was ignored), and a Coke for Nate. Jamie put on water for tea for herself, even though it was about a million degrees in there, and surely she didn't really want any. It was just something to do. Nate could read her.

Then she announced to the room at large that Trace was indeed Arley's father, and that he was passing through *town,* and would be staying for *lunch.* She said she'd seen him a couple of times at the *high school,* and that he'd wanted to see where they *lived,* and that seemed like a nice thing. Nate had never heard her talk like this, all in italics and with her breath so very high up in her chest.

Lunch would be tuna fish sandwiches on little wheat bread triangles, and celery sticks and little cubes of what the children called Monster cheese, which Jamie was industriously chopping up. Nate wondered why he hadn't found that hunk of cheese himself when he'd rummaged through the fridge that morning. He would have gobbled it right up.

They ate outside on the porch, and Nate tried to make casual conversation with Trace—like what kind of a name *was* Trace, anyway? Ah, it was really Tracey. But that had seemed like a girl's name, and so he'd dropped the *y.*

"Cool. Kind of goes with your profession, too, I would imagine," Nate said. The dude was giving him a blank look, so he added, "You know, the word *trace.* I heard you're in graffiti."

Trace laughed at that, but Jamie gave him a look. *Don't start with the jokes: in graffiti.*

He returned the look. *This is how men talk to each other. And by the way, this guy must have been a lot hunkier five years ago than he is right now, or I can't believe you ever let him touch you.*

Lunch was bad, he thought, but it wasn't as bad as it might have been. After they ate, Trace allowed himself to be dragged upstairs by Arley so he could admire his room and be shown all his treasures: his four foreign coins, a Sponge Bob Band-Aid still in its wrapper, a one-foot section of shiny brown audiotape, his broken cell phone. Christopher went along, too, since it seemed in a way that Arley's dad had been brought around specifically for his edification: Arley wanted to show that he had a father, too, one that could be paraded around and made to look at stuff.

After a few moments of hanging around Jamie in the kitchen, watching her in silence, Nate decided he'd take a trip upstairs as well. He found Trace standing at the door of the boys' room, listening as Arley explained about the kid whose cat rode ponies.

That old chestnut. Next came the story about the kid throwing up the orange circus peanuts—always a hit with Christopher and Arley, who fell over themselves in the telling. And then, because Arley's father was a visitor of the highest importance, they even lavished upon him all their best facts: a birch tree branch is nature's toothbrush for when you're lost in the woods; roundworms live in people's butts; the sun is really a star only it's just closer than the other stars; if you get lockjaw they have to kill you because you're going to die anyway; and if you pet a raccoon, you have to go right to the doctor and get twenty-three shots in the stomach.

"That's cool," said Trace. He looked out of place here in this bright, clean children's room filled with toys, his clothes all wrong, his eyes unfocused and bored. Nate stood watching him in the doorway, his arms folded.

"Dude," he said. "You need a ride back to town?"

Trace looked at him gratefully. "Yeah," he said. "My bike's at the school."

On the way back, they made small talk about Harleys and weather conditions and how Trace was now on the road, how it was good to be out of New York, yada yada yada. Nate could do this; it was part of what he was about, being chameleon-like and speaking the street talk. He could feel himself toughening up his language, becoming someone Trace could relate to.

When they got to the school, Trace paused, his hand on the door handle. "So, you're doing her now, is that it?"

Nate looked straight at him, tried not to look disturbed at the phraseology. "No, as a matter of fact, I'm not," he said. "Why? You want to get back with her?"

"Nah. Well, maybe. I just heard from some mutual friends that she was doin' all right. Living with an old guy who died. So I came by to see if she'd help me out a little, you know." He sighed. "I didn't tell her this yet, but—well, I did some jail time for my art, man, and well, some other peripheral things. Some drug stuff. Nothing major. Things got a little messed up after that. Let's just say I have some debts."

"She thinks you're here because you wanted to see the kid."

He blinked. "Oh, yeah! Well, sure. The kid. He's my *son,* what do you think?"

"Just so you know, she doesn't have any money," Nate said. "She's barely scraping by."

"Really," Trace said. He got out of the car. "Lucky she has you then, man. Thanks for the ride." He put his head inside the window and tapped on the door. "Be cool about the other stuff I told you."

"Right."

"HECKUVA GUY, YOUR ex," Nate said later.

"Yes," she said. She was crocheting—no doubt making some damn-fool thing for the kids, even though he had forbidden it. She'd taken all that forbidding as a joke.

"Kind of a surprise, I guess, seeing him again." He got down a cup for coffee, feigning nonchalance. "So, does he look the same, would you say?"

She eyed him suspiciously. "Well, he looks older if that's what you mean. He used to be much more put together and presentable, and *handsome*. Okay? Are you satisfied?"

"*I'm* satisfied," he said. "The question is, are *you* satisfied? I just wanted to know: are you thinking of getting back together with this guy?"

"You certainly have a way of getting right to the point," she said.

"That's because we don't have a lot of time here on earth." He laughed, feebly, but she didn't laugh. She did another row of crocheting, that hook flashing. She was moving so fast he thought she wasn't going to answer, but then she said, "I just think it's good for Arley to get to see that he does indeed have a father."

"Oh, *indeed* it is," he said, to mock her. "I've set the bar pretty high."

He stood there a moment more, watching her. Lately it had been so hard for them to be in the same room, and—well, he missed her. He missed those evenings on the porch with her, the times when they could just talk. He missed a lot, actually. His groin tightened. He wanted to tell her about Trace's having done jail time—did she know that? Did she know that he'd come because he thought she had money, and he needed some? He wanted—no, he ached to find out what exactly she *did* know. Should he just come out and ask her? Her fingers were flying around the crochet hook, and her hair was falling across her face, so he couldn't see her expression.

Naturally he said the worst possible thing. "Yeah, so you think he's showing up so he can put his name in for the Father of the Year Award? Because I just want to say, I think I've got that nomination all sewn up."

She didn't smile.

"I was being *ironic*," he said.

"I'm sure you were," she said.

"No, no. I just think that Arley certainly is lucky to at last find out that he has a *dad* in the world. I mean, I'm no expert on father-son relationships, as anyone could attest who's known me for even five minutes, but imagine the loss of him going his whole life without finding *that* guy—"

"Would you just stop it? Just stop it," she said. She put down the crocheting and turned and faced him and for a moment he was so surprised that he thought his heart wasn't going to start up again. Her face was red. "I am so sick and tired of you being so *ironic* and clever about every single thing! And I've had it with the way you act like we're all just sooo misguided and unenlightened, compared to the *fabulous life* you used to have."

"Wait, I never said—"

She stood up. "Let me finish, okay? *Would you just please be quiet for one full minute and let me finish?* It's awful and terrible and sad that your dad was bad to you and that you can't get over it—but get over it! It's not my fault, and God knows it's not *Christopher's* fault. You act like everything is out of your control, but you could make everything go your way if you didn't hold onto your stupid bitterness over your father. You choose to imagine him and me in some kind of love thing, and then you stomp around here, acting so *put upon* and sorry for yourself because you somehow think you're trapped here with this house. Why *are* you even here, anyway? What's keeping you here when you obviously hate every single minute of it?"

He put down the coffee cup on the counter. He felt light-headed all of a sudden. He said, "I do not want to hear anything you have to say on the subject of my father. You and everybody else have bought into the idea that he was some great and wonderful guy, and that I was the fucked-up one—"

"No!" she said. "No, don't tell me all that. Those are your *excuses* for the way you act. Don't you know that by now? Who cares whether he was the perfect dad or not? He's *dead* now, and you can't go back and fix it, even if you stomp around here and pout forever. And I don't want to know your stupid convoluted reasons. And I want to say one more thing to you, and then I'm going to get out of your way. I will *not* have you breaking my little boy's heart. Do you hear me? I *will not have it.*"

"Wha—? What are you talking about?"

"Oh, you know what I'm talking about. You know that Arley adores you, and I know it's quite a thrill to have somebody love you so much and want you to pay attention to him all the time—but the truth is you *don't* love him, and I will *not* have you breaking his heart by pretending you do."

This—now *this* stunned him. "I do nothing. I'm just a sitting duck when he comes around—"

"You do things with him and act all fake as if you like him, but I see the way you really feel. I see what you're doing. Do you know what he thinks? Do you even have any idea what he imagines to be true? He thinks he can love you enough and that he'll win you over and get you to stay here. That's what he told me, that he goes and sits with you so you'll stay. How pathetic is that? I mean, how awful and sad is that, that this little boy . . ."

Oh my God. She was crying now, reaching over and grabbing the roll of paper towels and wiping her face with one, sniffling. She'd gotten herself so worked up she was now beginning to sob. She buried her head in her hands and leaned against the counter. He felt like the wind had been knocked out of the middle of him. Women were always crying. His mother, Louisa . . . women were always going to pieces on him. But this couldn't be about him. This was about that idiot she used to be with. She was thinking of that dude, and then crying at Nate.

He stood and looked at her, and then she straightened herself up, dried her eyes, and glared at him. She had the meanest, cutest glare of anybody he'd ever seen, and it was hard not to want to laugh and go hug her when she put on that face. He started toward her.

"*Don't,*" she said in a low voice that was almost worse than the yelling. "Just stay away from me. I don't ever want you to touch me again. This is the last thing on earth that I need from you."

"Don't worry," he said. "Touching you is the last thing I was thinking of doing."

He turned then on his heel and walked out to the barn, feeling grateful for the coolness and peace inside. Funny how Harris seemed to be sitting there waiting for him, opening the door and ushering him into the coolness.

You see now, don't you, why I needed this sanctuary. Now you know what it's really like.

Ron Shiner came by the next day on his lunch hour to see if there was any trouble brewing that he might become a part of. He pulled up in his pickup truck and got out carrying a bag of subs. He seemed highly amused to find Nate outside, now painting the back stairs he'd built. It was, Nate had decided, his very last effort on the house. The new Realtor had said she was bringing over a prospective buyer that weekend, and she strongly suggested that since he wasn't going to put in a second bath—and he wasn't—then little things like the steps being painted might tip the balance in his favor.

Ron had been on vacation to the Cape with his family, and he had a lot of hilarious stories having to do with lobsters getting loose in cottage kitchens, helped by little boys, and funny stories about trying to have sex with his wife while the kids banged on the bedroom door. Then he looked around. "Where's Christopher?" he said. "I thought you'd be doing your usual male bonding."

"Yeah, well, I let him go with Jamie and Arley to the high school."

"Oh," Ron said. And laughed.

"What?"

"Nothing, man." He laughed again. "She's good with that kid, that's for sure."

"Yep. She is. Here, help me paint these stairs, why don't you? Here's an extra brush."

"Why? Are you too tired after all your adventures?"

"What are you talking about, adventures?"

"You and Jamie."

"There is no me and Jamie."

"Not even by now? What's wrong with you, dude? Did it fall off or something?"

"She was involved with my dad. Turns out he died in her bed. Without clothing. And, she's now accusing me of leading on her son, trying to make him dependent on me so that I can—I don't know—rule the world or something. Did you know that you can lead a kid on? I didn't even know that was a category of crime."

"Oh, yeah. Sure. Hey, that's a time-honored tradition with the single moms. In fact, that's how I got Ellen to marry me. I led her kid on until she fell for me."

"Yeah, well . . ."

"You're not into it."

He shrugged. "My dad. You know. Incest rule or something."

Ron laughed. "Doesn't apply here."

"Well, the yuck rule applies. And anything my dad was getting, I don't want. Just on principle."

Ron shrugged. "Well. I gotta say, man, that I don't believe it for a minute. I mean, so what if your dad had his clothes off? Naked doesn't mean sex. Jamie was not into him. And you really are showing a weird side here. I mean, this is life. Twenty-first-century life. You haven't been naked with a woman and not had sex?"

"When it comes to my dad, naked means sex."

"Listen," Ron said. "Let me just tell you something. You'd know if Jamie had been in love with your dad, you'd *feel* it. And anyway, my wife is good friends with Lucy, you know. And Lucy says that Jamie is in love with you, dude. So do with that what you will. I just thought you ought to know. I gotta get back to work. The livestock in this county require my services."

"Tell Ellen she is misinformed."

"Ha! Fat chance of that. When did you turn into such a suspicious old fart? Lighten up! Take things at face value."

After Ron left, Nate kicked the stairs as hard as he could, and the bucket of paint fell over and spilled in the dirt. Goddamn it. *This* was what his life was like. It summed it up perfectly. People like Ron Shiner—people who thought in black and white, good and bad—they had no clue about what was really going on in the world. They met girls and married them, and when it didn't work out, they got divorced. They didn't beat themselves up, they just met new women—maybe women with children—moved a couple of miles away, and resettled themselves. Along the way, they kept looking forward as though everything was unfolding in some expected, logical way. Ron sold *feed*. You want a bag of feed around here, you pretty much buy it from Ron. Over and over again. He remembers your birthday and your children's names, and what kind of beer you like—and you see him at the fairs and in church and coaching your kid's basketball team.

But life just doesn't work that way.

Nate stood staring at the half-painted steps, and then he sighed and went down to the paint store *again* and got more paint for the steps, and when he got back, lugging yet another gallon of brown, he put it in the barn and went into the kitchen, looking for something to drink. There was Trace Forrester, standing in the doorway between the dining room and the kitchen. Just standing there.

"Hey! Wow, man, you startled me. What are you doing in here?" Nate said.

"I—I thought you were Jamie," Trace said. "She and I were together and we were both heading over here, and I guess I got here first."

He was lying. Anybody could see he was lying. He was standing in an artificially straight way, with his arms close to his sides, as if he had something stuck in his shirt.

"Really?" Nate said. "So you must have been with her at the music school, where the boys have their lessons on Thursdays."

"Yeah, I was. I was at the music school."

"Or—oh, wait. Is it soccer practice on Thursdays? I do believe it is." He went over to the calendar, pretended to consult. "Yep, soccer practice. So you must have meant that you were at the *soccer field,* not the music school."

Trace gave him a level look.

"No matter. Either way. Care for a beer?" Nate said. "I've been thinking I didn't really get to hear about what else you're planning to do in this area. And also I want to know what you think of that Arley. Quite a boy you've got there."

"Yeah," Trace said. "He's a little fucker, all right." He laughed. "That's what my dad always called me. Highest praise going."

Nate laughed his fake oh-ho-ho laugh. "Well, now, you're like me. You've been gone from his life for a long time. I didn't raise my boy, either, and now I'm trying to catch up, make up for lost time. Tough, isn't it?" Nate handed him a cold bottle of beer and took a Coke for himself. He motioned him out to the porch and they sat down in the chairs.

Trace sat on the edge of the Adirondack chair, which was not easy, and drank his beer fast. Nate noticed he kept his left arm straight down close to his side.

"So you looking to get back together with Jamie? Is that what I'm hearing?" Nate said. He stretched out, made his voice sound slow and friendly, even though it was all he could do not to pick this guy up by the scruff of his neck and throw him in the shrubbery. He had never disliked a human being as intently as he did this one. But he knew he had to take this one slow and easy, just keep reeling out the line. He listened—trying not to wince—as Trace told him how much he'd always loved Jamie and the "little fucker." And then Trace started talking about how Jamie had just disappeared on him, left him during the most troubled time of his life, didn't even wait to find out that he'd gone to *jail,* and how he'd hoped to get things together, but she still owed him for not sticking by him when he was really in need.

"You know she met me when I was teaching. She's one of those girls who goes for guys when they're successful, but then, when they're down and out, she doesn't stay around," he said. After a while he sat back in the chair, asked for another beer. Nate got up and got him one.

When he came back out with it, he brought along a notepad and a pen. He handed both to Trace, who reached up automatically to take them. A leather pouch slipped out of his shirt just then and landed on the chair. Trace scrambled around to pick it up, but both his hands were holding things by now, so Nate reached down and picked it up for him.

There was some cash in it, he could see, a wad of bills—and then a bunch of earrings and necklaces and Jamie's little digital camera.

"Okay," he said to Trace. He cleared his throat. "Put down the beer, and I want you to write something for me. I'll dictate, and you write."

"This is not what you think, man."

"I'll dictate and you write."

"She gave me this stuff, man."

"*I'll dictate and you write.* Come on. What I tell you. Let's go."

"I'm not writing shit."

Nate put his foot up on the chair and stared down at Trace. "You will write exactly what I say, or I will humiliate you in front of this woman and your son. And then I will call the cops and have you taken out of here. Now get writing." He watched as Trace stared off at the woods beyond the pond, like he was calculating what it would take to make a run for it, and then, finally, he picked up the pen.

Nate spoke slowly: " 'Dear Jamie and Arley: I was called . . . out of town . . . and I must . . . return . . . to New York. I came by to tell you both . . . good-bye . . .' "

"No way."

"Way. Get writing. 'It's been great . . . to see you. I am sorry that I just . . . cannot stick around. Arley'—no, you idiot. It's A-R-L-E-Y. Don't you know your own kid's name? 'Arley, you have . . . a wonderful . . . mom who loves you very much. I will always . . . wish . . . that I could have been . . . a better dad . . .' "

"No!" Trace said.

"*Write* it."

He wrote.

" '. . . but this is good-bye . . . I got called for a job, and I have work that I must do.' "

Trace sighed loudly. "I don't want to put that last part."

"You have to put that last part. I don't want them worrying about you, or thinking they're to blame."

When he was finished, he said, "Look, all I heard was she was with some old dude who died, and she was living in a house and all that. I just need some money for paints. I wasn't going to do anything. I know you're fucking her."

Nate took out his wallet and calmly gave Trace two twenty-dollar bills, which he said was for gas money so that he could be sure Trace could get as far away from here as possible. He added that if he ever saw him again, he was probably going to kill him by cutting off both his arms and beating him over the head with them, and then burying his body in the bottom of the pond, where the Mafia used to come and bury the dead people that they never wanted to get found, as opposed to the ones they hoped would be found so they'd be an example for others.

WHEN JAMIE CAME home, she picked up the note off the table on the porch and read it without saying anything. Her hair was falling

down over her face, so Nate didn't know for sure what she was thinking. She read and reread it for a long time, and then she turned it over,
and then read it again. She must have read the damn thing ten times.
He stood carefully far away from her and watched as she folded it and
put it in the pocket of her skirt.

Later she cleared her throat and said, "So, did you see that note?"

"What note?"

"Trace left me a note."

"Oh."

"So you didn't see him when he came?"

"I was busy in the barn most of the day."

She didn't say anything, just stared out the window for a
moment. Then she shrugged.

He felt the sensation of words backing up in his throat. He'd like
to ask her if she knew that Lucy was telling people that Jamie was in
love with him. But how did you ask that? And then he remembered
one of Harris's rules of thumb: Talk doesn't mean shit. It's how a person acts.

And she was not acting as if she could even stand him.

Not that he blamed her. He could barely stand himself.

Lucy always said that if you want to prove that the universe has a sense of humor, all you have to do is pay attention to the way it makes everything happen all at once. And so it was that the phone and the doorbell both rang at the same time, and Jamie, who was home alone cooking dinner and obsessively going over the list for the jamboree hike the next day, ran to the door, grabbing the portable phone on her way. She was expecting it to be something simple, like the mailman with something that needed to be signed for, and so she opened the door and said, "Hello?" into the phone at the same instant.

On the telephone, Shana said, "You've got the job!" And at the door, a young woman in a business suit, with hair that was seriously moussed and fluffed up, turned from surveying the yard, thinking the "Hello?" had been for her, smiled and said, "Oh, hello. I'm Tina Oliver. Is Nate home?"

Jamie was flummoxed. The two events lined up in a kind of cosmic mismatch. In her confusion, she said to Tina, "Really? I got the job?" and into the telephone, to Shana, "Come in."

But then it all got sorted out. People laughed, she apologized and explained, introduced herself to Tina, and then listened, finger in the air, while Shana proudly went over the events of the board of trustees meeting, in which Shana had been praised for coming up with such a qualified candidate. And the job included the cutest little place to live—really, when could Jamie come and take a look at it? And the girls were going to spoil Arley; Shana herself couldn't wait to start buying him toys. Oh, it was going to be so exciting! They'd be together again at last.

Finally Jamie could hang up, and by then, she and Tina had walked all the way to the kitchen, where onions were sputtering in oil on the stove. Jamie had to run over to stir them, since it would not do to set the house on fire in front of Nate's fiancée, who was already looking around the place as if it might qualify for federal disaster relief. It was bad enough that Jamie was wearing her ripped jeans and a paint-spattered Bob Marley T-shirt, which was practically covered in cerulean blue, and that her hair was stuck up in one of those messy ponytails she made when she was painting.

She'd been alone in the house while Nate had taken the kids down to the pond, as she explained to Tina. What Jamie didn't say was that she'd hoped to get an early dinner so she could spend the evening obsessively checking and rechecking and making final phone calls for the jamboree tomorrow. Everything seemed in place, but what if she'd forgotten some essential thing that would make the whole day a nightmare? She was familiar with nightmares.

She took a deep breath. Quite possibly she was in one right now.

Tina said with a fake little laugh, "Wow. So dinner comes early in the country, doesn't it? In my world, this would still be lunchtime."

Jamie wanted to say something like "And exactly how did it happen that you managed to stray *out* of your world, if I may ask?" But she was going to try to be nice, so instead she asked if Tina wanted some iced tea, which she did. This was good. She put the spaghetti sauce on simmer, and then the two of them went out to the porch swing, where Jamie could get a chance to study the other woman. She wanted to take a good, long, scientific look at the woman whom Nate managed to sleep with and *not* have the reptilian withdrawal response to. Was it the perfect hair, the suit that looked as if it had never seen a wrinkle, or the way of seeming sophisticated, bored and lively, all at the same time? Who could know?

"I never knew this place was so big," Tina said. "There's a pond, you said?"

"Oh, yes," Jamie told her. "It's right there through those bushes and down a little path. Would you like to walk down there and see Nate?"

Tina made a face and pointed to her high heels. "Actually," she said, "I'm not much for tromping around in wetlands, so I was hoping you and I could have a little chat. Get to know each other a little bit." She took a sip of her iced tea. "*So!* You were his dad's girlfriend, right?"

"No," Jamie said. "I wasn't."

"Oh! I thought for sure that's what I had heard. But . . . well, you lived here with the dad. Nate said you were here when he came here, but that he'd never heard of you before that. I thought you were the live-in gal pal."

Nice one, Jamie thought. "Yeah. I lived here, but I wasn't his girlfriend."

"*Really.*"

Jamie regarded her with interest. "Have you never heard of a man and a woman sharing a house?"

Tina opened her mouth. "Well, of course I have. It's just I was sure that what I heard was that you and the dad were *together,* and then he died. And you've sort of stayed on. That was my *impression.* I'm sorry if I've gotten the wrong information somehow and offended you."

"Nope, I'm not offended," Jamie said. "I'm just setting the record straight because I get really impatient with people who can't seem to see that distinction, as you so clearly can. Lots of people just can't fathom how a woman can move into a man's house out of, you know, motives other than wanting to sleep in his bed. It just tires me out, is all."

"Oh, no, I understand perfectly. Now that you've explained it." She was silent, looking out at the pond as if she were trying to concentrate. Then she said, clearly going for a nonchalant tone but failing, "And now . . . well, now that the old man is gone, what are your plans?"

Jamie took a long sip of iced tea, which gave her an opportunity to glare at Tina over the glass. "Why do you want to know all this?" she said, making her voice very pleasant.

Tina gave her a level gaze. "Listen," she said. "I am simply trying to make conversation with you. It's what I do. I'm a salesperson, and people like to talk about themselves. That's all this is." She sniffed.

Jamie couldn't help herself. The job offer had made her feel a thousand different emotions, and she'd had no time to sort them out. Or maybe it was just that she felt cranky and bitchy at finally getting a look at the kind of woman Nate appreciated, *really* appreciated. But whatever it was, she was feeling small and mean and cranky. "Well," she said, leaning forward a little, "I think there's more to it than that."

Tina looked shocked, which was fun in itself. Really, this chick was so insecure. She was going to have to grow a backbone if she wanted to be involved with old Natey over the long haul. "What are you talking about?"

"Well," she said, evenly, "*I* think that you're asking questions because you want to know what's going on with me and Nate. Which is perfectly natural. I'd feel the same way if I came up to a house, unannounced, where my boyfriend lived, and there was a woman there who'd been living with him for—oh, nearly two months, between the separations. So I tell you what. Why don't you just ask me what you want to know right up front, and I can tell you what I want you to know about me, and then we won't have to be so nicey-nice with each other. I really don't like to play these little games. I never could figure them out, actually."

Tina blanched, and then took a deep breath and said, "I think you're doing fine." She took a sip of her tea and added, "Anyway, what I've *heard* about you from Nate is that you're a wonderful babysitter."

Jamie laughed out loud. The *babysitter?*

"What's so funny?"

"It's just that that was so perfect. You really are very adept. I can see where you'd be good at your job. All that reading people's minds and then disarming them that salespeople have to do. Now me, I'm just an artist. I'm not good at that *at all.* Maybe it's because I work mostly alone, and even when I'm teaching or something, basically all the talking just goes one way, so I don't get to do nuances very often." She took a sip of her iced tea and glanced at at Tina, who was looking bereft and defensive all at once, picking unhappily at a fleck of something on her slacks.

Suddenly Jamie was tired of the game. She remembered that she was leaving anyhow. None of this mattered; she couldn't even imagine why she'd cared enough to act this way—all about a man who was so screwed up that he couldn't face his own demons. She sighed. "Okay, listen," she said. "I am not your worst nightmare. Believe me. He and I are not interested in each other. And that conversation you heard when I answered the door was me getting a job in Vermont. I'm leaving in just a few weeks, and I expect that Nate and I won't ever communicate with each other again."

Tina was so transparent that her whole face flooded with relief, which she then tried to hide. "Oh!" she said. "Well. You know, I didn't really think that there *was* anything between you, you know. He's a faithful kind of man. It's just kind of a weird *situation,* you know, when your boyfriend has this *live-in* person that you don't even *know.*" She laughed.

"No, no, don't explain," Jamie said. "But I will tell you that the one you have to worry about is Christopher. He's the live-in who's going to put you through your paces."

"Oh, the kid," Tina said. "Well, believe me, I've met him, and my plan is that he and I will just love each other to death."

"Excellent!" Jamie said. "It's good you've got that thought out."

Tina stood up. "Is there a bathroom around here? I really feel like I should freshen up, you know?"

"Upstairs," Jamie said. "These old houses—they just put one bathroom in, so it's the one we all share. Anyway, don't mind the mess, okay? Go up the stairs, turn right, and then it's the first door on the left."

Tina went into the house, and for a moment Jamie let herself exhale and slump down in her chair. God, she was horrible. Mean and small and cranky and bitchy. But what the hell was this woman *thinking,* just showing up like this, and then acting as though she had a right to barge in and stake out her little territory, her Nate ownership? Christ, it was as if she was going to take out the deed on him and start flashing it around.

Had Nate even *known* she was coming? Jamie could not imagine that he had. No, this had all the earmarks of a major ambush. For a moment she thought about calling him on his cell phone, telling him the news. But then she figured it would be so much more fun—and informative—to see his face when he first came tromping up the path with the boys and saw his lovely Tina sitting there on the porch.

AND IT *WAS* fun. Well, at first, at least. Nate came walking up the hill, with the boys trailing behind him. He was carrying a bucket that Jamie knew was filled with dirt and earthworms. He looked ridiculously messed up and almost fried from the hot sun. Arley was dancing around him, going around him in circles like a demented little circus performer in his ladybug vest, while Christopher was skipping along beside them, looking down at the ground.

Nate had his there's-so-much-work-to-do-on-this-house scowl as he walked across the yard, taking a moment to glare at the barn, which had paint peeling off the sides, and to squint upward at the second floor of the house, which he'd painted in a slapdash way without doing the eaves or scraping—and then his eye came down to the porch, and there it was: an unmistakable blanching. Even from her seat on the swing, Jamie could see his eyes grow wide and his mouth form the words *Oh shit*. Tina must have seen it too, but Jamie had to hand it to her: she got to her feet and stood there bravely waving her hand like a queen on a parade float, which gave Jamie an ample opportunity to study her body, which Lucy would have called "a cute, girlish figure."

The boys must have been asking a question because Nate said something in a low voice to them, and then he stopped walking and stood there, a goofy expression on his face. He stretched out his arms, pantomiming surprise, then smacked his forehead. All excellent showmanship, just excellent. But when he came up onto the porch, he still looked stunned, like stroke-patient stunned. But then Tina rushed over and kind of fell into his arms and planted her mouth on his in a Hollywood lip-lock, and for a long, horrible moment Jamie thought she wouldn't be able to breathe normally ever again.

TINA SAID SHE wanted to eat out. At first she said this was to protect "poor Jamie," who hadn't been informed that there would be an extra dinner guest, and she shouldn't have to increase the amount of food she'd made. But when that protest was nixed by Nate, she then got a little coy look on her face and looped her arm into Nate's and said in a pouty little voice that, okay, she hadn't wanted to spill the beans just yet, but the truth was she had a "widdle surpwise" for him. She'd gotten them reservations at the Copper Beech Inn, the *Garden Suite*—and she'd had to practically sell her soul to get them, and oh, it was just *the* most exciting thing. Her face was animated now. Just think: the two of them, going off together like this, getting reacquainted. She walked her fingers up his shirt front, as if "reacquainted" was a concept he needed to have illustrated for him.

Jamie thought that Nate still looked stunned, but he finally seemed to get with the program and went upstairs to clean the worm dirt off his hands and to pack.

"Bring comfy clothes, darling—without worm juice on them!" Tina called after him. And then she turned to Jamie. "*Thank you,* Jamie, for being so understanding. We've just been apart sooo long, and I feel like I just need one tiny little weekend off with him before I start, you know, getting into my *role* as stepmother and acting all adult about things." She gave a simpering smile and looked over at the boys, who were squatted down in the yard examining their worms. "My, they're so cute, aren't they? I can see where you must have *so much fun* with them!"

"Oh, yes," Jamie said. "It's fun, all right." Well, it was.

"Children are just so . . . so *natural,* don't you think so? No hypocrisy to them at all. I just adore how they look at life. Such an appreciation for nature that all of us have lost."

For a moment Jamie felt like she might throw up. It had occurred to her that Nate's going away for the weekend meant that he wouldn't be helping out after all with the jamboree. He had been assigned a group of kids to lead on a hike. She was taken aback at how disappointed she felt. It was almost like a pain in her side.

But, really, it would be okay. All she was really feeling was irritation that now she was going to have to get on the phone and try to intimidate one more dad into participating so they wouldn't be short-handed. That's all. And by the time Nate came downstairs with his suitcase, she was totally over it. When Tina glommed onto his arm, chirping in baby talk about how they were going to have so much fun, Jamie was honestly happy to see the two of them leave.

No, really.

Even when he came back into the house and said to her, "I'm so sorry about the hike—" she just waved him off, didn't even look in his direction. That's how cool she was.

"It's fine," she said. "Don't worry about it. I'll find somebody else."

"Um, also, one other thing. Tina just told me that you got a *job* today. Is this the Vermont job?"

"Yeah," she said. "I got offered the job at the school after all."

"I thought you already had that job."

She sighed. "It was never finalized. Not until today."

"So you're taking it."

"Yes, I'm taking it."

"Did anybody ever tell you what the seasons are in Vermont? Nine months of winter and three months where the skiing's not so good."

"Ha-ha," she said. "Um, not to be rude or anything, but isn't there someplace you're supposed to be?"

"I just wanted to say that I'm sorry about the hike."

"It's okay."

He stood there hesitating in the doorway. "I guess this means I broke my promise."

"You're getting married to this woman. You have to do what she wants. Just go, will you? I'll sort it out. Believe me."

"Do you hate me?"

"Despise you. Now *get out*!"

"Great! I despise you, too. Have fun on the hike."

"Why are you doing this? Will you *go*?"

AFTER DINNER, SHE called Lucy.

"Is there any way you could come and lead a hike with me tomorrow? It's the jamboree, and Nate can't help because he's been dragged off by a baby-talking woman with sharp hair," she said. She had practiced saying this so that she wouldn't sound disappointed in the least—merely professional and concerned about the jamboree.

But Lucy wasn't having any of it. "Oh my God!" she said. "Tell me. Oh my God. Is this . . . his *fiancée*? At last? Oh, my poor baby sister."

"It is," Jamie said. "And it's totally fine. Merely interesting from a sociological point of view—you know, the kind of woman who could capture the so-called heart of Nate. And she's awful, just dreadful. I can see now why it never would have worked for him and me, if that's who he likes. Believe me, I'm fine."

"Wow," Lucy said. And then, "Wow again. Your life has certainly gotten interesting: first with Trace showing up and leaving again, and now Nate taking off with his fiancée. Are you really okay?"

"Of course I'm okay. I never really cared about Nate. And the best news of all is that I got the job in Vermont. Shana called today to say they'd decided on me."

"Oh," Lucy said. "Oh my goodness. Oh my. I don't know how I feel about this, now that it's happening. You're going to move away."

"I know." Jamie had a slight moment of nostalgia, but she pushed it aside out of necessity. "Look, we have to be strong about things. Life moves on, you know. You'd be the first to point out that I need to get things going again; can't just stay here in this house mooning after men. No, wait. That's what I'd be saying to you. *You'd* be saying: Throw yourself at the guy! Get more sex!"

Lucy laughed. "Yeah, well, I'm changing. You'll be glad to know that I haven't gone back to Dan, and not because of a lack of chances, either. I've turned him down. And—" She took a deep breath. "I've met this guy who's helping me draw up a business plan to open my own yoga studio, and I think I'm going to teach dance and yoga, and it's going to be called Yoga a Go-go. The art gallery downtown is thinking about renting me their upstairs."

"Yoga a Go-go?"

"Yes, and the best part is that I am not sleeping with the guy who's helping me with the business plan." She laughed.

"Excellent! And so will you help me with the hike?"

"Actually, I can't. As part of my training for this, I'm going to the hospital to do a yoga class with people who've had traumatic head injuries and are brain-damaged."

"But are you qualified for that? Teaching people with brain damage?"

"Darling. You've seen my dating life. I'm overqualified."

CHAPTER
32

The night was stuffy and humid, which made sleep nearly impossible. She thrashed around in the bed, and finally fell into a damaged, ruinous sleep at about three thirty, only to have her eyes fly open at four. Shit! She'd forgotten to confirm the reservation for the bus that was supposed to take everybody—all the parents and kids—to the state park. She lay there performing mental torture on herself for a while. Actually, it was Sue DeLucia who was supposed to be in charge of transportation, but at the last moment she'd gotten involved with some other damn-fool thing, and so she'd thrown it all back in Jamie's lap. Figured.

Shit, shit, shit. Why had she ever agreed to be put in charge of all this stuff? She was a woman who could barely keep her grocery list straight in her head, much less run a whole organization. *Hello?* She was the art lady. Didn't anybody remember that? Had she ever in any way indicated she wanted to be president of the organization, or even secretary? No. She was the one bringing in the chalk and the charcoal and the drawing pads of thick creamy paper. That was it: the extent of her skills.

She got up and paced and drank bitter coffee and paced some

more, and looked at her lists, added up the people who said they'd come, added them up again, considered calling a couple more just in case some of them didn't show, wondered when the bus company opened and if they could confirm a reservation in the middle of the night. And then she tried to remember whether Sue DeLucia had ever even *made* the reservation, or had that been something Jamie was supposed to do, too?

Was she confirming or reserving? Reserving or confirming? And how was she going to move to Vermont and leave Christopher? Could she take Harris's car? Life was going to be complicated. She'd need snow tires. She'd probably have to buy warmer clothes. Arley needed better mittens, that was for sure. She should have thought of all these things before she accepted the job.

Mittens. She couldn't believe she was up in the middle of the night, in *August,* fretting over Arley's mittens.

And where *was* the Copper Beech Inn anyway, and why did having a reservation there mean so much? The Garden Suite. What the hell?

She drank another cup of coffee, got dressed, then took off all her clothes and put on different ones, watched the sun come up, accepted the unhappy fact that it was probably not going to rain, which would have meant she could cancel this horrendous thing, and then went in to wake the boys.

PEOPLE WERE NICE about the buses. They could all pile into the various station wagons and SUVs, they said cheerfully. Joe Hansen even put the grills in the trunk of his massive car, and the Snows managed to find room in their station wagon for the hamburger meat and the buns. Jamie stood around in the commuter parking lot with her clipboard feeling dazed at the number of people milling around, the inane questions people were asking her, the kids darting in and out, playing heart-stopping games of chase among the parked cars, and

why was it that nobody was noticing how freaking dangerous that was?
Her head hurt. Lola Jarvis kept popping up in front of her wanting to
know if anybody had thought to bring plastic forks for the coleslaw
she'd made. Jack Fortner had thought to bring bug spray, and he wondered if they needed signed releases to put it on the children whose
parents weren't present. Ack! The Johnsons called on Jamie's cell
phone to say that their little Brandon was sick, and so the whole family couldn't come. Will and Diana Johnson were supposed to have led
a group on the hike, and with Nate being gone, now they were down
three adults. And as if this weren't worrisome enough, Sue DeLucia
had sent bottles of soda, which some parents frowned at, and nobody
had remembered to bring cups. Or ice.

At one point Jamie said, only half-jokingly, "Let's just all go back
home and back to bed. We can reschedule this hike for when the children are in their thirties."

And then Cooksey showed up. In uniform.

"I'm not here in my capacity as the *founder* of this organization,"
he told Jamie. "I've given up all that. It's yours now, and you can
wreck it if you want to. I'm here as the police chief, just to make sure
all traffic and safety protocols are being met."

"But do you have any jurisdiction outside of town?" somebody
called out, and Cooksey glowered into the crowd and said he had
jurisdiction wherever citizens of his town might go, particularly the
young citizens who were being led on something that was more of an
unnecessary worry than anything else. Jamie had a wild moment of
hoping he'd take out his badge and announce that hikes were illegal
and that they were all going to be arrested if they took one more step.

But of course he couldn't do anything that useful, and so it happened that everybody eventually sorted things out and people were
assigned to seats in each other's cars, and then they drove, caravan-
style, to the park, where they staked out picnic areas and where some
of the fathers pitched tents, then waited while Jamie ran around orga-
nizing all the children into little groups of eight hikers, complete with

two adults for each group. Even with the kids buzzing around, falling out of formation, hitting one another on the arms, and generally screaming and jumping around in excitement, she somehow managed to assign them all numbers and hand out whistles, and have the adults check to make sure they had their cell phones.

And one by one, the groups headed up the mountain in the early morning heat. Waves of humidity rose up from the parking lot. But wait—how had she miscalculated again? The group she was supposed to lead didn't have another adult to go along with her. It was supposed to be Nate. She thought she'd replaced him, but then the replacement hadn't shown up. Who was it supposed to be? She scanned the list, but of course, it didn't matter anyway. Earlier, Cooksey had groused for a while, and then gone ambling down the mountain to the ranger station. He was the only solution. She had to phone him. He was going to have to come along with her.

She swallowed hard, tried to convince herself there was some other way. She maybe should just try going by herself. But no, being in charge of six little boys alone—that was too much. She closed her eyes and punched in Cooksey's number, and told him the problem.

"You've really got yourself in a bind then, haven't you?" he said. And then he sighed heavily—and with deep satisfaction, she was sure—and said he'd come right back up and go with her.

"Hurry," she said. "I mean, if you don't mind." The other groups had already left, and Damon Rangle, the biggest boy in her group, wanted to run up the mountain, and was already heading out. She had to keep calling her boys back until, finally, Cooksey managed to make his way back to them, limping and groaning and walking about as slow as a glacier.

IT WAS ACTUALLY okay for a while, in an adrenaline-pumping kind of way. Cooksey was plodding along, huffing and puffing, and every now and then growling about how if he'd *known* what he was going to be asked to do, he'd have worn the right shoes. The boys were running ahead, trying hard to catch up with the others, and Jamie was somewhere in the middle, trying to tend to Cooksey, but more concerned that the boys not get completely out of her sight. She kept calling for them to slow down, which they did for a while—but, really, they were *kids*. And they were filled with about ten times the energy she felt would have been perfectly adequate. But, still, they were funny and curious, and loved being outside. Damon was the ringleader, she quickly realized. He'd go off the path every now and then, and she'd find him balancing on rocks or wading toward a patch of poison ivy, and have to rein him back in—but otherwise, things went smoothly.

She was tense, but in a good way. An aware, hypervigilant kind of tense. She could do this hard thing, and she could do all the other hard things, too: leave Nate and leave this life here, put all the past with Harris aside, and start her life over. She was *that sort of bear,* as Winnie-the-Pooh had claimed: capable and strong, not like Lucy, who was so dependent on the wrong man, who was even now still suffering over Dan's defection. She, Jamie, was so different! So wonderfully prepared and capable.

And then Arley had the worst asthma attack she could ever remember.

IT CAME ON suddenly, like a summer thunderstorm. One minute he'd been dancing along the path, walking backward, trying to avoid getting bumped into by Damon, who was spinning in circles, and the next, he was sitting on the ground breathing rapidly, his eyes filled with fear.

She yelled for the group to stop, but they were shouting and carrying on, and couldn't hear her. Cooksey was so far behind them on the path that she couldn't see him. She searched through her pants pockets for the inhaler, and then took off her backpack and rummaged through the outside and inside compartments. Nothing! But it *had* to be there.

"*Christopher!* Boys! Come back here!" she yelled, and to her surprise, they started returning, pushing and shoving one another as they walked, but, still, coming to her. Arley was wheezing hard now. She dumped the contents of the backpack out—there was a pen, wadded-up Kleenex, a tampon, some quarters, a Lego guy, and at the very bottom: the inhaler. When her fingers wrapped around it, she felt her whole body nearly collapse in relief—but when she ran over to Arley and shoved it in his mouth, nothing came out. It was empty. Empty!

"It's okay," she said to him. "There's got to be a spare here. Just take it easy." She searched her pockets again, her jeans, her backpack. Nothing. And where was Cooksey? She looked down the path again—where was that old man?

Her heart started pumping madly. What was she going to do? She was always prepared for this! She hadn't left the house in four years without patting both pockets to make sure there were inhalers. People laughed at how inhalers seemed to fall out of everything she owned. Two in her purse, two in her pocket, two in the car. That was the way she was.

But now, nothing. She reached for her cell phone, but she had no service on the mountain. She blew her whistle and shouted, but that didn't do any good, either.

She regarded the boys. Christopher looked gravely concerned. She knelt down next to him and tried to sound reassuring.

"Is Arley going to be all right?" he said, and she said, "Yes. Of course he is. I just have to somehow get an inhaler." She brushed back her hair. "Listen. Can you go back and meet Chief Cooksey for me? Will you run and find him?"

"Okay," he said.

"Run!" she said. And then called after him, "But be careful!"

She cradled Arley in her arms and kept trying to help him breathe. Damon had organized the other children in the group into a whip line, and they were laughing and snapping themselves until the last person fell down each time. She blew her whistle. They looked at her blankly.

"Come here, boys! I have something to tell you," she said. It seemed to take forever for them to stop playing and come to her, but finally they saw the panic in her eyes and came over.

"This is an emergency," she said. "I have to take Arley to the car, where I have his inhaler. And we can't all go down together because I'm going to have to run very fast with him. So here's what I need you to do: I need you to sit here on the path and wait. Chief Cooksey is going to be here in a second, and I need for you to mind him. Don't give him a hard time. He can't go fast. Can you do that?"

They nodded.

"Now, you can't go off the path, and you can't keep walking. You have to promise me you'll wait. Will you?"

Just then Cooksey and Christopher came into sight. She called down to them, as loudly as she could: "Frank, I've got to go to the car! Arley needs help!"

He looked like a very old man, struggling as he came up the hill. He was saying something to her, but she couldn't hear. She couldn't wait any longer. She gathered Arley up in her arms. Damon piped up that he knew the way to the castle, and he could lead them.

"No," she said. "No. You have to wait here with Chief Cooksey."

He grabbed hold of another kid's hand, and said, "Then we'll do the whip! Grab on!"

"Careful!" she said. And with Arley in her arms, she ran as fast as she dared, slipping on rocks here and there and feeling her lungs nearly bursting. Arley slumped against her, and every now and then she said, "Just take shallow breaths, sweetheart. You're going to be okay."

She wasn't at all sure that this was true, or that she should have left the boys with Cooksey, or if her cell phone really wouldn't work at any point on the mountain. Maybe she should have kept stopping to try, but Arley's eyes were closed, and all she could think of was a news story she'd once read about a kid dying of an asthma attack. By the time she got to the car, it was probably only twenty minutes later, but it felt as though a whole day had passed. She wasn't sure of anything anymore. People—not from their group—were milling around in the parking lot. She sped past them, feeling them look at her, this woman holding a gray little boy. Someone said, "Do you need help?" and she couldn't even stop to answer. Her heart was about to explode wide open, and suddenly a ranger appeared, but instead of coming to help her, he started running up the mountain, and word started circulating that a boy was in trouble.

"No, he's here!" she tried to say to a woman nearby, but words didn't come out, or maybe the woman just couldn't hear her. It had been forever, but she was almost at the car by now, and just as she got there, she heard the sirens and thought how lucky it was that some-one—but who?—had known to call for help for her. Had Cooksey managed to call?

Only, the sirens pushed right on by, taking the camp road, and she was left to unlock the car herself while balancing Arley, and at last she got into the hot car and put him down on the seat, which was too hot for his bare legs, but what could she do? Her fingers found the inhaler in the center console, and she put it to his lips and said, "Breathe in, Arley, breathe in," and she sat back and watched with relief as the pink started to slowly spread through his face.

Tears of relief came to her eyes. She didn't know for how long she sat there; she just wanted to stay there forever. Minutes passed, and she lugged Arley into the shade, took in several deep breaths, and that's when she noticed that something was terribly, awfully wrong. People were hurrying up the mountain, and the ambulance—the one that should have been for Arley—was sitting there bleating, with its red light circling around and around, and then she saw the stretcher coming down, carried by two men.

CHAPTER
33

The Copper Beech Inn was one of those places you'd like if you liked those kinds of places, was how Nate saw it. It was a little too precious for him, all the antiques and the carved dark wood and the flowered wallpaper and wall sconces and lace curtains. Lace curtains! The food, he supposed, was good—Tina certainly kept exclaiming over it, but then she was in an exclamatory mood. She was filled with excitement so strenuous it made him tired just having to react to it. She wanted to go antiquing, she said, and maybe on a ferry cruise to see the seals! Or the eagles! Or the lighthouses! Or something else that he didn't want to see very much. And then to a play! Yes, a play!

He was trying to be ardent and loving, the way a man in a soap opera would act, but the truth was, he hated surprises, hated the sensation of being carted off to a destination somebody else had chosen for him, and he detested lace curtains. And Tina was just so jolly and filled up with plans, none of which seemed to have anything to do with his reality. He realized with a kind of startled clarity that what he truly wanted to be doing was painting the kitchen or spending time with Christopher at the jamboree.

Which was a shock, really. He hadn't known until now how all that work had become front and center for him. He would have thought he hated it, but in fact, the monotonous scraping and peeling and tearing down had changed something in him, and then the building back up and repainting and resurfacing—well, it was a cliché, that's what it was. A stupid metamorphosis that he would deny if anyone accused him of it. Of liking physical labor.

His hands were rough now and dirty, dark and ropy, like he remembered Harris's hands being. Which was disgusting, really. How was it that he could sit in this inn, with its white tablecloths and candlelight and bottles of French wine for *lunch,* and yet have a thick line of black dirt underneath each nail? He wanted to point out this dirt to Tina. It was funny, really, when you thought about it, that he, Nate Goddard, had these weird-looking *hands.* Hands that looked nothing like his.

"You're awfully quiet," she said.

"I'm a quiet guy."

"What are you thinking about?"

"I'm thinking about why women always need to know what a guy is thinking."

She looked surprised, then hurt.

"No. I'm actually thinking about how dirty my hands are."

She made a face at him.

"You asked," he said.

"Oh, that's just because now you're a country boy . . . but all that'll change when you get back to your real work."

But wait. He hadn't been complaining about his dirty hands. And this was the third time she'd brought up what she called his "real work," and he realized that he had let it go the other two times and he didn't have the energy to talk about it now, either. In fact, he felt sleepy, even though it was only just noon, and they'd had lots of sleep the night before. He stared out the window of the inn, out at the sultry gardens, and he wanted to go outside and stretch out on the grass and never have to talk again. Could he do that, please? Could she go off to an eagle watch or a play or antiquing, for whatever good that was going to do her, when she'd only have to carry all the ridiculous things she'd buy on the airplane, for God's sake? And could he be permitted, oh, say, seventy-two hours of sleep without anybody wanting anything from him, most of all without his having to tell somebody how he *felt*?

When his cell phone rang, he felt too lethargic even to be surprised. As he picked it up, he had a momentary flash of Tina's turning away from him, her face bitter with disappointment—but then all that was gone in an instant, always to remain a fleeting, momentary impression, nothing concrete. It was merely the vestige of a day that had already turned sour but that was now veering off into something else altogether.

His son, the voice said, had been injured. He was at Middlesex Hospital.

THE SURGEON WAS world-famous, which somehow gave him the right to be both incoherent and jocular. "You probably think it's easy putting people's arms back together when they've done the whip on them," he said. "Fewer people would be doing the whip if they knew how rarely it works out well. Of course, these are children we're talking about."

He was standing in the waiting room in his green scrubs, still holding his mask. He had a glistening bald head, as though he'd surgically removed his own hair with such precision that no head whiskers sprouted there. Nate, who had finally quit shaking, thought of starting up again.

"What whip?" he said.

"Oh, you didn't know. That's right, they told me you weren't there." The guy put his knee up on the arm of the chair across from Nate and Tina, and proceeded to describe how the accident had happened, from a bone point of view. Apparently the children had decided to play Whip, as children have been doing for hundreds of thousands of years. It's the game where they form themselves a line and then run together and reverse direction so that the guy at the end of the line—in this case, Christopher—gets himself jerked so hard that he sometimes falls down, and then all the other children fall down, in this case, on top of him, onto a rock—and well, in Christopher's case, the arm bone took the brunt of it. So much so that it was broken in two places and was actually protruding through the skin, bringing with it all these little veins and muscles and tendons. The surgeon pantomimed things sticking out in all directions.

"Oh my God," Tina said. "Eww."

The surgeon nodded. "Exactly."

"So you were able to fix it?" said Nate, who felt he might lose consciousness.

"Oh, I fixed it all right," the surgeon said, and Nate forgave him everything: the incoherence, the jocularity, even the surgical removal of his hair. "He'll be fine. Just has to follow the rules for a while, take care of the thing. Not easy for a—what? Five-year-old, is it? He must take it easy. Which is *not* easy."

"No, not at all," Nate said.

"I just want you to know that lots of surgeons couldn't put an arm like that together again. It might have always been crooked."

"Yeah?"

"What saved him is that nobody touched him until the ambulance got there. I guess we're lucky the police chief couldn't move him. Almost certain that if an adult had picked him right up, the arm would have—I don't know—deteriorated is the technical term."

Nate had been told a bit about the circumstances. Cooksey had met him at the hospital and told him the whole thing, at first spinning it in a typical Cooksey way: Jamie had, in a moment of breathtaking irresponsibility, forgotten to bring an inhaler, and then she'd left the hiking group alone with him on the mountain while she'd taken Arley and run down the hill with him. And he'd been far away when she left, and the kids had gotten the better of him. All out of control, these kids. He'd looked away when he said that part, then cleared his throat, pressed his hand to his eyes, and started again in a husky voice.

"I'm not up to this anymore," he said. "A whole load of restless kids, never been told how to behave, horsing around up there and not listening to me. They don't respect authority, kids today," he said. "A police chief means nothing to them."

Christopher had been in surgery then, and Nate was in no mood to hear all this. Cooksey left for a while, paced the hospital corridors, called his wife, came back over twisting his watch around and around on his wrist. "Listen," he said. He looked like a balloon that was collapsing in on itself, eyes all sunken in and baggy. "I shouldn't have been up there today," he said. "But I've been thinking. This Jamie . . . well, what's she gonna do? She's got a sick boy, lots to think about." He stared off into space. "Life or death all the damn time. She had to do what she did. Lemme just say, if you want to blame her for this, it's probably gonna end up being *me* you should blame." He looked up with rheumy eyes that were red rimmed and horrible. Eyes from hell. "Because . . . I was the one right there, wasn't I? That's the kick in the head! It ended up being *me* in charge and not able to handle a bunch of little boys. How do you like that? Chief of goddamned police and I can't keep a passel of kids in line." He shook his head. "That's all I want to say."

"It was an accident," Nate said. But Cooksey was already walking out the double doors to the outside.

"I FIND IT interesting," Tina said, when they were alone, "that this *accident* happens when we have our first moment away together."

"Well," he said. He was so weak he didn't think he could move from the chair. Christopher was still in the recovery room, and Nate felt as though most of the life force had been removed from his own body.

"Don't you?"

"I think accidents happen when they happen."

"Well, I happen to believe there *are* no accidents. I think she maybe did this because she's jealous. I'm not going to say it was conscious or anything. She'd never intentionally hurt your son. I know that. But still . . . you go to an inn with me, and your son's arm gets broken worse than any arm has ever gotten broken in the history of the world. You do the math."

"Do the math?" he said.

"I'm *joking*. It's just an expression. I was being cute."

"What time is it?"

"Four thirty in the morning. Shall we go back to the inn?"

"Back to the inn?"

"Well, we have to spend the night someplace, and we did pay for the room."

"Christopher is in the recovery room," he said.

"Yeah, that means he's recovering."

He stood up and stretched. He couldn't look at her. "Why don't you go back? I'm staying here for when he wakes up."

"We'd come back first thing in the morning. And they'll call us if there's anything."

"No. I'll stay. You should go. Get some sleep." He sat back down and didn't look at her. He stared at his hands again, those dirty hands.

She sighed loudly. "And so now you think I'm a bad person for suggesting that."

"No. Not at all. It's just that—I need to be here now."

"Look, I made a mistake. I didn't know you wanted to stay here. I'll learn this stuff. Don't worry. I'll get to be a good stepmother, you'll see."

"Tina," he said. "It's *fine*. Even if you were his real mother, I'd still say you should go get some sleep. One of us should sleep."

"Well . . ."

"No, really. Go."

"Shall I go to the inn?"

"Sure. Why not?"

"Will you walk me out to the parking lot?"

"Why?"

"Because . . . you're a gentleman? And I'm a woman alone?"

"All right," he said. He sighed and stood up again. He had to hold onto the back of the chair to remain upright.

She gathered up her stuff, and he waited. He was so tired, but wired on worry and bad hospital coffee. He was wondering about Jamie. He'd spoken with her briefly on the phone before the surgery, and she'd said she was sorry. She said something about trusting people, how the thing she felt the worst about was that he had trusted her, and Christopher had trusted her, and she had let them down.

But no one could be trusted, he thought. Right now, shuffling down the corridor to the parking garage, with Tina at his side, he felt certain that he understood something basic now: Nobody could really be trusted to take care of you all the time. Nobody was ever going to be one hundred percent what you needed them to be. Especially not when something else they wanted was at stake. They'd have to let go every time.

This seemed to mean something, but he wasn't sure just what. It had to do with his father leaving his mother, and with him leaving home after Christopher was born, and with Jamie finding out she had to leave a whole group of kids in the woods.

And yes, even with Tina now. They reached her parked car and she looked at him like she already knew that something momentous had happened between them. Her eyes were opaque and cloudy. She'd go back to the inn alone, and sleep there in the big king-size bed in the room with the antiques and the flowered wallpaper, and maybe tomorrow she'd eat breakfast in the café, and the waiter might stop by and say, "And where is your gentleman friend?"

And what would she say, Nate wondered. Would she say, "Oh, his son was badly hurt in an accident yesterday, and he's at the hospital with him"? And would she hear what that really meant, that she was there pouring a cascade of golden syrup on her pancakes while she said that, or stopping to suck on a delectable strawberry?

"It was too bad," she'd say perhaps.

And would the waiter's expression cause her to at last understand what had just happened?

CHAPTER
34

It was the craziest thing: his thinking a boy could die of a broken arm. Of course Christopher wasn't going to die, but that's how it felt, here in this place of death. The nurses teased him sometimes. They said he could sleep at his own house, the boy was going to be okay. It hurt like hell, yes, but they kept him on pain medication. They would watch him. Nate could leave. He *should* leave.

But he couldn't. Once, he got up, thinking he'd go, but then he sat back down. He told one nurse, "No, I've been gone too much of his life as it is," and she gave him a quizzical look. He couldn't quite explain how he felt, as though he had entered into long, simple days that seemed to exist somehow out of regular human time. The hospital was its own peculiar little universe: always lit up, always populated by people who were awake and watching. Nurses came and went in shifts. It was a like a montage of days and long, placid hours. The world-famous surgeon came and made jokes and further congratulated himself on his prowess. Tina came back to visit and then caught a flight to wherever she had to go for her next sales call. Nate drank bad coffee and then one day realized he couldn't live this way and switched over to a healthy diet of fruit and tea and chicken sandwiches.

He slept in a chair that could somehow flip into another position and become something like a bed, though not a comfortable one. And therefore he spent many nights tossing and turning, or staring at Christopher's face in the dim glow of the night-light.

Sometimes the boy would wake up, stir in his sleep, and he'd see his father there, and kind of smile as he returned to sleep. These were fleeting not-quite-smiles, but Nate was heartened by them. And then he was heartened by the fact that he was heartened.

There was so much he did not know. He felt sleep-deprived and purified in a way, as if his brain had been scrubbed out with steel wool. Sounds, even the muffled dinging of the elevator bell or the sudden voice calling on the loudspeaker, startled him. A beam of light could take him by surprise, or the sound of a child crying from down the hall. He was locked into Christopher, and it felt as though he were using all his mind control to reach through to that little boy who was so much like he had been—and maybe still was: wounded and terrified, cagily watching the adults to see what would happen to him.

There were phone messages from Jamie, coming at first on his cell phone, and then from the nurses. Once he tried to call her back in the middle of the night, but he got her voice mail and didn't leave a message. He didn't know what to say anyway.

"Christopher," he said to his sleeping child, "we both have huge boo-boos. And I am going to sit here until I figure out how to fix them."

Instead of talking, though, he played Candy Land and Old Maid. He held straws in milk shakes up to his son's lips. He told knock-knock jokes and riddles. He read stories. He walked with him down the hall to the play therapist, where Nate tied his right arm behind his back in solidarity with his son, and they tried to draw pictures with their left hands and laughed at how badly they did. And that was the day that Christopher turned six years old and called him Dad.

. . .

JAMIE SHOWED UP on Christopher's birthday, even though Nate hadn't returned her calls.

She gave Nate a frightened-looking, apologetic smile and made her way over to the bedside, where she said, "Oh, Christopher! Look at you sitting up in bed and looking so well. I brought you a birthday cake and a present, honey. Can you open it?"

Christopher was delighted to see her, and Nate sat back in his chair and watched them together. She was calm and tentative, guilty as hell for what she'd done, obviously half-expecting that Nate might send her out of there. But he wouldn't. He felt buoyed by her presence, he realized. He could breathe again with her there. While she was there, he actually fell asleep on the cot, and when he woke up, she and Christopher were doing Legos together. He would hold the pieces up, and she would snap them together.

When she saw that Nate was awake, she kissed Christopher on the cheek and said she had to go.

Nate tensed up, hoping that she wasn't going to start apologizing all over herself and getting all maudlin on him. There were about forty thousand subjects he did not want to discuss anymore with *any-one,* he realized: Tina, his old job, the house, Christopher's accident, his dad, Frank Cooksey, blame of any sort, politics, funerals, Mustangs, the Copper Beech Inn, graffiti, people who tell lies, Howie, his mother . . . and Louisa's eyes, which were right now looking out at him from the face of his son in a way he'd never noticed before. And then he remembered that Louisa had died here in this hospital. After the accident. He could hardly breathe.

"How's Arley?" he managed to say.

"He's fine," Jamie said.

"Do you think you could bring him for a visit?"

"Okay."

"I miss the little dude."

From the bed, Christopher laughed. "*I* miss the little dude!" he said.

Jamie looked at him and laughed, too. "Okay, I'll bring him tomorrow," she said. She looked at Nate, a long, scary look that might mean she was going to start talking about feelings, and then she said, "Do you need anything?"

"No," he said. "Well . . . underwear. Do you transport underwear?"

"When that's what is needed, I do," she said.

The door closed softly behind her. .

THERE ARE NIGHTS that can't be borne. And that night was one of them. He thought about asking the nurse for a Xanax, but in the end, he decided just to walk. They let you walk through hospitals—that was the oddest thing. You could walk down the hall and into the lobby, outside to the circular driveway, where the parked cars were covered with dew, where two orderlies were smoking.

He'd stood out there smoking the night that Christopher was born. He and Ron Shiner, standing here leaning on Ron's car and smoking a cigar that Ron had brought over, even though it was gross. Louisa had yelled at him when he'd come back in, smelling like that. And Harris had been there, too. He remembered this with a little start of surprise: Harris driving up in the Mustang, parking next to him, leaning over and giving him a hug, teasing him about having a son.

"The Goddard boys grow up to hate their dads," he'd said. "So just be expecting it. That's all I'm saying. You do your best, and they hate you anyway."

He closed his eyes.

And then, what the fuck, five days later he'd been back at this hospital—hanging outside the emergency room, while they tried to work on Louisa after the car accident, or at least they pretended to. Acted as if there was a chance she didn't have fatal injuries, maybe because they knew she was a new mom. Or maybe it was because he was standing there sobbing so pathetically. He hadn't thought of that in years.

The night air was foggy and hot. He sat down on the concrete bench, feeling the tears that were backed up inside him starting to flow. All his worst moments had happened right here in this spot, right where he was now. His mother being sick. Louisa. And even Harris, giving his horrible little prophecy, unaware that he held any responsibility for Nate hating him. Deserving to be hated. *Making* him hate.

He'd been hiding from thinking about this for so long that he felt there was a frozen boulder lodged right in his solar plexus. All the highs and lows had been gone from him. He had waded through sadness and happiness both, without letting either one of them touch him.

This place. *This place.* How was it that he had to come back here again, that he needed to be standing in this spot in the middle of the night, his son four floors above him? His son who had played Candy Land with him, who now turned to him when he was in pain, who called him Dad.

It was horrible to try to think it through tonight. He couldn't. He just sat there, letting it all settle over him, and then he realized the craziest thing: He was happy. He was actually happy, like hallelujah happy. Stripped to the center of him.

Happy without fixing it. Happy without ever being able to figure out how Harris could have done those things he did. He didn't need to. Was it going to be this easy? He just needed to let it go, to realize that Harris was flawed and damaged but that he was also so treasured by the two people Nate loved the most: Christopher and . . . Jamie, for reasons he would probably never understand. He *loved* Jamie. He sat there for a long moment. He said, "Huh!" out loud, and one of the orderlies, who was heading back inside, looked at him and laughed.

"You goin' through it, dude, aren't you?" he said. "I've been watching you, and you really got some heavy shit goin' on."

"This is going to sound crazy," Nate said, "but I just realized I love the woman I've been living with."

"Just now? Right this minute?"

"Yeah."

"Well, that's pretty convenient," the guy said. He was a plump man with a balding head. "You already living with her and all. At least you won't have to move any boxes."

"I don't know if it's convenient," Nate said. "First, I've got to convince her that it's true and see if she'll have me, then I gotta convince her not to move to Vermont, get her to forgive herself for getting my kid injured, break up with my fiancée, quit my job, and finish painting the back stairs of my house. Oh, and I've got to master the inhaler once and for all. Her kid has asthma. Maybe, in fact, what I should do is learn to cure asthma. Tonight I feel like I could actually do that."

"That oughta work," the guy said. "She'll love you if you cure her kid. Maybe all you gotta do is want to."

"I just have to figure out whether to start doing all that right now or wait until morning."

"Hey, why wait?" the guy said. "This is the way I see it. This could be one of those moments you'll always remember, one of those days you'll tell your grandchildren about someday."

"You think?"

"And she might be up just waiting for you to call and tell her."

"Yeah, okay," Nate said. He got out his cell phone and looked at the guy. "I don't think I want you to listen to me grovel."

The man laughed. "Hey, man, we've all been to Grovel Town. Give it your best shot, and come find me later and let me know how it worked out. But I have a feeling she's waiting for you."

Which, as a matter of fact, she was.

"DO YOU KNOW what porn movies get wrong?" she said to him.

"What?"

"The love part. They never show what happens after the . . . you know . . . the sex—the breaking up and the coming back together. How tough it all is."

"Jesus. It's going to be really hard, isn't it?"

"Ha! Unbelievably hard."

"Could we pretend for a moment that it's all going to be easy and wonderful, just to get us through?"

"No," she said, and laughed. "But it's going to be crazy and wonderful."

"I want you to come down here now and be here with me. I need to kiss you in this hospital, to break the evil spell here. And I have to warn you: we may need to dance naked in the lobby, like we did in our kitchen. That seems very important right now."

"I'll come and dance with you tomorrow. For tonight, I think our love has to stand the test of time," she said. "It's an act of faith."

"Okay, but there will be so many more people around tomorrow. You might feel uncomfortable."

She was silent for a long time, and then she said, "You're really going to stay crazy, aren't you?"

"Yes," he said and closed his eyes, tasted the salt on his lips. Had he cried? He didn't think so. But he would, he could. "Yes," he said again. "Hallelujah."

ACKNOWLEDGMENTS

I have so much gratitude to everyone who helped me with this book, who read early drafts and volunteered to think hard about love and romance and how in the world people ever get together.

Many thanks to Shaye Areheart for her unending kindness and encouragement, and to Sally Kim, who showed great enthusiasm for this project—and to all the staff at Shaye Areheart Books, who help make an author's life smooth and serene. And of course, I adore my agent, Nancy Yost, who is with me every step of the way, guiding me and making me laugh.

I owe a great debt to Alice Mattison, Kim Steffen, Diane Cyr, and Mary Rose Meade, all of whom read early drafts and pointed me in the right direction. Leslie Connor and Nancy Hall allowed me to imprison them in my car and take them on looooooong drives while I detailed to them every turn and twist of the plot. Jim Emswiler told me how children deal with grief. Karen Bergantino discussed this book with me through endless early morning walks. And my step-mother, Helen Myers, who reads everything, was always willing to take my long-distance calls and help me figure out what my characters were all about.

My family has been unfailingly understanding throughout this process of writing and editing. My love goes out to Allie, Ben, Stephanie, Mike, Miles, Amy, Charlie and Josh for all the happiness you bring me. And to Jimbo, who stands by me every single day, even when I'm just possibly a bit of a lunatic.

1. Harris presents the story of how he came to be Christopher's caretaker by explaining that Nate was far too irresponsible to be a father, especially after Nate's wife, Louisa, died. However, when Nate speaks about it with Jamie, he claims that Harris didn't want him to be a part of Christopher's life and insisted on him staying far away. Why do you think Harris prevented Nate from being a part of Christopher's life? What would be his motivation in doing so? Do you think this was something that Nate believed in order to walk away relatively guilt free? Why?

2. By Nate's account, Harris was a horrible father to him, abandoning him and then ignoring him for much of his life. Why then would Nate and Louisa move in with Harris? Were the two men trying to reconcile or was it purely a necessity for the young couple? Why?

3. After Louisa's death, why would Nate leave Christopher to be raised by the father who abandoned him?

4. Arguably, Jamie is the most grounded and responsible character, despite her hippie inclinations. However, toward the end of the novel

Lucy says to her, "You're the one who does what she wants. You have your *art*. And you don't do anything you don't want to. Anything that's just for money. It's *me* who has to worry about the mortgage and the bills. I've always had to take care of you, even from the time we were little and you were too shy to get to know anybody. It's always been me, me, me!" (p. 270) How does this argument shed new light on Jamie's lifestyle? Did you believe Lucy? Why or why not? Did the argument make you see Jamie as irresponsible or rather as taking life as it comes and following her happiness? Do you think Lucy is jealous of Jamie? Why?

5. Chief Cooksey is also antagonistic to Jamie. Do you think his anger toward her is as simple as him wanting to protect Harris from a gold digger? Or does his viewpoint speak to something greater—some fundamental dislike of Jamie and her life choices?

6. When Chief Cooksey tells Nate about how Harris's body was found, why didn't Nate confront Jamie? Why did he choose to believe that Jamie had lied to him?

7. What did you make of Lainey Haney asking Jamie to rejoin the Campfire Kids as leader of the jamboree? What does her inclusion of Jamie say about the town and the viewpoint of the younger generation—especially in comparison to the views of Chief Cooksey?

8. There are so many character dichotomies throughout the text— Harris and Nate, Nate and Trace, Jamie and Nate, Jamie and Lucy, Jamie and Tina, and Christopher and Arley. However, rather than the pairs being simple foils of each other, they seem to share both similarities and differences, and all the characters have both good and bad qualities. What do you make of all these pairings? What are the similarities and differences in each of the pairs?

9. Describe the moment when Nate proved that he could be, and wanted to be, not only a provider for but a parent to Christopher. How

did he show that he could be a good partner for Jamie? When was that turning point?

10. Toward the end of the novel both Nate's and Jamie's lives fall apart. After arguing with her sister, Jamie is prompted to leave Lucy's house and become temporarily homeless, first camping by the pond and then squatting in the abandoned house. Meanwhile, overwhelmed with caring for Christopher and trying to maintain a long-distance relationship with Tina, Nate loses his job. What is revealed in their individual declines?

11. In this novel, even the house is a character. How do Harris's attempts to repair it, Nate's tearing it apart, and Jamie's squatting in it represent aspects of each person's character?

12. This novel seems to put forth the idea that people can change. Do you think that this is true? Who in the novel evolves most? What are the benefits or drawbacks of the characters' evolutions?

13. After Christopher breaks his arm in the whip line, Chief Cooksey tells Nate, "I've been thinking. This Jamie . . . well, what's she gonna do? She's got a sick boy, lots to think about. . . . Life or death all the damn time. She had to do what she did. Lemme just say, if you want to blame her for this, it's probably gonna end up being *me* you should blame." What led Cooksey to have this change of heart about Jamie? What has he learned?

14. The novel also speaks to the idea of family. What do you think constitutes a family? Were Harris and Jamie a family? Are Nate and Jamie?

15. As Denise Morgan outlines it, kissing games are the things in life one doesn't take seriously. Given that definition, what do you think is the significance of the book's title?

ALSO BY

Sandi Kahn Shelton

The story of two sisters who learn what they need to let
go of—and what they have to hold on to as tightly as they can.

A PIECE OF NORMAL
A NOVEL
$13.95 PAPER ($17.95 CANADA) • 978-1-4000-9732-6

One woman's complicated, infuriating, and mystifying family
might be just the thing to help her define herself on her own terms
and live the life she's always wanted.

WHAT COMES AFTER CRAZY
A NOVEL
$13.95 PAPER ($21.00 CANADA) • 978-1-4000-9730-2

Available from Three Rivers Press wherever books are sold